Grasping Minerva firmly by the arm, Blakeney hustled her across the square. "Can't you behave like a normal young lady? I was mad to agree to this walk."

"Nonsense. It has been a most interesting experience."

It occurred to him that a bride who wasn't a "normal young lady" might make life interesting in some ways. He looked down at her, calmly keeping pace with his stride that made no effort to accommodate ladylike steps.

Minerva was pleased by the consideration her reluctant betrothed paid her. Again she noted the spiderweb of lines extending from the corners of his dark blue eyes, a physical manifestation of his maturity. She had to admit, he really was very good looking. As she studied him in the gaslight, something odd happened. His expression, the quality of his regard, altered. In any other man she'd have read it as . . . desire.

"My dear Miss Montrose. Does a future husband merit a kiss?"

He held her gaze with unwavering heat for some moments, while she tried to interpret this unexpected turn of events. At the beginning of the evening she'd have sooner kissed a snake than Blakeney. But now?

"Why not?" she said slowly. "We may as well both find out what we are getting."

MIRANDA NEVILLE

Confessions
from an
Arranged Marriage

AVON

An Imprint of HarperCollinsPublishers

This is a work of fiction. Names, characters, places, and incidents are products of the author's imagination or are used fictitiously and are not to be construed as real. Any resemblance to actual events, locales, organizations, or persons, living or dead, is entirely coincidental.

AVON BOOKS
An Imprint of HarperCollins*Publishers*
10 East 53rd Street
New York, New York 10022-5299

Copyright © 2012 by Miranda Neville
ISBN 978-0-06-202305-6
www.avonromance.com

First Avon Books mass market printing: April 2012

Avon Trademark Reg. U.S. Pat. Off. and in Other Countries, Marca Registrada, Hecho en U.S.A.
HarperCollins® is a registered trademark of HarperCollins Publishers.

Printed in the U.S.A.

10 9 8 7 6 5 4 3 2 1

This one's for Becca.

Chapter 1

London, Spring 1822

Lord Blakeney wasn't in the ballroom. He wasn't even in the building. Minerva Montrose wouldn't care if he was on a ship to America.

When the stone-faced footman informed Miss Montrose that his lordship was nowhere to be found, it came as no surprise to her. If you asked her to name the men in the world guaranteed to be unreliable, the Marquis of Blakeney would be first on her list.

Never mind that the ball was at Vanderlin House, the London home of the Duke and Duchess of Hampton. Never mind that the ball was occasioned by her formal presentation to the *ton*. And certainly never mind that Blakeney, the duke's only son and heir, was supposed to open the ball with her. Minerva knew him well enough to be undisturbed by his failure to keep this particular engagement. Neither was she disappointed at the loss of a partner who would have younger debutantes grinding their teeth with envy. Her marital ambitions took no account of high rank.

"I don't think Blakeney's coming." Her brother-in-law, Viscount Iverley, looked so mournful Minerva had to smile.

"This must be the first time in your life you've been sorry for his absence," she said.

"I'd be just as happy if I never had to set eyes on him again."

"I haven't seen him for almost two years. I don't suppose he has changed."

Sebastian gave a contemptuous grunt. "He was an arrogant ass at the age of ten, with very little reason I may say, and he never got any better. He's an idiot without a worthwhile thought in his head."

"The duke and duchess are clever people. How did they produce such a son?"

"Perhaps he was dropped on his head by a nurse."

Sebastian's feud with his first cousin went back to their childhood, and winning Diana, Minerva's sister, from his old rival had done nothing to abate his dislike. Minerva adored her brother-in-law and shared his opinion of Blakeney's intellect. At another time the pair of them would have enjoyed a cheerful enumeration of the latter's many shortcomings, but Sebastian had something else on his mind.

"Do you suppose I shall have to dance with you instead?"

Minerva resisted the urge to tease a man teetering on the edge of desperation. "Only if we cannot find me another partner, preferably one who is both sober and capable of rational conversation. Blakeney, should he appear, is likely to be neither."

Sebastian's look of terror flickered to one of shrewdness. "The Member of Parliament for Gristlewick, I suppose. Does the fellow realize you are going to hunt him down and transform him, willy-nilly, into a successful statesman?"

Minerva lowered her eyes to her slippers with a modesty that would fool no one who knew her. "Mr. Parkes, if I'm not mistaken, would like to be Prime Minister, and I'm the very person to make it happen."

"Good luck to him. Which is he?"

This early in the evening the ballroom remained less than half full. Those present for the most part compromised political aspirants anxious to please the duke, rather than the merely fashionable members of the *ton,* who preferred to be fashionably late. Ignoring Adam's most famous London interior, which to Minerva's eye was merely white and gold with a lot of pillars, passing with indifference over anyone in a gown, her questing gaze sought a cluster of men in earnest conversation beyond the Ionic colonnade that divided off one end of the long chamber. "Over there." she said.

"The short sandy-haired fellow?"

"I'd call it light brown. I would expect you of all people, Sebastian, to appreciate a man who cultivates his intellect rather than his appearance."

"I take your word that the man is a paragon of learning. At the moment he'd impress me by coming to claim you for the opening dance."

"He won't do that. He has already engaged me for the second."

Sebastian looked back at her, anxiety visible

through his spectacles. "Then who are you going to dance with? You can't sit out the first set when this wretched ball is in your honor."

"Wretched? If it weren't for Diana increasing, you'd be giving the ball yourself."

"Don't remind me."

"It was very good of you to come up from Kent to support me."

"Diana made me. And she ordered me to get a report on the new fashions. How the devil am I supposed to do that? And now I'm supposed to dance."

Minerva patted his arm without a hint of mockery. Well, perhaps a hint. "Poor Sebastian. You should pity me too. I'd rather be conversing with all those M.P.s than leading off the dance. Cheer up. Here comes the duchess. Perhaps she's found me a partner." She tightened her grip on him lest he attempt escape.

Their hostess, the Duchess of Hampton, haughty and elegant in emerald green, joined them. "I'm sorry, Miss Montrose," she said. "It seems my son has forgotten his engagement." Only a thinning of the lips and a greater than usual coldness in her tone revealed the extent of her displeasure, but Minerva had no doubt the duchess was exceedingly angry at Blakeney's discourtesy. "It is only proper that a member of the family lead you out. Unfortunately the duke's heart does not allow him to dance." Her eyes rested on her husband's nephew. "Iverley. You must do the honors."

"I want to kill Blakeney," Sebastian muttered as he trailed her to the center of the room. "Not that there's anything unusual about that."

"Don't worry," Minerva said. "It's a dance, not an execution."

Having survived the first set without disaster, Sebastian limped off to find liquid refreshment and avoid being pressed onto the dance floor again. Minerva tended to share his dislike of dancing, but for a different reason. She had no trouble going through the steps, but during a pair of country dances with Mr. Thomas Parkes there was little time for discourse. Standing opposite in the line, she had ample opportunity to take in the agreeable appearance of the man, whom she'd long since selected as a potential husband based upon newspaper reports of his budding career. A little above average—only a man as tall as Lord Iverley would call him short—his height topped hers by two or three inches. His figure was solid without running to fat, and encased in evening clothes distinguished by propriety without excessive elegance. The admittedly sandy hair was thick and well cut and crowned agreeable, sensible features.

All in all, a most satisfactory picture. Minerva set no store by good looks. In her experience handsome men tended to be arrogant and self-absorbed. One of many reasons she had little time for Lord Blakeney.

Mr. Parkes examined her in return and she smiled encouragingly. As her sister Diana had often told her, men were dreadfully shallow about a woman's appearance and tended to be impressed first by beauty. She'd rather be esteemed for her intelligence, but Minerva was a realist. She knew people thought her pretty. If Mr. Parkes wanted smiles, she'd give him smiles. She believed him attracted to both her brains and her person and wondered how soon she could expect an offer. She'd like to be wed this season. There was a possibility the government would fall in the next few months and he would be embroiled in the excitement of the election. When that happened, Minerva had every intention of being involved as Mrs. Parkes.

At the end of the set, he offered his arm to escort her back to Lady Chase, her chaperone in Diana's absence. Her eager question about the Irish situation died half formed because his attention, like most of the others in their vicinity, turned to the entrance. A gentleman staggered through the double doors and skidded on the polished parquetry floor. At a distance of twenty feet, Minerva saw the newcomer preserve his balance by grabbing the shoulders of a large-bosomed, open-mouthed matron. Swinging her aside, his backward slide was arrested by the wall. Without a hint of embarrassment he slouched against a pilaster and scowled at the assembly.

He was as gorgeous as ever. A lock of dark blond hair with glints of gold flopped over a noble brow. No nose had ever been more perfectly carved, no jaw as firmly etched. The shapely mouth was full, sensuous, and sulky, matching the expression in his dusky blue eyes.

He'd always been a handsome devil but the sight of him filled Minerva with disgust.

Lord Blakeney had arrived.

Surveying the room, his glance came to rest on her. His lips twisted into a derisive half smile and their eyes met in mutual displeasure. He shoved his back away from the wall and ambled over to her.

"Our dance, I believe, Miss Montrose." He hadn't changed a bit.

Minerva felt a strong desire to slap his arrogant face. "Lord Blakeney," she said with the merest hint of a curtsey. "I believe *our dance* was over half an hour ago."

"This one will do just as well."

Mr. Parkes forestalled her response with a bow and a polite "my lord."

"Do I know you?" Blakeney asked.

"His Grace presented us at Brooks's last week."

"Right. I remember." Obviously a lie. He'd never give a second thought to a man he couldn't challenge to a fencing bout or horse race. Confirming her thought, he paid no more attention to the M.P. for Gristlewick but listened with an exaggerated air to the musicians tuning up. "I do believe it's to be a waltz." He proffered his arm. "Never let it be said I forget all my family obligations."

Minerva replied through gritted teeth and a gratified smile. "I assure you, my lord, you owe me nothing. As your cousin's sister-in-law, our relationship is negligible." Anyone watching would think her looking at him with pleasure, not noticing how her eyes slid over his shoulder to glance with envy and regret at Mr. Parkes, who had murmured his leave-taking and headed in the delightful direction of the Home Secretary.

Blakeney's eyes narrowed. "I meant my obligation to the duke and duchess. My revered parents. Your hosts."

So he didn't even pretend to be polite. Good.

Blakeney's manners might not have improved since Minerva last set eyes on him, but at close quarters she detected subtle alterations in his appearance. He'd aged while she was living in Vienna and he at the Vanderlins' Devon estate. Aged was perhaps the wrong word—he was only twenty-nine, or perhaps thirty, the same as Sebastian—but he no longer appeared quite the golden youth who'd courted Diana. She perceived a delicate web of lines extending from the corners of his eyes. When she'd known him before his grooming had always been impeccable. Now one of his stockings was wrinkled and his neck cloth askew. His hair brushed his collar, still damp and curling upward. He needed the attention of a barber. As he placed his hand on her waist she caught the fresh scent of verbena soap mingled with a strong aroma of brandy.

She supposed she'd better attempt to converse with the oaf. "My previous partner, Mr. Parkes, is a brilliant man with a brilliant future. I believe your father thinks very highly of him."

He guided her into the turn with just a hint of excessive force and much to her satisfaction she detected a wobble in his footwork. Her smile broadened. She'd succeeded in irking him.

He recovered adroitly with no more than a firmer press of his hand, warm on her waist through her silk gown. He danced well, she grudgingly admitted, even though she was pretty sure he was foxed. He must have shaved himself for he'd missed a bit, on the left jaw. Fair as he was, she wouldn't have noticed if she'd been more than the six inches away demanded by the waltz.

"Is your valet indisposed, or were you not at home when you changed for the evening?" An impertinent question that skirted impropriety, but there had always been something about Blakeney that made her lose her poise and behave like an unschooled savage.

The curve of his lips matched hers while his eyes lit with malice. "Since you ask, Miss Montrose, I came from Henrietta Street and the house of Mademoiselle Desirée de Bonamour." He spoke in deep mocking tones. Though there was no reason fair coloring shouldn't be accompanied by a low baritone, in Blakeney Minerva always found the combination incongruous. "She's a very hospitable lady. When I realized I was late she invited me to share—er—use her bath."

Infuriated with herself for blushing, she almost lost her temper. She wasn't the least bit interested in the Frenchwoman, universally proclaimed (though mostly out of earshot of unmarried girls) as the most beautiful in London.

"I suppose you seek to embarrass me by mentioning your mistress," she said.

"No," he said. "Just to remind you that I have better things to do than cater to the consequence of an ambitious miss."

"Then we find ourselves in perfect accord," she retorted. "I have better objects of my attention than a spoiled wastrel without a thought in his head except for sports." She favored him with a sweet and utterly insincere smile.

"Sports? Miss Montrose. I'm not thinking of sports now."

Minerva wasn't sure what the last riposte meant. He might be thinking of what he could be doing with his mistress, or, equally likely, that he'd like to kill his current partner. With four brothers Minerva was an expert at inciting the desire to commit violence. The smile she'd just employed could reduce the youngest Montrose to rabies.

She tried to read Blakeney's face, in case it became necessary to duck and avoid strangulation. "I wouldn't want to disturb your mental exertions, Lord Blakeney. I shall remain silent until we finish the waltz and may be done with each other."

"It will be my very great pleasure, Miss Montrose, never to dance with you again."

It took every ounce of her considerable willpower to keep a simper on her face and her feet off his; she was tempted more than once to stamp hard on the lout. She might have done it, by accident of course, if not for her doubt that her satin evening slippers would be able to inflict much pain on his big clumsy feet. Well not clumsy exactly. Even drunk they moved with deft precision after the one initial slip. His smile was as steady as hers, and from their expressions an onlooker would likely believe them to be enjoying the waltz in perfect accord.

They completed the set without exchanging another word.

Chapter 2

"**B**lake, old fellow." A well known and utterly unwelcome figure blocked his path.

The evening just got even worse. Bad enough having to attend a ball in his parents' house; worse that his presence was required in order to dance with the most pestilential female he'd ever known. He didn't care that Minerva Montrose was the prettiest debutante in London. He wasn't interested in prettiness, or debutantes, and above all he wasn't interested in Minerva. The girl had been a thorn in his side when he was wooing her elder sister. Not having her as his sister-in-law was a huge consolation when Diana threw him over for bloody Sebastian Iverley.

Now this. Just when he'd reached the relative safety of the dining room, but before he'd acquired badly needed liquid sustenance to top up the brandy he'd downed earlier. He looked down into the face of his enemy and resisted the impulse to rearrange the angelic features with his fist.

"Huntley," he said, with a curt nod.

"How are you, Blake?"

He turned to catch the eye of a laden footman. There were enough people seeking refreshment that he couldn't either hit or cut the scoundrel without drawing the attention of other guests.

"What, no handshake for your old school friend?"

Blake snatched a glass from the tray and responded with a brief, unapologetic grimace. It was good to keep his hands occupied. He scarcely trusted himself to speak.

Huntley gave the guileless smile that charmed so many, but no longer fooled Blake. "It's good to see you. You were away from town for so long. Two years is it? Your friends have missed you."

"Have they?"

"You should have let me know you were back."

"Why would I do that?"

"I understand, Blake, because I know how maladroit you are with a pen. I believe your handwriting's got even worse since Eton."

"Which is why you were so kind as to perform the task of writing those vowels on my behalf."

"As you know, I've always been present and willing to help my friend."

A cold wind buffeted Blake's heart. His "old school friend" was never going to let him go. He'd trusted the boy with his secret; the grown man had taught him the foolishness of relying on another. He took another draft of wine and stared at the man, who looked better than the last time they'd met. Plumper and healthier and dressed by a good tailor. Why not? He'd done well for himself.

"What do you want, Huntley?"

The reply to the bitter question came with blithe cheeriness. "Why, nothing. Merely a chance to renew our friendship, raise a glass, and talk over the good old days. You always called me Geoffrey then."

"Things change, Huntley."

"You weren't so haughty at school. It never mattered then that your father was a duke. Of course, I could be of use to you."

During all their years of friendship, why had he never noticed that Huntley was a sniveling whiner? It would have tipped him off to the man's fundamental dishonesty.

"I think I've more than repaid any past favors," he replied. "What are you doing in my father's house?"

"I was invited. I'm standing for Parliament in the Westborough by-election, don't you know? As a member of the duke's faction."

If he'd wormed his way into the circle surrounding the Duke of Hampton, Blake would never be rid of the little parasite. And any degree of intimacy between Huntley and his father could lead to disaster.

Huntley's expression was ever designed to invite trust and elicit confidences, but Blake read nothing but provocation in the innocent round features. Huntley knew he was worried and wanted to make him sweat, to beg even. Blake decided to disappoint him, at least for the moment. "Excuse me. I'm engaged for the next dance."

"I understand. Is it the smiles of the beautiful Miss Montrose that call again, or some other incomparable?"

Blake turned his back on the bastard and made for the exit.

"Enjoy yourself," Huntley called. "I'll still be here."

The encounter drained away his last drop of well-being. The day had been so satisfactory, especially the invigorating afternoon in Desirée's bed. Before he remembered he'd promised his mother to attend her damnable ball.

God, he wished he could return to Henrietta Street and his mistress's perfumed arms and silken body. She'd hinted at something new, although a week of almost nonstop Desirée had left him depleted. But delicious as she was in bed, she was also an amusing conversationalist without any intellectual pretensions. With her he could relax and laugh and never feel stupid. Ridiculous, since Desirée was shameless about her mercenary motives, but he was quite infatuated with his expensive new ladybird. Little wonder, perhaps, since the two years he'd spent in the country had been almost celibate.

And all because of Huntley, whose exorbitant demands meant he had to rusticate to pay his debts. Though there were aspects of life in Devon he'd enjoyed, he felt he deserved a little recreation unmarred by demands from young ladies, old enemies, or his parents.

If he left now he'd avoid his father's rebuke and his mother's reproaches for his late arrival tonight. He'd also ensure the parental admonishments would be all the sharper for being postponed. Worth it, perhaps, but Desirée had made it clear in her alluring way that she'd very much appreciate bracelets to match the ruby necklace he'd given her. With this new demand on his purse he'd better not anger the old man any more than he usually did, just by existing.

Still, he'd be damned if he'd go looking for trouble by returning to the ballroom and being forced by the duchess to dance with a marriageable virgin. Since the dining room was occupied by Geoffrey Huntley, he sought another refuge.

The small withdrawing room was unoccupied, but the table of drinks ensured someone would come in. The odds were overwhelming that, whoever they were, Blake wouldn't want to see them. He helped himself to an open bottle and slipped into the window embrasure, behind the curtains. It was a quiet and agreeably cool retreat from rooms overheated by bodies and candlelight. He could enjoy a bit of peace and quiet and complete the process of becoming foxed enough to face the duke without pain.

"There's no one in here." A well-known voice intruded on Blake's second glass of champagne. James Lambton was about the only person whose company he welcomed. He'd forgotten his friend had told him he would attend this infernal ball. He'd forgotten a lot today.

About to emerge from his hiding place, he stopped at the sound of a woman's voice. "There's no comfortable furniture either."

How amusing. Lamb was engaged in a tryst. And since he recognized the lady, Blake knew exactly the object of the meeting and what kind of furniture they sought. A bed for preference but a sofa, or even a large chair, would suffice. Just as long as it could accommodate a couple looking for a fast, furious fuck.

In his early London days he'd accommodated the lady himself during an assembly or two. The Duchess of Lethbridge wasn't much older than him in years, but surpassed him by decades in experience. Having produced three sons in as many years as a bride, her equally licentious husband let her do as she liked. What she liked was young men. As far as Blake knew, his friend had never been called upon to service the beautiful and lascivious duchess and this was his big chance.

"This won't do," she said. "Where else is there?"

"The library won't be in use during a ball."

"There's not enough time now. I promised I'd stand up with the Prime Minister. I'll meet you there in an hour."

Things improved. Minerva's next partners were more to her taste: a young peer, about to be seconded to the embassy in Vienna, who listened appreciatively to her impressions of that city; a junior secretary in the War Office. The fact that the Duke of Hampton was one of the leaders of the opposition party didn't stop members of the government accepting his hospitality. Mr. Thomas Parkes, a staunch supporter of the Hampton faction, had engaged her for a second set later in the evening.

"He must be serious," observed Juliana, the young Marchioness of Chase, "since he requested the supper dance."

"Are you sure you didn't do the inviting, Min?" Mrs. Tarquin Compton asked.

"There was no need," Minerva said, ignoring Celia Compton's needling. "He was waiting for me as the last dance finished and he would have stayed and talked, but he was hoping to have a word with the Prime Minister."

"He prefers a politician to you? How appalling! You should cut the acquaintance at once."

Minerva laughed. "I wouldn't have anything more to do with him if he failed to grasp such an opportunity."

"I hate to break it to you," said Juliana, "but your Mr. Parkes must have failed. The Prime Minister is waltzing with the Duchess of Lethbridge."

The three ladies looked with interest at the beauty in the arms of the country's premier. Minerva had promised to help Sebastian with his fashion report. "Would you call that pure white?" she asked. "I think the shade is a little creamier than my gown, but perhaps not. Mind you, that embroidered satin is hardly the kind of thing I would wear. She's practically naked on top."

Celia, who had refreshingly liberal notions of what was proper to discuss with an unmarried girl, made a noise that a rude person would call a snort. "The duchess is hardly a debutante. According to Tarquin she's enjoyed liaisons with half the good-looking men in London."

"Including him?"

"He claims not, says he wasn't handsome enough to tempt her. Nonsense of course, but I'm happy *he* wasn't tempted. What about Cain?"

The pursed disapproval of Juliana's pretty lips was spoiled by a twinkle in her eye. "I've never enquired. Better not to know what he got up to before we married."

Minerva glanced down at her own simple white silk with its net overskirt and the embroidered satin slippers below. A slight aura emanated from the toes, a familiar visual disturbance echoed by a faint ache behind her eyes.

"Bother," she muttered but not softly enough.

"What is it?"

"It's all right, Celia. Well, no, it isn't. I have a migraine coming. I know the signs."

"Truly?" Celia asked. "This isn't one of your convenient headaches, letting you sneak off to a secret meeting and plot the downfall of the government?"

Minerva managed a wry smile. "I'm a reformed character. All the time I was in Vienna I never got into a scrape." Hardly ever, she amended silently. No point worrying Juliana. "I wouldn't invent illness during a ball given in my honor. I'll admit I don't get real attacks very often, but when they come I can be in pain for hours."

"Is there anything you can do to stop it?" Juliana asked.

"I have my powders with me. Sometimes if I take one and lie down, it goes away. If I'm gone more than half an hour, please make my excuses to our hostess."

Half an hour and half a bottle later, Blake had an idea. He and Lamb had been torturing each other with pranks for years. Why not tonight?

The library at Vanderlin House, though far smaller than that at Mandeville, the country seat in Shropshire, was well stocked. Gilt spines glowed by the light of a single lamp, turned down low. Slipping in from the deserted passage, Blake couldn't appreciate the restful cool of the room with its faint odor of leather. Above the serried bookshelves loomed the ghostly marble faces of Greek and Roman philosophers. During visits to the library under the supervision of his tutors he'd often fantasized about shooting the smug bastards. Especially the Greek ones.

God, he hated Greek. He took a swig from his bottle and found it empty.

Narrowing his eyes, he assessed the odds of bowling it to bring down a bust of Plato. Easy with a cricket ball, but he wasn't sure he could control the spin on a flying champagne bottle. He almost missed the fact that he was not alone. A woman in white lay on the divan, provided for comfortable reading but handy for a less cerebral activity.

The duchess had arrived early.

A tall woman, her feet hung over the end of the padded bench. One gloved arm was draped over her eyes while the other trailed dramatically toward the floor. He very much doubted she was asleep. Rather, he guessed, she had invited Lamb to participate in one of her little games.

Wandering satyr surprises sleeping nymph, perhaps. Or—suitable to the library setting—visiting scholar ravishes the virginal daughter of the house. Pondering the possibilities aroused a little interest in him. Not much. He'd spent most of the past week in Desirée's bed. He was also quite drunk.

On the other hand, it would be amusing if Lamb arrived to find his position already occupied, so to speak. Childish but amusing. This was even better than surprising Lamb in flagrante. He stepped quietly across the room and squatted on the floor at the end of the couch, contemplating a pair of white slippers, made from silk with a swirly pattern. He corrected his balance by falling onto his knees, averted his eyes from the nauseating spirals, and looked at the duchess's ankles instead.

Very pretty. Blake had always had a weakness for a neat ankle, though he didn't recall ever taking note of Anthea Lethbridge's. Slender, well defined, and deceptively innocent in pure white stockings.

With the tip of his forefinger he traced the bone beneath the silk. She didn't move. He opened his hand and felt warmth under his palm. She twitched at his touch. He closed his hand around the tender limb and inched it upward. Her body undulated seductively and her legs parted a little, though from the rhythm of her breathing he'd think her asleep.

Sleeping nymph it was. Good acting.

With a hand on each ankle he gently drew the legs apart and leaned over to kiss the spot above her slipper, then, nudging at her skirt with his brow, he ran his lips up her inner calf.

The sweet heady scent of woman enticed him to explore further. He might not be in a fit state for the full performance—though that fact was now in dispute—but he could taste. And he knew the lady would appreciate his attention. Chuckling softly he raised the skirts and dove under until he was enclosed in a tent of silk petticoats. The soft skin of her thighs brushed his cheeks. Her fragrant heat was a siren call to his groin. The lovely duchess was going to receive double pleasure tonight.

She moved, stretched her legs out as though emerging from slumber. Then he heard the door-knob turn and remembered the existence of his old friend. Damn Lamb. He was early too.

"What?" The question was voiced in a blend of sleepiness and confusion, followed by a strangled shriek. Flailing hands beat at his head through the material of the gown and he hastily withdrew.

Sinking back onto his ankles he looked up to meet the outraged face of Miss Minerva Montrose.

"What are you doing?" she cried. She lay before him, her legs exposed to the knees.

His head swam and his mouth fell agape as they stared at each other in horror. Then in unison they turned to the door.

A parade that wouldn't have disgraced the fashionable hour in Hyde Park trooped into the library.

His mother, the Duchess of Hampton.

Lord Iverley, his first cousin, lifelong enemy, and Minerva's brother-in-law.

Lady Chase and Mrs. Compton, best friends of Diana, Minerva's sister, Sebastian's wife, and Blake's erstwhile fiancée.

James Lambton, looking surprised.

The Duchess of Lethbridge, looking amused.

And Lady Georgina Harville, the biggest gossip in London.

Chapter 3

Blakeney stood before his father, who had risen at his entrance and faced him across the dark carved desk. In the course of a century or so the duke's study, much larger than the library, had received most of the men who'd wielded any power in England, up to and including future monarchs. The furnishings, in the colossal style, had never changed in Blake's memory; they made a statement of the permanency of the power of the Vanderlin family, starting when the first duke built the Piccadilly mansion. On too many occasions the fourth and present duke had received his son in this chamber, always to remind him of his inadequacy as the future standard-bearer of the family influence. Many of his friends boasted of the birchings they'd received from their sires, but the duke never laid a hand on Blake. Touching was not something he did, either in affection or anger. Blake had often thought he'd prefer a steel rod on his back to the lash of his father's tongue.

"In a lifetime of idiocies, you've just committed the worst." The Duke of Hampton's tone emerged as dry and colorless as his face, pale from an existence dealing in the back rooms of politics, and capped by a head of hair Blake couldn't recall, even in his youth, being anything but gray, fading to white.

"You almost debauched a virtuous young lady. For all your *bêtises* I've never known you to be depraved."

He couldn't disagree, but it didn't make the duke's scorn any less painful. His father's opinion had always hurt, all the more because it was deserved. He felt like the lowest worm.

"I was drunk." He still was, he supposed, though he'd never felt more sober.

"That fact is the only excuse, and a poor one at that. I really thought, Blakeney, when you elected to spend two years away from London, that you'd grown up and had finally discovered an appreciation of your future duties. That I was wrong is a disappointment to me."

Blake's hands clenched behind his back in the classic stance of the guilty schoolboy. He hated that his sire could make him feel ten years old again, much too young and naïve to be inebriated.

"Miss Montrose is not the wife I would have chosen for you. I expected you to ally yourself with one of the great families, as I did with your mother. To find a wife, also like your mother, who was up to the task of being Duchess of Hampton. But it can't be helped. I cannot allow you to be responsible for the girl's ruin."

He wanted to argue, not because he disagreed with the duke's assessment of the position, but because it was couched in terms of his father's and his family's responsibility, and not his own.

"Miss Montrose's father is my closest neighbor and her sister is your cousin's wife. She was also a guest in my house this evening. The wedding will take place in a month."

With the impending slam of the prison door Blake found his voice. "Why so long? Why not tomorrow?" he asked bitterly.

The duke gave his I-can't-believe-my-son-is-such-a-fool look. "If you get Miss Montrose with child during the honeymoon, I don't want any questions about her virtue, or danger of confirming that you did indeed debauch her in the library this evening."

"Good lord, sir. Isn't talk of pregnancy a trifle premature?" Blake had scarcely grasped the fact he was to be a husband. His brain reeled from the identity of his bride. Fatherhood seemed too far-fetched.

"I hope not. We need an heir. There have been too few sons born to the Vanderlins during the past century. I have nothing against Thomas Vanderlin, but he's only a second cousin and I'd prefer to see the dukedom descend in the direct line. The best thing about Miss Montrose is the way the females in her family breed sons. Her mother has four, you know, and her sister two already, in only two years of marriage. And she is increasing again."

Amazing how His Grace could voice the most indelicate of sentiments in the same tone he'd instruct one of his political clients how to vote on a bill in Parliament. The muted satisfaction in the duke's voice made Blake slightly sick. Little as he liked Minerva Montrose, surely she deserved better than to be regarded as a brood animal.

"Is there no way out of this?" he asked. He'd never changed his father's mind about anything he could recall, but he had to try. "I accept my own responsibility, but I have no reason to believe Miss Montrose wishes to marry me."

"Not wish to marry you? I find that improbable." Before Blake could make the mistake of reading a compliment in the duke's astonishment, his father shook his head decisively. "I'd be sorry to have such a poor opinion of the young woman that she'd be reluctant to wed the heir to the Duke of Hampton. Whatever she may think of you, she must respect your family and future position in life. Your mother thinks highly of her intelligence or she would never have offered to give the ball in her honor."

"I wish she hadn't."

"I will speak to Iverley about the settlements. Your allowance will be increased at once, and more so once we have an heir."

"I'm permitted to take care of that piece of business myself? You mean there's something you and Cousin Sebastian cannot arrange for me?"

"I assume getting a son is within your capabilities. She's a very pretty girl."

Blake couldn't deny his bride's beauty, but his role as a stud filled him with no anticipation. She left him cold with her English pink and white looks, all blond and blue-eyed perfection, not to mention her openly derisive scorn for his character and intellect. He thought about Desirée: dark, exotic, experienced, and admiring. Ruby bracelets or not, he was going straight to her house once he escaped from this interview.

"One more thing." The duke hadn't finished with him.

"Sir?"

"Your mistress. Dismiss her."

"Damn it, sir. Why?"

"People must believe this a love match. There's no other reason for you to wed such a girl. Breaking with the Frenchwoman cannot matter to you. You've only been with her a week or two."

Three. Three weeks ago he'd managed to outcharm and outbid a dozen rivals for Desirée's favors in a chase almost as thrilling as a good foxhunt. But his dried-up old prune of a father would never understand. Blake had no idea if the old man had ever kept a mistress. Probably too obsessed by politics and power to suffer the weaknesses of the flesh.

If he obeyed his father, a grim future stretched ahead of him. Instead of Desirée's endless skill and creativity, he was sentenced to a lifetime of sleeping with a sharp-tongued little snip of a girl with no idea of how to please a man in bed, and doubtless little interest in learning.

Minerva's future floated beyond her control as her ambitions threatened to crash into ruins. She was helpless to steer her own fate. It all depended on that tenuous and delicate abstraction, her *reputation*.

Diana had often warned her to guard it as though it were a small helpless child. There had been occasions in the past when she'd put it at risk. Not in a major way, but just enough to gets its infant toes wet. And she—and her reputation—had survived.

But nothing she'd done, or dreamed of doing, equaled being caught with a man's head up her skirts. She wasn't even to blame, unless she could be faulted for misjudging her dose of powder and dozing off under the influence of the opiate. The unfairness of it pierced her to the core.

She supposed there was a certain ironic justice in the fact that she had, on occasion, feigned such a headache for her own purposes.

Damn.

The day after the ball her friends gathered around her in the morning room of Lord Chase's house. Everyone was willing to find a reason why she could survive Lord Blakeney's drunken advances without having to wed him.

"You don't have to marry Blakeney." Sebastian was the most vehement, Celia Compton almost as much.

"We will always support you, won't we Tarquin?" she asked her husband, who agreed, but Minerva detected some reserve in his response. Not that he would personally repudiate her, but Tarquin Compton was a better judge of worldly opinion than anyone else in the room.

Juliana poured her a cup of tea and offered her silent sympathy. She'd already apologized profusely, and quite needlessly, for failing as a chaperone. There was, in Minerva's opinion, no one to blame but Blakeney. And she did. How could he have mistaken her for that woman?

Damn.

"I wish Diana were here," she said. "She'd know what to do."

"So do I," Sebastian said. "If she hadn't stayed in the country we'd have held your ball at our house and this wouldn't have happened because," and his voice gained a rough-edged savagery, "I wouldn't have let my bloody cousin Blakeney over the threshold."

What he left unsaid was that he'd managed to get Diana with child a ridiculously short time after the birth of their second son, Nicolas Jenson Iverley. Thanks to him she was vomiting in Kent instead of chaperoning her sister in London.

"You don't have to marry him," he said, as though repetition would make it true.

Juliana walked over to the window for the fourth time. "I see Cain in the middle of the square. Now we'll hear Lady Moberley's opinion."

Lord Chase, always known as Cain to his friends, had gone to canvas the opinion of his aunt, a lioness of London society.

"Well?" Four voices, almost in unison, greeted his entrance. Minerva dared not speak. She had some inkling how a prisoner at the dock, facing the gallows, must await the verdict of the jury. She rose from her chair and fixed her eyes on the marquis.

Cain exhibited none of his usual cheerful charm. His blue eyes were sober and he shook his head.

"I'm sorry, Minerva." She was grateful he didn't

beat about the bush. "My aunt believes that you will never be received again in the highest circles unless Blakeney weds you."

"Does she believe I *let* him do that to me?"

"It doesn't matter. There's not a soul in London who believes you either innocent or unwilling. Or rather, not a soul who wants to believe. It's just too good a story."

"Lady Georgina Harville has been spreading it, I suppose. She always hated Diana."

"The tale being told over the teacups is that you pretended to have a headache and went off to meet Blakeney in the library."

"That's ridiculous. We don't even like each other. Surely there's something Blakeney can do to make up for this, besides marrying me." She almost spat out the last two words.

Tarquin offered his ruling. "As a gentleman he can do nothing less. You can refuse his offer, of course, but people will remember. There'll always be a taint attached to your name."

The walls of the Chases' spacious room seemed to close in on Minerva as she strode back and forth and contemplated her unwelcome future. She faced an existence utterly different than she'd planned since she'd first become enthralled by politics at the age of eight. Reading the account of Lord Byron's speech in the House of Lords in support of the Luddites had opened up a world of injustice beyond the peaceful backwater of Mandeville Wallop. Ever since, she'd burned to make her mark on the world. Instead of a worthwhile life spent supporting her husband in the betterment of their country, was she to wed a dissolute idiot with whom she had nothing in common?

That she would eventually be a duchess was of little consequence. The days of the aristocracy would pass, had perhaps already passed. Reform was in the air and could not long be postponed by the interests that fought it. In the future power would be with the bold, the brilliant, the self-made. Minerva wanted to be one of them.

Celia and Juliana gathered about her, trying to make the best of things.

"Blakeney was always amiable to me," Celia insisted, "that summer at Mandeville. I never had the least reason to dislike him."

"I never thought he was as brainless as people say," Juliana chimed in, "even if he wouldn't know the Gutenberg Bible from a Minerva Press novel." Lady Chase had a tendency to judge everyone in relation to antiquarian books.

Sebastian listened with disfavor to these excuses, which Minerva herself found quite unconvincing. "Women! Always ready to forgive a handsome face." He had never forgiven Blakeney for wanting to marry Diana, or for boyhood bullying. "I should call him out for what he's done. Or I could just kill him."

"I understand your sentiments, old fellow." Tarquin placed a staying hand on Sebastian's shoulder. "But all you'd do is cause a bigger scandal and upset your family. And Minerva would be no better off than she is now."

"What about that other fellow, Min?" Sebastian asked. "Parkes, was it? Doesn't he want to marry you?"

"Our courtship hadn't got to that stage. We've only known each other a couple of weeks."

"Suppose I call on him? I'll offer him a large dowry and the support of every connection I muster."

Minerva doubted Parkes would accept, and she wouldn't respect him if he did. "I thought I'd be able to assist him in his political career. Under the present circumstances I'd be nothing but a drag on his advancement." She shook her head in amazed despondency. "Blakeney has ruined me. I have no other choice."

Chapter 4

The engagement between The Marquis of Blakeney and Miss Minerva Montrose, to counterbalance its scandalous origins, was conducted with the greatest degree of ceremony. Some of the formalities were more acceptable to Blake than others.

The worst was having to ask Sebastian Iverley for permission to address his sister-in-law. Not that he had anything to say in the matter. The duke had got together with old Owl and agreed that, under the circumstances, it would take too long to apply to Minerva's father in Shropshire. So Sebastian acted in Mr. Montrose's absence and gave his consent to the match in a manner that made it clear he'd just as soon throttle Blake.

The feeling, as always, was mutual.

The proposal itself was performed in the presence of his father and Lord Iverley in the drawing room at the Marquis of Chase's house in Berkeley Square.

He asked Minerva (thankfully not on one knee) for the great honor of her hand in marriage.

The honor was all hers, she replied with a curtsey.

He begged not to be kept in suspense. She accepted his offer.

He expressed his enormous relief that she had condescended to make him the happiest of men.

She gave him her hand. He kissed it, rather hastily.

The play went off without a hitch, neither forgetting the prescribed lines.

His last hope, that she would prefer any alternative to marriage to a man she'd always openly disliked, was dashed. Failing a miracle, he and Minerva Montrose would shortly be bound together as long as they both should live.

Something about London life Minerva could never adapt to was the propriety of being driven ridiculously short distances. Impatient by nature, she preferred to walk and never minded hopping over the gutters and avoiding horse droppings. This evening the short distance from Berkeley Square to Vanderlin House in Piccadilly would have been much quicker on foot; an altercation between the drivers of a brewer's dray and a high perch phaeton blocked the exit from the square.

She therefore had more than a few minutes alone with her fiancé, who had arrived with the ducal town coach and a ceremonial complement of footmen to escort her to dinner with his family. The generous dimensions of the vehicle allowed the engaged couple to avoid all danger of physical contact while sitting side by side on the well-padded bench. Minerva stared out of the window, where the quarrel proceeded noisily with no sign of ending.

"When do you expect Diana to arrive?" Blakeney said, abruptly breaking the strained silence.

"Not before tomorrow evening. Perhaps the day after. She tends to be most unwell in the mornings and Sebastian won't let her travel unless she feels better."

"A very solicitous husband, my cousin."

"Yes he is. He and Diana are very happy together."

He failed to detect her defiant tone, or chose to ignore it. "I had the impression our relations were conspiring not to leave us alone together. In Iverley's absence I expected a different protector for you."

She turned to face him for the first time. His flawless features were so lacking in expression it had to be deliberate. He must be feeling something; anger or remorse were possibilities. Or both.

"Am I in danger of being ravished in the streets of London?"

The provocation hit its target and elicited a discernible wince. "Never," he said. "I learned my lesson there."

"You mean, to make sure you have the right woman before you start . . ." she trailed off, unable to think of a delicate way of putting it.

"Precisely."

"Do you make a habit of slipping out of ballrooms to engage in . . . ?" It was beginning to annoy her that she didn't possess the proper vocabulary for this conversation, or to conduct the conversation in a proper fashion. As it happened, she knew several words for the activity, none of them repeatable in polite society. Since Blakeney doubtless knew even more, it was illogical that she couldn't bring herself to utter them. "Do you often get drunk and attempt to . . . *do that* to ladies you find lying about in libraries? Good lord, you put your head up my . . ."

"No," he cut in to her swelling tirade. "I do not. And I'm sorry. I owe you an apology."

"Yes," she said. "You do."

"I've tried to make recompense in the only way I can."

"I wish I could say I appreciate it, but marriage to you was not the goal of my life." She wrestled with her anger, sought a measure of grace. "I suppose it wasn't your plan either."

"No, but I have to marry someone. I was engaged before . . ." his voice trailed off.

"Were you about to mention that you once proposed to my sister?"

"Yes," he said. "But I thought it might be indelicate."

"Indelicate or not, the fact that you were once engaged to Diana won't go away. Are you still in love with her?"

"No."

Minerva believed it. In fact she'd never thought him in love with Diana. His brief unofficial betrothal to her sister had been spurred by the latter's fortune, inherited from her first husband. But he'd certainly been attracted to her, another dark beauty like his current mistress.

Her own fair coloring was completely different. Not that she'd ever, in her entire life, considered trying to win Blakeney's attention. She'd always known him to be handsome, beautiful even. Viewed objectively, there could hardly be a better looking man in England. But he had nothing she wanted in a spouse and apparently he felt the same way about her.

"Look," he said, "it appears we are to be wed whether either of us wishes it or not. Can we start by trying to be polite?"

A reasonable proposal, but not one she was yet ready to accept. She stared straight ahead, lips pursed. Her still sharp anger battled a rational desire for civil relations with her spouse. In the dim confines of the carriage she was very conscious of his masculinity and what that meant in terms of marriage. In theory she knew what happened in the conjugal bed, but she'd mostly thought about the less intimate aspects of the wedded state. Added to her discomfort was the recollection of her shock at waking up and finding a man's head touching parts of her she'd never display in public. Good Lord. Inches farther and he'd have been at her . . .

Was she really going to go through with this marriage? Wouldn't it be better to say no and live with the consequences? She wished with all her heart that she could turn back the clock, return to the optimism with which she'd arrived at Vanderlin House for the ball. She'd been poised to seek the useful future she'd planned for years. Thanks to the careless advances of this drunken lord, it had all turned to ashes. She blinked back tears of rage and continued to say nothing.

He reached out a hand to cover hers and even through their gloves she flinched at his touch.

"I'm sorry." He pulled back as though burned. "Why did you accept me? I expected you to refuse."

"Wanted me to refuse, you mean. I'm so sorry but, hard as the decision was, I preferred you to the ruination of my reputation and a lifelong banishment to the country." She held her forefingers half an inch part. "By this much."

"I didn't think you cared that much for the opinion of the world. I've witnessed occasions when you demonstrated little care for your precious reputation. Like the time you were arrested for attending a seditious meeting."

Blake no longer sounded conciliatory. It was too bad that he knew about some of the little problems she'd run into in the past, notably the time two years ago when the magistrates had raided a gathering of political reformers she'd sneaked out to join.

"My arrest was completely unreasonable," she said crossly, "and very likely illegal. Besides, it was hushed up. What you did to me in the library can't be. Now I can never achieve my ambition in life. Do you realize I was about to become engaged to a young man with a brilliant political career ahead of him? Obviously I am no use to any other man now. I am regarded as the Marquis of Blakeney's leavings."

"I'm sorry," he said again. "I wish I could make things different. I wish there was something I could do."

"I don't suppose you'd like to be Prime Minister?"

He shuddered visibly. "God, no."

That's what she thought.

Though a small family party, half a dozen liveried and bewigged footmen attended to the needs of the five diners. Enough leaves had been removed to reduce the table to an almost domestic size, making the dining room at Vanderlin House with its gilt coffered ceiling and ornate velvet drapery appear more than usually cavernous. Blake couldn't remember ever passing a convivial evening there, and he expected tonight to be no exception.

The duke took his place at the head of the table in a chair that resembled a throne. When Blake and his sisters had crept out of the nursery to explore the forbidden wonders below, he'd sit there and pretend he was the king and demand the girls curtsey to him. Sometimes they did, especially Amanda, the youngest. The older girls treated him with less respect. None of the three was present to celebrate his betrothal. Aside from Minerva, the only guest was his brother-in-law Gideon Louther, Maria's husband and the duke's chief parliamentary henchman.

Minerva, seated in the place of honor to the right of the throne, was being subjected to his father's most flattering attention. The old man possessed a good deal of old-fashioned charm when he cared to exercise it, which wasn't often and never on his own son. The duke wanted something from her, of course. Blake sensed his lips curling into an involuntary sneer. Louther and the duchess were al-

ready exchanging political gossip so Blake listened
to his father ascertain whether his future daughter-
in-law preferred *potage à la reine* or *à la russe.*

"We must make sure the servants know your favorite dishes," the duke said.

"Thank you, Your Grace. You are very kind."

"Not at all. Since one must eat, one may as well
enjoy it, especially in one's own home. Vanderlin
House will of course be your home much of the
time."

"Not for many years, I trust."

"In less than a month you will be living under
my roof. You must speak to the steward about
any preferences you have about furnishings too. I
daresay the duchess will show you the rooms after
dinner."

Blake, in midsip, almost spat out his wine.
"Here, sir? Here? We have no intention of living at
Vanderlin House."

"Of course you will live here. There's plenty of
room and your mother will be able to instruct Minerva in her future duties. You too. It's time you
played a more active part in the affairs of the dukedom. With the election likely this year you should
be working with Gideon on our prospects."

"If you need my help, let me have the management of Mandeville. I proved myself capable in
Devon."

"Live in the country, Blakeney? Can you think
of nothing but horses and hunting? You wouldn't
wish to live outside London, would you, my dear?"

The duke didn't expect Minerva to answer,
which was just as well since there was no tactful

response she could give without contradicting one of the two men.

"Naturally we shall live part of the year in London," Blake said. "In our own establishment." *A very small part of the year,* he promised silently.

"The business of the Dukes of Hampton is the business of the nation and has ever been so. It's time you gained some respect for our family tradition. You are, after all, our future."

"Perhaps I don't wish to follow tradition. Perhaps I see a different future."

"History is greater than the petty concerns of one man." He glared at Blake, the faded blue eyes still fierce in his papery face. "I will not allow the work of generations of Vanderlins to end with me."

And that was why the duke wanted them here, why he wanted this marriage. An heir, a different more satisfactory heir. It must gall him that Blake, whom he never trusted with anything, had to be the instrument of getting the son. But after that, he had no doubt, his father would wish to control him.

Blake wasn't going to live at Vanderlin House being instructed by Gideon. And it would serve the duke right if Minerva lacked her family capacity for producing boys. Instead of arguing, which was pointless, he answered his father's challenge with a careless shrug and addressed his soup. He'd chosen the *consommé* over either of the *potages* and wondered if there was a pun in there somewhere. *Consommé . . . consummation . . . or not.*

There was one sure way of foiling the duke's plans for this marriage.

Conversation of the kind he'd been hearing all his life washed over him: Who would get which office or bishopric or ambassadorship? How would so-and-so vote on which bill? Who should have one of the parliamentary seats over which the family held influence or sway? Who deserved the family jewels, to be "elected" to one of the Vanderlin pocket boroughs? Blake paid scant attention.

What would the duke do if a year passed, two years, with no sign of a child of either sex, let alone a son? Would he blame his worthless son? Women were usually held responsible for lack of fertility.

A name penetrated his thoughts.

"Remind me, Gideon, who we are supporting in Westborough?" the duke said.

"Geoffrey Huntley."

"Can he afford it?"

"It appears so. He is using his own funds. I implied we'd find him an easier seat if he doesn't win Westborough. It'll be a hard-fought election and it won't come cheap. I'm pleased we do not have to pay the expenses this time."

The duke nodded his approval and Blake enjoyed the irony. He wished he could tell his superior father that he was, indeed, paying for Huntley's election, with income from his estates by way of his son's allowance and a little ungentlemanly extortion.

So it went on, with little or no contribution from himself, till the long meal was over. His betrothed wife drank it in. She'd always been as drearily obsessed with politics as any proper Vanderlin. After a while she ventured a remark which was received with approval and encouragement.

Blake had to admit avid interest added animation to her insipid beauty. He'd always known she was clever. Just like the rest of her family, even her sister, though Diana never flaunted her brains or Blake wouldn't have considered marrying her. Just like his bloody brilliant cousin Sebastian, whom Diana had preferred.

Almost since he could remember, Blakeney had wondered why he was the only stupid member of a family famous for superior intellect. Perhaps he'd be doing the Vanderlin line a favor by letting the dukedom go to his cousin. He didn't think his bride would mind. In the carriage she'd made it clear she was far from forgiving his error. And she'd flinched in disgust when he touched her hand.

He didn't think Minerva would complain if he neglected to consummate the marriage. Hell, she'd likely be overjoyed if he never visited her bed.

Minerva was used to the Duke of Hampton's principal country seat. She'd grown up on a small estate next door. Vast as Mandeville House was, familiarity let her see the massive mansion in reduced perspective. The first sight of Vanderlin House had astounded her. She scarcely believed a family could own a house so large in the middle of London, where even couples as wealthy as the Chases and the Iverleys lived in relatively modest, though spacious, houses. The Piccadilly residence was large enough to house the population of a small town and, judging by the ever-present number of liveried servants, it did.

When the duchess had offered to give the ball

for her in Diana's absence, she'd refused to be intimidated. But living in this gilded palace was another matter. Ridiculous.

Every room was designed to impress and couldn't have presented a greater contrast to her childhood home: shabby, cozy Wallop Hall with its low ceilings, cramped quarters, and dogs.

Ridiculous, and a little alarming.

Since the disaster in the library she'd steadily refused to look beyond the wedding ceremony when she became the Marchioness of Blakeney. Between that event and the rest of her life lay the consummation. She'd been curious about marital relations in an academic sort of way; it seemed the sort of thing a girl should know. But once she'd wormed the truth out of Celia (Diana having always very meanly declined to inform her until she was betrothed) she'd lost interest. Diana and Celia seemed to like it, but the business all sounded odd, messy, and possibly unpleasant.

And not at all the sort of thing you wanted to do with someone you didn't like.

At the end of the meal the duchess led her to the drawing room she used every day, a high-ceiled room with plentiful gilt plasterwork, but modest compared to the series of reception rooms used for big entertainments. With a fire in the grate and the curtains drawn it was as close to cozy as any part of Vanderlin House Minerva had yet seen, and that wasn't very close at all. The apartment was a perfect match for its mistress: handsome, elegant, and chilly.

"I had thought," the duchess said as they settled

on tapestry-covered chairs, "to show you the quarters the duke has decided on for you, but I think they are better seen by day. Let's settle down and talk informally. Do you like this room?"

"Very elegant."

"A good size for everyday use. There's one very similar in the west end of the house which will be yours."

Minerva hoped it had more comfortable seating. Though Diana often scolded her for it, she liked to put her feet up on a sofa and read for hours. The duchess appeared never to so much as bend her spine.

"Naturally for formal entertaining you will use the principal rooms," she continued.

Though Minerva dreamed of being a great hostess, she found the idea of receiving hundreds of people in this vast house intimidating. Her ambitions were on a smaller scale.

"Don't worry, my dear. We have an excellent staff so there will be no need for you to concern yourself with the mundane details of domestic arrangements."

"You know, Your Grace, Blakeney and I have not discussed where we shall live. I had the impression the duke's kind offer of rooms here came as a surprise to him."

The duchess swept aside such an insignificant obstacle as her son's opinion. "He will do as he's bid." Her voice dropped to a confidential level. "The first time you dined at Mandeville, after your sister wed Iverley, I was impressed by your grasp of national affairs."

"Thank you."

"It was why I offered to have your presentation ball here. And because of the duke's affection for Iverley, of course."

"I was most grateful."

"Perhaps not so grateful anymore?" Minerva thought there might be a hint of mischief in the duchess's question, the first she'd ever detected in that formidable lady's demeanor. She wasn't sure, and even if there were, she couldn't think of a suitable reply. She kept quiet and waited.

"As I am sure you realize, the wives of great men have important parts to play in affairs of state. If we are clever we women can exert great influence."

How often Minerva had said the same thing, in almost the same words, to her family and friends. For the first time in days her heart beat with excitement instead of rage.

"I am the very person," the duchess continued, "to instruct you in your future role."

About to fall on her knees, at least figuratively, and beg her future mother-in-law to let her study at the feet of the master, another thought brought her up short. The duchess spoke of the wives of great men and the Duke of Hampton was one, by most measures. He had been deeply involved in the affairs of the nation for two score years and held numerous offices. He'd almost become Prime Minister back in the last century.

Minerva, on the other hand, was to be the wife of Lord Blakeney. And anyone with less resemblance to a great man was hard to fathom. "But . . ." she began, striving for a tactful way to tell Blakeney's mother that he probably wasn't statesman material.

Her compunction was wasted.

"Blakeney has never been up to the task he will inherit," the duchess said with brutal candor. "He will need your help if he is to perform his future role with any degree of competence."

"I am flattered by your confidence but under the circumstances I believe I have very little influence."

"A clever wife has ways of making herself attended. And since your other duty is to ensure the future generations of Vanderlins, the interests tally nicely."

Greatly as she respected the duchess, Minerva thought she'd better stand up for herself.

"I do not think the methods you suggest," she said carefully, "will win Blakeney's affections since he has no interest in me that way and I have no experience at all."

"Of course you don't! But you will. Lucky you are such a pretty girl."

"And if I should be in the position to persuade him, how can I make him attend to matters for which he has no predilection?"

"Despite his behavior, including the incredible foolishness that has brought us to this pass, I do not believe my son to be a truly stupid man."

"Of course not," Minerva murmured. She wasn't entirely sure the duchess was correct. As far as native wit went, Blakeney might not be lacking. But she'd never had a discussion with the man that wasn't idiotic by her standards. She hated talking about sports.

"If only he would work harder, but he is lazy.

From earliest childhood he refused to apply himself to his schoolroom lessons. His idleness was ever a disappointment to his father."

Perversely, Minerva had a sudden urge to defend her fiancé. Nothing about Blakeney had ever struck her as lazy. On the contrary, he appeared to suffer from an excess of energy, which he expended in physical activities. And he was good at them. Little as Minerva might share the passion, she'd grown up with a hunting-mad mother and knew you didn't become a brilliant horseman, and owner of a first-rate stable of hunters, without the expenditure of considerable effort.

It also didn't seem right to hear the duke and duchess disparage their son because he didn't care to follow their path. Her own parents had never discouraged their six children from following whatever direction appealed to them, and as a result the six of them ended up with a dizzying variety of interests and occupations. William and Margo Montrose might be surprised by some of their children's choices, but they regarded all of them with enormous affection and pride.

Blakeney's attitude to the affairs of the country baffled Minerva. She recalled his indifference to the terrible massacre of Peterloo a few years earlier. How could he not care, especially when he'd been brought up in the very center of English political life? Hazily she wondered if years of proximity could have actually fostered indifference.

For the first time she felt a stirring of curiosity about Blakeney, what kind of man he was, and how he'd reached the age of thirty as that man.

Chapter 5

The carriage drew up at the door and Blake could hardly wait to get out of Hampton House and breathe the free, if smoke-tainted air, of the streets. He'd drop his betrothed in Berkeley Square, dismiss his father's servants, and take a hackney to Covent Garden. Or maybe he'd walk. His limbs felt cramped, his chest tight, a common physical response to the company of his father. The best remedy was a hard gallop over open fields, or a bout of fencing or boxing. Absent either possibility, the company of Desirée would relieve his restlessness. The duke hadn't put a precise date on his mistress's dismissal.

Minerva ignored his hand as he offered to help her into the carriage. "Could we walk?" she said.

He glanced down. "In white slippers? I wouldn't give odds on them reaching home unsoiled."

"I should care, but I don't. I have a fit of the fidgets only exercise will ease."

Blake had rarely felt so much in harmony with the girl. "Very well, Miss Montrose. Take my arm and watch where you step. And let's try not to get either robbed or arrested."

"I have every confidence you are capable of saving me from the former fate. As for the latter, I wish you'd stop bringing that up. I was very young then, and I no longer do such foolish things."

"When my sister Amanda got into trouble at that age it was usually borrowing the older girls' gowns or ogling the footmen. I don't recall her breaking any laws."

"And I shall endeavor not to do so again between here and Berkeley Square."

He dismissed the carriage with a few words and they made their way out to Piccadilly in silence. When they reached the corner of Devonshire House Minerva dropped his arm and skipped on ahead.

"We should turn here," he called.

"No," she said over her shoulder. "I want to keep walking. I'm never allowed to walk around London at night."

"That's because it's not safe for a lady."

"I am sure you are well able to protect me."

He caught up with her right under a streetlamp so was favored with a clear view of a smug little grin. Abandoning hope of a quick escape to Covent Garden, he soon learned she had a particular destination in mind.

"Not a good idea," he said when she turned at the narrow entrance to White Horse Street.

"I want to see Shepherd's Market at night. I read about the old May Fair where all sorts of wicked things happened, but during the day there's nothing but food stalls."

Blake shrugged. The riotous fair had been abolished decades earlier, although the area retained its

odor of notoriety. Minerva was likely to see nothing worse than a few ladies of ill repute. If she was
shocked, so much the better. Still, he seized her
arm and held her firmly at his side.

As they approached the market square, a couple
of prostitutes eyed them curiously. Blake noticed
his companion return their gaze and wondered if
Minerva knew what these women were. Mercifully
she was, for once, quiet, until one of the street-
walkers, a bold piece with a heavily painted face,
stepped directly in front of them.

"Lookin' for a three-in-a-bed, are you?" she demanded. "Or I can find a stallion for your lady if
that's her taste. Mind you," she continued, lowering her eyes to Blake's groin, "I bet a well-hung
cull like you can take care of us both."

Minerva's response to this interesting proposi-
tion he would never know. Just as he backed away
from the thrust of the trollop's ample and mostly
uncovered bosom, he felt a disturbance at his back
and swung around, grabbing a wrist just as its
hand extracted the purse from the tail pocket of
his coat.

"Caught in the act," he said with satisfaction.

The thief was small and wiry and wriggled like
a trout on the line while emitting a stream of ob-
scenities. The whore, probably his accomplice,
turned and fled.

"Quiet in the presence of a lady. You're coming
with me to find the Watch," Blake said. "Miss
Montrose, stay close. I need both hands to manage
this rogue." He tossed her his recovered purse.

His betrothed could not, of course, be expected

to behave like a normal female. She neither succumbed to the vapors, for which Blakeney was profoundly grateful, nor expressed shock and outrage at the attempted theft. Instead she ignored his command and moved to face the blaspheming pickpocket whose arms Blake had firmly twisted behind his back.

"Let him go," she said.

"What?"

"He's little more than a boy."

"That's right, miss," the rogue said, ceasing to struggle in Blake's grip. "Let me go. I never done anything like this before but my mum and little brothers and sisters is starving."

"For Heaven's sake! You're not going to credit such . . ."

She interrupted him. "Let him go. Please. There's no harm done and you still have your money."

With a mental shrug, Blake decided to comply. Dragging the miscreant to Piccadilly to track down a representative of London's somewhat haphazard law enforcement wouldn't be easy, and having both hands occupied would leave Minerva unprotected or—just as likely—free to get into trouble.

"If you insist," he said and released the thief.

"Thanks, guv."

"Thank the lady."

"Thanks, miss. How 'bout a shilling to buy supper for the little 'uns?"

"Don't press your luck."

At Blake's threatening move the lad took to his heels and melted into the alley from which he'd come.

"Let's get out of here." Grasping Minerva firmly by the arm, he hustled her across the square and through to the better lit civilization of Curzon Street.

"It's coming back to me what a cursed nuisance you are, Miss Montrose. Can't you behave like a normal young lady? I was mad to agree to this walk."

"Nonsense. It has been a most interesting experience."

He occurred to him he agreed with her, and his protests were mere bluster. A bride who wasn't a "normal young lady" might make life interesting in some ways. He looked down at her, calmly keeping pace with his stride that made no effort to accommodate ladylike steps.

"You didn't believe the pack of lies that boy told, did you?" he asked. "Far more likely he's part of an organized ring of thieves."

"Far more likely, but we can't be certain. And the law makes no distinction between a starving boy who steals a loaf of bread and a practiced criminal. Either way he could get sent to the gallows or the hulks. Who are you and I to judge and condemn that youth to such a fate?"

"Is lawlessness the only alternative?"

"Reform is the alternative."

And off she went, speaking of theories of justice and bills in Parliament, Bentham and Cobbett, and Elizabeth Fry, prisons and public education. To his astonishment, Blake found himself interested. He enjoyed hearing her discuss public business without reference to political maneuvers, realizing his father's affairs always seemed to concern the wrangling of the ministry, Parliament, and party. Minerva had the knack of presenting facts in a clear but entertaining fashion, omitting excessive verbiage and getting straight to the point. After a lifetime of hearing and blocking out such discourse, he paid close attention. She made these matters sound truly important. For the most part he listened in silence, only venturing a question or two.

"Is the new prison on the Millbank a great improvement?" he asked.

"Better than Newgate or the hulks. But the prisoners don't stay there long before being moved on. Until Parliament acts there will be no true justice."

By now they'd reached the south end of Berkeley Square, almost at the Chases' house. Minerva came to a halt and turned to study his face. Under the light of a gas streetlamp, blue eyes blazed with an intensity that belied the pallid perfection of her features.

"I do believe you care, Blakeney," she said. "I would never have thought it. Let me send you some pamphlets on the subject."

His heart sank. Pamphlets. She wanted him to read pamphlets. It was like being at school again.

She carried on, oblivious to his discomfort. "When you read the details you cannot fail to be touched by the horrors visited upon these unfortunates. No one could."

He needed to change the subject, fast. Though it went contrary to his resolution earlier in the evening, he could think of only one way to do it.

Minerva was pleased by the attention her reluctant betrothed paid her. According to previous experience, Blakeney never showed curiosity about anything but hunting. While he courted Diana they'd suffered interminable accounts of the pursuit of foxes. Perhaps the intervening years had effected a change in his frivolous outlook.

Again she noted the spiderweb of lines extending from the corners of his dark blue eyes, a physical manifestation of his maturity. She had to admit, he really was very good looking. As she studied him in the gaslight, something odd happened. His expression, the quality of his regard, altered. In any other man she'd have read it as . . . desire.

"My dear Miss Montrose. If I have to listen to such dry stuff, let it be from the lips of a pretty girl. Or why not put those pretty lips to better use. Does a future husband merit a kiss?"

He held her gaze with unwavering heat for some moments, while she tried to interpret this unexpected turn of events. At the beginning of the evening she'd have sooner kissed a snake than Blakeney. But now?

"Why not?" she said slowly. "We may as well both find out what we are getting."

His breath caressed her cheek. "In the interests of discretion," he murmured, his deep voice descending to a basso profundo, "and because I don't wish to have to answer to Lord Chase at swordpoint, I suggest we move away from the lamp."

He offered his arm in an oddly formal gesture and led her to a dark spot in the center of the square. The garden was large enough to provide a refuge from urban noise, even in this exclusive neighborhood. The racket of hooves and wheels on cobblestones, music and chatter emerging from the open windows of a mansion, faded into the distance, leaving the murmur of a soft breeze through new leaves and the discordant song of a nightbird.

Minerva wondered how many lovers had hidden among these trees to steal a kiss. But she and Blakeney weren't lovers. She waited curiously with unwonted passivity as he placed one hand on her shoulder and tilted her chin with the other. Unable to read his expression in the dark, she closed her eyes, sensing his body heat, the scent of starch, his warm breath lightly laced with wine.

She envisioned that shapely sulky mouth as it touched her, lips soft and firm, brushing the breadth of hers. She gave an involuntary smile. It felt good.

He came closer and she opened to his unspoken request, mingling her breath with his, enjoying his gentle sucking on her upper lip. He knew what he was doing.

Responding to her participation, he lowered his hands to part the velvet cloak she wore over her evening gown, then drew her in close so his clothing—fine wool and crisp linen—caressed the exposed skin of her chest and neck. Her flesh tingled.

"Now," he whispered. The word wafted between her parted lips, followed by his tongue, teasing and stroking the tender skin within. Minerva found herself being thoroughly kissed by someone she recognized as a master of the art.

Her head began to buzz and, fearing she might

faint, she held onto his head, and learned the golden locks were as silken to the touch as the eye. She tried to analyze the experience, define the taste of the kiss, but it was like nothing she recognized, neither sweet nor sharp. It tasted . . . physical. And very good. Her thoughts dissolved along with her breath.

Then, quite abruptly, he set her aside and stepped back so she had to clear her muddled head and find her balance in a hurry.

"Thank you, Miss Montrose. You kiss as prettily as you look. Now let me see you to Lord Chase's door before you succumb to the dangers of the night air."

The words sounded genuine and were delivered with a winning smile, but she didn't feel complimented. By the time she took formal leave of him in the hall of the Chases' house she knew why.

It wasn't the first time Minerva Montrose had been kissed. In the spirit of research and a liberal education she'd accepted embraces from a couple of gentleman, one of them a highly attractive Austrian count. She'd carefully selected him for the experiment, knowing him a hardened flirt and quite uninterested in marriage to an English girl of moderate fortune. In an anteroom of a Viennese ballroom, after a superb waltz, he'd kissed her every bit as thoroughly as Blakeney had just done. Unlike Blakeney the young Graf had emerged from the embrace panting with a flattering degree of desperation.

Not so her betrothed husband. If Minerva judged correctly, he had been scarcely affected by her. Yet he'd initiated the encounter with theatrical seductiveness.

Theatrical indeed. Thinking back on it, she believed he'd proposed the kiss to change the subject. He was trying to avoid something, very likely her conversation, which hurt a little. She'd thought him engaged by the subjects she found so engrossing. Her kisses, apparently, were no more fascinating to her future spouse, and this also irked her. For she'd found him a much better kisser than the Austrian, and it piqued her vanity to be found wanting.

Chapter 6

Blake had given his mistress her congé, but they hadn't yet parted. Desirée couldn't understand why parting was necessary, especially once she grasped that marriage would greatly improve the state of his purse. She had a very French attitude toward the institution of matrimony.

"Of course," she said, stretched out on the mattress of her large, lace-trimmed bed. "I don't understand why *monsieur le duc* did not arrange a marriage for you before. It seems quite strange that you must wed this *jeune fille d'aucun importance* just because of *un petit scandale*."

Stark naked, Blake stood over her and helped himself to the coffee that had been delivered to the chamber, along with the midday sun. He didn't ask how she knew about the *scandale*. The members of the demimonde always knew at least as much about their beau monde counterparts as the highborn gossips of Mayfair.

"The point isn't the scandal for me. It's that I ruined her prospects for another respectable match."

"She has done well for herself. Better than she could expect. She must be very pleased, *je crois*."

"Miss Montrose? She thinks she's far too clever for me."

"If she is so clever she knows she has made *une alliance superbe*."

"No. She dislikes me, thinks me a fool."

Beneath his protests a seed of doubt was sewn. It bothered him that Minerva Montrose might be coming around to the worldly benefits of their marriage. Why should he care? Wouldn't it be better if he and his bride found grounds for mutual accommodation? The source of his disquiet niggled the back of his brain. During their nighttime adventure in Shepherd's Market he'd softened toward her, even liked her a little. That she should continue to despise him for his stupidity yet enjoy the material advantages of being a Vanderlin seemed intolerable.

He thought of their kiss, initiated by him for reasons that had nothing to do with desire. For a girl who entirely lacked experience it had been a fair effort. She hadn't kept her lips clamped shut like a trap. Her body—and he admitted the excellence of her figure—had melted under his mild caresses. For a moment he'd looked forward to his coming duty of taking her to bed. Until he remembered he wasn't going to.

He looked down at the Frenchwoman, displayed shamelessly for his visual delectation. He'd never before had a woman who shaved or plucked every hair that wasn't on her head. And she was full of tricks.

"*Viens, mon cher,*" Desirée demanded in her most lubricious tone.

He set aside his cup and returned to bed.

An hour later he lay on his back, lightly panting, happily spent, with some new French words in his vocabulary.

"*Mon amour,*" she whispered in his ear. "To part would be a tragedy. After the wedding *voyage* is over, you will come back to me."

"You should find a new protector," Blake said without much enthusiasm.

"Is she beautiful, your fiancée? As beautiful as me?"

He raised himself onto his elbow and looked down at the flawless features, knife-sharp cheekbones, and full carmine lips.

"Miss Montrose is exceedingly beautiful," he said and was rewarded with a sulky pout that made him think of the uses of a skilled mouth. She hadn't made him wait for the ruby bracelets, which should be ready for delivery from the jeweler in a day or two. Alas, they would be her farewell gift.

"You will forget Desirée. You love this *jeune fille,* this English virgin." Almond-shaped black eyes filled with tears, arousing admiration for her acting and an inkling of interest in another bout.

"No."

"Then come back to me. What is it to her, as long as you give her jewels and children?"

"Give her jewels!" he yelled and jumped up from the bed. "What time is it?"

Once again Desirée had made him late for an appointment at Vanderlin House. This time his parents' summons was for the purpose of surveying his new living quarters and deciding which of the family jewels should be assigned to the use of his bride.

Not that he had any intention of setting up house under the ducal noses, but he hadn't yet evolved his strategy for resistance. Time enough after their wedding trip to Paris.

He scrambled through his ablutions and into his clothes. It wouldn't be the first time Minerva had seen him unshaven. Neither, alas, would it be the last.

"After the honeymoon . . ." Desirée reminded him as he gave her a quick parting kiss.

"I'll think about it," he said.

Minerva liked pretty clothes, but not enough to spare much time for them. When Diana had insisted on ordering dozens of garments in preparation for the season, Minerva left most of the decisions to her knowledgeable sister and made sure she had something to read during the fittings. The modistes became accustomed to Miss Montrose standing with her nose in a copy of *The Reformist* magazine while they pinned and tucked and hemmed around her.

Despite her indifference she knew she was one of the better dressed ladies making her debut that year. Her sole regret was her stubbornly frivolous golden hair, and she envied her sister's rich brown locks. The young daughter of her Viennese hosts had compared her to a flaxen-headed doll. The little girl meant it as a compliment, but Minerva had taken a dislike to the wide-eyed simper on the face of the toy. After that she refused to have her hair curled, preferring to wear it in neat braids pinned around her head.

As for jewelry, she was content with what she had: a necklace of small pearls presented at birth by her godmother; her parents' confirmation gift of a gold cross and chain; a modest pearl set of brooch, bracelets, and eardrops from Diana and Sebastian. They went with everything and required little thought.

Even Diana's lavish jewelry collection didn't prepare her for the extent of the Duke of Hampton's possessions. Boxes and cases were heaped high covering every inch of the desk in the duke's study, whence they'd been hastily removed by a procession of three or four footman under orders from Blakeney's mother. She didn't say so, but clearly the duchess had realized the library, the scene of the late unfortunate incident, might not be the best location for a ceremony accepting Minerva as bride to the heir to the dukedom.

Not that the heir had deigned to appear. Minerva had arrived at the appointed hour and enjoyed a tour of her future quarters without the participation of the man who was to share them. She ought to be insulted, she supposed, but found it easier to answer questions about her taste in bed curtains without the presence of the man who would have the right to join her behind the drapes.

Aside from the duke and duchess and herself, the only attendant in the study was a very old man, whose sole duty seemed to be the care of this impressive treasure. Minerva had never heard of such a specialized servant and had no idea what his title might be. He wore a footman's wig but rather than livery he dressed like a clerk. He seemed to know his part in the ritual. He made a selection from the array of boxes, opened it, and placed it before the duke's eyes with a deferential air. His master would either shake his head or, less often, gesture for the duchess to see the contents. If the latter agreed, Minerva's opinion was sought.

Many of the pieces were old-fashioned and not, to her ignorant eyes, attractive. At first she tried to murmur something noncommittal but when an uncommonly ugly antique bracelet was added to the pile of items to be given to her, she decided she'd better make her feelings known if she wasn't to end up with a box full of unwearable horrors.

"Thank you, but it's not to my taste, ma'am," she said, barely repressing a shudder at a brooch of frightening brown and yellow stones.

The duke waved the piece away while the duchess looked at her with a glimmer of respect, and began to take a more active part in the proceedings.

"Diamonds," she said. "You must have a diamond set. They are always useful."

Despite having managed her entire life without such a convenience, Minerva obediently considered two different necklaces with matching earrings and bracelets. Not for the first time she wished Diana were there. Her sister would know exactly what to choose. Not wishing to appear greedy, she picked the set with the smaller stones. Then she expressed admiration for a pretty collar of cameos that had the virtue of simplicity.

"A lovely group," her future mother-in-law said.

"Those are ancient Roman gems I bought on my Grand Tour," added the duke. "I had them made up into a necklace for my mother."

"You mean these carvings are almost two thousand years old?" Minerva asked. "The faces look quite modern."

"I always thought that myself. Some of the subjects are known. Two or three of the men are Caesars. There's a record of the names somewhere if you would care to see it."

"Thank you," Minerva said politely, despite only a cursory interest in Roman history. The duke displayed unusual animation, as though his gift to his mother held some importance for him.

"Is it in the case? Give it to Miss Montrose."

The Steward of the Jewels, as Minerva had mentally dubbed the attendant, silently handed her a folded paper. The foolscap sheet bore a drawing of the necklace, with about half the cameos identified by name in a neat copperplate. Beneath was inscribed a paragraph about each historical character.

"'Livia, the wife of Emperor Augustus.'" Minerva smiled. "I never thought to wear the image of an Empress of Rome."

"Are you going to adopt the lady's habit of ruthlessness?" asked a voice from the doorway. "Should I be alarmed?"

"Blakeney," said the duke, his tone plunged from balmy to frost. "You honor us. Pray come in and close the door."

Blakeney sauntered forward and bowed to his father, managing to convey derision in the obeisance. Not troubling with an apology for his tardiness, he greeted the ladies with a kiss on the hand apiece.

"My dear Miss Montrose," he drawled over her knuckle, "are you planning to run the Roman Empire from behind the throne?"

He was only being provocative. Surely he had no idea that had always been her plan for marriage, down to almost those very words. Surprised to find him so well informed about Roman history, she glanced again at the paper in her left hand and read the paragraph to herself.

She smiled sweetly. "Like Livia and Augustus I look forward to fifty-one years of devoted matrimony."

"A very proper sentiment," said the duke. "You shall have the cameos."

"My grandmother's antique necklace," Blakeney said. "I remember her wearing it and telling me the stories behind the gems. I never knew my grandfather, the third duke, but I do remember the duchess as an old woman. Like my mother she was younger than her spouse."

Minerva had known the Duke and Duchess of Hampton by sight since she was a child. She'd always regarded them as deeply venerable and extremely old. Now she covertly examined the couple with greater attention for their appearance than she'd ever accorded before. The duke had to be well into his sixties, given what she knew of his career, which was almost everything. If anything he looked older, his face lined and gray, and with a stoop of the shoulders as though he carried the burdens of the world. The duchess looked as healthy as Minerva's own mother and about the same age: not many years above fifty.

"The dukes of Hampton always marry much younger women," Blake went on. "The ten years difference in our ages is nothing. I'd have to wed a child to stay in the family tradition."

"A singularly foolish remark," said the duke. He turned to Minerva with a warm smile that seemed a deliberate snub of his son. "Now, my dear. Do you think you have enough baubles?"

"More than enough, sir. You and the duchess are very kind."

Blakeney approached the small table on which the Steward of the Jewels had placed Minerva's selections, searching for something. He pushed aside the flat box containing the cameos to open the larger one beneath. The diamonds. He set his shoulders back and looked his father in the eye. Minerva had never seen her fiancé so . . . intent. She looked from the younger man to the older and, for the first time, saw the resemblance. In his youth the duke must have looked very like Blakeney. Now he seemed wrinkled and pale in contrast to his son's vigorous, golden glow. A fleeting notion of an old king challenged by a young prince tickled her brain, but she couldn't place the reference.

"The George I amethysts are not here." Blakeney's statement sounded like an accusation.

The duke said nothing.

"And the Queen Anne pearls? Why does Miss Montrose have these puny diamonds instead?"

"They are not puny . . ." Both Blake and his father ignored her interruption.

"Miss Montrose," the duke said calmly, "shall have the use of all the family jewels in due course."

"Why not now?"

Minerva couldn't see what Blakeney had to be angry about, yet clearly he was upset. She moved across the room to take his arm, the first time she'd touched him uninvited.

"Their Graces have been more than generous. They've given me everything I could possibly need. I have no desire to deprive the duchess of her jewels."

Blakeney's muscles were tense under her hand. "There's no question of depriving *the duchess* of anything."

Minerva sensed undercurrents in the exchange. Perhaps Blakeney thought she minded because she wasn't being festooned in pearls and amethysts, but she found it hard to believe he cared.

The Duke of Hampton had long been one of the statesmen she admired the most and, though she'd told herself she needed to try, she hadn't yet broken the habit of thinking Blakeney the next thing to an idiot. He was engaged in some kind of contest of wills with his father, something beyond the kind of masculine strife she was accustomed to observe among her four brothers. Blakeney's paternal battle appeared to be more serious. Did it merely arise from the duke's disappointment in his son's indifference to weighty matters of state? Minerva could understand such displeasure. Yet she couldn't help feeling there was a greater conflict at work and she was curious to discover it.

*   *   *

The amethysts had been a wedding gift from
George I to the second duke. The pearls had been
in the family even longer, dating from the time
when Queen Anne had enjoyed a brief but violent
friendship with the beautiful young wife of the
first Marquis of Blakeney, before he was created
duke for his steadfast support of the Hanoverian
succession.

Both heirlooms were the traditional perquisites
of the heir's bride. By fobbing Minerva off with
insignificant trinkets, the duke demonstrated his
contempt for his only son.

Blake was used to that. To his surprise some of
his anger at the snub was on behalf of his fiancée.

*Miss Montrose shall have the use of all the
family jewels in due course.*

That clever young lady might be oblivious to the
duke's meaning, but not Blake. The duke was stat-
ing that Minerva, with her insufficient connections
and fortune, would only be fully welcomed into
the Vanderlin family when she'd produced a son.
Or even two.

Blake was rather charmed by her naïveté. She
had no idea she'd been given inferior jewels. He
also felt some compunction that she wouldn't be
earning the good ones any time soon. When he col-
lected Desirée's ruby bracelets, he noticed a magnificent emerald and diamond necklace in a glass
case.

"A copy of one owned by the late Empress Jo-
sephine and made in Paris," the jeweler said, only
too happy to demonstrate the most expensive item
in his shop to a customer known to be about to

have immediate, rather than future, access to a handsome fortune. "With the war well behind us we have no need to avoid French fashions."

"Indeed not," Blake said. "I'm off to Paris myself in a week or two."

"With such a necklace a lady would have no trouble holding her own, or even surpassing, the French ladies."

Blake left the premises with the bracelets for his mistress in one pocket and a wedding present for his bride in the other.

He reached his rooms to find that someone had delivered a parcel for him. Any expectation of pleasure vanished when his man told him it came from Vanderlin House. He didn't bother to open the duke's note. As promised or threatened, his father was making another attempt to prepare Blake for his illustrious future by setting him a course of study. He picked up the first of a thick sheaf of pamphlets and allowed himself a little grin. Minerva, at least, hadn't made good on her kind offer to provide him with improving literature. Perhaps there was hope for them yet.

He'd better give it a try. Every now and then he suffered an attack of hope that a miracle would occur and he would be able to appreciate one of these earnest tracts, full of matters vital to the future of the nation.

He poured himself a glass of sherry for fortification and turned to the first page.

The smell of ink on cheap paper assaulted him. Small print and long words danced before his eyes.

Ten minutes later he stood up and pitched them into the fire, glass and pamphlet both.

Chapter 7

When Sebastian deemed his wife well enough to travel up from Kent, Minerva was reunited with her sister at the Iverleys' house in Portman Square. Once the children had been kissed and admired and settled in the nursery with their attendants, Diana lost no time in hustling Minerva to her boudoir for a tête-à-tête.

"I'm so sorry, my darling," Diana said, drawing Minerva down onto the sofa with her and holding her hand. "It's all my fault."

"Why? Because you didn't marry Blakeney yourself? Do you expect me to believe you regret wedding Sebastian because of what has happened to me?"

"Hardly! Though I'm glad to see your misfortunes haven't rendered you incapable of impertinence. I meant if I'd been well enough to attend to your presentation myself, the ball would have been here. There would have been no chance of Blake trying to seduce someone in the library because Sebastian wouldn't have let me invite him."

Minerva rested her head on Diana's shoulder, as she had so often as a child. Finally in company with the one person in whom she might fully confide, she felt none of the need to scream with anger or weep with fear she'd been suppressing.

"What's done is done," she said. "I must make the best of it."

"My dearest Min! The maturity of the sentiment does you great credit. Lift up your head so I may look for gray hairs."

"After all, Blakeney is heir to one of the most powerful political families in England. He may not be very clever but perhaps that's for the best. I shall guide him." She wished she felt as confident as she sounded.

"That's all very well, but Blake's not just a dynasty. He's a man too. And I think you'll find when you get to know him he's not all bad. I wouldn't have considered marrying him if he was."

"You thought you were in love with him because of his looks!"

"True. Mostly. But I like him too. I always have. Sebastian has his own reasons to loathe him, going back to their childhood, but he's getting over it."

"Not that I've noticed. He wanted to kill Blakeney after the ball."

"Blake did behave abominably. I was so furious when I heard about it."

"He thought I was the Duchess of Lethbridge, I understand that. I understand that men have mistresses, too. I've been trying to tell myself he didn't mean it."

Diana's arms tightened about her. "Poor Min. I don't know what to say. Try and forget it. How have you been getting on with him since?"

Minerva shrugged. "We've only met a few times. We have been pleasant to each other."

"Nothing more?"

"We had one conversation about criminal justice reform, but since then he's shied away when I talk about anything interesting."

"Interesting to you, you mean."

Min grinned back at Diana. "Of course."

"You used to complain about his hunting stories. Have you had to suffer a lot of them?"

"Not one." Min stopped to think about it. "How very odd. He's mentioned horses a couple of times, but no hunting. He's been living in Devon for a year or two. Perhaps they don't hunt there. If not, I don't know what he was doing there."

"He sold his hunters when he left London. The duke keeps him very short of money but that will change now. Sebastian made sure of it when he negotiated the marriage settlement. You needn't worry."

"I wasn't worrying," Minerva said absently. Blakeney had always been hunting mad, yet apparently he'd given up the sport, just like that. She added it to the compilation of odd facts she was amassing about her husband-to-be.

"What about the duke and duchess? Have they received you kindly?"

"The duke and duchess could not have been more gracious. Dining at their table and hearing the latest political news from its very source is thrilling. I can't believe I am to live at Vanderlin House."

"Is that settled then?" Diana asked. "Did Blake agree?"

"I've seen my rooms. Our rooms." Minerva replied. It was true that her fiancé had been silent on the subject of their abode. *Silence meant consent, didn't it?*

"I think it an excellent sign that the duke and duchess are so cordial in their welcome. If they respect you, Blakeney will too."

"They are giving me a lot of jewelry."

"Tell me about it." Diana's eyes lit up at the mention of one of her favorite subjects.

When it came to describing jewelry, or clothing, Minerva inevitably disappointed her fashionable sister. "Some diamonds. And some other things. I can't remember, there were so many. You'll have to wait and see them when they've been cleaned. Although," she added, "they didn't look dirty to me."

"I don't know Blakeney's parents well," Diana said. "Sebastian likes them."

Min frowned. "I like them, I suppose, and I admire them. But they aren't very warm. Not at all like our parents. In fact they are quite cold with Blakeney."

"I'm sure it's just ducal formality. Since Blake is to marry into our family, I suppose we'd better get him used to the Montroses. I shall give a dinner."

"Rather a small dinner since it's too far for Rufus and Henry, and Mama and Papa aren't coming to London for the wedding." Minerva's parents hated to travel. They'd written that they'd see Blake and Minerva in Shropshire, when they returned from Paris and came up to Mandeville House for the summer.

"Will's only a few miles from London and we'll send for Stephen from Harrow. Four Montroses can make enough of a racket to let Blake know what he's in for."

Minerva tried to imagine Blakeney fitting into a gathering of her noisy, opinionated family and failed. Not that her fiancé was a man of excessive formality, but conversation among the Montroses raged fast and furious, quite unlike Blake's rather dégagé attitude. His stance in company tended toward semi-inattention, punctuated by the occasional cynical comment.

He had hinted at a more serious side during their walk home from dinner at Vanderlin House, then belied the impression with his kiss in the middle of Berkeley Square. She shook her head in bafflement and blushed at the recollection.

Diana regarded her with interest and drew the right conclusion. "Has he kissed you?"

She nodded.

"How was it?"

"It was pleasant." Min didn't want to admit how much, even to Diana. As for the odd physical sensations she sometimes got in Blakeney's presence, it was merely her body's reactions to a good-looking man. True, she'd met plenty of good-looking men without getting so much as a quiver of desire in her chest, let alone her belly, but Blakeney was probably the handsomest man she knew. It was natural and quite involuntary, like a sneeze in a dusty room.

"It's good you find him attractive. You'll enjoy bedding him, and if you enjoy it he'll enjoy it. Bed isn't everything, but mutual satisfaction there can help smooth over differences in other areas of life. I always said I'd tell you all about marital intercourse once you were engaged, and it may as well be now."

"As a matter of fact I know quite a bit."

"Why am I not surprised? I had a feeling Celia and you had a few interesting chats."

"I read a book too." At the time, Minerva had found the outlandish games played by men and women in *The Genuine and Remarkable Amours of the Celebrated Peter Aretin* cause for mirth. Two years later she wasn't so sure.

"Books are all very well, but you can't ask them questions when you don't understand something. I'm going to be frank with you. I believe Blake to be a man of sophisticated tastes when it comes to women."

"Did you . . . ?"

"Absolutely not. We never exchanged more than a kiss or two."

Min nodded in considerable relief. Her forthcoming nuptials were complicated enough already.

"Gentlemen expect their brides to be virtuous," Diana continued. "Some men like them to be ignorant too. They enjoy playing the tutor in the bedroom. My first husband was like that. I do not believe Blakeney is one of those. The more you know, the happier you'll both be." She smiled. "You can get a man to do just about anything after a good bout of lovemaking."

Minerva felt less confidence than she had on any subject in years. The kiss she'd shared with Blakeney had affected him much less than it had her.

She thought about parliamentary and criminal reform. She thought about children working long hours at dangerous tasks for pitiful wages. She thought about the number of parliamentary seats controlled by the Duke of Hampton and his influence in the country. Influence that would one day be wielded by Lord Blakeney. She thought about influencing Lord Blakeney.

Never one to shrink from a challenge, she stiffened her spine. "I suppose I'd better listen to your advice," she said.

William Montrose, the eldest of Minerva's brothers, was a very large man, topping Blake by two or three inches in height and at least three times as much around the chest. His brawn was obviously helpful for hacking his way through jungles in pursuit of rare plants, and for beating up men who had the temerity to look up his sister's skirts. Blake seized his hand and shook it vigorously.

"It's been a long time, Montrose. I recall you are a fair boxer. Would you like to put on the gloves with me at Jackson's some time?" Better to let William expend his violent impulses under circumstances where Blake's superior science and speed would make the contest an equal one.

William's glare dissolved into a reserved smile with just a hint of a threat. "I'd be delighted, Blakeney. My felicitations, and I trust you will treat my sister well."

Though invited to a family dinner, the guest list had been expanded to include the Iverleys' friends, the Chases and the Comptons. The group was small enough for informality. Not that the Montroses went in for ceremony. As his neighbors in Shropshire he'd always been a little acquainted with the family, and well aware of their reputation for eccentricity. No one at the table appeared at all surprised when Stephen, the youngest, threw a piece of bread at his brother in response to a mild insult. Even the haughty and exquisite dandy Tarquin Compton merely ducked, and brushed a falling crumb from his coat.

Diana Iverley was a talented hostess and Blake wondered if his future wife shared her sister's aptitude. He wouldn't mind more evenings like this one, but couldn't imagine such an event in the lofty apartments of Vanderlin House. Even Cousin Sebastian, usually so hellishly serious, seemed relaxed at his wife's table. He and Blake had exchanged polite, if not cordial, greetings, and proceeded to ignore each other by silent mutual agreement.

After an enjoyable discussion with Stephen about estate management, he turned to his betrothed.

"Well Miss Montrose," he began, hoping to forestall another conversation about the prospects for a dissolution of Parliament. "How did you enjoy the play last night?"

"Very well, thank you, Lord Blakeney. It was very gracious of the duke and duchess to invite me."

"Did you prefer the tragedy or the farce?"

"I've never been fond of *Macbeth*. I don't find it at all probable that Lady Macbeth would go mad like that. I should think she'd be too busy running Scotland."

"You shock me, Miss Montrose. Do you con-
done murder?"

"Don't be absurd, Lord Blakeney. I am happy to
say that regicide is no longer a necessary or feasible
route to power."

Amazing the way the girl managed to bring any
discussion around to her favorite topic.

"I think you'd better call me Blake," he said
hastily.

"And you'd better call me Minerva."

"Your family call you Min."

"That's such a childish name."

"Perhaps I'll call you Minnie."

"If you do I'll have to kill you. Or call you
Arthur."

"No one has ever called me Arthur. How did
you even know it's my name?"

Minerva's perfect little mouth pursed into a
pout of a smile. "There are no secrets from Mr.
Debrett."

This hint of mischief piqued Blake's attention.
She was appealing when she wasn't being deathly
earnest. Knowing only too well what *interested* his
future bride, it might be to his advantage to find
out what *amused* her.

"So if you don't think much of *Macbeth,* do you
enjoy comedies?"

"I do. I adore Sheridan's ingenuity and wit." Her
perfect little nose wrinkled. "The farce last night
was idiotic and not at all witty."

"You didn't appreciate the pirates stranded on a
desert island?"

"Pirates are all very well, but what was Harlequin doing there? And performing poodles in neck ruffs?" Her blue eyes twinkled with mirth. "Don't you think it strains credulity to find an entire pantomime troupe in the middle of the ocean?"

"I don't think logic is the main object of these entertainments." Blake wondered if he should mention that the display of ankles by the females in the company was the major attraction, and one he could appreciate.

"Of course," she said, lowering her voice and leaning in confidentially. "I expect you enjoyed the girls. My brothers would have."

Touché, he conceded silently. Could Minerva Montrose actually be flirting?

"Were they pretty?" He angled his head so their lips were less than a foot apart, bordering on the intimate.

She held her ground and met his eye, though her faint blush told him she was a little embarrassed. For all her confidence, Minerva Montrose was a novice when it came to playing the coquette. She was also, he had to admit, every bit as pretty as any of the dancers.

He dropped his voice to a murmur. "I didn't notice any handsome girls. On the stage."

"How very dull for you," she said gamely.

"I wasn't bored," he said, and summoned his most seductive smile

This time she couldn't hold his gaze. She drew back, her cheeks scarlet. "Neither was I. The company in the box was excellent. I enjoyed meeting your old school friend Mr. Huntley."

She was clearly flustered by his attention, but

she couldn't have said anything more guaranteed to break the flirtatious mood and sour Blake's temper. He'd been trying to put that particular encounter out of his mind.

He leaned back in his chair and stared straight ahead. "We make all sorts of friends in our youth."

His discouraging tone seemed to restore her poise. "I found Mr. Huntley agreeable and sensible."

He shrugged, not daring to say what he really thought of Huntley, in case he gave a hint of the truth.

"I understand he comes from an ordinary family," Minerva continued, "and his grandfather was a merchant. He was quite open to me about his origins when he told me about the by-election he is contesting."

When the blackguard had invaded the duke's box, it had taken all Blake's restraint not to cause a scandal by tossing him into the pit. He'd stepped out into the passage to regain control of his temper and missed the fact that Minerva and Huntley had spoken at length. His gut tightened, worrying what his "old friend" wanted with his fiancée. Nothing good, that was for sure.

"Huntley told me he decided to stand for Parliament," he said.

"What's wrong with that?"

"Nothing, I suppose. I've never had much time for politicians. Seems they're all jockeying for advancement."

"Just because a man needs to make his way in life, it doesn't mean he cannot also act for the greater good. Not everyone is fortunate enough to be born into wealth and position. Our public life needs men of talent, regardless of their birth. But perhaps you disagree."

If she expected him to respond to her challenge with a defense of hereditary government, she'd be disappointed. Blake had always been alive to the irony of his place in that system. Many people, starting with his father, found it ludicrous he had been born to inherit power and responsibility. He heartily concurred.

As did his future bride. "It's shocking the way, as Shakespeare said, that some men are born to greatness and yet deserve it so little." The amazing thing was, she spoke without any edge of malice. She looked at him as she spoke, obviously had him in mind, but had no idea her words might be interpreted as a personal attack. Her expression was one of alert interest.

"That's arrant nonsense, Juliana." Iverley's outburst fell into a moment of quiet around the table and saved Blake from the need to respond. "That binding is seventeenth century or I'm a Dutchman."

"Total twaddle, Iverley," replied Lady Chase. "Any idiot can see it's Elizabethan."

"Sebastian's off again," Minerva said.

Blake groaned. "Books!"

"Oh please, no!" added Stephen Montrose.

The three of them spoke almost simultaneously, then burst out laughing.

"Sebastian and Juliana will be at it for ages now," Minerva said. "They used to hate each other. Even though they are friends nowadays, and she's been allowed to join the Burgundy Club, their relations tend to be argumentative."

Sebastian, Tarquin Compton, and the Chases were members of a society of book collectors, not an organization Blake had ever been in danger of joining.

"And does Lady Chase generally win?" he asked.

"I neither know nor care. I'm afraid my interest in antiquarian books is slight. Or nonexistent."

"There's no need to apologize to me," he said, drawing another smile from her. "I couldn't agree with you more."

Stephen made a gagging noise.

In this gathering of bibliophiles it felt good to be with Minerva and Stephen, in shared scorn for the pursuit of book collecting. Although in his case scorn wasn't quite the right word. Dread rather.

His relief was short-lived. William Montrose and Celia Compton were also talking about books, but the kind one read. Or rather the kind everyone else read. Their exchange about their preferred novels by the author of *Waverley* degenerated into a table-wide debate. Blake learned that everyone in the room, even his scholarly cousin, his high-minded betrothed bride, and her youngest brother, read all the most popular novels of the day. Opinions on *Ivanhoe* and *Rob Roy,* Miss Edgeworth, Miss Austen, and Mrs. Radcliffe were tossed across the room like Stephen's bread.

Blake sank into his seat and yearned for invisibility. He'd spent his entire life avoiding such discussions and chosen his intimates from those who derived their amusement from less elevated pastimes. In his future he saw no escape. He faced the truth that he was doomed to join a family with a passion for the written word.

What would these literate people think if they knew he'd sooner attempt to swim the English Channel than plow through one of Sir Walter Scott's endless volumes?

What would they say if they realized that their newest member, a grown man of thirty with a famous name and the finest education England had to offer, could barely read? That he could only decipher a simple printed page with the greatest of difficulty?

Blakeney knew that many people, starting with his own father, thought him stupid. Almost no one knew for certain that it was the absolute truth.

Chapter 8

Getting drunk was very tempting. The decanters of port and brandy being passed around the table were far friendlier than the men at the table. The ladies had left, leaving Blake at the mercy of the Montrose brothers, Iverley, and his friends.

Since the disaster with Huntley, Blake avoided drinking to excess. Come to think of it, the last time he'd overindulged was the evening of his mother's ball for Minerva.

Look where being drunk had got him that time. He pushed away his glass without taking a sip and resigned himself to dealing with potentially hostile company in a state of sobriety. He was saved by the arrival of a footman with a request that he join Lady Iverley in the library.

What was it about libraries? Why did people have to have so many damn books?

Diana received him alone.

"Is this wise? May I expect my cousin to burst in and knock me down?"

Diana laughed. "I told Sebastian I was going to

speak to you after dinner. He promised to behave."

"I assume that's only if *we* behave."

"You have no more desire to misbehave with me than I do with you, so don't pretend otherwise."

"You know I've been pining for you ever since you so cruelly threw me over."

"I know nothing of the kind. And a good thing too, since we are to be brother and sister."

Diana came forward, took both his hands and kissed him on the cheek. "Welcome to the family."

"I'm sorry," he said. "I never meant to compromise your sister."

"I know that, Blake. Now sit down and let us talk about it. First tell me how you are. I haven't seen you since you were at Mandeville two summers ago."

"I've been living in Devon, managing the estate there."

"And does farming suit you? You are looking well."

"I enjoyed having something useful to do. But I'm glad to be back in town for a while."

"Did your rustication have anything to do with that little money problem you had?"

"Thank you for your loan. I'm sorry it took so long to repay." If she noticed he hadn't answered the question she gave no sign. "Did you tell your sister about it?" he asked.

"No, I didn't think it my business to do so. If it's something she should know, I trust you to tell her yourself. If not, I think we should both forget the matter."

Blake found himself relaxing. He'd always felt

at ease with Diana, one reason he'd wished to marry her. He had to admit Minerva was the more beautiful of the sisters. Judged dispassionately, Diana's face was ordinary. Her appeal derived from a luscious figure, shining dark hair, and impeccable grooming and dress. The only feature she shared with Minerva was their wide, clear blue eyes. Aside from her large fortune, he'd always thought her eminently beddable. Not that he ever had bedded her, alas, before she was swept off by the loathsome bookworm Sebastian. An outcome that Blake still didn't entirely comprehend, though he supposed it had something to do with love.

He reminded himself that she'd been an experienced widow when he courted her, while Minerva was a virginal miss. In their conversation that evening there'd been a hint of sensuality, a suggestion that his bride could be aroused to passion. It crossed his mind that not bedding her might cost him something. Also, by frustrating his father's plans, he would injure his bride, who must expect motherhood as a result of marriage. Fatherhood wasn't something he'd ever much considered, but he, too, might like to have an heir some day.

He felt his resolve waver. His decision had been made in a moment of anger at his father, perhaps in too much haste. If they continued to get along as well as they had this evening, it would be difficult, foolish even, to hold to it. The emerald necklace was in the pocket of his greatcoat. He'd intended to present it to her after dinner, in front of her family and friends, as a public token of goodwill. He should seek a private audience instead.

"Blake! Pay attention."

"I beg your pardon. What were you saying?"

"I hadn't started yet. I want to talk about Minerva. She's a good girl and I think you can be happy together. She wants to put the—er—manner of your betrothal behind you."

"I'm glad."

"She's much younger than you."

"Ten years is not an uncommon difference in ages. And she seems very self-assured."

"Min has always been grown-up for her years but that doesn't mean she knows as much as she thinks she does. She tends to be impulsive and get herself into scrapes. Sometimes she needs to be saved from herself."

This was the first suggestion, in any discussions of their marriage, that Blake could bring anything to the union apart from his name, his fortune, and his virility. The thought of guiding his all-too-clever fiancée warmed him, gave him an unwonted feeling of protectiveness.

"You mean," he said with a grin, "bailing her out of prison as needed?"

"I trust," Diana said repressively, "that Min has outgrown such indiscretions. Not that you were any help rescuing her. Thank God for Sebastian."

"Yes, thank God."

"Stop it, Blake. You never really cared for me and he had a reason to hate you. *You* at least should be over your quarrel."

What could he say? No one, with the exception of Amanda, knew why he'd detested Sebastian on sight, the perfect cousin, brought in by the duke to set an example of intellectual attainment to his idle, dunderheaded heir.

"I will, of course, do my best to care for my wife. I wish we could be wed under better circumstances. I know she'd rather have a clever man as a husband."

"She's quite come around to it, you know. She has always wanted to be in the thick of the political or diplomatic world. What family occupies that world more thoroughly than the Vanderlins?"

"None," Blake said.

Diana continued, blithely unaware that she could hardly have found a thing to say that would make him *less* enthusiastic about his bride. "Her ambition since she was quite a child has been to be a political hostess. She's so excited about going to live at Vanderlin House and training under your mother for the position of duchess. She'll be the greatest help and credit to you. In fact, you really couldn't have chosen a better wife."

A chill seeped through his veins. The last thing in the world he needed was to be "helped" with his accursed ducal future. All he wanted was to forget it.

A sense of injustice, so powerful as to be almost physical, hit him. The marriage had seemed bearable when it was equally unpalatable to both. He'd been prepared to search for some kind of mutual accommodation with his bride.

Instead, far from reluctant, Minerva was apparently getting everything she wanted: Vanderlin House and the great influence and power of the Dukes of Hampton. She made no bones about the fact that her husband-to-be was undeserving of his inheritance. But it wouldn't stop her enjoying it.

And he, Blake, what did he get?

Money. He got money and plenty of it, ironically, thanks to the efforts of Sebastian Iverley who had negotiated hard with the duke on behalf of his sister-in-law. After a lifetime of being kept on an allowance that was meager considering the extent of the family holdings, and two years of penny-pinching, Blake would enjoy all the appurtenances of a rich man's heir.

But it came with strings attached. He had to dispose of a mistress who satisfied him, wed an irritating miss ten years his junior who would have no idea what to do in bed, and please his implacable parents by siring as many children as possible.

The oblivious Diana drove the final nail in the coffin of his good intentions. "I know Min doesn't have the fortune or connections the duke desired, but I believe he will see, has already seen, that Minerva is the perfect wife for you."

Two days before the wedding the jewelry was delivered to Portman Square where Celia Compton took tea and gossip with Minerva and Diana in the latter's boudoir.

"I can't wait to see what Minerva chose," Diana said, opening a box with a cheerful avidity that couldn't have presented a greater contrast with the formality of the scene at Vanderlin House. "Oh, this is lovely."

The case contained the Roman cameos. Gratified to have her taste validated by her fastidious sister,

Minerva explained the history of the necklace.

"When you get to Paris," Diana said, "you must have a gown made to wear with them. Dark rose, I think. Puce looks liverish with your hair."

Celia shrieked. "Lord, this a beastly thing." She had found the ugly bracelet. "Are these cornelians, Diana?"

"How could you, Min?" Diana said with an eloquent shudder. "You'll just have to lose it."

"I could drop it in the gutter, I suppose."

"I hear they have very deep gutters in Paris," said Celia. "And huge French rats that eat rocks. What other horrors did you pick?"

The ladies fell on the jewel cases and as they examined the booty their comments became both politer and quieter. Minerva realized her sister in particular was distressed, but didn't understand why.

"Where are the major pieces?" Diana asked.

"There's a whole set of diamonds. Necklace, bracelets, and so forth."

"It must be in here," Diana said, cheering up as she reached for the largest case. "Oh. They're quite small."

"Are they?" Minerva asked. "They seem large enough to me."

Diana shook her head. "Does Blake know which jewels you've been given?"

"Yes."

"And he was satisfied?"

"Well, he did say something about some pearls, and amethysts I think. The duke said I'd have them later. Why?" She could see Diana was upset.

"Never mind. It probably isn't important."

Minerva had never seen eye to eye with her sister when it came to the importance of fashion. As far as she was concerned the diamonds, and everything else, were quite adequate. She was more curious about her bridegroom, of whom she'd seen very little since the Iverleys' dinner party.

Her hopes of building a cordial alliance with Blake had been depressed by his behavior since that evening. They'd had fun at the table. They'd agreed to address each other informally. He'd threatened to call her Minnie, which, while not a good thing in itself, was the kind of teasing she associated with a warm close family relationship. And surely there was no closer family relationship than that of husband and wife, nor one in which warmth, even heat, was more desirable. The way his deep, heartfelt laugh affected her body made the latter a real possibility, at least from her point of view.

They'd returned to the drawing room where the party continued a lively discussion of the latest novels. Minerva had noticed her fiancé's dark blue eyes had a tendency to glaze over when the topic was the minutiae of government she found so fascinating. This being a reaction she'd observed in others, she was quite ready to feed him her favorite subject in small, manageable morsels.

But novels? A man as frivolous as Blake should enjoy them. It wasn't as though the Montroses or their friends went in for the moralizing tales of Hannah More. What could be more enjoyable than Scott's dashing adventures? Blakeney hadn't offered an opinion on any book.

He'd taken his leave at an early hour and the Chases and the Comptons, though they tried to hide it, were embarrassed for her. Probably thought he'd left to spend the night with his mistress. The idea was surprisingly painful. Since their flirtatious exchange at dinner, she had been looking forward to slipping off to the library with him for another kiss. Since then they'd never been alone and Blake had made no effort to change that state of affairs.

"Did Blake say anything to you about the jewels?" she asked Diana. "Do you have reason to think there's something odd about them?"

Diana shook her head. "As I told you before, we had a very amiable chat."

"I may be able to throw light on the matter," Celia said. "Lord Hugo's valet was in Rundle & Bridge at the same time as Blakeney. Perhaps I shouldn't go on. I don't want to give away secrets or spoil a surprise."

Whatever it was, Minerva decided she'd rather know. "I don't much care for surprises."

"According to Lord Hugo, Bennett saw Blake buying some very expensive trinkets. Two ruby bracelets and an emerald necklace."

"Hmm, rubies," said Diana. "I'm not sure they will suit Min. But you'll look marvelous in emeralds. I'm so glad to hear Blake is doing the right thing by you. You must pretend to be astonished when he gives them to you."

Minerva felt a glow of pleasure. She might be indifferent to the size of gems, but not to gifts from her future husband. Thank goodness she'd found the perfect gift for him. It wasn't expensive but she knew he'd love it. She had it specially bound by Sebastian's bookbinder.

"You were right to tell us, Celia," Diana said. "I was already confident, but now I have no doubt everything will be fine once Min and Blake are married."

"You are not going to be married!" Sebastian appeared at the doorway looking furious. He strode into the room, Tarquin Compton at his heels. Ignoring his wife's greeting and shaking off her restraining hand on his arm, he stood over Minerva's chair. "I won't let you marry that man."

"Goodness," Celia said, "whatever happened must be serious to drag you two away from a book sale."

Tarquin dropped a kiss on her knuckles. "I thought I'd better come in case Sebastian decided to make a detour and kill Blakeney on the way here."

"Sebastian!" Minerva said. "I wish you'd stop glowering and tell us what's the matter. What has Blake done now?"

"That idiot Winchester, who gossips more than an old woman, saw him in a box at Covent Garden last night with Desirée de Bonamour."

"Oh." The pleasant glow turned to ice in her veins.

"And that's not all. The *lady* was wearing the ruby necklace he gave her last month."

Diana interrupted. "That was before . . ."

"*And* a pair of ruby bracelets he bought *last week*. Bad enough he keeps a mistress when he's to be wed in three days. But to flaunt her publicly like that! It's an insult to you, Minerva. I'd like to call him out and I may do so when I go and tell him your wedding is off. At the very least I'll knock him down. I owe him a black eye."

An enormous calm settled over Minerva. While Sebastian roared, Diana and Celia clucked, and Tarquin looked elegantly grim, she let them fade from her consciousness as she set her mind to the question of her future.

She had to decide now if she was to be wed the day after tomorrow. She considered her options and they hadn't changed. Nothing was any different than it had been that horrible morning when she realized she was forced to wed a man she despised. Except that it was, because back then she'd had no expectations. Her view of Blake and their marriage had shifted. Without really acknowledging it, she'd thought she could have everything she wanted, and more. She'd believed in the possibility of the kind of respect and affection her parents shared, and Sebastian and Diana, and their friends. How foolish! Lord Blakeney was neither capable of affection nor deserving of respect.

If she broke the engagement she'd still be ruined. She'd still be doomed to a life in the country and no chance of living her ambition to affect the future of the nation and the course of history.

"I'll marry Blakeney," she said, blinking back an angry tear. "It isn't as though any of us ever believed him to be a saint. I don't see that I have a choice. I'm sure he'd be delighted if I cried off but I won't do it. Why should I be disgraced and he get off scot-free?"

Chapter 9

The marriage, by special license, took place in the drawing room at Vanderlin House. Neither party wished for a large affair. A handful of friends and relations on both sides witnessed the union of Arthur William Gerrit Vanderlin, Marquis of Blakeney, a bachelor, and Minerva Margaret Montrose, spinster daughter of William Montrose of Mandeville Wallop, Shropshire.

All present agreed that they were an extraordinarily striking couple, matched in blue-eyed golden beauty that exemplified the best of English aristocratic looks. The bride wore a simple but elegant morning gown of yellow muslin with a gold cross and chain as her only adornment. Her demeanor spoke of a calm self-assurance, admirable in a girl of nineteen who had landed the decade's greatest marital prize. Not one hint of unseemly triumph marred her porcelain prettiness.

The bridegroom, if you knew him well and observed him closely, appeared to have drunk too much the previous night.

* * *

They were getting ready to leave, so they could catch the Calais packet from Tower Pier. The just-minted Lady Blakeney was surrounded by females, hugging and weeping and no doubt plying her with advice about the wedded state. Her new husband stood a little apart with James Lambton, whom Blake had invited to stand as groomsman, despite the fact that he was, in a way, responsible for the whole hideous occasion.

He envied Minerva the support of her brothers and sister. Maria was in attendance, with her husband Gideon Louther, but he'd never been close to his eldest sister. Amanda, the youngest of the family, was in Edinburgh, staying with the middle girl, Anne, and her Scottish earl husband. Among numerous letters of good wishes and felicitations, Amanda's was the only one he read. Writing in neat capital letters and keeping her missive mercifully brief, she conveyed her best love and wished him every happiness.

Just two people knew of his shame, and Amanda was the only one he trusted. Blake missed her very much, but it was better to have her absent. She'd be weaving tender fancies about his bride, even though she and Anne had certainly heard the truth from their mother. Utterly loyal in her discretion, she'd often urged him to reveal his secret to the family, and would certainly want his bride to know.

Never. Minerva, Marchioness of Blakeney wanted him only for his position in life. If she knew the whole truth of his absolute inadequacy she'd despise him more than ever.

"Blake, a word with you." Gideon Louther approached, looking purposeful. But then he'd rarely seen his brother-in-law wear any other expression. "You're off to Paris," he said, drawing Blake aside. "What are you going to do there?"

"Since I've never been there, I don't know. I expect I'll find out once I arrive."

"Maria always tells me the dressmakers there surpass any to be found in London. I suppose Lady Blakeney will enjoy the shops."

Lady Blakeney. The name sounded peculiar spoken aloud.

It had been the duchess who suggested they take the wedding trip to Paris, and Blake agreed without resistance or resentment. The last thing he wanted was to be immured in the country with his bride and no other distractions. In this he felt certain she would be in entire agreement.

"I know the duke has sent word to the ambassador, Sir Charles Stuart. Should you wish for company, you and Lady Blakeney will be received everywhere."

"Oh, good."

"French society has regained all its brilliance since the end of the war."

"Really?" Blake was more interested in the brilliance of French horseflesh. Through friends in the Jockey Club he had introductions to a couple of breeders. And thanks to his marriage he had the funds to restock his stables with the best.

"While you're there you might keep your ears open. I'd like to hear your impressions."

Gideon's casually delivered request caught his attention. Gideon had never shown the least curiosity about Blake's opinion on any matter. "My impressions of what?"

"King Louis is in poor health and won't last much longer. His brother Charles, the Count of Artois, will succeed him. Since he's a man of little tact and extreme authoritarian views, there are many of us who expect him to try the patience of his subjects. It's quite possible the Bourbons may lose the throne again."

"Hah!" Blake said. "Having gained the habit of disposing of their monarchs the French may decide to keep in practice."

He detected a note of surprise in Gideon's approving nod at this not particularly brilliant observation. "Precisely. And there are two possible replacements for Charles. The Duke of Orleans is the more likely and the more acceptable to us. But there remains a strong strain of Bonapartism among the French. Bonaparte's son, the Duke of Reichstadt may live in Austria, but there are those who would like to see him Napoleon II, Emperor of the French, in fact as well as name."

"We wouldn't like that, would we? How old is this dangerous pretender?"

Gideon looked annoyed. "No one stays twelve years old for ever. Besides, the point is not the boy himself, but his allies. What we wish to know is who, among the French notables, would be prepared to support his restoration, and who would prefer the Orleanists."

"That's all very interesting, Gideon, but what has it to do with me? Correct me if I'm wrong, but I believe it's the job of our ambassador there to gather and report such information."

"Correct me if I'm wrong, Blake, but you do know we are in opposition."

"I may be slow but even I don't need a decade to notice that the other fellows are in power."

"Not for much longer, we hope. And when we take over I expect to be Secretary for Foreign Affairs. It is of considerable use to me to receive independent reports from the European capitals. Anything I learn that puts me a step ahead of the government gives the party an advantage."

"I'm flattered you should think me capable of discovering anything the embassy has missed. Actually, I think you may be a touch demented. No one ever talks to me of such stuff."

"Exactly! No one expects you to care for anything but frivolity. Tongues that would be guarded to the presence of other Englishmen may wag freely in yours."

"Finally my stupidity may be put to use, you mean."

"Your reputation, rather. If I thought you stupid I wouldn't expect you to recognize a fact worth reporting."

Good Lord. Kind words from Gideon. If he wasn't stone-cold sober he'd be almost flattered.

"I don't need to tell you to keep this to yourself."

About to ask if he should mention it to Minerva, Blake held his tongue. He could imagine how gleefully she would latch onto the task. He wanted to do it alone, prove to himself, to Gideon, and perhaps even to his bride, that he wasn't entirely useless. He also took a slightly malicious pleasure in depriving her of the kind of intrigue that would delight her. Let her wait until their return to London to become the leading lady of the opposition.

"Don't worry, Gideon," he said, with his most winning smile. "There's no one better when it comes to keeping a secret."

They reached Calais soon after dawn. Minerva was a good traveler, but even the best cabins on board were hardly luxurious and the crossing had been a trifle bumpy. Minerva assumed the lack of comfort had saved her from the attentions of her bridegroom the night of the marriage. Although she didn't sleep well, her rest in the narrow berth was undisturbed by a nocturnal visitation from Blake. She had girded herself to endure what happened between them, but couldn't deny her relief at the postponement.

They were met at the dock by Mr. Fussell, the courier hired by the duke to ease their journey to Paris. He escorted them to Meurice's Hotel to eat breakfast, while he took care of their passports, the unloading of their luggage, and the exigent French customs officials. Although Dessin's was the more luxurious establishment, he believed my lord and my lady would be more comfortable at Meurice's, where all the staff spoke English and the fare was just as visitors from across the Channel preferred it. Few French inns, he explained in dismay, served beer with meals and the tea was often undrinkable.

Minerva hated beer, and the chocolate, which she preferred to tea anyway, was good. She and Blake ate eggs and ham in virtual silence. His sullenness was, in her opinion, uncalled for. She had reason to be aggrieved. He had been seen in public with his mistress less than a week ago. Yet he responded to her polite attempts at conversation with monosyllables. With the important exception of the marriage vows, they'd barely exchanged a word in days.

Well, she had nothing to apologize for and it was his turn to make an effort. Luckily she had a book with her to occupy the journey to Paris.

Their silence was broken when Fussell returned and asked if they preferred to travel at a leisurely pace and spend an extra night on the road, or press ahead and sleep at Abbeville. In a desire to reach their destination as quickly as possible, they were as united as the most devoted newlywed couple. Abbeville it would be.

The Paris road was in decent repair, the hired animals swift, and the posting inns where they changed horses efficient. After a few hours they made a longer stop to take refreshment at a sizable inn and were shown into a coffee room with a blazing wood fire.

Minerva walked over to the hearth to warm her hands and a gentleman arose from a nearby chair. "*Ne vous dérangez pas, je vous en prie,*" she said.

"I know better than to sit in the presence of a lady," he replied in English. "Take my seat. It's nearest to the fire."

"Thank you, sir, but I prefer to stand after sitting in the coach for so long." She smiled at the man whom, from his style of dress and speech, she guessed to be a commercial traveler. "How did you know I was English? I thought my French accent was quite good."

"Excellent, madam, but most of the customers at the Hôtel d'Angleterre are English." From his tone she gathered this was a matter for rejoicing.

"It appears to be a comfortable establishment. It's not often one sees a wood fire."

"All too often in France there's no fire at all. There's a dearth of fuel and the French don't approach the ingenuity of our countrymen when it comes to the extraction of coal."

"Indeed." Minerva hid her smile at the fellow's national pride. She had a feeling there was little in France he would allow to be superior to the English version. "I have found French food to be quite excellent so far."

He shook his head sadly. "It's almost impossible to find a proper roast or beefsteak unless you know where to go. I'd be glad to offer my assistance to a fellow countrywoman. Allow me to introduce myself. Joseph Bell, at your service."

"Why, thank you, Mr. Bell." She thrust out her hand and shook his heartily. "I am . . . Lady Blakeney."

The effect was startling. He dropped her hand and his jaw, looked with alarm at Blake, over by the window, and almost doubled over in a deep bow.

"I am honored, my lady. My lord, I do apologize for my presumption."

Blake had seemed more interested in activities out in the yard than his bride's conversation. He turned around to examine Mr. Bell, who appeared quite terrified. Minerva, adjusting her internal vision to see her husband through the eyes of a stranger, understood why. With his height of over six feet enhanced by a tall beaver hat, he towered over the little traveler. The multicaped greatcoat and gleaming top boots, worn with casual perfection of cut and fit, reeked of limitless wealth and aristocratic self-assurance. Used to looking at Blake and finding him merely annoyingly handsome, she now saw he might also be intimidating. Having no idea whether he would object to a low-born stranger hobnobbing with his wife, Minerva intervened to protect her new acquaintance.

"There's no need, Mr. Bell. Lord Blakeney will be as grateful as I am for your assistance, won't you, my lord."

Blake responded with an affable nod. "Certainly. You must tell us all the dangers we face in French inns."

Bell bowed again, even lower, rather to Minerva's disapproval. As a believer in the principle of equality, she felt such obeisance excessive when no longer required for reasons of self-preservation.

"I have been traveling the roads of northern France for three years now and I could tell you stories that would curl your hair. The dirt and the cold I've had to suffer! I couldn't count the times I've been given forks encrusted with old food. And served nothing but insolence when I complained."

"Dear me, how shocking," Blake murmured and Minerva thought she detected a curl of the lip, a glint of amusement in his eye. Not wishing to hurt the little man's feelings, she hastily pressed him for further tales of horror.

"Well, my lady, I'll tell you the worst thing about French inns." Minerva held her breath. "None of the bedchambers are furnished with . . ."—he paused for dramatic effect—"carpets!"

"Admit it," Blake said ten minutes later when they settled back into the carriage. "You weren't expecting him to say *carpets*."

If he thought her mealymouthed he was doomed to disappointment. "Certainly not. Neither were you. You were as relieved as I to learn that we are not going to find ourselves in rooms without chamber pots." She blushed anyway because that night they would, presumably, sleep in the same room. And aside from the other thing that would happen, the question of chamber pots was not one she'd considered about sharing a bed with a man. She supposed there'd be a screen, but they could still *hear* each other.

Blake noted her blush. Was it caused by the reference to one private function of the body, or to another which she must be expecting to take place tonight? If the latter, he felt a faint malicious pleasure of which he was a little ashamed. They were, after all, sharing a moment of amusement. He decided he wouldn't spend the last hours of the day's journey in silence, with her reading and him looking out of the window.

Had he been alone, he might have had recourse to his own book. Minerva's wedding gift of a handsomely bound collection of Pierce Egan's sporting essays touched him; at the same time it made him cringe. He knew he'd enjoy it, but he couldn't risk having her notice how laboriously he read, how infrequently he turned the pages.

"Do you often strike up conversations with strangers?" he asked.

"I find I learn the most interesting things from them. When I traveled to Vienna our party crossed France in the public *diligence* and I met all manner of people. Traveling in your luxurious coach is more comfortable but less educational."

"I don't think you'll learn much from Mr. Bell other than the superiority of all things English."

"Who knew that carpets were so important? I don't suppose, of course, that you've ever had to suffer a night in a room with a bare floor."

"There you are wrong. The duke didn't believe in coddling. The nurseries at Mandeville and Vanderlin House were sparsely furnished, and unheated, except in dead of winter. I also passed several happy years in the luxurious setting of Eton."

"Bad was it? My brothers make Harrow sound worse than Newgate Gaol."

"We yield nothing to other schools when it comes to misery and privation."

"Rufus always said they made school uncomfortable as a practical demonstration of Greek history. How the Spartans lived."

"Oh yes, your brother the great scholar. Fluent in how many dead languages?"

He shifted restlessly. Of all the humiliations of his education, classes in Greek had been the worst. None of the methods he'd invented to disguise his inability could save him from the Greek alphabet, or get him beyond the lowest level of Greek studies. His father had been at his most scathing on that subject. Even the mention of Greek made Blake's hackles rise.

Minerva looked a little surprised at his tone. "Personally I think the study of Latin and Greek is a waste of time for most people. Rufus is a scholar and exploring ruins in Turkey, but why should farmers, and lawyers, and merchants learn them? It would be far more rational to educate them in modern languages, mathematics, and natural science. It makes me glad I am a woman so I wasn't made to study the classics. I can't abide philosophical speculations either."

"I'm not one for abstractions myself."

Minerva nodded vigorously. "Give me the practical details that affect people's lives. That's why I enjoy meeting strangers and learning about them."

"I should apologize for taking you in a private coach then. Had I known I'd have arranged for us to travel by stagecoach. I'd like to have seen the duke's secretary's response to such a request."

"It doesn't matter. I've been reading *Galignani's Guide to Paris*."

Blake had the urge to try and impress his wife, probably a fruitless exertion. "It is possible to learn about the life of the people by observing the countryside."

"What do you mean?"

"Looking out of the window as we travel, I've noticed fields of barley."

"Yes?"

"But no vineyards. Which means that the local people very likely drink beer rather than wine."

"Which means Mr. Fussell could be wrong! What fun. At the next inn we must ask for beer. Or rather you must. I can't stand the stuff. What else?"

"The woods are very fine. Excellent timber."

"Oh." She didn't appear to be interested in timber.

"The villages along the road are small and the houses for the most part mean. From which I would conclude most of the inhabitants are peasants."

"No yeoman farmers?"

"I've glimpsed a few châteaux but very few houses of a middling sort."

Minerva's eyes gleamed. "Which means the reforms of the Revolution have had no noticeable affect on the rural economy here."

And off she went, discussing the French legal system and comparing it with the English. Blake was beginning to find her lectures enjoyable. They required little participation on his part and, as long as she wasn't thrusting further reading on him, he was happy to hear what she had to say. He occasionally ventured a question and she actually consulted him over details of English land law.

Late in the afternoon, when they pulled up for a change of horses, Mr. Fussell, who followed the coach in a hired chaise, along with Blake's valet and Minerva's maid, came to the window to assure them this was the last stop before Abbeville and they could look forward to the comforts of the Hôtel d'Angleterre in little more than an hour.

"Another Hôtel d'Angleterre?" Blake asked.

"This road is so well traveled by the English," the courier explained, "that excellent inns have been established along the route to meet the needs and tastes of our countrymen."

"It might be amusing to investigate the tastes of the French. What do you think, my dear?"

"Is there another good inn at Abbeville?" Minerva asked.

Fussell appeared astonished at the question. "Well, my lady. I wouldn't recommend the Tête de Boeuf but the Hôtel de France enjoys a good repute."

"The Hôtel de France sounds perfect."

"But I hardly think it would please your ladyship. I know for a fact that the bedchambers lack carpets."

Since his bride was too overcome with giggles to speak, Blake stepped in. "In that case, Fussell, we shall most certainly spend the night at the Hôtel de France."

Chapter 10

Though her brothers—and most other people who knew her—would have dismissed the possibility, Minerva was feeling shy. As the Hôtel de France drew nearer, conversation became sporadic and eventually faded to silence. Minerva couldn't think of a thing to say because she was too busy thinking of what she would *do* that night.

Theoretical knowledge of relations between a man and a woman was all very well, but at Abbeville she would have to engage in them. She, Minerva Montrose or rather Minerva Vanderlin, Marchioness of Blakeney, was finally going to do some of those things (pray God, not all of them on the first night) with this man. With Blake.

Never in a million years would she have dreamed of ending up in this situation. She'd plotted to prevent Diana from marrying Blake because she believed him to be shallow, conceited, and lacking in intelligence. And now he was her, Minerva's, husband.

Rocking along the French roads in the fading light, he lounged in his corner of the carriage, greatcoat open to reveal the careless elegance of his traveling clothes, one booted foot propped on the opposite seat. His thumbs were hooked into the pockets of his waistcoat and his eyes closed, though he wasn't asleep. No wedding-night nerves for her husband, but then he knew what he was doing.

She'd never denied the appeal of his appearance. Taking advantage of his inattention to stare at him, she observed that, despite his golden fairness, his eyelashes were long and dark. Perhaps her favorite feature in this very good-looking face was the mouth, shapely lips that could look sulky or sensual or both but were now curved in the faintest of smiles. A shiver of excitement rippled through her chest as she remembered their one kiss, and contemplated its repetition.

She didn't love her husband and she wasn't glad she'd married him. She didn't even respect him, though she'd been surprised by some of his thoughtful responses that afternoon. But, the truth struck her, she wasn't loath to consummate her marriage. Nervous, yes, but not reluctant.

She dressed carefully for dinner. As Blake helped her into her seat at the dinner table, his fingers brushed the skin revealed by the low back of her evening gown, arousing gooseflesh at his touch and a glow in her cheeks. In her imagination she felt those hands, smooth and well cared for but neither soft nor feminine, touching other parts of her. Parts that were now suitably covered by forget-me-not blue sarcenet and the finest lawn undergarments. She blushed some more.

The waiter handed them each a list the size of a London theater handbill on which was printed the bill of fare.

"What would you like to drink?" Blake asked her. "Will you join me in some wine, or would you prefer something else?"

"I'd like wine," Minerva said, deciding an injection of courage from a bottle wouldn't go amiss. "Will you have beer?"

"Not tonight. For breakfast, perhaps."

Although the waiter, like the rest of the staff at the Hôtel de France, spoke only French, he understood the exchange and left to fulfill it.

"Goodness," Minerva said. "There must be over a hundred dishes listed here. How are we to choose?"

"I'll leave it up to you." He put the paper on the table with hardly a glance.

Planning a meal was the kind of thing married ladies did, but interested her not a whit. When the duchess, her mother-in-law, had told her she need not trouble herself with domestic details she'd been pleased. Now she was being tested with very little chance of passing the examination.

"What dishes do you like?"

"Everything," he said unhelpfully. "I eat everything."

The menu was divided into several sections, each offering a dozen or more choices. Although a few of the words were unfamiliar, she understood most of them. It struck her she hadn't yet heard Blake speak a single word of French, though he must have studied the language. All Englishmen did, even when at war with France. True, there was a vast difference between learning in the school-room from books, and speaking and understanding a foreign tongue in conversation with natives. Minerva's German was excellent after her year in Vienna and her French almost as good, but only because she'd made the effort to seek out French speakers and practice.

Had Blake managed to pass through Eton and Oxford without learning enough basic French to read a list of dishes? Given what she knew of her husband's unscholarly disposition, she had to admit it was possible.

The waiter returned with wine and she asked him to bring them a selection of their best cuisine. Apparently this was the right thing to do. He began to speak with great animation of *Jambon de Bayonne* and *Fricassée de Poulet* and the freshest, most tender local vegetables. Minerva agreed with everything he suggested, much to the pleasure of the Frenchman who was quite young and handsome despite an exaggerated moustache. His assurances that milady (and milord) would enjoy everything the Hôtel de France had to offer were accompanied by languishing looks and lavish compliments on her beauty. Blake might not understand a word the Gallic Lothario said, but he got the idea and scared him off with a scowl.

Though jealousy had always struck her as an illogical emotion, the hint of possessiveness heightened her anticipation. A plan that had been lurking in the back of her mind took solid shape: to win her husband away from his mistress and make something more of their marriage than mutual toleration. She swallowed a mouthful of wine, then another, and it still seemed like a good idea.

Before the waiter brought their soup, she'd run through her mind every hint she'd garnered from her elder sister on the enticement of gentlemen. Unlike every other area of her studies, this one she'd neglected. She'd been a witness to Diana's efforts to entice this very member of the male sex. Unfortunately she recalled her sister listening with feigned fascination while Blake droned on about endless days in the hunting field in pursuit of the fox.

Perhaps there were limits to what she was prepared to endure to win her husband's attention!

But she drew the broader lesson from Diana's example: let a man talk about himself and what interested him. She could appreciate that, since she loved to talk about the things that aroused her enthusiasm. Her brothers had been known to mimic suicide by hanging after ten minutes of speculation about some parliamentary maneuver.

"You've been living in Devon," she said. "Tell me about it."

The food was good and the knives and forks clean. Blake found nothing to complain about in the Hôtel de France other than the impertinence of the waiter. After a pleasant afternoon he looked forward to dining with his bride.

He could hardly complain of the picture she presented, sitting across the white linen expanse of the table. Her gown in some soft silky material brought out the clear blue of her eyes and showed off the excellence of her figure: a slender neck, breasts high but short of voluptuous, graceful shoulders and arms. Flawless white skin was set off by a string of small pearls that caused him a twinge of compunction about the emerald necklace, stowed in his luggage. He couldn't decide whether to give it to her.

She listened with flattering attention to his description of the improvements he'd made during his self-imposed exile in Devon. Her animated responses were multiplied by the mirrors that lined the walls of the hotel dining room, offering him a variety of angles from which to admire her classical profile and fair beauty. Her hair was dressed without the fussy curls favored by fashionable ladies, simplicity making her look older than her years.

Something shifted in his view of her. She was no longer Diana's tiresome little sister whom he'd been force to wed. The new Lady Blakeney was a grown woman and a fascinating one. A woman he desired. The discovery was unsettling and unwelcome. It complicated the decision he'd made about the course of their marriage.

"You've made a study of estate management," she said as the long meal drew to a close. Who would have guessed Minerva Montrose would address him with a measure of respect?

"I suppose it's my occupation, if I have one. I hope my father will let me have the running of Mandeville now. What else am I to do to be useful?"

The china blue eyes grew wide. "The Dukes of

Hampton have been deeply concerned with the business of the nation. Surely you will wish to continue the tradition?" The note of reproach was muted but unmistakable.

"Do you know how the Vanderlins achieved their exalted position?"

"The first one came to England with William of Orange in 1688."

"Gerrit Vanderlin, the best looking man in Holland. It's said the ladies swooned when he first appeared at the English court."

Minerva's snort expressed her opinion of such weakness. "But he was a brilliant man! He didn't enjoy William's confidence because of his looks."

Blake smiled at her naïveté. "You think not? Very fond of a handsome man was William."

He was happy to see he'd managed to confound his bride, though he couldn't tell whether it was shock at his ancestor's inappropriate friendship with a monarch, or merely the suggestion that the Vanderlin political dynasty had been founded on something other than merit.

He was also glad of the reminder that his major asset in Minerva's eyes was his ancestry. For a while he'd made the mistake of believing she saw him as a man and not merely a Vanderlin.

There was something she needed from him in order to become fully a Vanderlin herself. He derived a certain pleasure from the fact that she hadn't yet worked it out for herself. For all her intelligence and grasp of politics, Blake didn't believe she understood her place in the Vanderlin firmament. Until she had a son she was a very small star indeed. Inconsequential and unlikely to be permitted the least degree of influence. Ironically she needed his manhood if she was to prove her worth and conceive the much needed heir. She wasn't going to succeed any time soon.

She examined a tray of pastries and selected a tiny cherry tart. Her shapely mouth closed over the glistening ruby sphere and she took a bite. As he watched her slender white throat swallow the morsel, and a pink tongue sweep away a crumb from her lips, he felt desire stir, fortunately concealed by the table linens.

Even if his feelings for his wife had softened, he still wished to disappoint his father. He would not go to her chamber that night.

Her bare feet on the earthen tiles gave Minerva a new appreciation of carpets. She dismissed her maid and jumped into bed. Aside from the floor, the night wasn't cold and she left the old-fashioned casement window ajar. Instead of getting all the way under the blankets, she sat back against the pillows, covered only to the waist. She spread her loose hair, crinkly from being unbraided, over her shoulders and wondered how to arrange her arms in an alluring manner. After experimenting with two or three positions she felt silly, and less attractive by the minute.

She wished she'd paid more attention to the chatter of girls in Vienna and London when they talked about pursuing men. She'd scorned such tactics, wanting to be chosen for her character and intellectual talents. The joke was on her, because she had married a man who had no time for either.

She thought of the way Sebastian's face lit up when Diana entered a room, of the warmth in his gaze as it followed her every move. It occurred to her she might enjoy the same things from a man and to envy her sister's ability to inspire them.

She couldn't even bring herself to think of all that Diana had said about the marriage bed. For the first time in her life Minerva felt truly unsure of herself, eager for Blake's arrival and what would happen that night, and terrified that her ignorance would cause her to do something wrong and disgust her handsome, experienced bridegroom.

She looked down at the shadow of her nipples showing through the fine lawn of her nightgown and thought about the size of her breasts. Didn't men prefer them larger? Why else would stays be designed to push them upward and enhance the swell? Snatching the blankets she covered herself to the neck.

She heard footsteps in the adjoining room, occupied by her husband. An exchange of words with his valet competed with noise drifting through the open window. The sounds of wheels, hooves, harness, and horses were common to inn yards in every country. They mingled with the calls and chatter of patrons, ostlers, and maids, undistinguishable but unmistakably French.

How long did it take a man to prepare for bed? Less time than a woman, she would have thought. He didn't have a complicated hairstyle to be taken apart and he didn't wear stays, at least Blakeney didn't. She felt a slightly hysterical giggle arise, thinking of various gentlemen she'd met who tended to creak when they moved, signaling the presence of corsets to contain excess flesh.

Deciding she'd feel better in the dark, she blew out the candle on the table next to the bed, and waited. The sounds next door ceased and she expected any moment that the connecting would open to admit her bridegroom.

Time passed. Five, ten, fifteen minutes? She recalled their earlier parting. Once the covers were removed she'd risen from the table and stated her intention of retiring to bed, since the day had begun early and they'd dined late. He walked her to the door and said he'd stay for a last glass of wine. He hoped her room was comfortable and she had everything she needed, despite the lack of a carpet. She was too nervous to laugh at the joke. He kissed her hand. Very proper and gallant.

Had he said anything about seeing her later? She rather thought not, but surely it had been implied. Weddings were followed by beddings. All the information she possessed was very clear on the point. She waited.

And waited.

Chapter 11

Honeymoon. Minerva happened to have looked up the word in Johnson's *Dictionary*.

The first month after marriage, when there is nothing but tenderness and pleasure.

The famous doctor's definition bore no resemblance to the week that had passed since her lonely vigil in the Abbeville Inn.

There had been no chance to interrogate Blake about his unaccountable failure to join her that night. The next morning he'd hired a horse and ridden all the way to Paris while she occupied the coach in solitary splendor. When they spoke, which wasn't often, he was perfectly polite and maddeningly elusive.

On arrival in the French capital, they moved into a handsome Faubourg St. Honoré apartment arranged by the Duke of Hampton. The spacious accommodation spread out over the entire floor of an *hôtel particulier,* as the noble mansions of Paris were called. The count who owned this one had moved to a modern house in the St. Germain quarter, leaving the faded glory of his graceful old family home to tenants.

Although not given to timidity, Minerva couldn't find the words to ask her husband why he'd chosen not to consummate their marriage. *Why haven't you bedded me?* would do it, but she couldn't quite form her mouth around the sentence. Her fury at Blake and frustration at her own helplessness increased as the days passed.

What in the name of heaven was the matter with him? And what was the matter with her?

The French seemed to be damnably fond of mirrors in their furnishings. Almost ubiquitous in the cafés and restaurants that were such a feature of French life, they also covered the walls of every public room in the rooms occupied by Lord and Lady Blakeney. Even after a week in France Blake wasn't used to catching sight of himself at every turn of the head. Never particularly fond of his looks—as a boy he'd always thought dark coloring more manly—he was beginning to hate the sight of his own face.

The positive side of the array of glass was that he was able to look at his wife without appearing to stare. She looked very beautiful that morning. Perhaps there was something about the Parisian air, but she seemed to grow more appealing each time he saw her.

"Good morning, my lord," she said, taking a seat at the table and accepting chocolate from the manservant, one of several domestics who came with the apartment. She barely accorded him a glance, instead picking up the French newspaper that waited at her place.

He couldn't really blame her. After failing to appear in her room in Abbeville, he'd taken the coward's way out. He'd never offered an explanation and she hadn't asked for one. As for his reasons, he became less confident of their validity by the day. He couldn't flatter himself his continuing absence from her bed was much of a hardship for her. He, on the other hand, was beginning to think his decision had been a very bad idea.

Things seemed different away from England. Even in Devon he hadn't felt so free of his father, for the estate there belonged to the duke. But something in the atmosphere of Paris, the existence of the sea between himself and his destiny, filled him with a sense of optimism he'd been scarcely aware of lacking.

"What are your plans for today?" he asked.

She glanced over the top of the paper and regarded him as though he was a piece of refuse in the gutter. Not encouraging.

"I doubt you'll be any more interested in my daily activities than I will," she said.

"Why don't you try me?"

With an exaggerated sigh she lowered the gazette. "I have a dress fitting this morning."

What was so annoying about that? Women always liked new clothes, didn't they? "New clothes, splendid."

"My interfering sister set me up with her maid's cousin to visit a dressmaker in the Palais Royal. It's a ridiculous waste of time, but I'll never hear the last of it from Diana if I refuse. And it's not as though I have anything else very interesting to do."

"I thought you'd called on some of the ladies attached to the Embassy."

"I have, but sitting with them is no more exciting than paying morning calls in London. I daresay there are some evening parties among the diplomatic set, but they hesitate to invite us."

"Why?"

"Because the rumors of our love match reached Paris. One of the ladies implied we must wish to be alone together at night." She wrinkled her nose.

"I'm sorry about that."

"I set her right, I assure you."

"Perhaps invitations will start arriving now."

"I notice the lack of invitations doesn't stop *you* going out after dinner. But men can always do what they want."

Blake wondered how he could improve her mood. Not only was he remorseful that she was finding her visit to the French capital so dull, he also needed her help. Judging by her baleful stare she'd just as soon drop him into the River Seine as share a crust with him if he was starving.

The servant reappeared at his elbow with a large envelope on a silver tray. He frowned at the address. "It looks like an invitation, my dear. Why don't you open it and see if it's something that will get you out at night."

" 'Monsieur et madame le marquis et la marquise de Blakeney,' " she read. "Not from the ambassador, or anyone English." He glimpsed a gilt fleur-de-lis on the card she pulled out. "Oh my goodness! It's from the Tuileries. We are summoned to the King's reception on Tuesday."

"Are we, indeed? There you are."

"It's not an evening occasion. King Louis receives diplomats and distinguished foreigners every Tuesday afternoon."

"How do you know these things?" he asked.

"I read the papers."

"What do you know about the King's brother Charles?" he asked before she could start doing so again. After a week of pursuing introductions and frequenting the fashionable cafés that were the Parisian equivalent of London clubs, he had to acknowledge he needed help.

"The Count of Artois? It's said he isn't as easygoing as Louis. He leads the Ultras and is opposed to any liberal reform. Many Frenchmen would prefer not to see him succeed. But it's highly unlikely that Fat Louis will outlive him. Then we shall see whether he can hold onto the country."

The effect of his question—and her answer—on Minerva's appearance was extraordinary. It was as though a magician had breathed into the veins of a sullen ice princess and transformed her into a creature of heat and light. Blue eyes emitted sparks of excitement, her cheeks grew flushed, and her bow-shaped mouth revealed pearly white teeth as it formed cogent thoughts with admirable speed and fluency.

The sight of those red lips transfixed him. Visions of them doing things other than talking invaded his brain. He beat them back and concentrated on the words, as she spoke of the Duke of Orleans and the remaining Bonapartes. He'd always been good at learning by listening, and she could tell him what he needed to know.

She stopped to draw breath and looked at him

closely. He'd cultivated the art of looking unconcerned while his brain concentrated on taking in verbal information. Had his bland mask failed him?

"What is Artois to you?" she asked.

"I'm curious about the factions that want to replace him, that's all," he said, as he might about the prospects for a boxing match or horse race.

"Well, that must be the first time." She eyed him with open suspicion.

Since he was getting nowhere on his own, he told her what his brother-in-law had asked him to find out.

"It's so unfair! You know nothing and he gives you a wonderful mission like that. And I, just because I'm a woman, have to go to dress fittings and drink tea with ladies."

"I was hoping you would help me. We could start at the Tuileries reception. I don't know where to start looking for secret Orleanists or Bonaparte sympathizers."

"I don't see what you can expect to learn when you don't even know French."

"What makes you think that?"

"I noticed how you avoid anything written in French. The menus in the inns, the newspaper. Even that card of invitation."

He froze for a moment. Minerva was far too observant. If he contradicted her now she might draw the correct conclusion: that it was only the *written* word that gave him trouble. "I'll never discover anything without your assistance," he said in a humble voice.

She gave him a kind nod. "I'll do my best to help you. I speak German too, of course, and Napoleon's son lives with his mother in Vienna. I may be able to discover something from the Austrian delegation."

"That's an excellent idea. But even with my limited powers of communication I believe I may be able to turn up something among the French gentlemen I encounter. With your advice, of course."

"I expect you will." Her voice reeked of condescension. "As Sir Gideon told you, no one will expect you to be interested in French politics. It all comes down to patronage, of course. I recommend you look for hints that people are dissatisfied with their position at court and their standing with Louis and Charles."

"Thank you."

"Don't forget that Orleans has several sons too. You may meet some of them and observe their associates."

Her superior tone aroused his sporting instincts. "I'd like to propose a small wager. More of a contest really. Let's see who can identify the most Orleanist or Bonapartist supporters."

"Very well," she said. "What's the prize?" From her smirk she regarded it as money in the bank.

"What would you like?"

"I don't know. I can't think of anything I want at the moment."

"Very well. A favor to be named later."

"And you?" she asked, confident she'd never have to pay up.

"The same."

"Done."

"May the best spy win."

Lady Elizabeth Stuart, the wife of the British ambassador, told them about the new historical tapestries in the Tuileries Throne Room. Minerva wished she wouldn't. The illustrious French monarchs admired by the present king—Saint Louis, François I, and Henri IV—interested her not a whit.

Blake didn't even pretend to look at the wall hangings. He was surveying the crowd for anti-Bourbon subversives. She pulled on his arm to draw his attention and smiled sweetly.

"Did I tell you I saw the King's carriage driving through the streets yesterday?" she asked. "My goodness he does drive fast."

"He does that because it gives him the illusion he's taking exercise," the ambassadress said.

"Truly? No wonder they call him Fat Louis."

"I met him once," her husband said. "My father took me to call on him at Hartwell."

"What was he like?"

"Affable. And fat."

How could Blake sound so laconic? Had he no idea how fortunate he was to have met Louis XVIII during his exile in England?

Sir Charles Stuart hurried over to warn them that the king and his party were on their way. "When he addresses me I shall present you. He will tell you he wishes you well. He uses the same words to everyone and hardly ever says anything else."

"It's all a matter of his tone of voice, I suppose," Minerva said.

"Precisely, Lady Blakeney. Much thought goes into the interpretation of those few repeated words. I compliment your instinct for diplomacy."

A rustle of expectation, followed by a hush, heralded the royal entrance. As Louis made his way through the crowd Minerva had ample chance to examine him. Simply but richly attired, she learned little from his appearance. His expression was agreeable but distant and gave little away. "*Le Roi se porte t'il bien,*" he said. The same words to each person he addressed.

Affable. She rather thought Blake had it right. *And fat.*

The king greeted Sir Charles, who begged leave to present his companions. She and Blake curtseyed and bowed respectively, deeply and in perfect coordination. When she rose and lifted her face the king was smiling.

"We have met before, Lord Blakeney," he said in excellent English. "I remember when your good father brought you to Hartwell. Walk with me a little and give me news of the Duke of Hampton."

Surprise rippled around the huge chamber. Members of the king's entourage stood aside to make room for Blakeney. Minerva moved to accompany him but was stayed by Sir Charles Stuart's hand on her arm. She watched them walk into the dividing crowd, who looked astonished at King's unusual condescension to a foreigner, and were clearly speculating as to its significance.

Minerva asked the ambassador to introduce

her to some members of the Austrian delegation. Blake might think he had an advantage due to a childhood visit. All right, a very grand childhood visit, not the kind of thing that ever happened to her at Wallop Hall. But she wasn't without her own resources, not least of which was an excellent command of German. While her husband was occupied by the king and surrounded by die-hard loyalists, she would be making the acquaintance of those who knew Napoleon's widow and son.

"Have a delightful time." Minerva waved from her seat in the salon where, as usual, she was nose deep in a newspaper. "I can think of few worse ways to spend a day than exploring a dilapidated stable."

"That's hardly the way to describe a building that accommodated two hundred and fifty horses and five hundred dogs. I'm sorry the party is gentlemen only. You'd enjoy it."

"I think you must have mistaken me for my mother."

"No, I most definitely haven't done that."

"Go," she said, shooing him off. "Go and talk to men about racing. Men who are courtiers of the Count of Artois and would never abandon the legitimist cause. I, meanwhile, will be pursuing other avenues."

She looked delectably smug, no doubt contemplating victory. For a moment he wavered. When the Duke of Montillou had proposed the expedition to Chantilly he'd been pleased. Not only did the stable sound like a sight any horseman would want to see, he also learned that Artois was a keen amateur of horseflesh and his circle would put Blake in touch with important breeders.

He wondered if she was sorry to be left alone for two days. It wasn't much of a honeymoon, for either of them, but as a man he had more freedom to go out. He felt a pang of guilt about abandoning her every evening after dinner. Although he could claim altruistic motives for his excursions, he couldn't deny he was enjoying himself. Tomorrow he'd turn his attention to improving relations with his wife, as well as the other task he had to perform. Winning their little contest would be undeniably satisfying. Minerva would also be impressed. To his surprise it had become important to him that she not think him a worthless fool.

On impulse he walked over to her chair, pushed aside the paper, and kissed her cheek. "I should return by midafternoon tomorrow. We could go riding."

Minerva was convinced there was something she didn't know about her husband. In the Tuileries Throne Room, while she made the acquaintance of members of the Austrian nobility visiting Paris, she covertly observed Blake after he was released from the royal presence. He conversed with several different gentlemen and they didn't appear to be the kinds of superficial exchange one had in a language one barely knew. Of course, this was a gathering of diplomats, so perhaps his acquaintances all spoke English.

Now he'd set off for a day and a night in the company of a party of Frenchmen. He'd told her he wanted to talk about buying horses, business she knew from her mother demanded all one's wits. Wouldn't it be normal to be apprehensive about conducting such negotiations across a language barrier? And if he did indeed speak French, why would he try and hide it from her?

The minute she heard the front door to the apartment slam, she tiptoed through the connecting door from her room into his. The apartment had no dressing rooms but her bedchamber was enormous, with plenty of space for a large armoire and chest of drawers as well as a dressing table well supplied, like the rest of the house, with mirrors.

Blake's room had the same tall windows overlooking the gracious little garden at the back of the mansion. It was a bit smaller than her own, though the bed looked larger, and much tidier. Her maid had given up trying to control the books and papers that she accumulated like drifting autumn leaves. By contrast almost every surface in his room was bare. A single volume lay on a table near the bed, along with a water carafe and a decanter of wine. She snatched it up and recognized the red leather binding. It was the book she'd given him for a wedding present.

She held it for a moment, pleased that he kept it by him, though why would he not? Egan's *Boxiana* was a treat for any gentleman of sporting tastes. The book fell open to the white ribbon bookmark. He'd read two pages. As far she could see, it was the sole reading matter in the room and certainly not written in French. Did the man never read a newspaper? Even her mother read the racing news.

The dressing table bore only a pair of silver-backed brushes. With the ruthlessness that made her younger brother's life an open book, she opened drawers and rooted through the contents, finding small clothes and the accoutrements of a gentleman of fashion: cuff buttons, fobs, handkerchiefs, and such. Nothing surprising or revealing.

She picked up a slim card case, distracted by an intricate design of silver and lapis lazuli, and finally found a piece of paper, a letter stowed away beneath. She'd unfolded the single sheet before her action gave her pause.

What was she doing? It was one thing to have a look around the room at whatever was openly displayed. Looking in drawers was more intrusive and, now she considered the matter, she felt guilty. Blake was not her brother. And to read a private letter without permission? She wouldn't even do that to Stephen. Quickly she refolded and replaced the paper, but not before she observed that the writing was all in capital letters, as though addressed to a child who'd scarcely learned to read. The discovery dissolved a tension she hadn't even been aware of feeling. It was unlikely to be a love letter written in such a juvenile manner.

About to close the drawer and cease her prying, she noticed a large flat case tucked into the back. The contents made her gasp. Even a woman as little interested in jewelry as Minerva couldn't fail to be impressed by the exquisite emerald necklace.

She cast her mind back to the day Sebastian had burst in with the story of Blake and his mistress and the rubies. She—and everyone else—had assumed then that the emeralds he'd purchased were intended for the same woman.

And yet, here they were. And here she was, in Paris, with Blake, while Mademoiselle Desirée de Bonamour was not. If that was her real name, a fact Minerva highly doubted. Perhaps she'd returned to Lancashire or Cumberland or some other prosaic spot from which she'd emerged.

Celia Compton, a reliable source of information about things proper ladies weren't supposed to know, had told her gentlemen often gave their mistresses expensive parting gifts. Perhaps that's all those ruby bracelets had been.

She raised fingers to the spot on her cheek where Blake had kissed her good-bye. It was cool to the touch but warm in her imagination.

The necklace might be a wedding present. If Blake had decided to behave in a husbandly manner at last, Min would welcome it. She would find the courage to ask for an explanation of his previous neglect. It wasn't like her to be so timorous.

Her fingers moved to her mouth, lightly tapping her lips and eliciting memories of a certain kiss. Instead of asking Blake why he hadn't come to her bed, perhaps she'd make the move toward intimacy herself. Although rather apprehensive about how to go about it, it suited her temperament to take the initiative.

She put the necklace back where she'd found it, made sure she left no sign of her intrusion, and returned to her own room to await her maid. While Blake wasted his time with a lot of horse-mad men, she'd be following up a very promising lead. She looked forward to taking the first prize in their contest.

And had an idea of what she would ask for.

Chapter 12

Minerva was in the salon when Blake returned, rather later in the afternoon than he'd intended. He stood in the doorway for a moment, taking in the scene. Aside from the gilt plasterwork and mirrors, the walls were decorated with paintings of classical temples and abundantly blooming rosebushes among which wandered ladies, gentlemen, and cherubs dressed in the modes of the last century. Although to be precise the cherubs wore only wisps of cloth, the perennial fashion for junior angels. In contrast to the sugary frivolity of her background, his wife seemed the epitome of restraint in a simple gown of some blue and white striped stuff. Seated on a gilt and brocaded sofa that complemented the rest of the furnishings, she looked serene, pretty, and unpretentious.

How agreeable to come home to such a sweet creature, Blake thought, then grinned at such an inapt description of Minerva, Marchioness of Blakeney. For a start, the wholesome spouse of his fleeting imagination would doubtless be occupied by her embroidery. He couldn't swear to it, but he'd be astonished to learn Minerva had ever wielded a needle in her life. She probably didn't paint in watercolors or play the harp either. Instead, predictably, she sat with a litter of paper on her lap and a pile of books and magazines on the sofa. She was reading a letter with frowning concentration when his arrival distracted her.

"I'm sorry I'm late," he said. "I fear it's too late to ride out now."

In his experience women became fractious about unpunctuality. She dismissed his offense with glorious and unfeminine unconcern. "Never mind that. I have good news for you. And look at all the invitations that have arrived for us." She pawed through the mess on her knee. "Tonight we are asked to a reception by the Prussian ambassador, a literary soirée to hear readings by several poets, and I daresay there are more."

"Splendid," he said, planning avoidance tactics. "We can decide which we prefer later."

"Oh, I'm sure we'll have time for more than one."

"I want to tell you about my expedition," he said firmly.

She set aside her letters and sat up straight. "You had a enjoyable time?" she asked, though he could tell her question was merely polite.

"There must have been a dozen gentlemen in the party, including a couple of English sportsmen, Armitage and Thornton, both good friends of mine. They were invited over to offer advice on setting up a French Jockey Club and getting some quality horse racing started in France."

"Really?" Minerva's reaction was bored—and predictable. It amused Blake that he began to know just what would elicit her enthusiasm. She wasn't expecting to hear anything of interest about a lot of men talking about horses. He decided to play with her a little.

"The Revolution set back the progress of the sport in France," he began, clasping his hands behind his back and pacing about the room.

"Oh?"

"Horse racing is, after all, an aristocratic sport."

"Oh."

"The breeding of first-rate horses demands care and almost unlimited funds."

Her eyes grew dull but, as he waxed lyrical about the care and training of thoroughbreds, they gradually began to glow, but not with joy. Five minutes later she looked as though she'd like to beat him over the head with a riding crop. It was time to put her out of her misery. Although she wasn't going to be precisely happy when she discovered how many favors she owed him. Never mind. She looked especially fetching when annoyed.

"Of course the main point of the trip was to see the Great Stables. I've never seen anything so magnificent. They are like a palace for horses. The prince who built them in the last century believed he would be reincarnated as a horse. I suppose he thought he was providing himself with proper quarters for his future life."

A noise in the back of her throat told him what she thought of that piece of nonsense.

Now they were getting to the good bit. "The

Prince of Condé, it was. The present owner of Chantilly, the Duke of Bourbon, is the last of the line and the son of the Duke of Orleans is his heir."

He expected her to grasp the significance of these members of the French royal family, but she was no longer listening. Instead she rose to her feet and glared at him.

"Will you stop?" she burst out. "I told you I had news and all you do is go on and on about horses. You're worse than my mother. It's my turn to talk."

His news could wait. She was going to have a big shock and the lingering anticipation would make him savor her chagrin all the more. She would learn that her husband wasn't as much of a fool as she'd thought. He'd be fooling her, of course. If she ever found out the truth she'd never see him as anything but a pitiful idiot. A weight settled in his stomach as he contemplated the odds of getting though a lifetime without her learning about him. Not good.

He shook off the shadow of fear that he was used to ignoring. "I apologize for monopolizing the conversation," he said with feigned remorse. "Please, sit again and you'll have all my attention."

He joined her on the sofa, close enough that their knees brushed. He took both her hands in both his and looked down at her with his most soulful gaze and his best coaxing smile. "Tell me what you've been doing for two days. Tell me all about it."

She'd been dying to tell him what she'd learned and had nearly burst her stays while he went on and on about those wretched equines and their dreary owners. What felt like the last hour, though she knew it hadn't been that long, reminded her of the bad old days when she and Diana had listened to Blake bore on about hunting.

Now, when she was at last getting her chance to speak, he distracted her by sitting too close and holding her hands and *looking at her.* She'd never experienced deep blue eyes focused on her with such intensity. Her heart beat faster and her stomach fluttered and she felt her control slipping away, as though she might do something without forethought. Like kissing her husband. And though she'd decided the day before that she would kiss him again, she'd also decided it would be at a moment of her own choice. This was not the moment and she would not succumb to her unruly impulses.

Breaking the lock of their gazes, she snatched free her hands and edged away from him up the sofa. She took a deep breath to clear her head. "While you have been jaunting around with your horse-loving friends, *I* have been putting my time to good use."

"Embroidery?"

"Espionage."

"Sounds hazardous."

"No more dangerous than drinking tea with the wife of the Austria ambassador."

"Spilled tea can burn badly if very hot. I'm sure the Austrians serve tea hot."

"I made the acquaintance of Princess Walstein."

"How charming for you. Does she have a firm grasp on her teacup?"

"She has a firm grasp on her friendship with the Austrian royal family. She's a friend of the Empress Marie-Louise."

"Remind me . . ."

Minerva turned her head sharply. Could he possibly have forgotten the significance of Napoleon's widow, or was he simply being annoying? His features were set in bland incomprehension but she thought she detected a glimmer of laughter in his eye.

"The former Empress of France."

"Oh."

"The mother of the Bonaparte heir."

"Of course.

"Princess Walstein is a close friend and member of the imperial household. I can guess what she's doing in Paris."

"Buying new clothes? Meeting her lover?"

"Women do think of things besides clothes," she said. "And lovers."

"Pity."

It was time to take control of the conversation. "I believe Princess Walstein is here to investigate support for the restoration of the Duke of Reichstadt as emperor."

"Or to buy clothes."

"I'm not making this up. I have reasons to think so. I observed her in close very close— conversation with the Duke of Mouchy-Ferrand."

"Oh yes, my old friend Mouchy."

"Do you know who he is?"

"Haven't a notion."

"It's a Napoleonic dukedom. His father was a general who managed to avoid taking sides after Bonaparte's escape from Elba by claiming illness and remaining at his country estate."

"Very sly."

"Well, it turns out he really was ill," she said. "He died on the day of Waterloo. It means his son never had to state his preference. In fact, after the Restoration the new duke was a member of the Ultras, the Count of Artois's conservatives."

"Doesn't sound like much of a Bonapartist to me."

"He must be very clever. I can't think of any reason why he'd be speaking so earnestly with the Princess. In German too, so no one would understand. Everyone else present was French and, as far as I can tell, very few of the French speak German. Luckily I can. I heard them arranging a private meeting."

"Is she pretty?"

Minerva gave up in disgust. He refused to take her seriously, but she knew she was right. She had her ideas about how to discover the reason for that meeting.

"Scoff if you want," she said, "but I'll get proof that the duke is a Bonapartist and you will owe me a favor."

Blake leaned in and lowered his head close to hers. "I'll look forward to it," he murmured, his breath warm on her cheek. "And I look forward to *your* favor."

"I don't owe you one," she said, disgusted that her voice was a little wobbly.

"In fact you do, Minnie."

"Don't call me that."

"I'll call you anything I like. Since you owe me four favors, you are not in a position to argue."

Minerva scuttled over to the far end of the sofa

to avoid his proximity and the way it muddled her brain. With a good three feet between them, she tried to make sense of his claim and failed.

"Four? What do you mean?"

He grinned at her, odiously smug. Also odiously handsome. What was one to do with a man who made one's body quiver at his gaze? She was not a foolish female, to be distracted from important matters by well-cast features and a roguish smile. And dark blue eyes.

It took more to impress Minerva Montrose— she still couldn't get used to thinking of herself by her new name—than looks, however exceptionally fine. She admired a man for what he achieved, not the face he was born with.

Blake held up his left hand, palm forward and fingers splayed, interrupting her view of that handsome face.

"Four," he said and rattled off a string of names, counting them on his fingers. She recognized the names, of course, all prominent members of the circles of King Louis XVIII of France and his heir and brother, the Count of Artois. "I met them all at Chantilly."

"How nice for you. What does that prove?"

"Did I mention that the Duke of Orleans joined the party for the tour of the stables and dinner?"

"You met the duke?"

"He lived in England for many years, you know. He seems a delightful man. Very keen on horse racing."

Minerva couldn't believe his luck. Men and their sports! "Is that all you talked about?"

"A group of men want to start racing at Chantilly and he is speaking with his cousin Bourbon, the owner of the estate, on their behalf."

"Is that all?"

Half an hour later she was convinced.

"I wouldn't call it proof," Blake concluded. "Short of asking them directly if they'd like to see Louis Philippe made king, or intercepting secret communications, I don't see how there could be. But I think Gideon will be pleased with the information and that, after all, is the object of our researches."

Minerva nodded slowly. She couldn't argue with that, neither did she wish to. "Excellent work," she said. "I concede your victory."

"Thank you, my lady. I'll admit I was lucky."

"I don't believe in luck. You saw the opportunity and seized it. *That's* what luck means."

"I disagree. I'm beginning to think I was very lucky the night I mistook you for the Duchess of Lethbridge."

"Oh." Her voice wobbled. "Are you flirting with me, Blake?"

"I'm trying, but you're quite hard to flirt with. You don't take compliments well."

"If you mean compliments on my face, I don't care for them."

"It wasn't your face I was complimenting."

To her dismay she felt herself blushing hotly. Could he possibly be referring to the part of her body he'd been investigating that night?

"I meant," he said, and judging by his sly smile he'd read her thoughts, "that having a clever wife isn't such a bad thing. Far from it."

She'd never felt less clever in her life. "What are you going to claim for a forfeit?"

"I would like to choose where we go this evening."

"Very well," she said over a pang of disappointment. She'd thought he might ask for something more . . . intimate. "I really hope you're not going to pick the poets."

"Not a chance. And I don't fancy the Russians."

"Prussians."

"Not them either."

"No? There'll be all sorts of interesting people there."

"I'd like to take you to dine at a restaurant or café. It's quite usual for ladies to eat out in public here."

"Do you mean *ladies?*"

"Yes, indeed. Ladies of impeccable birth. And when did you become so high in the instep?"

"I'd enjoy that. I'd have a chance to see some of the ordinary citizens of Paris."

"I'd thought we might try one of the fashionable spots, but if it's ordinary people you want, then I think we'll go to the Café de la Paix in the Palais-Royal. Unless you fancy the Café des Aveugles."

"The Café for the Blind? What an odd name."

"It's located in a dark cellar. I fear it may be too low for your taste."

"What do you know of my taste?"

He threw up his hands. "Not much. For all I know you'd enjoy it immensely, but I'm not sure I can guarantee your safety there. The Café de la

Paix should be disreputable enough to broaden your education without risking death."

She leaped to her feet. "What time do you wish to leave? I must change," she said, suddenly giddy at the prospect. An evening in a disreputable café, in company with a man, was a new and thrilling experience.

He caught her hand before she could leave. "There's no hurry. Things begin late here." He leaned over and dropped a light kiss on her lips. Her heart thudded. "And Minnie—"

"Don't call me that."

"Don't overdress."

For a wild moment she considered going out in nothing but her petticoats. The thought of Blake seeing her in dishabille excited her.

"Nothing too rich for an evening in low company," he added.

Chapter 13

The Café de la Paix was like nothing Minerva had ever seen. Set in a barely converted theater, complete with stage and boxes, it was packed to capacity with the kind of people they would never have encountered among the Prussians, Russians, or even the literary set.

For a start, few of the females in the place could be categorized as "ladies" except in the most generous definition of the word. The combination of boldly exposed bosoms and bolder face paint left her in no doubt that these exotic creatures were sisters to the prostitute who had propositioned them in Shepherd's Market. Their escorts appeared to be either men of commerce or overdressed dandies of a raffish cast. Mingling with this disreputable crowd was a slightly more sober element, very likely small tradesmen and their wives out to enjoy the free entertainment provided for the price of a drink or a light meal. An orchestra played without remission on the stage but the principal attraction of the place was the ropedancers, who performed feats of daring on a wire strung diagonally across the auditorium.

Minerva held her breath when a pretty girl in a wide knee-length skirt took off with graceful steps across the expanse of the chamber. She imagined the smashed crockery and broken bones if a dancer ever fell onto the tables below. The patrons in the pit area stared up with eyes and mouths agape, especially the men. Looking up the dancer's skirt, Minerva thought, covering her mouth to hide a giggle.

"What?" Blake regarded her with quizzing look.

"I was wondering what she wears under her skirt." The kind of remark she'd make to her sister and even her brothers. So what was wrong with speaking thus to her husband?

"I wouldn't know," he said, but something in his air—a touch of exaggerated innocence—told her that he might, in fact, be cognizant of the undergarments worn by members of the dancing profession.

The dancer reached the point closest to their box, one of the most luxurious on the second tier. Though a few feet above them, from their vantage point it was possible only to see her flesh-colored stockings. Then she stopped, braced herself, and tumbled, heels over head, sideways on the narrow wire. Minerva's attention was divided between admiration for the girl's courage and agility, and distinct relief at the discovery that she wore tightly fitting hose, all the way to the waist.

"Is your curiosity satisfied, Minnie?"

"Quite so. And don't call me that." She couldn't put much vehemence into her protest. To her horror, she was beginning to get a guilty pleasure out of the silly nickname. Impulsively she reached out her hand to touch his arm. "Thank you for bringing me here. I'm enjoying myself."

Mr. Thomas Parkes would never have brought her here.

The thought came out of nowhere. Nor could she even imagine raising the subject of intimate garments with him. But that was because he was a gentleman of solid worth, not a frivolous aristocrat. Yet the frivolous aristocrat had taken her out of his milieu and, at her request, brought her to a place where she could mingle with people quite beneath his touch. In all the time she'd known him Blake had never appeared to set much store by his grand position. She'd always assumed it was because he took it for granted. That he was so secure in his superiority he needn't trouble himself with it. Unless he truly didn't feel superior. She had always had a low opinion of his character and abilities, after all. Perhaps he shared her view. And if he had a modest view of his own worth then, paradoxically, her own assessment of him would have to be adjusted upwards.

She felt confused, an unwonted state of affairs she attributed to the champagne she'd drunk. That was another new discovery. She really liked champagne.

The waiter, who'd withdrawn after bringing the wine, entered the box. To Minerva's interest, though not much to her surprise, Blake conducted a conversation with the man in serviceable if not elegant French about their meal.

"Why did you tell me you couldn't speak French?" she asked once the man had left.

"I told you nothing of the kind."

"But you let me think so."

"I like to live down to people's low opinion of my intelligence."

"That seems very foolish. Anyway, I already guessed you spoke French. Even with Englishmen present, most of the talk at Chantilly must have been in French and you could never have learned what you did without understanding it."

Blake merely smiled and refilled her glass.

"Why do you pretend to know less than you do?"

"Just perverse, I suppose. Most people pretend to know more than they do."

"I don't." She paused. "At least, I don't think I do."

He brought his face close to hers. "You think too much, Minnie," he said.

Her eyes fixed on his half-smiling mouth. Her breathing quickened, her lips parted. Then he drew back. Of course he wouldn't kiss her in public, would he? She wouldn't want him to, would she?

"Have some more champagne and remember this: I'm just as stupid as you've always thought me."

"I don't exactly think you stupid."

He looked at her with skepticism written clearly on his face. It was just as well the waiter returned with a laden tray. She wasn't sure what to say.

Parisian cafés didn't serve formal dinners. Blake had ordered an array of dishes from those offered by the waiter: various hors d'oeuvres, savory and sweet pastries, cheeses, and fruit.

Having long since confirmed that Mr. Fussell's derogatory comments on French food were nothing but patriotic prejudice, Minerva fell to with enthusiasm, hoping food would soak up some of the champagne and stop the unruly fluttering that afflicted her body.

She wore the simplest evening gown she had with her, an off-white muslin suitable for an informal dinner in the country. The sleeves were very short and she felt exposed in the light garment, as though clad in gossamer. Her skin felt sensitive in a way that was new to her, alive and shimmering. She hoped it was caused by the heavenly bubbles of French wine and not by the proximity of a handsome English marquis, who lounged in the chair next to her and watched her eat olives with a faint smile on his lips. When he caught her studying him she jerked her head aside.

To still the thud of her heart, she concentrated on the crowd, which grew rowdier as the evening progressed. The tempo of the music seemed designed to warm the blood and set bodies moving to its rhythm. In the center of the pit a woman danced on a large round table, displaying all of her ankles and a good deal of calf. Her tablemates cheered her on and clapped along with the beat, except for one man whose face was almost buried in his companion's ample and barely covered bosom. To her surprise her own seemed to ache in sympathy and she rather thought her nipples might be hardening under her gown. She averted her regard from the couple and noticed that none of their neighbors were giving them a second look. Public kissing wasn't likely to trouble the clientele of the Café de la Paix.

"What do you suppose these people think of us?" Minerva said.

"What do you mean?"

"Although you are informal tonight, your dress proclaims your wealth and position. You are obviously a man of means and fashion. No one could mistake you for anything else."

"I'm not sure that's a compliment. What about you?"

"I am dressed too simply to be the wife of such an important man, yet I hardly match the other 'ladies' in the place, most of whom I take to be courtesans. I probably look like a schoolgirl." She was rather disgusted with the notion of appearing so young and naïve, and felt a fleeting regret that she wasn't wearing one of her elegant ensembles from the Parisian dressmaker.

Blake appeared to give the matter some thought. His answer when it came was matter-of-fact. "I guess that most of the men here envy me for being able to afford a beauty so great she needs no adornment."

For a moment the overblown compliment flummoxed her, until she grasped his meaning. She laughed in disbelief. "You mean they think I must be a courtesan *because* of my plain dress?"

"Naturally, if our relationship were to progress, I would furnish you with some expensive and ostentatious jewelry."

She raised her hand to her modest pearl necklace. She'd thought about wearing the Vanderlin cameos but they'd seemed too fine. She remembered the emeralds she'd found in Blake's room. And the rubies he'd given to his mistress, a real courtesan. Logically there was no reason to mind greatly about the latter. But the thought threatened to spoil her evening and she pushed it aside. Instead she might as well learn something. Knowledge of the way the world worked was always worth acquiring.

"Let's assume that we have just met, before any gifts have changed hands. What would you do?"

Blake shifted his chair so that his leg brushed hers at every slight movement, unless she stiffened her muscles and consciously avoided contact. She forced herself to relax and sensed his thigh disturb the thin layers of cloth against her skin. He put his left elbow on the table and rested his head on his fist, turning his neck to face her.

"Well?" she said, nervous and excited at his proximity.

"I would woo you."

"Why?"

"Mistresses need wooing, just as much as wives."

More than wives. At least in her case. Being courted in a romantic sense had never been her dream, but it occurred to her she might be missing something.

Then he touched her. The light trace of his fingers over the back of her ungloved hand shot a quiver up the length of her arm. And Minerva, ever a girl of ambition, realized she wanted to be courted by her husband.

Blake wasn't sure what he was doing. The

object of the evening had been to improve relations with his wife. As he got to know Minerva he found he liked her, despite some of her irritating traits. Now he realized he wanted her, quite badly. There'd been several moments tonight, and earlier, when he'd almost lost control and progressed from gentle flirtation to full seduction. She sat there, the picture of fair youthfulness in her modest gown, and instead of a girl he saw a siren. Edging closer so the details of golden locks and bright eyes hardly mattered, he basked in the clean fragrant heat and was unable to resist touching the soft skin. His fingers limned the fine bones, the tender knuckles. Her hand was small for a tall woman, and businesslike. With her slender body one would expect long fingers. Instead they were on the short side, not ungraceful but quite sturdy with well-shaped nails trimmed short. The left hand hung at her side, and the right, which he continued to lightly caress, was unadorned. A practical hand for a practical lady.

He didn't believe Minerva was unaware of her beauty; she was too intelligent for that. But it wasn't important to her. He'd never known a woman so lacking in vanity and he found it commendable, and even exciting.

"Have you ever been in love, Minnie?" He guessed not. She was too busy with the business of the world to concern herself with romantic dreams like most young girls.

"Certainly I have."

Touché. Just when he thought he had her measure. The answer didn't please him.

"With whom? Or is it a secret?"

"I'll tell you if you promise not to tell my brothers."

"It'll be just between ourselves. Who was this fortunate fellow?"

She pursed her lips and her eyes sparkled. "Caleb Robinson."

He knew the name, but how? Was it some tedious political aspirant who haunted the corridors of Vanderlin House? Then it came to him and he relaxed.

"Robinson! The blacksmith at Duke's Mandeville."

"The handsomest man I ever met. I fell in love with him when I was eight years old."

Blake let out a crack of laughter. "I'm afraid you have a rival for his affections."

"I'm sure I have many, including his wife. Who in particular?"

"My younger sister, Amanda. She fully agrees with your assessment of his bulging muscles and black curls."

"What makes you think I wasn't attracted to his intellect, his conversation, and his sterling character?"

"Just a guess."

"As it happens," she said with an enthusiasm that managed to be both innocent and lascivious, "you are correct. I never missed a chance to go to the forge when one of our horses needed to be shod."

"I will say," Blake said, "that the man is a genius with horses. Very likely has Gypsy blood."

"Who cares about horses? I liked to watch him beating the hot iron with his hammer."

"My sister would envy you. She would never have been allowed to visit the forge. Robinson always came up to the Mandeville stables to shoe the horses."

"It's funny, isn't it, that we lived near each other for so long and yet our acquaintance is so slight. I know most of our neighbors far better. Of course, I always knew who you were."

"What did you think of me?"

"I thought you very handsome." He felt absurdly pleased. "What did you think of me?" she asked.

"I had no idea of your existence."

What some women would take as a snub, Minerva accepted with equanimity. "I didn't expect you had. I was a girl, and ten years younger. It's not as though you were in the habit of visiting us."

She didn't need to point out the reason: the ducal Vanderlins held themselves aloof from the local gentry. The Duke and Duchess of Hampton were too busy about their own vital affairs to pay more than ritual attention to the less important inhabitants of Shropshire. Their children were guarded carefully. As a boy, Blake had at least been free to wander the park and village, and to ride with the hunt. The daughters of the house rarely escaped their governesses. Amanda, his faithful ally, had only been able to develop her youthful tendre for the blacksmith because he, Blake, helped her occasionally escape.

"I'm surprised your sister confided in you. Did you tease her about Mr. Robinson? My brothers would have been unmerciful."

"Amanda doesn't keep any secrets from me."

"Brothers are wonderful, though that's another thing I'd never tell any of mine. I'm glad you're a good one."

"Amanda is a good sister, easily my favorite."

"I look forward to meeting her and exchanging reminiscences of unrequited love."

They smiled at each other and a spiral of warmth curled around his heart. For all their difference in station, growing up within three miles of each other made them fellow countrymen. A wave of longing for Mandeville engulfed him. He'd always been happier there. In London, huge as Vanderlin House was, he'd never been able to escape the presence of his father and the weight of expectations he could never fulfill.

"We'll try and lure Amanda back from Scotland," he said. "She loves Mandeville as much as I do. We'll spend the summer there."

"And then back to London in the autumn," his wife replied. "I can hardly wait."

He rested back in his chair and turned his attention to the scene below. He wondered what Minerva thought of the open lust displayed by some elements of the crowd. She showed no sign of shock, neither would he expect her to. In all the time he'd known her she'd never hinted at the prudishness of the average young miss. But he guessed she knew little or nothing about physical love and he doubted she had any great curiosity either. She certainly hadn't seemed upset by his absence from her bed.

"Blake."

"Yes?"

"Do you think anyone would notice if you kissed me?"

He really needed to stop making assumptions about her.

"We're seated well back in the box and the lighting is weak," he said with feigned disinterest. "I shouldn't think anything we did would draw much attention, unless someone looks at us directly."

"Would you like to kiss me?" Was that a hint of diffidence?

"Why do you ask?"

She leaned closer, and though her approach was too matter-of-fact to be flirtatious, it didn't stop his body responding as to the advances of an expensive courtesan. On the contrary, there was something exciting about such directness. He'd never known Minerva Blakeney to be coy and she wasn't starting now.

"I owe you a number of favors and I hate to be in debt," she said.

"Since you are the debtor I think you should offer the payment."

After a little thought she nodded. "What would I have to do to discharge one favor owed? How long should a kiss last?"

"It can be a mere peck, and let me say right off that wouldn't be enough. Or it can last for hours."

"Hours? What about breathing?"

"You breathe through your nose."

"I see." He watched her close her lips tight and experiment. Then she smiled.

"Let me propose a contest."

"Are you sure you want to lose again?"

"I haven't lost the other one yet. I'm merely behind." She frowned at him. "Don't look so sure of yourself. I shall overtake you. And I'll win this one too."

"What's the challenge?"

"I will kiss you and that will pay one of your favors. For one minute. Is that long enough?"

"It seems fair."

"And then the kiss will continue and whoever stops first loses."

He couldn't help it. He ran a finger along the bow of her upper lip, plump and satin smooth. "Done," he said hoarsely.

The lip rose beneath his touch and he felt her breath mist his finger. "I knew it would appeal to your sporting instincts."

"Whilst you, my lady, haven't an ounce of competitive spirit."

"Let's start. I shall be doing the kissing at first so you must count to sixty and let me know when the minute is up. Nudge my arm or something, because of course we may not speak."

"You have this all planned, don't you?"

She stood up and took a healthy swig from her glass. For courage, he fancied. She wasn't as brassy as she appeared. And he, though he hadn't taken in a quarter of the wine he needed to be foxed, was a little punch-drunk himself.

"I thought it would be more discreet if we stood in the shadows. Not," she said waving an arm at the raucous crowd, "that anyone would likely care *what* we do."

"There's probably *something* we could do to shock them."

She blushed and walked to the rear of the box. "Come."

"Where would you like me to stand?"

She wrinkled her nose while she thought about it, then positioned him with his back to the wall. Taking his head in both hands she drew it down and gave him a quick trial kiss. "Start counting."

She began slowly, delicately nibbling at his upper lip with an intermittent shy touch of tongue at the seam of his mouth. *Eleven, twelve, thirteen,* he counted silently. Then she fitted their mouths together and began to draw on his. *Twenty, twenty-one.* The pressure grew and he felt her sucking his breath from his barely open lips. *Twenty-eight, twenty-nine.*

When she widened the kiss, brought her tongue into full play, he stopped noticing her technique and let his senses drown in humid heat and champagne-laced sweetness.

Thirty-eight, forty-two . . . He lost count and didn't care. All his powers of concentration were needed to remain passive. Minerva Blakeney, née Montrose, knew how to kiss and how to kiss well, and he couldn't wait for the next stage of the challenge.

He had no idea if the full minute had passed and he didn't care. To hell with it. He'd grant her the victory and they could get on with the real contest. He swung her round to exchange positions. "One to you," he whispered against her lips and thrust his tongue deep into her mouth.

Minerva had no time to savor her victory, and little inclination to do so because she was pleasurably, ecstatically engaged in the next challenge. Kissing a passive Blake had been fun, but being shoved against the wall and ruthlessly possessed took excitement to new levels. Their previous kiss in Berkeley Square, good though it had been, had nothing on this one. She felt giddy with delight.

She forced her scrambled brain to function. It was important for this kiss to last a long time, both for a second victory and because, win or lose, she wasn't anxious to stop soon. Breathe through the nose, she thought. Yes. Lips locked? She wouldn't want to lose by default because she couldn't keep her hold on the kiss. Though Blake's mouth was bigger than hers, somehow their lips were perfectly aligned. She'd swear not an atom of air would escape them.

The gentle rhythm of his breathing, felt rather than heard, was in counterpoint to her own, the harmony of lovers. Lovers. The word pierced her consciousness and jolted her heart. Is that what they were, she and Blake? Lovers as well as husband and wife? It seemed so unlikely, but also so right. Without volition she hummed with satisfaction and surrendered herself to the joy of her lover's ravishing kiss.

She felt pleasurably engulfed. His lower arms lay flat on either side of her head and his hard sportsman's body enclosed her, pressed her against the velvet wall of the box. Her breasts stiffened under his weight and her legs sensed the muscles of his through their thin covering of muslin and petticoat. She moaned and returned his kiss stroke for stroke then moaned again, louder, when one powerful thigh nudged hers apart and he rubbed his groin against hers. The hardness against her soft private place set her glowing and aching inside. She pushed back and drew an answering moan from him.

The world receded to two bodies locked as one, sharing the same air. Far away, wild music played on, the tune changing several times, the only measure of time passing. But the Café de la Paix seemed in a different universe from the one inhabited by them, the universe of Minerva and Blake. Thoughts swirling and jumbled, she felt breathless and faint and lost to sensation. She wanted it to last forever and she wanted something more. Her hands laced his hair and massaged his skull, but she pulled one loose and brought it down to grasp one of his firm buttocks and tug him closer to her, sending a message that came from pure instinct.

Every inch of him stiffened, not excluding the hard bulge she rubbed with her belly. He broke the seal of their mouths. "Oh, Minnie!" he groaned and grasped her own bottom, pulling her up on her tiptoes and tight against him, grinding his pelvis into hers at the same time as he covered her face and neck with hard, fast kisses. "Oh, Minnie," he said again, his face now plunged into the space between her aching breasts. "You are going to kill me."

"Blake," she whispered. "I've won."

It wasn't supposed to be a crow of triumph. To tell the truth she didn't feel much glee. Discontent rather, if it meant the kiss was over. She'd have been happy to continue another hour or two. She shook her head in wonder that the whole extraordinary business could be summed up in a single short word. Kiss. He raised his head and looked at her, blue eyes dark and blazing, though with what emotion she couldn't guess. She craned her neck, trying to find his mouth again, but he stepped back, leaving her body chilled. His breathing, like hers, was uneven and labored.

"Very well done, my lady," he said with a strained smile. "Another favor redeemed."

"One more to go." She invested the phrase with more competitive relish than she felt.

"I think we deserve some champagne after our exertions."

She wanted kisses, not champagne. Why didn't he feel the same way?

He took her right hand in both his and raised it for a lingering buss on the palm. She felt better. "Let us sit," he said and guided her into her chair, sat beside her, not too close but not too far, and poured them both more wine.

"To a most stimulating competition," he toasted. The suggestive tone accompanied by a lingering gaze set her body quivering again. Perhaps tonight they would at last consummate their marriage.

Blake stopped at the door to his wife's chamber. She swayed a little. Too much champagne, he judged.

"Good night," he said, brushing her knuckles with his lips as though taking leave of a dowager. "I trust you will sleep well."

"Er . . . good night." She appeared confused as she examined his face, slightly bleary-eyed.

She expected him to follow her in, or come to her later. It was what he wanted, had wanted all night. He'd had to break off that astonishing kiss and concede victory. It was either that or take her against the wall in a public place. He'd needed some distance to control himself.

At that moment he had made his decision. To hell with his father. He would woo her into bed.

He'd never pursued a woman so lacking in experience and he wanted to take his time. It might take days, but they had time. There was a reason they called it a honeymoon. She was willing now, also a little foxed. It occurred to him a slight alcoholic numbness might help with her virginity, but he wanted their first time to be memorable.

And if getting Minerva with child (a possibility though not his principle goal) was the result, he wasn't doing it to please his father but to please himself. And his bride. He'd also discovered a surprising ambition. When he took possession of Minerva she was going to come to him not because of the duty of a wife, but because she wanted him, and respected him too.

Making her want him was the easy part. He could read the messages of her body. Respect was much harder, perhaps even impossible.

Chapter 14

Minerva woke with a slight headache. She'd been a trifle inebriated when finally getting to bed in the small hours. She must remember that champagne, delicious as it was, needed to be taken in moderation. She rang for her maid and asked for a cup of tea and dry toast in bed, her usual morning chocolate seeming too rich for her fragile state. While awaiting sustenance she considered the disappointing conclusion to a marvelous evening.

He'd deliberately conceded the contest, she was now sure. She didn't believe for a moment that Blake, who possessed the endurance of a bruising huntsman, couldn't have kept kissing for much longer. But he'd redeemed himself by chatting most charmingly over champagne. Nothing of great substance was said, but she had to admit her husband was entertaining when it came to small talk. After they'd eaten and drunk their fill, and compared the skills of a succession of ropedancers, none of whom fell into the crowd, he'd suggested they move on to a different establishment.

The Café des Chinoises also offered music of

a delightfully low kind and the decorations were matched by its staff, pretty young women in Chinese costume instead of the usual waiters. After sharing another bottle of champagne, which Blake declared inferior to that at the Café de la Paix though Minerva was beyond such discrimination, they'd ended the evening with ices at Tortoni's.

Blake was an assiduous escort, consulting her wishes, helping her tenderly through doors, up and down steps, and in and out of the carriage. He whispered compliments, setting her ears a-tizzy beneath his lips, kissed her hand frequently, and never lost a chance to gently tease her and call her Minnie.

His absence from her bed was more of a mystery than ever.

Her maid came in with a tray.

"Has His Lordship risen?" Min asked.

"He went out over an hour ago."

Min looked at the clock on the mantle, surprised at how late it was and slightly peeved at Blake. She'd hoped they'd do something together that day. The presence of a note on her tray allayed her annoyance, until she tried to read it.

She'd never seen his handwriting before, apart from his bold one-word signature on various settlement papers and the record of their marriage. It was absolutely execrable.

She stared at the single sheet, unable to believe a grown man with a superior education could produce such illegible chicken scratches, even when writing in haste. She couldn't tell if his spelling was that of a six year old with an incompetent governess, or his writing so bad it just appeared that way.

"Dear Minnie," the note began but it looked like "Daer Minei." If he was going to saddle her with the dreadful nickname let him at least spell it right. "I've gone to see a man about a horse." Or rather "hores." The next part was even worse and it took some time to decipher the message: that he intended to return in the afternoon to take her riding. The clearest part of the brief and unsatisfactory missive was the signature.

Just when they were beginning to enjoy something resembling a honeymoon, he'd left her to go and see a horse (or *hores*). With his luck the seller would turn out to be Napoleon Bonaparte's best friend and Blake would draw ahead in their contest again. Not that she hadn't enjoyed paying Blake his favors, but it would be even more fun to have him in her debt. Besides, it was unjust, ridiculous, and humiliating that she, with her years of study of politics and diplomacy, should be defeated by a man whose main interest was horses. Who couldn't even spell!

How was she to eavesdrop on Princess Walstein's secret meeting with the Duke of Mouchy-Ferrand that afternoon? The pair of them had arranged to meet at the duke's *hôtel*. Minerva had discovered its location, on the Ile St. Louis, and she'd learned that a duchess existed and was in residence. To her mind that meant the Princess would make an afternoon call on the lady of the house, then slip away to do her business with the duke.

Minerva rejected the idea of infiltrating the

Mouchy household disguised as a servant. The challenge of speaking servants' French with an Austrian accent appealed to her strongly and she abandoned the plan only after prolonged thought. Pretending to be the Princess's maid might win her access to the establishment, but she'd be shown immediately into the presence of her so-called mistress and her deception exposed. In the end she decided to call on the Duchess of Mouchy-Ferrand under her own name. After all, duchesses needed to stick together and she was practically one herself now. Once admitted to the Hôtel Mouchy, she had every confidence in her ability to improvise.

Fortunately an elaborate promenade gown of royal blue silk had been delivered from the Parisian dressmaker. Worn with an ermine tippet, blue kid gloves and slippers, and a *chapeau de velours* so elegant even Minerva couldn't help being impressed, she looked every inch a high-ranking noblewoman. Diana would be proud of her, she thought, as she took a last look in the hall mirrors on her way out.

Emerging from the hired carriage in the courtyard of the Duke of Mouchy-Ferrand's mansion, she had her own footman, one of the French servants belonging to their apartment, announce *la marquise de Blakeney* and swept into the hall with her nose in the air, far too important to utter so much as a word to insignificant lackeys. The bewigged functionary who admitted her was duly impressed and meekly led her to a large salon, rather fussily furnished with gilt furniture. A vast crystal chandelier, suspended from a frescoed ceiling, seemed to dominate the room, dwarfing the salon's sole occupants.

The elder of two ladies, a plain, stout woman of rubicund complexion who almost burst out of her overdecorated gown, turned out to be the duke's mother, widow of Bonaparte's general. Minerva's intelligence had told her the old duchess, in far-off egalitarian days, had been the daughter of a butcher. By contrast her daughter-in-law was very pale and slight. She came from an *ancien régime* family and the current duke had wed her after he inherited, in a hurry to enhance his royalist credentials.

The two duchesses received Minerva with civility, though baffled by her presence. She wasn't sure they believed the rigmarole she spun of having been recommended to call by the Duchess of Hampton because of a complicated connection through a series of friends and relations, most of whom didn't even exist. But they were confused by her tale, impressed by her excellent French, and too polite to argue.

It occurred to Minerva she might be able to discover something of the duke's political predilections from the ladies. She would also enjoy a firsthand account of Napoleon's court from the old duchess. But asking the French about their Bonapartist past was most definitely not *comme il faut*. So she endured fifteen minutes of small talk while furiously wondering how she was going to find the duke. She'd heard him mention three o'clock to the princess but, with only a few minutes to the hour, there was no sign of him. Would his Austrian caller be shown directly to whatever room he occupied?

"I had the pleasure of making the acquaintance of *monsieur le duc* at the Austrian Embassy," she said finally. "Will he join us this afternoon?"

The question, which to her seemed perfectly innocent, was ill-received. The young duchess looked as though she'd been struck, while her mother-in-law answered with a brisk *"non"* and gave Minerva the look her own mother would bestow on a mongrel who came sniffing round her prize foxhound bitch.

Luckily for her plans—since she was momentarily nonplussed by the reaction—a large party of callers arrived: more ladies, a couple of gentlemen, and several children. Unlike her they were expected and appeared to be members of the family, but not from the aristocratic side. A great deal of jolly greeting of *cousins* and *cousines* went on, reminding Minerva a little of her own boisterous family. In the commotion she was able to excuse herself, implying an unspecified call of nature.

From visiting the British Embassy and a couple of other great Parisian houses, she had a basic grasp of the way French *hôtels* were arranged. She expected that the duke would have his own suite of interconnected apartments, most likely on the opposite side of the court from the state rooms. She made her way around, by way of a long painted gallery, her slippered footsteps deafening to her ears on the parquetry floor. To her relief she didn't encounter any servants, a fact that was perhaps significant in itself. If the duke had a private meeting to plot treason he'd have ordered his staff to keep away. Leaving the gallery, she discovered a door open to a modest-sized room, furnished as a study. She entered softly, ready to claim she'd got lost if the room was occupied. She was rewarded by the sound of a voice from an adjoining chamber, female and speaking in German.

She was straining to make out any words, when distracted by a new sound. Someone in the passage coming nearer. Someone walking quickly, wearing boots, and making no attempt to disguise his approach.

There was something to be said for honeymoons, Blake decided as he returned to the apartment, eager to see Minerva again. One part of him feared she'd been disgusted by his note. He could have left word with the servant, but he wanted to make the message personal, to assure her he hadn't just abandoned her without a word. Since this morning he was full of optimism, he'd decided to take the risk. With luck she was feeling fond enough of him to attribute his terrible handwriting to carelessness. Plenty of his fellow Etonians had penmanship equally bad, despite being able to read perfectly well.

He went straight to his room, not wishing to present himself to Minerva in his dirt after a morning in the stables, followed by a bout of fencing with Armitage. He'd awoken feeling itchy and sluggish and in need of exercise. Since childhood he'd been accustomed to expend most of his energy in physical activities where he excelled, as opposed to the intellectual pursuits at which he so dismally failed. His tension was certainly exacerbated by his abstinence from one particular physical release.

Soon, he promised himself. *Soon.*

Once he'd washed off the sweat and changed his clothes, he raced to the salon and found it empty save for a servant attending to the fire. An enquiry about the whereabouts of milady elicited the news that she'd taken the cabriolet and left him a note. The disadvantage of writing as a means of communication was that one might be expected to read a response.

Blast the woman! He'd picked up some unsavory gossip about the Duke of Mouchy-Ferrand at the fencing club and wanted to warn her before she dashed off, like a greyhound to a hare, to catch a Bonapartist. It was possible that Mouchy was a sympathizer of the late Emperor; Blake had heard nothing to indicate otherwise. More certain were the duke's imaginative amorous habits. Blake's regrettably innocent wife might find herself in a situation far more troubling than a few hours in a London magistrates' jail.

With something like panic he perused the sheet of paper. Her writing, though neat and even, was not in the capital letters he found easiest to read. Neither was it as brief as his own earlier epistle. He took a deep breath and tried to relax. Otherwise he'd waste precious minutes watching the words and letters dance before his eyes in a meaningless jumble. Because he was looking for them, the words emerged. Mouchy-Ferrand. And surely the word before was "*hôtel.*"

He sent a servant to summon a fiacre and set off for the Ile St. Louis. He managed to decipher most of the letter en route, confirming his choice of destination. The signature drew a smile: Minerva Blakeney. She hadn't written that very often. The salutation was the formal and correct "my lord." Minnie could be very proper in some ways, but underneath lay the heart of a rebel. He wondered if she could be persuaded to join him in flouting his family and its tradition of keeping its collective finger in the nation's pie.

The Hôtel Mouchy was one of those very large Parisian mansions, every bit as grand as Vanderlin House, but possessed of more charm and grace. The fiacre entered the court and deposited him at the steps to the surprisingly modest main entrance, alongside Minerva's cabriolet. A majordomo confirmed that Milady Blakeney had indeed called. Shown to a drawing room he found a chatty family gathering, but no wife and no sign of any gentlemen who answered to the description he'd been given of the duke.

He left abruptly and doubted his presence had even been noticed. "Where is the duke?" he demanded, and when the lackey showed a tendency to object he applied double persuasion: with one hand he picked up the man by his collar while the other slipped him a *louis d'or*. Impressed by Blake's muscles, the value of the coin, or both, the man supplied the information he needed.

Chapter 15

Minerva thought fast. If found by a servant, she was confident in her ability to bluster her way through an explanation of her presence in a private area of the house. But she really wanted to overhear the potentially treasonous communications being exchanged in the next room. And suppose it wasn't the duke and the princess in the next room? What if the owner of the house were to discover her?

Moving almost as fast as she thought, she grabbed her skirts and tiptoed across the room to a tapestry-covered screen near the empty fireplace. As the approaching footsteps came in from the corridor, she slipped behind it, just in time.

She heard the newcomer stop inside the room. Holding her own breath, it was quiet enough to sense his.

"Minnie?" The word came softly.

Blake?

"Minnie. You may as well come out. I can see your feathers."

To her intense annoyance she'd misjudged the

height of the screen, or rather forgotten she was wearing a bonnet with extra tall ostrich plumes that had cost five *louis* apiece. She stepped out of her hiding place and scowled at her husband.

"What are you doing here?" she whispered crossly. "And how did you know it was me? This is a new hat."

Blake raised his eyes to the ceiling. "You're the only person I know who'd do anything this mad."

"Keep your voice down," she said, though he spoke barely above a murmur. "I'm trying to hear what's happening through there."

"No, Minnie, you are not. We're getting out of here. There's no time to explain." He started in her direction but she dodged him, closed the door into the corridor, and fixed her ear to the door into the next room. Holding Blake off with the flat of her hand and a ferocious glare, she heard two voices this time, one of them male, still speaking in German. Agog with anticipation she tried to make sense of the words coming through the solid panels.

"You are a very bad dog." At least, that's what it sounded like.

Then a noise like a woman imitating a bark, and a shuffling sound. Minerva shook her head in bafflement and put her finger in her ear, to make sure it wasn't blocked with wax.

"Lick my boots!"

What?

"What?" Blake had reached her side and was crowding her in the door embrasure.

"Ssh!" She got down on her knees and peered

through the keyhole. It was a large one and she could see quite a lot of the adjoining bedroom. In her view was the lower half of a gentleman's body, from waist to boots, and she had no difficulty recognizing the somewhat stout figure of the Duke of Mouchy-Ferrand, even without a sight of his florid complexion and heavily pomaded curls. The shuffling noise resolved itself into Princess Walstein, on hands and knees and wearing only her undergarments, crawling into view and preceding to obey her master's command. She really did lick his boots.

Minerva slumped back onto her heels. She considered herself hard to astonish, but this did it. When Blake pushed her aside she put up no resistance. He took her place at the keyhole, let out a ghost of a whistle, and began to shake with silent laughter.

"What are they doing?" she mouthed, but he was too overcome by mirth even for sign language.

Then Mouchy-Ferrand snapped another order, loud and clear. "Into the study. I want you on the desk." Those handsome boots, presumably licked clean, began to walk. In the direction of the room occupied by Blake and herself.

Without considering what the duke intended, she scrambled to her feet and pulled on Blake's hand, not giving him a chance to argue. "Hurry. They're coming in here. Behind the screen."

She backed in and they made it just before the door opened. Minerva tore off her hat and hurled it to the floor. Since the space was barely wide enough to hide two adults from view, there was no question of squatting or kneeling. An anxious glance sideways and upwards confirmed that the top of the screen cleared Blake's head, but only by a slim whisker. She returned her head to its natural position and found her nose banging against his chin. Her bosom, despite its modest proportion, thrust into his chest, and their toes touched. When she tried to lean away from the contact only his hands on her hips saved her balance.

Shaking his head and miming the word "no" he hooked his arms firmly about her waist, giving her no chance to escape.

Not that she wished to. Had they not been in such an awkward predicament she might have enjoyed herself. As it was, she clung to his shoulders and the hope they'd escape this place without exposure and public shame. Private embarrassment was inevitable, if they had to overhear more of *monsieur le duc* and the most noble princess's peculiar games. Being an incurable optimist, she hadn't given up on the idea that after they concluded their doggy fun they'd have a revealing conversation about the restoration of Napoleon II to the French Imperial throne.

But first the noble lady, particular friend to an empress, bumped into the room on all fours, barking and yapping as she went. The duke ordered her to bend over the desk. Blake and Minerva were treated to the sound of ripping cloth, then of bare flesh being firmly spanked, accompanied by further barking mixed with cries of pain that sounded, somehow . . . pleased.

Thanks to the shocking book she'd borrowed

from Celia Compton, Minerva thought herself well informed about unusual varieties of bedroom activity. She'd never heard of anything like this, nor could she imagine why a woman would enjoy being humiliated and beaten.

Why, then, did she feel hot and achy and desperately aware of her husband's body pressed against hers? She tilted her head again and discovered humor mixed with heat in the dark blue eyes. Her heart gave a little fillip and her chest felt full. She might have fallen backward had he not been holding her. She wrapped her arms around his neck and held on tight. For balance, of course. A smile she could only describe as evil crossed that beautiful mouth.

Then it began.

First, quite casually, one hand dropped from her waist to her bottom, giving it a gentle squeeze. An indignant glare was met with self-satisfied denial on Blake's face. His other hand followed suit. As he kneaded he also pulled her against him and she felt hard evidence of his own interest. She resisted the urge to push forward and rub herself against him. This was not the time nor the place!

Blake apparently thought otherwise. Her next sensation was of a breeze about her ankles and her calves. She dropped a hand to bat him off as he lifted her skirt, a fruitless effort. She dared not fight for fear of making a sound. His warm palm found her stockinged knee, gave it a quick squeeze then traveled north, past her garter to tickle the bare flesh of her leg. Her wriggling attempt at escape did nothing but intensify the ache between her thighs and the stiffness of his member, straining against her lower belly.

She was furious and excited and there wasn't a thing she could do. Lord Blakeney was going to suffer the sharp edge of her tongue, just as soon as she could safely give voice. In the meantime she contented herself with finding the lightly bristled skin of his inner jaw and giving it a nip with her teeth. She had to acknowledge his control in keeping his reaction to a silent wince. For a moment or two they stood motionless and she believed he'd decided to behave himself.

Then his hand moved inward and upward, between her thighs and under her drawers.

When contemplating the seduction of his wife, an idea that had occupied his mind much of the day, Blake had envisioned his own large bed as the location. Standing upright in a tight corner, in the same room as a couple indulging their own sensual larks, hadn't been part of the plan. Obedience games and spanking were not anything that appealed to him, and he would have expected his bride to be horrified.

Not for the first time Minerva proved of sterner stuff. Surprised, yes, but by Jupiter he actually thought she was a little aroused by the odd behavior of their unwitting host and his guest. And what started out as teasing provocation on his part threatened to get out of hand. Did she think biting his neck was the way to repel his advances? He had to swallow hard not to laugh out loud.

As his hand crept up the satin skin of her inner thigh, she wriggled to escape but his arm about her waist restrained her. No more than he did she wish to be discovered. She was in his power and, if he wasn't mistaken, reluctantly enjoying it. Soft curls tickled his questing palm and when his middle finger forged inward she squirmed and succeeded not in dislodging him, but in widening her entrance enough for his digit to slip into the heat. Wet heat. Yes, indeed.

Her breathing grew heavy against his chest and her eyelids lowered. She squirmed again but this time, surely, to encourage him, to rub herself against his probing finger. When he obliged her by finding and pressing on her clitoris she emitted a soft breathy sigh, but it didn't matter. Out in the room the Princess Walstein was reaching some kind of peak and becoming very noisy.

Not that he paid much attention. He was engrossed by the girl who was blossoming into womanhood in his arms. He just wished they'd hurry up and finish and go away so he could get Minerva out of here and across Paris to that bed. He didn't want to knock over the screen and cause an international scandal. Regretfully he removed his hand, let her skirts fall. He sensed rather than heard her protest and forestalled it with his lips. He already knew she liked kissing and she'd got better at it. Not content with mere contact, she at once opened to him and sucked eagerly on his tongue at its first entrance. Much as she approached life, there was nothing halfhearted about the way she kissed. It wasn't doing a lot for his control, however. He wrapped his arms about her in an effort to confine them in the smallest space possible.

The Princess stopped yapping and the only sound in the room was panting. He and Minerva simultaneously stiffened and drew apart. Dragging his gaze from her just-kissed mouth, he met her eyes, big and dreamy, but within seconds alert when the other pair began a brief spoken exchange. Despite knowing no German, Blake guessed at a couple of Anglo-Saxon sounding words that his linguist wife probably didn't understand.

Do it somewhere else, he begged.

His prayer was answered and two pairs of footsteps receded from the room. Half a minute passed as they looked at each other with widening smiles, then Minerva nodded.

He backed out, tapping her head to remind her to rescue her hat, rather the worse for wear for being trampled. Hand in hand they crept across the room, past the half-open door to the bedroom, whence came a new set of ecstatic noises, and into the passage. Once they made it round the corner to the long gallery, they stopped as one and succumbed to mirth.

"Oh my goodness, Blake." Minerva shook as she put on her hat in front of one of the inevitable mirrors and tried to arrange the battered feathers. "I thought I'd die in there."

Blake was almost doubled over, trying not to laugh out loud and attract the servants. "You're mad, Minnie. Quite mad. You need a keeper."

"Nonsense. I had a very good plan. It would have worked too."

"You mean if that pair were, in fact, discussing the restoration of the Empire."

"Hush! They still may be." He met her eyes in the mirror and raised his eyebrows. "Well, perhaps not. What a very strange couple. What they were doing can't be normal."

"Not to my taste."

She gave up on her bonnet and turned to face him in the flesh. "No?"

"The whole dog thing is ridiculous."

She giggled. "I couldn't believe it."

"But I can imagine being overcome by the desire to spank you."

"Don't you dare!"

"I'd like to put you over my knee and smack you hard."

She didn't know whether to believe him. Incredulity battled indignation in her features.

"But only to discourage you from foolish starts like this."

A hand to her shoulder prevented her stalking off in a pet. "Let me remind you what's to my taste, Minnie," he said softly and took her mouth in a light but lingering kiss. Their breath mingled through slightly parted lips. His desire, barely dampened by the business of escape, roared back. "Let's get out of here," he whispered.

Ten minutes later he assessed the design of the French cabriolet. Exposed to public view in the two-seated open chaise, he was unable to kiss her all the way home. The carriage was not, however without its erotic possibilities. From the waist downward they were protected by the leather apron hood. He placed his hand on her knee, exploring the delicate rounded joint through the stiff silk of her gown.

"Why did you come to find me?" Obviously her mind was not in quite the same place as his.

His caress switched to her thigh. "You have to ask?"

"I left a note."

"Yes you did."

"So why?"

His palm pressed between the thighs, feeling her heat through all the layers of feminine garments. To his pleasure her legs parted and she issued a little gasp.

"I came to find you, Minnie," he whispered, close to her ear, "because I couldn't wait for you any longer."

Later, Minerva thought. She'd ask him later. For the moment she'd think about the delicious sensations created by his hot breath on her ear and his hand down below. Earlier, behind the screen, when he'd actually touched her under her clothing she'd almost cried out with shock and pleasure. It wasn't nearly as good with drawers and petticoats and skirts in the way. She reclined against the meager padding of the cabriolet's seat and thrust her groin forward into Blake's touch. And wanted still more. She grasped the back of his hand and pushed down hard.

"That's it, Minnie," he said. Shivers traveled down her body and joined the even more powerful waves that built deep inside her. Staring ahead, she stared at the back of the driver and wondered fleetingly if he had any idea what was happening in his vehicle.

Not that she much cared. Coherent thought was

beyond her capability. All she could do was grind herself into his touch in pursuit of some unknown, unnamed goal. Her eyes closed, her breathing deepened. She yearned.

With a jingle of harness the carriage jerked to a halt, along with all the delicious sensations of Blake's touch.

"We're here."

"What?" She felt she'd awoken from a beautiful dream.

"Come," he said and his voice sounded as wobbly as she felt. He swung her down to the street and only his hold on her waist prevented her tripping on the cobblestones. At a pace that bordered on the unseemly, he took her by the hand and hurried her into their building, up the sweeping staircase to their apartment.

"Milady is unwell," Blake informed the footman who met them in the hall. "She must go to her room at once."

"I will send in her maid," said the servant.

"No need," Blake snapped and dragged her down the passage.

"This is your room," Minerva objected. "What will he think."

"I can guess and I don't care. By God, Minnie, do you have any idea what you do to me?"

She liked the sound of that. "I think it may be the same thing you do to me."

"Good. Turn around."

Before she could argue, he was at her back, undoing buttons. He kissed her nape, rousing blissful shivers as he slid the silken sleeves down her arms and the gown rustled to the floor. She arched backwards against his chest. "More," she said.

"Oh yes, Minnie. There will be plenty more, I promise. And there's a whole lot more of you I want to see. Starting with your hair." Fingers, blunt yet deft, threaded into her head, seeking and discarding pins, loosening the plump braids, combing out the locks and arranging them down her back. "Like a golden stream," he murmured.

There was something exciting about having him behind her. Without the sight of him, the touch of his hands and lips and his caressing tones affected her acutely. Hard to imagine there'd been a time she'd loathed the very sound of his voice. Now each word he uttered gave her a sensual thrill. She closed her eyes to enhance the feeling. Unusual too was the acceptance of a certain passivity, letting him do what he would and lead the way. She stood quite still while he wrestled with the laces of her stays and raised her arms obediently when he tugged them over her head. Blake knew his way around a woman's clothing. Shift and drawers followed, leaving her almost naked.

With a hand trailing around her waist he walked in front of her and looked, from her blue kid slippers, her white silk stocking and garters, past the fair hair covering her sex, and lingering at her breasts. Fingers reached out and stroked one with an air of reverence and wonder, evoking a delicious shudder. "Minerva." The word spun like a silken skein. "Truly a goddess. You are well named." His thumb rubbed rough over her nipple and the ache in the breast echoed that of her inner passage.

Finally their eyes met and instead of being embarrassed as she might have expected, she felt beautiful and powerful because this magnificent man was regarding her with unmistakable desire. And though being naked in his fully-clothed presence made her feel vulnerable in a delightfully wicked way, she reached for the end of his neck cloth and pulled.

"I want to see you too," she said, her cool tone belied by her racing heart.

He smiled his beautiful smile and, without breaking eye contact, removed his coat and tossed it onto a chair. "Whatever you wish, Minnie." And at that moment she knew she really liked him to call her by the silly name, and also that she'd never, ever admit it.

"Don't call me that," she said, but in a gravelly voice that sent a contrary message.

"Here, Minnie." He handed her his neck cloth and started on his waistcoat.

"Let me help." And while she slipped silk buttons from their holes she tilted her head to invite his kiss and somehow their mouths were still joined as he shrugged the waistcoat off. She would have undone the buttons of his trousers but he stopped her.

"Not yet," he said, his breathing a little rough and his eyes darkened to indigo. Instead he raised his arms and she tugged loose his shirt and helped pull it over his head.

Never had she seen a more wondrous sight than the muscled contours strewn with golden hair. She stepped back a pace to admire him and extended a trembling hand.

"Touch me, Minnie. I want you to touch me. Everywhere."

"Yes," she breathed and felt warm skin over flesh that jumped beneath her palm as she explored his athlete's broad shoulders and chest, the flat disks of his nipples, down the ridges of his abdomen to the iron-hard flat stomach. Her own chest felt heavy and full. In a burst of pent-up longing she reached her arms about him, hugged him hard, pressing her face into the center of his breast, feeling soft hair beneath her cheek and a piquant masculine scent in her nostrils.

His hand came up to her head, stroking her hair with careful tenderness. "I think," he said, "it's time we went to bed."

He stripped off the covers and she lay on her side on cool linen, watching him remove his boots before he joined her.

"Why are you still dressed?"

"It's your first time, Minnie. It'll be better for you to go slowly. If I'm not . . . free, I'm less likely to do something I regret."

"What?" Minerva felt quite pouty about not seeing the rest of him. Now that she'd got this far she was curious to see a man's prick. Especially Blake's prick.

"Never mind. You'll understand eventually. Relax and leave it all to me. I promise you'll enjoy this much more if you're truly excited."

"I'm already excited. I was excited when you touched me in the Hôtel Mouchy. I was excited in the carriage. I'm excited now. How excited can I be?"

He swooped in for a hard laughing kiss. "Much more than you are now. The fact that you're testy and capable of sensible speech means you've a long way to go to be ready."

"I'm sure I'm ready now."

"Did I say *sensible* speech? For such a clever girl, Minnie, you talk a lot of nonsense."

Rather than bite off his head for this outrageous statement, Minerva decided to let it go. She had to admit that in the present instance Blake knew what he was doing. Diana had suggested Blake would prefer an experienced lover, but he seemed to be quite content with her ignorance for the moment. She'd feel more confident applying her theoretical knowledge once she had some experience with the fundamentals. And though she was now looking forward to the event so much she couldn't conceive of any pain, Diana had warned her the first time might not be pleasurable.

His mouth quirked in a grin that made her stomach flip. "I've told you before, Minnie, you think too much. It is now my duty as your husband to render you mindless."

Over the next who-knew-how-many minutes Blake proved he had talents beyond the sporting, unless lovemaking was a sport, in which case he could add it to his list of championships.

With hands, lips, and body he caressed every inch of her skin, bringing her to a state of mindlessness and beyond. Whoever would have thought breasts would be so sensitive to touch? That a man sucking on one's nipples would send needles of bliss shooting down her torso? That the rough cloth of his trousers against her naked skin would thrill her so? When his fingers once more entered her private core she moaned with joy, thrusting upward to meet his stroke and grabbing his wrist to warn him not to stop, not to dare stop. With wicked skill he teased her, building a rhythm as his finger worked the route to her inner passage while his thumb flicked on that hidden nub, which swelled to giant proportions in her head until it occupied her brain to the exclusion of all else.

"Please, please," she begged, straining against him, tense with desire for something just beyond her grasp.

"Be still, let go," he whispered.

She focused her entire mind on that one aching spot.

"Let go," he said again and softly kissed her mouth, and she did, and flew off into a dark, silent place where only pleasure dwelt.

When she returned to the world Blake was propped on his elbow and his expression could only be called a smirk.

Though growing late, there remained sufficient light to see clearly. It was odd to be in bed when it was barely evening. She glanced down at his trousers. Boldly she placed her hand on the prominent bulge. It twitched under the cloth and he let out a groan.

"Does that hurt?" she asked, surprised. She would have thought otherwise.

"Lord, no. It's too good. I'm going to remove these now."

He swung off the bed and made short work of

the buttons. As he slid trousers and drawers down, his prick—the only word for it she could recall—sprang free. It was a bit larger than she expected and extremely buoyant.

"May I touch it?"

"Better not, if we intend to dispose of your virginity today. You, my lovely little Minnie, have brought me to a sorry pass."

He nudged apart her legs and, telling her to bend her knees, settled between them. With his splendid body covering hers she felt deliciously surrounded. The hair on his chest softly rasped her breasts and set her nipples atingle. He rocked in the cradle of her thighs and rubbed his prick, hard yet soft and very hot, along the damp crease of her entrance and she felt desire return. She wriggled a little, and bobbed her head up for an encouraging kiss. Down there she felt an emptiness that needed to be filled. He guided his member into place, probing at the entrance to the unbreached passage. She gasped with excitement, and then with pain as he entered. He felt too big and it hurt. All pleasure vanished and she whimpered.

"I'm sorry, Minnie," he whispered against her lips. "I'll make it quick."

She supposed he kept his word, but the first sharp thrusts felt like a dagger. They seemed to go on and on, as the pain eased to dull discomfort. At last he stiffened, threw back his head with an incoherent cry, and collapsed on top of her. She felt a gush of heat inside her, his seed she realized.

Instead of feeling sated bliss as she had after he'd pleasured her with his hand, she was a little irked by his weight. Far from mindless, thoughts whirled through her brain. His legs were hairy. The pleated silk lining the bed canopy had a small stain. She might be enceinte. Fond as she was of her nephews, she had no desire to produce progeny at Diana's pace. Besides, she had lots of things she wanted to do before pregnancy slowed her down.

Blake rolled off her and onto his back. He was panting softly and looked quite happy. Minerva tried to be reasonable. He had taken the trouble to make her happy earlier. And it wasn't his fault she was virgin and it turned out to be true that the first time hurt. But she didn't know if she could bear to ever do it again. Supposing it always felt this bad?

She lay beside him for a while and felt worse and worse. Even though her attempt to catch a Bonapartist had been an abject failure, she would have accounted the day a success, if an unorthodox one, up to the last quarter of an hour. Blake and she had felt like a real honeymoon couple, laughing and flirting and making love. Now she was full of doubts that she would be able to enjoy the marriage bed and satisfy her husband with his endless experience of beautiful, skilled courtesans. Especially when she remembered Diana saying that men were more satisfied when a woman enjoyed it.

She couldn't stand to think that he was lying there considering her inadequacy. She had boundless confidence in her ability to manage the public business of a lady of influence but discovered a most undesirable streak of uncertainty when she considered herself as a bedmate. If she'd pleased him, why didn't he say anything?

His breathing changed. She bolted upright. He was asleep!

The servant should have been in to light the fire and the lamps and draw the curtains. Minerva felt her cheeks grow warm because the household must know what she and Blake had been doing. She'd never really thought about how much servants knew of the most intimate habits of their masters. They must have noticed that Lord and Lady Blakeney had not, until this moment, shared a bed on their honeymoon. A fresh source of humiliation.

She got down from the bed, pulled on her shift in the fading light, and found a candle and tinder.

Peeved as she was, her heart danced a little jig at the sight of Blake stretched out, his skin golden against the pure white sheet. Nursing the flicking light she bent over the bed, the better to admire his glorious naked male body. A story of Greek mythology came to mind, of Psyche so overcome by the beauty of her sleeping husband, the God Eros, that she dropped wax on his chest and almost lost him forever.

She straightened and took a step back just as he opened his eyes and blinked at her. "Minnie," he said, barely awake. "I nodded off. What time is it?"

He rolled over with the easy athleticism that was even more pronounced naked than when he was clothed, and sat on the edge of the mattress.

She looked away, suddenly shy. Instead of being thrilled by their state of undress, she felt exposed and awkward. "I don't know. It's almost dark."

He retrieved the loose top sheet from the pile of

bedding and pulled it over his lap. "How are you, Minnie?" He smiled and held out a hand to her. She took it, a little stiffly. "Are you sore?"

"I'm all right."

He dropped a kiss on her palm. "It'll be better next time, I promise."

"It was fine." She felt like crying and she wasn't about to let that happen, having no idea how Blake would interpret such a sign of feminine frailty. She had no idea herself. Her emotions baffled her.

He stared at her, warily she fancied. "Are you hungry? I am."

"I suppose."

"Shall we dress then, and see what's for dinner?"

He stood up, holding the sheet around his waist with one hand and giving her a quick awkward embrace with his other arm. She endured it briefly and without reciprocation, then tore herself away.

"I'll see you in the dining room," she said.

Chapter 16

Blake had always enjoyed the time after lovemaking when he and his partner, sated and happy, could relax and talk about silly and insignificant things. He hoped Minerva's unwonted silence stemmed from her status as a new nonvirgin. All his lovers had been women of experience and he believed they'd enjoyed themselves. Many of course had been paid to do so, but he didn't think they'd feigned pleasure. He wasn't pleased with his own performance this evening. Once he'd entered her he should have slowed down, given her time to adjust. The wet heat of her virgin quim surrounding his cock has been too much. He couldn't ever recall losing control like that and he couldn't find the words to explain it.

If he'd hoped the consummation of their marriage would usher in a new era of understanding and harmony with Minerva, he couldn't flatter himself the golden age had yet begun. Despite his best efforts to entertain her, by midway through a dinner conversation exceptional for stilted triviality and long silences, he would have welcomed a disquisition on parliamentary tactics.

Almost. He wasn't quite that desperate.

"No luck with proving Mouchy-Ferrand a lover of Bonaparte, I guess. Too bad." If he couldn't amuse her, he'd annoy her instead. Anything was better than indifference.

"No."

"Never mind. With another month in Paris you're bound to find another candidate."

She cast him a challenging look and he was glad to see she hadn't sunk into a decline. "Certainly I shall. Even though I have the disadvantage of not knowing a lot of horse-mad men."

"Life's unfair."

"Why did you follow me to the Hôtel Mouchy?"

"One of the horse-mad men told me the duke is famous for being unscrupulous with women. I was worried about you. Quite rightly so. I thought you'd grown out of these dangerous impulses."

"Thank you," she said with a curt nod. "Though I would have been fine. It didn't seem to me that the princess was unwilling. Very strange."

"Supposing they had been plotting treason, as you hoped. Suppose they'd caught you spying?"

She dismissed the question with a shrug. "If I had been detected, I would have thought of an excuse."

The more he considered it, the more concerned he became. Minerva had a confidence in her own powers that he envied, but one day her lack of caution might—would—lead her into serious trouble. He only hoped he'd be there to prevent it.

"I'm glad I came after you, Minnie," he said softly with a melting look across the table.

She didn't melt. "As I said, there was no need.

I'll call on Princess Walstein again. But I must say, it'll be hard to think of her in the same way."

At last the tedious meal came to a close. "Would you like to go out this evening?" he asked. "We could try one of the other cafés. Or Tortoni's again. You liked the ices there."

"I don't think so, Blake. I think I'll retire early. I'm very tired." She blushed and looked away. "And rather sore."

That was that. Not that he would have asked for or expected to have her again tonight. But he knew plenty of ways to give and receive pleasure without penetration, including one she'd already experienced. He was tired himself and would welcome a chaste and companionable night in a shared bed. He opened his mouth to suggest it, but nothing in her behavior at dinner suggested she'd welcome his company in any way.

"It's still early. May I offer you a *partie* of piquet?"

"No thanks. I'll read in bed for a while before I sleep."

"In that case, my dear, I'll bid you good night."

He retired to his own room with a glass of brandy and picked up Pierce Egan's *Boxiana*. Although he couldn't read in the same room as her, it gave him pleasure to be sharing her activity, especially the book she'd given him. Winning her respect required more than lovemaking.

But he couldn't summon the calm he needed to decode the words. His head was elsewhere. After half an hour he put on his hat and coat and went for a long walk in the mild Parisian night.

He returned soon after midnight with new resolve. His bride was simply going to need a bit more wooing, that was all. Tomorrow he'd devote himself to her entertainment and after an extravagant dinner at Very's, reputedly the best restaurant in Paris, he'd present her with the emeralds, taking the jewelry route to the female heart. In fact, remembering that the necklace came from a famous French jeweler, he'd go out early and see if he could find matching bracelets.

He'd gone out without her.

Resolutely refusing to regret she'd rejected his invitation, Minerva applied herself to her book and found it hard to concentrate. Giving up, she blew out her candles and settled back in bed, wishing she wasn't alone. It was foolish to be upset by a painful experience she'd expected to be painful. She'd allowed shock to overcome the pleasurable— extremely pleasurable—events that had preceded it. Remembering what Blake could do with his hands got her hot and far from relaxed and it must have been very late when she finally drifted off to sleep. She'd been listening for his return in the adjoining room and heard nothing.

She woke with new optimism and a measure of self-disgust. She'd let herself get into what her brother Stephen called a funk. Minerva Blakeney didn't allow *anything* to quell her. She rang for her maid with special energy.

Milord, she learned, had gone riding. He'd given orders to let her sleep and would return in an hour or two. She was sorry not to be favored with an incomprehensible note in his appalling handwriting.

She drank her chocolate and took a bath, before dressing in another new ensemble and enjoying a hearty breakfast. With still no sign of Blake, she wandered into his chamber and made straight for a particular drawer. She hadn't thought much about the emerald necklace, but now she wondered why he hadn't given it to her.

It wasn't there. Had she mistaken the drawer? No. There was the card case and the letter. Her fingers itched to open it, but no. She would not so lower herself. There were a dozen good reasons why the necklace had disappeared. She just couldn't think of them at the moment.

Her half-formed suspicions seemed absurd when Blake reappeared late in the morning, seized her by the waist and swung her round. "Put on your bonnet, Minnie," he said, brushing a fast hard kiss on her lips. "Let's walk in the Tuileries Garden."

The public gardens adjacent to the royal residence performed the same function as Hyde Park at the fashionable hour. The paths were full of elegant walkers enjoying a fine afternoon. They nodded to several acquaintances before being accosted by Lady Elizabeth Stuart, who complimented Minerva's new gown.

When the conversation of the ambassadress and her friends turned from fashion to diplomatic gossip, Blake excused himself.

"I see Thornton on the other side of the circle," he said. "I'll return in a quarter of an hour."

Lady Elizabeth had some intriguing news from London and Minerva was unaware of time passing, nor of their group's progress around the basin and into the *Grande Allée*.

She scarcely noticed the riders and carriages on the broad avenue, until the reaction of those on foot drew her attention to a particularly elegant vis-à-vis drawn by a showy white horse. The equipage drew to a halt and was quickly surrounded by half a dozen gentlemen. The occupant was a woman whose style of dress, while extravagant and stylish, proclaimed her no lady. Dressed from head to foot in white velvet (Minerva shuddered to think of keeping it clean), the only color in her outfit was red: a red feather adorning a tiny white velvet hat perched on top of gleaming black locks. And a pair of ruby bracelets over her pure white gloves. The woman was utterly ravishing and vaguely familiar. Minerva was fairly sure she hadn't seen her in Paris, so it must have been London.

"Who is she?" she asked one of her companions.

"La Bonamour. She used to be the mistress of the Marshal Saint-Victor but then she went to London, or so I heard. I didn't know she was back."

Desirée de Bonamour it appeared, was not only a genuine Frenchwoman, she was also in Paris. With a sinking heart Minerva recognized the golden hair of one of the courtesan's thronged admirers. He'd removed his hat and was saluting his mistress's hand.

Minerva knew all about mistresses. Well, not all but quite a lot. She knew married men had mistresses, especially wealthy noblemen. She'd known Blake might not have broken with Desirée de Bonamour before their wedding, and still she'd married him, for her own reasons. At that point she'd accepted his infidelity with composure, if not pleasure, as the way of the world.

She wasn't going to accept it now. Not for one single second. She knew the proper thing for a wife to do, whether complacent or not, was to pretend public ignorance of a husband's other "interest." Too bad. Her chest swelled and a rushing, pounding noise flooded her brain and excluded every other thought. A quick "excuse me" was all the leave she took of Lady Elizabeth before she marched over to the carriage path, just as Blake turned away from the woman. He saw her approach and guilt was written all over his face.

"Min . . ."

"Don't dare call me that," she jabbed under her breath and then raised her voice. "My lord. I think I'd like to go home. There's a disagreeable stench in the vicinity."

The woman actually had the nerve to laugh at her feeble insult. Never mind. She saved her best work for her husband, as soon as she had him alone. He was the one she was angry at. And she was glad— rapturous—to see him look white about the gills.

"I think that's for the best," he said quietly. "Gentlemen," he said, replacing his hat. She'd have slapped him if he said another word to *that woman*. "Minerva." He offered her his arm. His sleeve beneath her glove was as welcome as a slug on bare skin.

As they walked away a buzz of chatter arose in English and French. Not a soul present would long be unaware of their identities. *How could he?*

"I take it you recognized the lady. I'm sorry. I wouldn't have that happen for the world. I didn't realize you were close by and it seemed churlish to ignore her greeting. We were once . . . close."

"Once?"

"We parted company before our wedding."

"Really?"

"Truly. I had no idea she was in Paris."

"I don't believe you."

They'd left their company well behind so, not seeing a soul she knew, she dropped her arm and shook it as though it had touched something vile. Blake grabbed her shoulder and spun her round to face him. He looked gorgeous and sincere, the lying bastard.

"It's the truth," he insisted. "Until a few minutes ago I hadn't set eyes on her in weeks."

"Since a certain night at Covent Garden?" she said sweetly. "Three days before our wedding."

"You heard about that, did you? I'm sorry for that too. There was a reason. Not a good one and I'm not proud of it, but that was the last time."

Her snort expressed her disbelief. She tore away from him and marched along the path as fast as her legs could carry her, which wasn't nearly fast enough. He caught her with insulting ease. "I don't know how to convince you if you insist on disbelieving me. But you can't have any reason to think I've been seeing Desirée in Paris because I haven't."

Did he think her a fool? "Hah! What about the first week we were here? You were out most of the time."

"I told you. I was trying to make contacts and

fulfill Gideon's mission. I got nowhere until you started to help me." He was trying to turn her up sweet. He knew as well as she that all he'd had to do was find a few horse lovers and Orleanists poured out of the stables. "Please, Minnie. Please believe me."

Damnably she wanted to, but she wasn't such a fool. "You bought emeralds," she cried. "And not for me. Did you give them to her this morning?"

"How do you know that?" His eyes narrowed. "Have you been searching my room? What were you doing?"

At once she realized her mistake in mentioning the necklace. As a veteran of fraternal quarrels, she knew the importance of never laying herself open to counterattack. On the defensive, she shot back. "And now I understand why you never came to my bed. Should I respect you for keeping faith with someone, even if it's your mistress and not your wife? Have you decided now that you may as well have both?"

"No! I have not betrayed you with Desirée."

"Then why didn't you . . . you know . . . until yesterday."

He bit his lip. "I was angry about our marriage."

"You think I was so thrilled? It wasn't my fault you compromised me. But I was ready to make the best of things rather than face ruin."

"I didn't want to get you with child. I didn't want to give my father the satisfaction of an heir to the dukedom. And I'll admit I was angry with you too. It was a lesser consideration, but I wanted to deprive you of the satisfaction of carrying the future Duke of Hampton. I'm sorry. It was petty of me."

This made no sense and her anger abated a degree in her bafflement. "Why would I care? I mean, I would expect to have children eventually, but I'm not especially anxious to do so."

"Because only when you bear a son will you be truly accepted by the family as worthy of being a duchess. Didn't you wonder why you weren't given any of the good jewels?"

"I'm not interested in jewels."

"But you want power, don't you? The jewels are emblems of the family's power and influence that you hoped to wield as my bride. Only when you've done your duty and produced a son will you be allowed all the privileges of the future duchess. Until then—and you'll forgive me for saying this, it's my father's view and not mine—you are merely a young woman of little fortune or birth who managed to capture me."

She panted with rekindled rage and the exertion of walking at full speed. "You have not the slightest idea what I believe or what I wanted of life. If you think I'd rather be married to a man whose merit comes only from his birth, you couldn't be more wrong. I admire a man who advances on his own merits." That wiped the arrogance off his face. "As for being a duchess, the wife of a duke, and the mother of another—it is to me a matter of supreme indifference." She stopped walking, folded her arms, and stuck her nose in the air.

To her gratification, Blake's voice lost its reasonable tone. "Hah! You say that, but you know it's unlikely you could have wed anyone who will wield the kind of sway my father has. He controls over a dozen seats in Parliament and influences as many again. I may not want to do what he does, but I know the kind of power I'll inherit. You're a very clever woman, Minerva. You know this and it's what you want."

The grain of truth in his accusation struck a nerve and made her angrier. "You pompous ass!" she yelled. "You don't know me at all. I despise the power of the aristocracy, the corruption of a system that gives a single man so much power. When true reform comes, the nobility will be nothing and England will be ruled by the common man. The only use I have for aristocratic power is to use it against itself."

Instead of becoming angrier, or cringing in shame, he had the gall to sound intrigued. "Does my father know what you think? By God, Minnie. You're a Radical. Does he know that?"

She made herself speak calmly, to try and get it into his fat, ignorant head that they were talking of matters more important than his family issues. "The duke is a man of great vision who has fought to change things, even against his own interest. I revere him for that. But he's old-fashioned. He sees gradual and limited changes, which will leave much of his inherited influence intact. I don't think he understands that the forces of change are too strong to control and he will eventually lose everything. Unfortunately, I doubt it'll happen in his lifetime."

This time his response truly surprised her and

she wondered if he'd lost his mind. "Why are you laughing?"

"My father has outwitted himself, the old devil. He thought he was getting the family a broodmare with the bonus of a little political knowledge to help his poor idiot heir. Turns out he's let a fox into the henhouse." He grabbed her by the waist and before she could struggle, swung her in a circle. "I'm glad I married you, Minnie. I can't wait to break the news to my venerable sire."

"You irresponsible blockhead!" she spat, shoving at his chest until he put her down. "It's all just a game to you. An idiotic male grudge match with your father that matters not a whit to anyone else. I don't know what you have against him and I don't wish to. My concern is the future of England and the English people."

"And you called me pompous!" He wasn't laughing anymore.

"Better pompous than irresponsible. You were born to a position where you could do some good in the world, and as far as I can see you've done nothing to prepare for it. You don't read the newspapers or study the issues of the day. You don't even try! You may be handsome and you may know all about horses but I made a huge mistake in thinking you might be worth more than that."

Now he wasn't laughing at all. He walked the short distance home without uttering another word, his mouth white and set into an ugly grimace. Despite her own fury she was disquieted at his palpable anger, so cold and controlled compared to her own. Could she be in the wrong?

Surely not. Even if she was mistaken about Mademoiselle de Bonamour—and she didn't believe it for an instant—everything else she'd said was true and fair. Wasn't it?

Nevertheless, by the time they entered the apartment she felt chilled and depressed at the ruin of her day.

The ruin of her life.

Blake stalked off to his own room, but returned before she'd finished removing her bonnet. "Here," he said, thrusting a familiar case in her hand, together with another smaller one which she opened. Matching bracelets. Just like Mademoiselle de Bonamour. Minerva couldn't decide whether to throw them in Blake's face or apologize.

As she wavered, a knock came at the door and the footman admitted a gentleman. She recognized him from her visit to the Embassy, one of Sir Charles Stuart's senior attachés.

"Lord Blakeney." He bowed. "My lady. I have bad news. The letter came by diplomatic courier, but another dispatch brought the news to Sir Charles and he desired me to acquaint you with the facts directly." He handed Blake a sealed letter. "I'm sorry to inform you that the Duke of Hampton has suffered a seizure."

"His heart?" Blake asked.

"So I understand. He is not expected to live long. I have been instructed to help with arrangements for your immediate return to London."

Minerva's hand crept over and took her husband's free one. He stared at the inscription on the envelope like a man who has received a death sentence.

"From my mother," he said. His words were enunciated crisply but his voice was devoid of expression. "Would you be so good as to read it, Minerva, while I discuss our journey."

Chapter 17

Held up by a flooded bridge near Beauvais, it took Minerva five days to reach London. She prayed that Blake, traveling ahead on horseback, had made it in time to see his father.

Incessant rain followed her across the Channel and onward from Dover. The gutters along Piccadilly worked overtime, their efficiency threatened by the thick layer of straw laid down on the street to muffle the clatter of carriage wheels and preserve the peace of the invalid in Vanderlin House. The absence of signs of mourning at the entrance, or on the servants' liveries, reassured her that the Duke of Hampton still lived. Her short term as Marchioness of Blakeney would continue a little longer. The idea of becoming a duchess and mistress of this, and half a dozen other mansions, seemed unreal.

The atmosphere in the house was one of sobriety and anticipation. Standing in the gilded hall at the foot of the great staircase, surrounded by bowing footmen with somber faces, she wondered where she should go. This was her home now, but she wasn't even sure if she could find the way to the suite she'd only seen once. She wished Blake would appear, and dreaded it.

After the news of the duke's illness arrived, all their conversation had been of practicalities. She'd offered to ride with him but, excellent horsewoman as she was, she couldn't keep up with his speed and stamina and had acknowledged the fact. She stayed to supervise the transportation of their possessions and servants from Paris. The honeymoon was over.

Hanging over her were two facts. She and Blake were new lovers. And they'd just had a blazing row. She wasn't sure which was paramount and both made her nervous about their coming reunion.

She'd had plenty of time on the road to ruminate. She admitted to herself that she'd said some hard things to her husband. Not that she thought all of them unjust, but she'd been less than tactful in their expression. In fact she'd been beastly. She had survived dozens of arguments on the practice and philosophy of politics, and prided herself on an ability to make the kind of rational case of which many men thought a woman incapable. Blake had driven her to an unprecedented rage and she didn't know why. Neither had she any idea how to approach him.

Her own uncertainties aside, she was concerned for him. Despite the complexities of his relations with his father, which she didn't understand, he must surely be affected by his parent's grave illness. She suddenly longed for her own father and a comforting embrace from that cheerful and loving eccentric. The contrast between William Montrose and the Duke of Hampton couldn't be greater and, for all the duke's material advantages, she rather thought she'd been dealt the better hand.

A footman took her traveling cloak, but the butler who'd greeted her with a respectful "My lady" had vanished. Within a few minutes a young woman entered the hall.

"Lady Blakeney," she said with a deep curtsey. "I am Amanda Vanderlin. Let me show you to your rooms. I'm afraid your suite is full of painters so we've prepared one of the guest chambers for you."

This was Blake's favorite sister. If Minerva hadn't recognized her, she would have known by the strong family resemblance.

"I'm glad to finally meet you, Amanda. I've seen you often over the years. We may even have met at a public day at Mandeville."

For a moment Amanda seemed disconcerted by the familiar address. Then she smiled and looked very like Blake at his most charming. "Of course we've met. Those public days are rather hideous, aren't they? Everyone seems so stiff and proper and embarrassed to be there."

"I wish we were meeting at a happier time. How is His Grace?"

"Not well. We fear he may not last the week."

"Where is Blake?"

"He's sitting with the duke now. So is my sister Anne, Lady Kildarren. Our mother is resting after being with him all night."

"I'd like to see Blake," Minerva said. "Does he know I'm here?"

"Filson will inform him. Meanwhile, let me take you upstairs. You must be weary from the journey."

While she washed off the dust and did her hair, Amanda told her how things stood. "Anne and Kildarren and I arrived from Scotland yesterday. Maria and Gideon Louther have been here most of the time, but they've returned to their own house for a while. I can't really believe it. My father has had a bad heart for a long time, but he never showed any weakness. At nearly seventy years old we shouldn't be surprised, but he's always seemed immortal and invincible. My mother says he has weakened, but I've seen so little of him in recent years."

Minerva squeezed her sister-in-law's hand for a moment. "I can see how distressing it must be. I've been very little at my father's house in the past two years and this makes me realize how much I miss him. I am glad that marrying Blake means I shall be only three miles from him and my mother at Mandeville."

They'd barely settled in the morning room when Blake entered. "Amanda," he said, sounding harassed. "Where is Gideon? The Prime Minister is threatening to come and pay his respects and I don't think the duke is up to it. Gideon will know how to fend him off."

Minerva stood. For an aching moment their eyes clashed and she thought he was pleased to see her. A tentative smile died unborn when he offered her a formal bow.

"Minerva," he said tonelessly. "I trust your journey was comfortable."

All she could do was murmur a commonplace. His hair and clothing were less than pristine. Dark shadows under his eyes emphasized his pallor and spoke to his exhaustion. She had an urge to smooth back a stray lock from his brow, but nothing in his manner suggested he'd welcome the gesture.

"Do you have everything you need?"

"Amanda has been most kind."

An awkward silence descended as Blake took in the sight of his wife. Amid the cold formality of Vanderlin House, rendered even grimmer than usual by the circumstances, she seemed young, vibrant, and very beautiful, like a fresh bloom in a catacomb. He was foolish to be glad she'd arrived. How could he take pleasure in the presence of a woman who despised him? While he faced the dread and grief of his father's last illness, their quarrel and the words she'd spoken haunted him. Because they were true. He was about to step into his father's shoes and be revealed in all his inadequacy.

He remembered the way she'd taken his hand when the news reached them in Paris, the calm efficiency with which she'd read his mother's letter aloud. He had no doubt he could rely on her for any assistance he requested. Minerva would be a dutiful wife. Though not an obedient one. The thought induced an inner smile, the first he'd had in five days.

The humor didn't reach his face and quickly faded from his mind. He didn't want a dutiful wife, but the point was moot. Whatever type of spouse he wanted, he had one already and she stood before him, expectant.

"What can I do to be useful?" she asked.

He shrugged helplessly. "Not much. All we can do is wait."

The butler came into the room to deliver a letter and announce a visitor. "Lord Iverley."

Minerva welcomed her brother-in-law with a kiss on the cheek. Heaven forbid that he, her husband, should merit such enthusiasm.

"Blakeney."

"Sebastian."

The cousins greeted each other with their usual coolness.

"Louther says the duke wants to see me."

Of course. His father wouldn't see the Prime Minster. But the nephew he'd always admired and loved, who had all the intellectual attributes Blake lacked, Sebastian Iverley he would see. If Blake were a bigger man he'd take him upstairs himself and witness the last meeting between his father and the man he wished had been his son.

"My lord." The butler held out the letter. "This was delivered from Windsor."

The king himself had written. "It requires my immediate attention," he said to his cousin. "Filson will show you up to the duke's room. Amanda, will you come to the study with me? I need your assistance."

He was glad of an excuse to escape. He didn't know what to say to Minerva beyond trivialities. Their quarrel felt like a great barrier he needed to dismantle or climb over, but he had no idea how to do it. Neither, at this time, did he have the energy to try.

Left alone, Minerva tried not to be put out that Blake had turned to his sister before his wife for help. Was she going to have to make the first move to restore amicable relations?

When she thought about their last exchange in the streets of Paris she felt uncomfortable and confused. She couldn't understand why she'd been quite so angry. It wasn't as though either had entered their marriage willingly. Why did she care so much about his manipulations, or even his mistress? Things she'd said about his lack of concern for matters of importance were true. But she couldn't deny she had said them in an ill-mannered, cruel way.

Applying her experience with her own family, especially Stephen, her closest in age, might help. They'd had dozens of vicious quarrels and they settled themselves in one of two ways. If things became virulent, violent even, a parent, nurse, or tutor might intervene. At which point brother and sister forgot their disagreement and united against the interfering authority. As they grew older, pinches and hairpulling ceased and verbal fluency improved. They'd argue each other to a standstill (or Minerva's victory), refuse to speak to each other for half an hour or half a day, then carry on as though nothing had happened.

Neither of them, in her recollection, had ever apologized beyond a muttered, "I'm sorry." She had little experience with the concept. And she could hardly compare her relationship to her brother with Blake, with whom she'd shared a bed and would share a lifetime. Being married was turning out to be a lot more complicated than she'd imagined.

"Will you read to me?" The duke's white hand trembled as he pointed to a brown leather book. His father's presence had shrunk to that of an old sick man of no special power.

The first time he'd seen him lying there, Blake had been shocked at how insignificant he looked. The huge room itself, dominated by the ancient bed of carved oak, had drawn most of his unwitting attention. Over all the years he'd never visited the room. The duke's children had no part in his intimate life.

During one of the stilted conversations they'd endured since then, he'd learned the bed had come from Holland with Gerrit Vanderlin, the first duke. It seemed to have swallowed up the once tall and proud figure, just as family tradition dominated his father's life.

Either Blake or his mother or one of his sisters attended the duke at all times, more often than not several of them. In addition, his brothers-in-law were often there, especially Gideon. And always a servant or two, and a doctor.

Today the duke had dismissed everyone but Blake. He could be thankful there would be no witnesses to his humiliation. With a hollow opening in the pit of his stomach he took the volume and opened it.

"Greek," he said with relief.

"Herodotus."

"You know I was never any good at Greek. The person you need is Cousin Sebastian."

The duke gave no sign he'd noticed the bitterness Blake couldn't keep out of his voice. "No matter. Your mother read to me from *The Times* earlier, but I find I don't much care for the news. It's hard to be interested in present events when I shan't be here to witness their outcome."

There was nothing to say. The doctors had told the duke he had only a few days to live at the most, and his father was ever a realist.

"I'd rather talk about the past. I've been thinking about my father."

Blake prepared for another lecture on past Vanderlin glories. He'd heard many in his life and he supposed he could survive one more.

"I was twenty-two when he died. Like you I was abroad. The news of his last illness reached me in Rome. Unlike you I didn't get back in time to see him."

"I'm thankful I was no farther away than Paris."

"I was about to leave for Greece. I never got there, you know. I never saw it."

"Did you want to?"

"More than anything I ever wanted. I fancied myself something of a classical scholar in those days." Regret filled his voice, a sentiment Blake had never associated with his father, who'd always appeared boundlessly confident and self-satisfied. "But it was not to be. I was Hampton and there were expectations."

Blake braced himself for a final harangue on his own inadequacy. Instead the duke's faded eyes regarded him a pensive expression. "I'm sorry I can't live longer and spare you the dukedom a few more years."

"Don't you mean you wish the dukedom could be spared me?"

"Don't jest about it, Blakeney. It's not a burden to be carried lightly. If I've sometimes been hard on you, it's because I wanted you to be prepared. I fear you are not ready for what you must face."

"I have never seen you display any discomfort in your position."

"I had a good many years to grow into it. And everything became easier once I found your mother."

In thirty years Blake had never heard his father even approach a discussion of his personal affairs. He wasn't precisely eloquent now, but something in his voice when he mentioned his own marriage conveyed a depth of emotion his son hadn't suspected.

"I'm sorry I've been a disappointment to you, Father," he said, the first time he'd ever addressed the duke in such a familiar fashion. "I wish I could have made you proud."

A small rare smile creased the duke's pale lips. "You have. You did well in Paris. I didn't expect you to identify those friends of the Duke of Orleans in such a short time."

"I should have guessed. That task was your idea, not Gideon's."

"I thought it was time to give you something to do. You justified my confidence."

"But I didn't really do anything, did I? You already knew those names." Blake shook his head at his own blindness. Far from doing anything useful, he'd merely managed to stumble through a very easy test.

"Had your time in Paris not been truncated, I

have every faith you would have found new and valuable information for us."

"If my wife had anything to say in the matter, I have no doubt of it."

The duke looked interested. "A very clever young woman. I hope you are getting on well with her. I'd like to think you will be as content as I have been."

"She certainly is clever."

He couldn't talk about Minerva now. He'd scarcely seen her in the two days since she arrived at Vanderlin House. He knew he needed to resolve their quarrel and he wanted to find a way for them to live in harmony. But at the moment it was more than he could manage. There were too many other demands on his time and attention.

"She is young," the duke said, "but my duchess was younger. Only seventeen when we wed and I was fifteen years older. I have never wanted another woman."

"You never kept a mistress?"

"Not after I married. I hope you will not either. It's one reason I made you dismiss your bird of paradise. I've forgotten her name."

"Desirée de Bonamour."

"An improbable name."

"Not the one she was born with."

The duke actually chuckled. "My first love was an Italian girl called Guilietta Giglio. Juliet Lily in English. Charming girl. I was quite heartbroken to leave her behind."

"In Rome when . . ."

"Yes. Something else I lost when my father died. But I forgot Guilietta quite quickly."

"Did you forget the other thing? About being a Greek scholar?"

"Not entirely. I maintained a few interests that were mine as a man and not as Duke of Hampton. You must do the same."

Blake saw evidence of his father's passion in the room: a battered bust of Homer, a graceful urn decorated in terra-cotta and black. There were symbols of classical learning all over the ducal residences. He'd taken them for granted and occasionally hated them.

"It won't be Greek I'm afraid. As you know, I could never even master the alphabet."

"You are a fine horseman, one of the best so I am told. You should be proud of that."

"I do know my horseflesh." In fact his father had criticized him for extravagance in his stables. "Pity I don't have much notion of politics."

"I believe Lady Blakeney could help you in that aspect of the Vanderlin affairs."

She'd certainly like to, he thought dourly. "I thought that was what Gideon was for."

"Gideon is a good man but he's a follower, not a leader. You must learn to decide for yourself. In the end you are the duke and responsible for the outcome of your decisions. It's one of the disadvantages of power." His voice trailed off and he looked frailer than ever. "I've always had a great deal of power and I've tried to exercise it for good."

Loath to cut off the most intimate conversation he'd ever had with his father, Blake knew he couldn't let it go on much longer. With profound sadness he stood up and dared to take the duke's hand. "I want you to know that I shall do my best for the family, and for the country too."

"I believe you will, my son. You have a long life ahead of you and things change. Your goals in life will not be the same as mine, nor should they. Let me give you one more piece of advice. Remember this: in politics there are no final victories or final defeats. The next day things will be different and you must adapt to new conditions." Another frail smile. "Rather like the hunting field."

The duke's voice was fading. "I believe I shall rest now. I'm glad we've had this talk."

"Yes, rest, father. I'll sit with you until my mother returns."

The duke settled back into the pillows and closed his eyes. Within minutes his shallow breathing told Blake that he slept. He sat beside the bed, looking at the face that always appeared cold and immovable. Everything seemed different. Not only was his father old and weak, he was also human.

Blake felt a wave of regret that only now was he offered a glimpse of this side of him. Now that it was too late, he felt this was a man to whom he might have confided his secret. Instead, he'd always offered the most powerful reason for hiding it.

He reached for his earliest memories of his father and discovered what he had forgotten: approval and even a restrained affection. The valued heir, he'd been brought to the duke's study each day. He had a faint recollection of infant games. Things changed when he grew old enough to read and his tutors reported his lack of progress. Bafflement changed to anger as years passed. Instead of affection he received punishment for idleness: birching from his tutors and scoldings from his parents, far more terrifying because of the weight of his father's disappointment. His mother, who supported her husband in all things, regarded him with sorrowful despair. Her distant dignity, even when her children were small, had repelled any impulse to ask her for help. Only when Amanda was old enough to learn had he finally mastered the letters of the alphabet and their meanings.

He had been taught to read by a five-year-old girl. With his little sister he could achieve the state of calm that brought sense out of the chaos of the symbols. By that time he had been written off as irredeemably stupid, the dolt who, by accident of birth, must inherit the leadership of a family famous for brilliance. Amanda had been helping him ever since. Except when he went to Eton.

That's where Huntley had come in, leading ultimately to disaster.

Suppose he'd told his father. Suppose he'd explained his inability to master the simple act of reading, instead of taking every measure to disguise it. He knew why he'd never been tempted. As long as he was perceived as lazy rather than brainless he had a chance to one day win his respect. Laziness could be cured; stupidity was forever.

He had one last chance. He would never have considered it without this afternoon's surprising exchange, but he was overcome with the urge to be honest with his father at the last. He formulated a confession in his head and waited. On his deathbed he did not believe the duke would reject him.

He hoped for a final blessing before he took up his father's burden.

Half an hour passed and Blake felt at peace with his decision. He sat in the quiet room overlooking Vanderlin House's ample garden, insulated from the noise of London by thick walls and curtains. Only the ticking of the mantel clock competed with the gentle breathing of the dying man.

Then something altered.

He leaped up and ran to the door, calling into the passage for the doctor. He rushed back to the bedside and heard only the clock. Groping for his father's wrist he sought a pulse, in vain. He pulled his watch from his fob pocket and convulsively polished the gold back against his waistcoat. Setting it against his father's nostrils elicited not so much as a hint of mist.

He stood aside, without hope, as the doctor hurried in. The pricking behind his eyes gave way to unshed tears.

The doctor stood up. "Your Grace," he said. "I regret to inform you that His Grace has passed away."

Within minutes the room filled. His mother, kneeling at her husband's bedside, weeping, with Amanda beside her. Maria and Anne and their husbands. The senior servants. A royal equerry who had called on behalf of the king. His own wife standing at the back of the room wearing an expression of unwonted hesitation. Their eyes met and he meant to reach out to her. He wasn't even sure if his hand moved before he was interrupted by Gideon.

"We talked about various contingencies, but the final decision about the arrangements will be yours, Hampton."

For a wild moment he thought his father hadn't died, after all. Then he realized the name was now his.

Chapter 18

Waiting for the Duke of Hampton's funeral, Minerva felt her life slowed almost to a halt. In all her youth she would never have chosen to spend so much as half an hour in Shropshire over London, having been bored to tears in the country. But now she wished the duke was to be buried at Mandeville instead of Westminster Abbey. Vanderlin House felt like a luxurious prison.

The family had, after some discussion, agreed the king's offer of the Abbey was too great an honor to be declined. Minerva was not consulted. She wasn't consulted about anything much. The duchess was almost prostrate and kept mostly to her own rooms. Blake's sisters and their husbands were polite without being warm. Only the staff treated her with deference. They knew the way the wind blew and recognized that she was, in fact, now mistress of the house. If not for the oddity of being addressed as Your Grace by the countless servants, she would scarcely credit she was now a duchess.

She didn't feel like such a lofty personage and

wondered if she ever would. Some attention and acknowledgement from the new master would have helped. But she saw little of her husband, and when she did he was never alone and constantly beset by people demanding opinions or decisions.

Minerva thought he looked pale and unhappy. He must surely be in a state of grief. And he had suddenly become a public figure as well, the head of the Vanderlins. Minerva would have gladly lent her assistance, but it was never demanded. With relations between them unresolved, she didn't know how to offer. The pall of grief in the house cast down even her buoyant spirits, especially since she found herself in the unusual position of not knowing what to do.

Beyond her initial condolences they'd spoken little. It was an extraordinary state of affairs that she, his wife, felt she had no right to intrude on his grief without a sign from him. But theirs was hardly an ordinary marriage.

Blake spent much of his time sequestered in the duke's study with either Gideon Louther or Lady Amanda. Left to her own devices, Minerva designated herself the task of dealing with the stream of visitors. The hatchment bearing the Vanderlin coat of arms was draped with crepe and hung at the entrance to the house. This sign of mourning would have deterred callers upon the demise of a lesser figure than the Duke of Hampton, but anyone important—and many who wished to appear so—ignored custom and paid respects to the passing of the duke.

The house steward and butler, whose decades

of service gave them greater knowledge than she, decided which visitors could be turned away and which had to be accommodated. Dressed in deepest black—she had one mourning gown made for the death of an uncle two years earlier—she took possession of one of the drawing rooms to receive peers and bishops, cabinet ministers and Members of Parliament. She became adept at deflecting suggestions that they should see her mother-in-law or her husband.

The latter was much in demand. These men of gravity, who'd had nothing in common with the sporting Lord Blakeney, were desperate to cultivate the acquaintance of the new Duke of Hampton, his captive parliamentary seats, and his powers of patronage. Minerva confined her remarks to polite commonplaces, but mentally she took notes.

Dinner after the funeral was eaten almost in silence. The service and interment in the medieval aisles of Westminster Abbey seemed to have squeezed the last drop of animation from the bereaved. The duchess remained in her rooms and the late duke's children seemed weighed down by their grief. Blake occupied the ornate thronelike seat that had been his father's.

The first dinner after the duke's death, he'd hesitated to sit there. "You are duke now and must take your father's place," the duchess had insisted, leading him to the head of the table. He'd started to argue, as though reluctant to accept the seat and all that it symbolized, then acceded. Minerva had quietly taken a place at the side of the table, again refusing to put herself forward until Blake invited it. His accusation that she was some kind of power-mad harpy still rankled. Yes, she wanted the power her new position could give her, but to do good, not as an end in itself. She was determined not to give Blake reason to repeat that particular charge.

Blake? She didn't even know how to address her husband. He was now "Duke," "Your Grace," or "Hampton." The other members of the family already addressed him by his new title. They called her "Duchess."

Tonight he looked ashen with fatigue, a shadow of his physically exuberant self. But that wasn't the only change. Minerva observed him at the head of the table, his evening clothes of unrelieved black emphasizing his fair coloring. There was a distance, a hauteur in his demeanor, as though he were slipping into his new role. As he courteously offered soup to his sister Anne on his right, she recalled the first time she'd dined at this table, seated in the place of honor now occupied by Lady Kildarren. She could not have imagined then that her care-free, careless fiancé could be so utterly transformed by assuming his position.

A pang of longing for a few happy days in Paris pierced her heart. They'd been too short and ended badly. In their transformed circumstances she wondered how to regain that brief accord.

Rather than spend another silent evening downstairs with her sisters-in-law, she retired to her room after dinner and paced for over an hour, fiddling with her hairbrushes, trying to read yet unable to concentrate. The next day, she decided, she would begin to make her place in this new world. She'd never asked to be a duchess, but that was what she was and she wasn't going to sit around another day in a state of limbo. And if her husband wouldn't break the ice between them, she would make the first move.

She was half asleep when the mattress moved and arms gathered her in and turned her around.

"Ssh," he said, claiming her lips and holding her against him. His hands caressed her back and thighs and bottom through the thin cambric of her nightgown and she felt his erection pressing against her belly.

"Blake," she murmured, the word soundless beneath his plundering mouth. He kissed her long and deep, demanding her silent cooperation. She gave it gladly, meeting his tongue stroke for stroke, pushing into his embrace, kneading his buttocks and pulling him closer.

She was hot and aroused and beyond thinking what the arrival of her husband in her bed meant. All that mattered was he wanted something and she wanted to give it.

It was quick and not particularly pretty. He wrestled up the skirt of her nightgown and checked her for readiness with a quick swipe of his fingers. Then he entered her without ceremony, pressing her down into the mattress and settling into a strong steady rhythm. She wasn't excited the way she'd been before, but neither did it hurt. His member slid smoothly inside her and she felt an agreeable fullness. After a few minutes it might have developed into a more powerful sensation, but instead his thrusts came faster, his breathing accelerated and, with a cry that sounded like agony, he stiffened and all his weight collapsed on her. She felt the hot gush inside her and a different damp heat on her chest, where his face lay.

Her husband was weeping.

She stroked his arms and shoulders and his damp, silken hair, rained kisses on any bit of him her lips could reach, and murmured something stupid. For once in her life Minerva felt less than her years. What words of consolation could she offer, who'd never known a moment's grief? With mind and body she tried to project comfort and perhaps her efforts succeeded. After a while he slipped off her, but held her close, his arms about her middle and one rough heavy leg over her own limbs. His breathing told her he slept. She kissed his mouth again and settled into slumber.

When she awoke she was alone.

Chapter 19

It was terrifying how much correspondence came to a duke. Blake took his seat behind his father's desk and regarded the three piles.

Hetherington, the duke's political secretary for the last two decades, pointed at the largest. "Those are letters of condolence, with my answers, ready for your signature."

His signature. That he could manage.

"The second pile are congratulations on your accession."

"Really? That seems a trifle indelicate."

"I think you will find, sir, that they are phrased *most* delicately."

"And?" Blake enjoyed Hetherington's dry sense of humor.

"The writers will wait at least another fortnight, a month even, before begging for any favor."

"Men of tact and refinement."

"Indeed. I took it upon myself to answer them in my own name, since press of business doesn't allow Your Grace to respond directly."

"I couldn't have put it better myself. And those?"

"Those are from your fellow dukes, members of the royal family, cabinet ministers, and your father's intimate acquaintance. You will wish to honor them with personal responses."

It was the last thing Blake wished to do, and the pile, though smaller than the others, still looked dauntingly large. He stretched out his legs and wished he was somewhere else, preferably on horseback. Not for the first time, he considered taking Hetherington into his confidence.

Not yet. Disguise and prevarication were so ingrained he couldn't bring himself to make the confession.

"You're a hard taskmaster," he said instead. "I hope they'll all appreciate the honor when called upon to decipher my ugly scrawl." He pointed to the sheaf of foolscap in Hetherington's arms. "What is that? More long, detailed reports for my entertainment?"

The secretary responded with a brief laugh. "As requested, I have made and attached a brief summary of the salient points of each one."

"Very brief, I trust."

"But there are a few you will want to read yourself."

"I doubt it."

"None of them is long."

"Splendid. You shall read them aloud to me while I sign these letters."

Having inked the nib of his pen, he seized the first from the pile, then stopped. Long practice with his signature was no help. He'd never signed himself *Hampton*. Luckily the first letter was easy.

Even if it came out backwards it was the same. He inscribed a bold H and let the remainder of the name drift into an illegible squiggle.

"Nearly signed it 'Blakeney,' " he commented to the watching Hetherington. "Carry on."

Practiced as he was at taking in information aurally, he had little difficulty grasping the import of the reports and deciding what to do. It was the way he'd worked with the land steward in Devon and he would set up the same system with Blenkinsop, the secretary who managed business from all the other estates. "Anything else?"

"Just the question of the duchess's pin money."

"I thought that was covered by her jointure."

"I meant Your Grace's wife."

He had a wife, a fact of which he was only too aware.

"The sum specified by her marriage settlement may not be sufficient now."

"Double it, then. Do you think that will be enough?"

"More than generous. Shall I inform Her Grace?"

"I'll do it."

He needed to speak to her. He'd stolen into her bed like a secret lover, leaving before dawn. Stricken by overwhelming sorrow, he'd avoided any other source of emotional stress. It was all he could do to present a brave face to those who expected him to behave like a Duke of Hampton, and even more to those who expected him to fail. Once his father was laid to rest he looked for some relief, a sense of finality, and found none. He'd gone to his wife's room because he was desperate for human contact. He intended only to hold her, but he'd been seduced by her scented heat, her tender flesh, and her kisses. Their congress had been quick and uncomplicated. For him a momentous physical relief had triggered an answering release of mental tension. Weeping wasn't something he could recall doing since childhood and he didn't like to think of it now. But deep inside he had to admit the tears had helped, as had her incoherent words of consolation. Before falling into a deep sleep with Minerva in his arms, he'd been in a state of serenity.

Their quarrel in Paris hung heavy on his mind. She'd said some harsh things and what tormented him was how many of them were true. Not about his former mistress; he'd broken with Desirée before the wedding, after the appearance at the theater, which was intended principally to thumb his nose at his father. But when she'd called him ill-prepared for his future role she'd been right. If she only knew how much.

"Where is Her Grace?" he asked his secretary.

"I believe she's receiving in the yellow drawing room."

Amanda had reported Minerva's sterling work protecting the rest of them from importunity before the funeral. He'd walked by one day and glimpsed her through an open door, fair, slender, and dignified in her clinging black gown. He'd thought at the time she looked too young to be a duchess. But if any visitors thought to take advantage of her inexperience and attempt encroachment they were going to be out of luck. Minerva, Duchess of

Hampton, had steel in her and not far beneath the surface. His lips twitched, feeling rusty, as though they hadn't smiled in weeks.

He had no intention of being embroiled with any tiresome callers. He rose and tugged on the bell-pull. It rang a little way down the passage where a footman was always on duty to see to the duke's requirements. "As soon as Her Grace is free, ask her to join me," he bade the servant. And observing a hint of uncertainty in the man's face, added "The young duchess."

Whatever—or whoever—occupied her, she didn't appear at once. Instead Gideon Louther entered, bursting with news.

"Doggett died!" Gideon announced.

Clearly he expected a reaction. "How sad," Blake said. "Who the devil is Doggett?"

"The Member for Warfield Castle."

"Ah." Even Blake knew the significance of that. Warfield Castle was a splendid place, a ruined medieval castle set within massive earthwork fortifications dating back to the Dark Ages. In the fourteenth century it had been an important place, doubtless bustling with soldiers, merchants, and monks. These days most of the inhabitants were sheep, but it still, by ancient right, sent two representatives to Parliament. Manchester, England's second largest town, sent none. Warfield Castle was the rottenest of rotten boroughs. The election of its Members of Parliament was in the hands of one man: the Duke of Hampton.

"I have a list of possible candidates. We must think carefully." Gideon didn't need to explain that this was a major prize. He started throwing out names and discussing their merits and drawbacks.

Blake wasn't much interested. "There's no hurry, is there?"

"Since it seems a general election is imminent, there may be no need to hold a by-election at Warfield."

"An election? At Warfield Castle?" Minerva entered the room. He had wondered how long she would maintain the restrained, almost meek, demeanor and he had his answer. The opinionated aspect of her personality was back in force. Her high color in marked contrast to her black dress, she brimmed with indignation. "So that a couple of shepherds can send a man to Parliament while big cities send none. It's disgraceful!"

"We're all agreed on that, Duchess," Gideon said soothingly. "In order to reform Parliament we must have enough votes, you know. And we can't afford to be fussy about where they come from."

"Is that so, Sir Gideon?"

Gideon took her question at face value. "We shall make sure our new Member for Warfield Castle will vote for the abolishment of his constituency. You needn't worry."

"Thank you so much for explaining it to me. You've set my mind at rest."

"Happy to be of service."

Blake almost laughed at Minerva's barely suppressed irritation and Gideon's earnest obliviousness.

"May I know who the candidates are?" she asked.

"We're still composing the list, Duchess," Gideon said. "I just heard of the vacancy and brought the news to Hampton." Blake had tried to get his brother-in-law not to call him Hampton, but in vain. Gideon refused to use the short form of the old title he'd had since birth.

Minerva narrowed her eyes at Gideon. She did not appreciate having such basic facts explained to her, and in such a condescending manner. Doubly irritated by his presence, a disappointment since she'd hoped to finally see her husband alone, she turned to Blake. "You summoned me?"

"I requested the pleasure of your company. Would you be so good, gentlemen? Duchess, please sit down."

Minerva took the chair next to the desk. As soon as they were alone Blake sat across from her, leaned forward, and put both hands on the desk.

"I'm doubling your pin money," he said. "You'll need it now."

Was that all? Her previous allowance was far greater than any sum she could spend. "Thank you," she said. If Blake wasn't going to bring up Paris, she would have to. As she sought the right words he preempted her.

"I want to apologize."

"For what?" She felt a little panicked. Was he admitting he had been seeing his mistress? In her heart she'd desperately wanted to believe his denials.

"For last night. I shouldn't have come to you like that."

"You have the right. You are my husband."

"I don't want to share your bed because I have the right."

Minerva touched his hand with the tips of her fingers, all she could reach across the expanse of polished wood and paper. "I'm glad you came. I shouldn't have said what I did in Paris. I'm sorry."

"You were upset about a woman who should never have even come to your attention. I can only repeat that there is no longer anything between us."

They fell into an uneasy silence. She was glad to hear him say that, very glad, but the quarrel had ended up being about much more. She couldn't think of a sensitive way to bring up what they'd said about his father. As for her charge that he wasn't up to the task before him, she approached it obliquely.

"If there's anything I can do to assist you with the affairs of the dukedom, please let me know." She looked longingly at the piles of letters and reports. Who knew what fascinating matters they contained?

"Thank you, Minerva. My father's secretaries are bringing me up to snuff. And Amanda has been helping me."

Minerva was developing a severe jealousy of her inoffensive sister-in-law. Filling the parliamentary vacancy at Warfield Castle was the kind of down-to-earth politics she loved and there was nothing she'd like better than to hear the list of possibilities and offer her opinion. Her extremely knowledge-able opinion, if she did say it herself.

An unwelcome instinct she couldn't ignore told

her this wasn't the moment to charge in and make demands. Their truce was too fragile. She bit her tongue and waited.

"You will have plenty to do learning the duties of a duchess."

She'd never asked to be a duchess but she hoped she could wield the kind of influence her mother-in-law possessed. It was forcibly brought home to her that such power derived solely from the duke and she could only possess it with his consent. How bitterly disappointing that Blake seemed to have no intention of sharing his business with her. His lack of trust hurt too. Making up their quarrel hadn't returned them to the closeness she'd felt in Paris.

Patience, she told herself sternly. Patience, alas, had never been numbered among her virtues.

"I must finish reading these papers," he said with a sigh, "or Hetherington will be after me."

He stood and walked over to her side of the desk, taking her hand and raising her from her chair. The interview was over. With a courtly nod he brushed his lips over her knuckles, sending a delicious shiver up her arm. A lock of hair flopped over his forehead and she itched to sweep it back. A pang of desire pierced her as she recalled their intimacy of the previous night. While it offended her sensibilities to use seduction rather than logic to achieve her ambitions, it would be no hardship.

If Blake wanted her to learn to be a duchess, then that's what she'd do. She'd be the best duchess the Vanderlin family had ever seen. And there was one particular duty she had in mind.

Chapter 20

Another grim family evening concluded with Maria and Anne playing a piano duet. They'd been no more than passable in the nursery and they were pretty bad now. Sitting in the music room, a chamber decorated to impress and awe rather than entertain, Blake discovered a new sympathy for the beasts in the Tower menagerie. Trying to ignore the itch in his feet and the assault on his ears, he let his eyes dwell more pleasurably on his wife. Their exchange that afternoon wasn't exactly a meeting of true minds, but he was ready to put their quarrel behind them. Would she welcome him in her room tonight? She appeared to listen to the music while reading the newspaper upside down on a table. While not the most remarkable of accomplishments, it wasn't a distraction he could achieve.

When the party rose to disperse for bed, she didn't wait for him to bid her good night.

"Shall I see you later, Duke?" she asked, softly enough not to be heard by anyone else.

"If you wish for my company," he replied cautiously. He couldn't flatter himself their earlier exchange had been more than adequate in repairing their relations. Too much remained unsaid. Minerva was disappointed by his refusal of her assistance, but he couldn't let her observe his struggles to wrestle the sea monster of ducal duty. Not until he had his disguises and evasions firmly in place. As for admitting the truth to her, he'd considered and rejected the idea. One day perhaps, when he'd proven to himself and demonstrated to her that he could manage his role.

"I shall look for you in my room in due course, then," she said with a sultry smile. He'd never known Minerva to be sultry. It pricked him right up.

A formal conjugal visit being outside his experience, he prepared with special care. With a clean body and smooth face he walked down the passage, glad not to meet a late lingering servant. The point of connecting bedchambers struck him as never before.

He half expected a curtain lecture on rotten boroughs, or an interrogation on his powers of political patronage. Instead she rose at his entrance and offered a tentative smile of welcome. In a simple white nightgown, her hair in shimmering gold ripples over her shoulders, she looked like a princess in a nursery tale, a virgin awaiting a unicorn. She wasn't, after all, far removed from that untouched state. Her beauty sent a message to his already eager cock, though shy and virginal had never been qualities that appealed to him in a woman.

Shyness was not Minerva's prevailing trait, the word termagant better describing her everyday character. But in the present case he was indubitably the expert and it pleased him to lead the way.

Without saying a word he walked over and gathered her close. Her vitality seemed to soak through his dressing robe into his flesh. When she raised her head to him he accepted her unspoken offer. It was a kiss of exploration, of new lovers who don't know each other's ways. Had he bedded her after the wedding, in the hotel in Abbeville, it might have been like this. He would set aside the memory of the fervid first coupling in Paris that had ended so badly, and last night's emotion-thick release, the details of which he could scarcely recall. They could start fresh, but without the shattered maidenhead to spoil her enjoyment.

Despite an aggressive erection, he felt no great urgency. With all the time in the world he caressed her firm little breasts, perfect in size and shape, palming the stiffened peak through fine cloth, her response igniting his passion.

He kissed her until her breathing shortened and her body sent out waves of heat. "Come to bed," he said, soft and low, then swept her up and carried her to the mattress, kissing her and murmuring praise all the way. "Get under the blankets."

She obeyed and stared up him with wide curious eyes, her mouth parted in a sensual invitation. He blew out the bedside candle, as he might have on their first night, slipped off his robe, and slid between the cool sheets to join her.

Removing her thin nightgown seemed almost a violation of her innocence. He also found her clothed body against his nakedness incredibly arousing. His bollocks roiled with excitement, his cock strained against her belly. Determined to ensure her pleasure he kissed his way down her neck, causing it to arch into his touch. His hands moved down from her bosom, exploring her through the soft cloth, cupping her covered sex, which thrust into his palm, a physical manifestation of Minerva's demanding personality that made him softly chuckle.

Finally he pulled her skirt to the waist and sought the heated cradle. A finger found her quim damp and slick, her clitoris hard and swollen beneath his thumb. Her climax took some time, his own somewhat less. As he moved inside her she put her arms around him and offered him kisses, but didn't speak. The only sounds she made throughout were little huffs of breath and muted cries of delight. After they finished she curled up against his chest and he fell asleep with her in his arms.

Blake began to think he could manage this duke business. He bounded into the ducal study after breakfast, sat himself down at the historic desk, and positively whipped through the memoranda Hetherington had prepared. His secretary had a neat hand and Blake was becoming accustomed to it. His summaries were admirably brief, his recommended courses of action sensible. After an hour only a handful remained where he needed more information before making a decision, and a couple more he needed Amanda to read aloud to him. There were still a few personal letters to write.

Writing was easier than reading. He could do it

quite quickly and he'd long since become practiced at scrawling such an appalling mess that no one would notice the irregular spelling, or the way letters sometimes emerged from his pen back to front. He dashed off a note to the Duke of Lethbridge who, he was pretty sure, wouldn't even attempt to decipher it. The good duke was as busy with his illicit amours as his duchess was with hers.

The Duchess of Lethbridge was, indirectly, responsible for Blake's sunny mood that morning. If it wasn't for her he wouldn't possess a duchess of his own and that would be a pity.

Damn, he felt lucky today, better than he had since the news of his father's illness: relaxed, full of vigor, and ready for anything. After a night of debauchery with an experienced and innovative mistress, Desirée for example, he'd be a little tired. Bedding a delicious young thing in a state of sobriety had sent him to sleep happy and replete.

And she hadn't made him talk about anything.

Maybe his wife had been possessed by something. Not a demon, obviously. Could one be possessed by an angel? Blake's theology was hazy on the idea, on which he wasted little speculation. Since having an amenable wife was not likely to be a lasting state of affairs, he might as well bask in it.

Intending to do a little basking, he tipped back in his chair, put his boots on his desk, and crossed his ankles. Not very ducal he thought. But he was a duke now and anything he did was, by definition, ducal. He emitted a happy sigh and basked away until interrupted by Filson.

"Who is it?" he asked, waving aside the card proffered on a silver tray.

"Mr. Geoffrey Huntley, Your Grace."

There went the pleasure of the morning. "I don't want to see him."

The butler gave a tactful little cough. "He was insistent, Your Grace. I would have turned him away, but I recall he came here with Your Grace on exeat from Eton once. I thought Your Grace might wish to receive an old friend."

He'd throw something if he had to hear the phrase "old friend" again in connection with Geoffrey Huntley.

"Show him in," he said.

He could tell Huntley to go to hell. He no longer had to keep his secret from his father. But he already knew he wouldn't. Why else had he agreed to see the man?

One day he might not care if the world knew the Duke of Hampton was barely literate, but it was too soon. He needed to establish himself in the position, learn the ropes, and win respect. He didn't want Minerva to know, not yet. So he'd discover Huntley's new price for his silence and decide if he could bring himself to pay it.

"Blake," the miserable slug said once the butler had announced him and left. "Or Hampton I suppose I should call you now."

Huntley was being insolent, of course. It was quite improper for a man of his insignificant status to address a duke by name. Huntley would certainly have addressed his father as Your Grace. Blake didn't care much for such distinctions, though he supposed he ought to now. And it would sound petty to demand his due. He took his feet off the desk but aimed to project the insolent self-assurance that came to him on the back of a horse or in the fencing saloon. He waited in silence for his enemy to make the first move.

Huntley appeared not a whit discomposed. He looked around for a chair and, when Blake didn't offer a seat, sat without invitation. "So you're the Duke of Hampton now. I visited Mandeville last year on a public day, since you never saw fit to invite me. Splendid park you have there."

Once he'd regretted not being able to invite his closest school friend, unacceptable to the family by reason of his undistinguished birth. Now he felt distaste that Huntley had polluted the place. "You haven't come to make small talk about the glories of my estate. Get to the point."

"Very well, we'll talk about me. Did you hear about the Westborough by-election? I lost." Huntley grinned with the breezy self-deprecating charm that people always saw as evidence of honesty. "It cost me a great deal of money, you know. Thirsty devils, those electors. Must have emptied a brewery at my expense, but it turned out they preferred the other party's beer."

Blake looked bored.

"Louther promised if I stood for Westborough and lost they'd find me a better seat this time. Westborough pretty much cleaned me out."

"I wonder if they'd have said that if they knew where you got the money."

"I told Louther I'd had a lucky run at cards."

"Lucky?"

"Are you implying that I cheated at piquet?" Huntley had always been good at the wounded look. It had won him acceptance in games of cricket and football from which athletic limitations excluded him. Just one wistful sigh and Blake would insist his friends let Huntley play. At the time it had seemed a fair exchange; now he recognized early training for extortion.

"The card game was fair, I grant you that."

"And you were drunk, Blake. You can't hold that against me."

No. Blake took responsibility for his own inebriation that night. And might well have signed the fraudulent I.O.U. anyway. His reading wasn't much better cold sober than drunk. There wasn't any point arguing about the past. "What do you want?"

"Warfield Castle. You know what that is, don't you?"

"You want to be my handpicked candidate for the rottenest borough in England."

"I want a Parliamentary seat that won't cost me anything and you have one in your gift."

"And?"

"That's all."

Like hell it was all. "Why should I give you this prize?" Blake wanted Huntley to spell it out.

"As a small token of gratitude for all those essays and exercises I wrote for you. It's such a little thing. I'm sure you wouldn't wish your beautiful new wife to know why her husband is incapable of writing her a billet-doux, or reading one either." He picked up a sheet of paper from the desk and began to read out loud. Or rather began to stammer a disconnected string of meaningless sounds. It was an exaggeration, but not by much. Blake let him have his fun without cramming the paper down his throat.

"It's such a little thing," Huntley said. "And will cost you nothing."

"Until the next time you want something from me."

"Think of it, Blake. If I'm the member for Warfield Castle you'll be my patron. I must vote as you wish and never speak ill of you. To do so would be ruin. We both get what we want. I get my career; you get my silence."

Blake tried to consider the ramifications. Was what Huntley said true, or was he opening himself up to endless demands? And could he live with himself?

In the short term he probably could. He'd buy himself time and at least he wouldn't be forcing the party to accept a candidate they didn't want. Gideon seemed to like the fellow.

He stood up abruptly and rang the bell. "I must consult my advisers," he said. "I'll let you know."

Huntley opened his mouth to argue, then thought better of it. He knew he'd won when Blake failed to give him an outright refusal.

Chapter 21

"**W**ho is Sir John North?"

"A third cousin, by way of the late duke's mother." Minerva made a note, awed by the way the duchess had generations of Vanderlin connections at her fingertips. "He is looking for a recommendation for his younger son at the Horse Guards."

"Send that down to the duke's secretary. Hetherington sees to military matters."

There was a lot to being a duchess Minerva had never considered. Though to be fair it wasn't a subject she'd wasted a lot of time on. When her mother-in-law invited her to the duchess's suite—soon to be Minerva's—she'd been intrigued to discover, in addition to a bedroom, dressing room, and comfortable sitting room, a chamber set up as a very efficient office. Since the family was in strict mourning, there were no merely social invitations to answer. But the greater part of the duchess's correspondence was appeals for charity, and reports and requests from huge numbers of relations in every part of England. Already many letters were addressed to Minerva. The changing of the ducal regime took place with brutal speed.

Minerva couldn't tell how Blake's mother felt about her demotion to dowager. She was as efficient as ever and perfectly friendly in her distant way. An air of depression spoke of her grief at her husband's death, not that she confided anything of her personal feelings.

Not every letter Minerva received was from the Vanderlin side of the family. Branches of her own family seemed pleased to number a duchess among their relations. Connections from both her father's and mother's side wrote to her, cousins who'd never paid the slightest attention to her before. As the days passed she began to understand the Duke and Duchess of Hampton's position at the center of a web of alliances, a system of mutual favors that benefited all. In return for Hampton patronage, the dukedom was paid with loyalty and influence. On a political level Minerva had always understood it, but she was fascinated to see it work close-at-hand.

Not that the feminine office of the alliance was directly involved in political decisions. Her virtual exclusion from Blake's office continued to chafe. Once the mourning period was over Minerva would be attending entertainments and giving her own. Then she would develop the power of the political hostess that had always been her ambition. She'd seize it for herself, with or without her husband's cooperation. Meanwhile she learned the less public but nonetheless vital part of her job.

With her egalitarian leanings she couldn't help feeling a certain disapproval, in principle. On the other hand, if she could help Cousin James's curate son find a living that would enable him to marry, she was glad to help.

The handsome allowance Blake had awarded her no longer seemed so outrageously generous. A duchess had demands on her purse Minerva would never have guessed. Having the means to contribute to worthy causes and personal appeals was an unexpected benefit of her position. She made a note to send a generous gift of money to her cousin Lucy who was about to make her modest debut, and another to the Middlesex charity hospital.

It was as well to be busy, otherwise it would be harder to stick with her resolution about how to treat Blake. She didn't interfere with his business and she welcomed him into her bed every night. And while she hadn't yet achieved the level of rapture of that afternoon in Paris, before her tiresome maidenhead ruined the experience, she found sleeping with her husband entirely enjoyable and felt she was getting the hang of the business.

Instead of giving her correspondence her undivided attention, she occasionally found herself staring into space while her mind wandered to earthy thoughts. And when she caught sight of Blake during the day, especially if he came into a room when she didn't expect him, an odd churning affected her from the chest to deep in her belly.

Nevertheless, because she had so little leisure, she missed reading in bed. It was all she could do to keep up with the newspapers, and Sir Walter Scott's latest romance lay unopened in her chamber. One evening she excused herself early from the after-dinner gathering in the drawing room. Hurrying through her bedtime preparations, she dismissed her maid and spent ten minutes cutting open the pages of the first three or four chapters of *The Fortunes of Nigel*. With a sigh of pleasure she snuggled down under the blankets, set her candle in the right spot, and opened the book. She hadn't even turned the first page when Blake came in, clad in his dressing gown, and stood next to the bed.

"You retired early. Are you tired?"

She lowered the volume. "I wanted to read. This new novel arrived days ago and I've been too busy to start it. Why don't you get a book of your own and join me?"

"Read yours aloud. I'd enjoy that."

The beginning was a little slow, but Minerva was soon caught up in the tale of London in the reign of James I. Judging by Blake's quiet attention, so was he.

"There's more than meets in the eye in young Lord Nigel's trip to London," he commented when she stopped for a rest, his air of surprise confirming the impression from a few weeks ago that he wasn't much in the habit of reading novels.

"Of course there is. We've only just started. Scott's stories are always long and complicated."

"I lay you odds Nigel is going to fall for pretty Miss Margaret, the watchmaker's daughter."

"In that case he had better succeed in mending his fortunes."

"You're always so practical. I thought ladies were only interested in love stories."

"Not this lady. Why don't you read for a while? My voice is tired."

Because they were slouched against the pillows in relaxed camaraderie, arms touching, she noticed a momentary tension in him, so quickly passed as to be barely perceptible. Then she felt his lips at her temple. "I have a better idea," he murmured.

"Really?" She loved having her ear kissed. His hot breath and swirling tongue sent shivers through her.

"Much, much better," he said and removed the volume from her hands.

"Are you sure you wouldn't like another chapter?"

"I'll write my own. I'll be Nigel and you can be Margaret." He untied the ribbon at the neck of her nightgown. His hand, warm and strong, sought her breast.

"I don't think Sir Walter Scott writes this kind of book." Even as she arched into his clever caressing hand, a fleeting sense of familiarity tickled her brain. There'd been another occasion like this: that evening in Berkeley Square, their first kiss. Deflection. Blake had kissed her to distract her from something and he was doing it again.

He pinched her nipple and a pang of desire shot straight to her lower regions. She was distracted, all right. "Perhaps he should start. Scott. Writing this kind of book." Then he kissed her and she lost the inclination to speak along with all interest in the fortunes of Nigel, or Margaret, or anyone else's but their own. "Don't stop," she protested when he released her lips.

On his knees, he loomed over her with an evil glint in his eye. Oh, she did like Blake when he was wicked.

"Are you fond of this nightgown?"

He wanted to talk about her attire? "It's just a nightgown."

"Not for long." His hands grasped each side of the opening over her breasts. With one rip the garment divided, leaving her exposed from neck to toes, an act of masterful arrogance she found shamefully exciting. His patent admiration of her body made it thrill with longing.

She reached up and shoved at his silk robe, anxious to reach *his* unclothed body. She loved the texture of his skin over the contour of his muscles, the way they seemed to come alive under her hand. And she loved his hands on her. He kissed her again, deeper, and she threaded her fingers through his hair, pulled him close, devouring him as his hands worked her breasts. Finally he pulled away.

"No," she objected.

"Ssh. You'll like this." Blake tossed aside his dressing gown. He never wore a nightshirt as far as she knew. His torso glowed golden in the candlelight and her heart, as usual, lurched at the sight of his male beauty. She sunk almost onto her back against the pillows as he tugged away the shredded remnants of her nightgown and tossed them aside.

Gently parting her legs, he knelt in front of her exposed and vulnerable body. In the flickering candlelight they gazed at each other. His face was grave and intent, his breathing a little labored and his member jutted out. Except for the first time, they'd always made love under the covers, so Minerva was pleased to get another good look at it. She felt a little shy as his eyes scanned her from head to toe. Then he leaned forward and, supported by outstretched arms on either side of her, he kissed his way down her body, sucking on each nipple, tickling her rib cage with his hair as he explored the indentation of her naval. She giggled a little, never having thought of it as an erotic zone. She also felt a little apprehensive at the proximity of his mouth to her private parts. Was he going to carry on his kissing descent?

The answer was yes. His lips on the tender flesh of her lower belly sent tingles through her. "Be still," he ordered, as her pelvis twisted upward. Then he edged back and opened her with his thumbs and, yes; he did. He plunged his tongue in.

The feeling was indescribably wonderful: wet, supple heat stroking and sucking and driving her to delirium. She pushed into him, silently urging him on. Involuntarily her hands went to her bosom, which was aching with desire. With her thumbs she tweaked her own nipples in time with the strokes of Blake's tongue below. Mindless with pleasure she lapsed into concentrated relaxation and felt the tension grow and crest until she exploded into a state of shuddering bliss more intense than she'd yet experienced. She'd had no idea that a man, this man, could make her feel so splendid. Her husband possessed his own variety of genius and she was grateful. Grateful she'd married him.

When he entered her still throbbing passage, his strong repetitive thrusts renewed her urgency.

It was a slower ascent and took a long time. The skin of his torso grew damp and hard breathing and groans of exertion filled her ears. She grasped his buttocks and met the slow rhythm of his movements. She was panting herself and she was sure the sound wasn't pretty but it reflected the way she worked her way into their union, grinding her hips, using her muscles to clench his member with every inward drive. When the moment came it was on a scream of mingled frustration and joy and once more she tumbled into ecstasy.

"Minnie," he called through his groans. "Minnie, Minnie, Minnie." The name jerked out with an accelerating beat as he drove to his own completion. An extra glow of happiness filled her at the sound of the name he hadn't used since Paris.

"So?" he asked after a few minutes, when they'd both recaptured their breath. They lay side by side under the sheet, holding hands. "What did you think of that?"

"I think you sound quite smug. And I think you deserve to. It was utterly delicious."

He grinned, more like his old carefree self than he had since his father's death. "There's nothing like it after a hard day's work."

"Did you have a bad day?"

"Not worse than yesterday. Or the day before. Or the day before that. I feel more exhausted by six hours of ducal correspondence than I do after a week's hunting in cold weather. I have more respect for my father now. I had no idea how much the old man did."

"How can I help?"

"You have enough to do on your own, my dear. My mother tells me how hard you are working."

"I'd *like* to help," she insisted.

He nuzzled her neck. "There'll be plenty to do once we have to go out in public again. I must confess I quite enjoy our state of mourning. I don't have to worry yet about taking my seat in the Lords. That's a horror I won't have to face until next season."

To Minerva, who could think of nothing she'd enjoy more than taking a seat in either House of Parliament, this was a stark reminder of their differences, despite their recently demonstrated compatibility in one area.

"Thank Heavens we'll be at Mandeville soon. The bad thing about being almost confined to the house is the lack of exercise. I can't wait for a decent gallop in the park."

"This house is big enough to keep me healthy. Today I discovered a whole new wing. Did you know you have three elderly ladies living upstairs who never leave their rooms?"

"The great-aunts. They've lived here forever. They used to come down for dinner but they prefer to stay put now. The youngest one can't be a day less than eighty. I called on them yesterday and they scolded me for not bringing you to meet them. I'm glad you found them on your own."

"I haven't yet managed to discover exactly how many people work here."

"I hope it's not too much for you."

"Hardly. Your mother assured me I need not concern myself with domestic details, like menus and housekeeping, unless I wish to, which I don't. If I need something, or perceive a problem, I have only to mention it and someone sees to it. How could I complain?"

"So it's not too terrible being Duchess of Hampton?" Blake sounded unsure of himself. "I know you didn't want it."

"Don't make me laugh. Everyone thinks I'm the luckiest girl in the world."

"But you don't."

"I manage," she said gruffly. "Especially if all our days end like this one," she added, realizing she'd sounded ungracious.

"Any time, Minnie. Let me know if there's anything else I can do to make things easier."

Minerva shifted up onto her elbow and gave him a lingering kiss. "Well," she said, "you can tell me who you're considering as the next member for Warfield Castle."

A light seemed to go out behind his eyes. "I'm probably going to give the seat to Huntley, my old Eton chum."

"I had the impression you didn't like him much."

"I don't have to like him. This is about politics not friendship."

That was an attitude she could understand. "What are his views of the issues? Where does he come down on the details of reform?"

"Gideon thinks he's deserves it. Let's not talk about this now."

"I'm coming round to Gideon, but I don't think he's always correct in his judgment," she said.

He pulled her down and started kissing the

junction of her neck and shoulder. "Gideon isn't a patch on you, Minnie. In so many ways."

As it happened, this was a particularly sensitive spot, which was some consolation. Still, it was intensely frustrating to be so close to a center of power and have so little part in it.

Chapter 22

A few days later, in the middle of the afternoon, Minerva found herself at loose ends. The duchess was closeted with her daughters; Anne and her husband were leaving for Scotland in a few days and Minerva rather hoped Lady Amanda would go with them. She, Blake, and his mother would travel to Shropshire for the summer.

She wandered down to the duke's study to see if she could pick up any political gossip. Or, if her husband didn't want her help with his work, he might be up for a spot of Walter Scott. She wasn't sure she ever was going to be able to think of the novelist in the same way.

The room was empty but she wasn't disappointed. The eternal presence of servants grated on her and sometimes made life at Vanderlin House unbearable. She felt herself continually on display. Alone there for the first time, she looked around and imagined the statesmen who must have sat in those chairs over the past century, making history. A cabinet contained a collection of Dutch porcelain, perhaps brought from Holland by the first

duke. She didn't know enough to judge the date of
the pieces. The pictures were mostly portraits from
different eras, but not formal ones: family groups
in oil or watercolor added a personal touch and
softened the grandeur of the room. One day perhaps, a depiction of Blake, her, and their children
might take their place in the historical pageant. The
late duke's interest in the classics was represented
by a glass-fronted bookcase filled with the works
of Greek and Roman authors. Though splendidly
bound they looked well used.

It struck her that Blake had yet to make his
mark. Paintings of horses and sporting books,
she thought with amusement, would be likely additions. Not that she had ever seen Blake with a
book in his hands, a fact she still found odd. She
couldn't imagine a life without reading.

Feeling a little guilty, she tiptoed over to the
desk where the usual neat piles of paper lay. He
had a system, she observed. Each report had a
brief précis attached with a pin. Not in Blake's
scrawl but obviously written by one of the secretaries. A few others had notes in capitals, in a
hand she recognized. The same letters she'd seen
on a paper hidden in a Paris drawer. Amanda's,
she guessed, glad to know that the letter her husband treasured had come from his sister, not another woman.

Reading a report from a Member of Parliament,
holder of one of the Vanderlin seats, she saw that
the secretary had done a fair job of summarizing
the contents, but Minerva had her doubts about
the method. It might be efficient with regards to

Blake's time, but she couldn't help wondering what subtleties he missed by not reading them himself.

"Your Grace?"

She jumped at Mr. Hetherington's greeting and hastily replaced the papers on the desk. "I was looking for the duke," she said.

Mr. Hetherington informed her that His Grace was in the ballroom, which seemed an odd place for a summer afternoon. The sound of clashing blades told her that Blake, deprived by the state of mourning from sessions at the boxing or fencing saloons, had imported a swordsman. Instead of going in, she took the stairs to the gallery for a better view.

With a tight padded jacket and close-fitting pantaloons Blake's figure showed to great advantage in his wife's opinion. She enjoyed watching the bout as much for the view of his body as for the demonstration of grace and skill by a pair of evenly matched fighters. With only a rudimentary knowledge of the art, she could tell Blake was a superb fencer, combining speed, agility, and strength. Each flash and clash of the swords, so fast as to be almost invisible, was accompanied by shouts and grunts. The combatants wiped the sweat from their foreheads after every violent exchange and Blake's blond hair clung to his skull in darkened hunks.

Minerva hung over the railing in shameless admiration. In years past she'd seen Blake compete in a horse race and knew him to be a rider of unparalleled skill. She wouldn't mind seeing him box too. It was always a pleasure to watch an expert at work, no matter what the avocation.

Her entertainment was interrupted by a cough. "Duchess?"

She dragged her eyes from the spectacle and turned to face Sir Gideon Louther.

"Sir Gideon," she said. "Since we are brother and sister, do you think you could bring yourself to call me Minerva?"

"I would be honored." He inclined his head and looked pleased. Sir Gideon was over twenty years older than her, a distinguished Member of Parliament for most of her lifetime. His subtle deference was a reminder of the level of importance she had attained for no good reason. Minerva had always wanted to exert influence, but she had imagined she would have to earn respect over time, not muddle into it by falling asleep in a library. Nevertheless, she wasn't foolish enough to disdain the opportunity fate had presented. And she knew Louther had spent a good deal of time in the duke's office over the past days. Perhaps he would be a source of information her husband refused to share with her.

"What can I do for you, Gideon? Or did you come to watch the fencing?"

"I need to speak to Hampton about something urgent. But it concerns you too. I hope you will see things my way."

How interesting.

"It's the party. As I'm sure you know, Minerva, perspicacious as you are, there is more than one opinion about the form parliamentary reform should take." He was certainly buttering her up, preferable to having him explain things as though she were an ignorant fool.

"As many plans as there are reformers. Perhaps more."

"Precisely. The most radical of our number will not get their way, and it's to be hoped we won't have to settle for a façade of reform that improves nothing. As one of the party's leaders in the Commons, it's my job to help forge a consensus, especially with the General Election imminent."

"Let me offer my commiserations. Is it going well?"

Having had ample opportunity to observe her brother-in-law since her return from Paris, Minerva suspected not. Gideon was an intelligent and shrewd man but she didn't see him as a natural leader of men, unlike their late father-in-law the duke, who had that quality in abundance.

"I'm concerned that we may fall into disarray before we even get to the election."

"You said you wanted my help. What can I do?"

"Every summer the late duke invited a large party to Mandeville. It was one of his tools to forge alliances and cement loyalty."

"I am well aware of the scope of Mandeville entertainments. Remember I lived most of my life just outside the park. With the family in mourning it will be quiet this year."

"I've come to beg Hampton—and you—to set aside your scruples and invite the usual guests to Mandeville this summer. I'm not exaggerating when I say the future of the country depends on it."

"I'm spent." Blake gasped, bent almost double and dripping sweat. His opponent, one of the best fencing masters in London, panted just as hard. Blake was proud to fight him to a draw. "Thank you," he said, mopping his face then cleaning off the damp haft of his foil. "That was excellent. Can you come back on Thursday? I leave for the country the day after but I'd like to get in one more session. I was rusty at the beginning today."

As he regained his breath and hilted his weapon, he became aware of a buzz of voices from the gallery. Minerva in a blue gown was a sight to gladden his racing heart. What a splendid ending to the afternoon it would be to find her in bed. He'd give her a hint, a suggestion she favor him with a chapter or two of Scott. He wondered when she'd arrived. He'd performed well and it pleased him to think of her watching.

Instead of paying him the least attention, she was speaking to Gideon with great energy. Whatever those two were hatching, Blake would probably dislike. The sooner he got her out of London the better.

The pair of them concluded their exchange with conspiratorial nods. "Hampton," Louther called. "Wait there. We're coming down."

His wife said nothing. She looked her most animated and handsome, no doubt as a result of a fascinating chat with Gideon. Then she engaged his eye and pursed her lips in a quick but unmistakable kiss. His interest in a bedroom meeting burgeoned.

Ten minutes later the day was ruined, and so was the summer. He'd always loathed the mass invasion of politicians at Mandeville. Last summer the thought of what he was avoiding had sharpened his enjoyment of the season in Devon. And now, instead of using his state of mourning as an excuse to pass July and August riding around his estate, visiting congenial and undemanding country neighbors, and spending a great deal of time in bed with his wife, he would have to endure tedious meals in the state dining room and listen to endless political jockeying.

"What about my mother?" he asked desperately. "We cannot expect her to tolerate a full house at Mandeville so soon after my father's death."

But the duchess, appealed to later, was no help. "I've decided to go to Scotland with Anne and Amanda. I've put up with politics all these years for your father's sake. Now I'd like to spend some time with my daughters and grandchildren. Minerva is quite capable of taking my place and it will be better for her to do so without me looking over her shoulder."

He could dig in his heels and refuse. He was, after all, the duke. He could tell the party and every squabbling member of it to go to hell and leave him and his family alone. But he discovered an inkling of attachment to the Vanderlin tradition, just enough to give him pause.

One member of his family, one he was anxious to please, glowed with ill-concealed excitement at the prospect of acting as hostess.

"Thank you for your confidence in me, Duchess. It's up to the duke to decide." Minerva turned to Blake. "If you don't wish to entertain so soon after your father's death then we shall abide by your decision. I know you are looking forward to a quiet summer." He gave her credit for effort. She was trying to be understanding and compliant while dying to beat him about the head and *demand* he say yes. "Gideon has convinced me it's essential, but no one could fault you for refusing."

Except her. He feared he'd never hear the last of it if he said no.

"Very well. They can come. But only for a week. Ten days at the most. Any longer would show disrespect for my father's memory."

She looked as though she wanted to embrace him, which would have been satisfactory. She also began to chatter on about who should be asked, how many guests the house could hold, and who could be safely snubbed. It dawned on him that having said yes, he still wasn't going to hear the last of it.

He escaped to the garden, taking Amanda with him.

"What did our mother mean, that she was going to Scotland with you and Anne? Surely you're coming to Mandeville for the summer."

"It's time to get back."

Something akin to panic gripped him when he realized Amanda was deserting him, when he needed her more than he had in years. As children the duke's daughters had a separate schoolroom and a governess. Five-year-old Amanda had come to him, begged her older brother to help her with the alphabet, using a set of letters printed on pasteboard squares. Though accustomed to treating his younger sister with lordly scorn, he'd agreed in the desperate hope that by teaching her, the symbols would begin to make sense to him. It worked, up to a point. He still got some of them confused but as she learned he imitated her. The trouble was that she quickly outstripped him in skill. He didn't know if she realized it, or whether her worship of her brother blinded her to his inability. One day he'd asked her if she could keep a big and terrible secret. She'd nodded, with serious eyes, and she'd been his faithful ally ever since.

"Please don't go. I need you here," he said.

"There's a reason—someone—I wish to get back."

"Amanda! Do you have a suitor?" She nodded, self-conscious and pleased. Despite inheriting the Vanderlin looks—and a Vanderlin fortune—the youngest daughter had a reserve that kept others at a distance.

He wanted his favorite sister to be happy, though he was sorry she might end up far away in Scotland. "It says much for your powers of resistance that you reached the age of twenty-seven unwed. I'd have thought our parents would have pushed you into a match, as they did for our older sisters. I know our mother presented you to many prospects."

She grinned. "Many, many prospects. But the choice was always mine, as long as a candidate was eligible, of course. The same for Maria and Anne. Both of them were pleased with their husbands and are happy in their marriages."

Having always assumed Maria had made a political alliance arranged by the duke, he considered the Louthers in a new light. Over the years, whenever he ran into him, Gideon had given him news of Maria and their four children. He enjoyed hearing about the escapades of his nephews and nieces, but he thought Gideon only spoke of them because Blake wasn't interested in politics. He now found it believable to think of Louther as an affectionate family man, his reports the testimony of a proud father.

By long ingrained habit, the notion of a proud father generated an inner tension and disquiet. But then he recalled that last conversation with the duke. That, and Amanda's words, helped explain why his father had never insisted on negotiating a marriage for him.

"I like your wife," Amanda said. "She's very clever. I think you should take her into your confidence. She can help you far better than I."

"I will, one day. But not yet."

He looked around the garden, a well-tended haven in the center of London. Even the high walls couldn't entirely dampen the noise of traffic, or exclude the dust that floated in and marred the green of the plantings. "I can't wait to get to Mandeville. We'll have a little time there before the guests descend. Perhaps the right moment will arise to tell Minerva."

Amanda squeezed his arm. "I believe you should. But even without her help or mine, you'll manage."

"At least Sebastian Iverley won't be there. For all his faults he's no politician."

"But he is your brother-in-law. Poor Cousin Sebastian. We were so horrid to him. I feel quite ashamed of the way we treated him as a boy."

"I suppose I do too. Yet whenever I see him, I remember the way the duke brought him to Mandeville to be an example to me. He always makes me feel like an ignorant fool and I can't get beyond my dislike."

Later in the day, Minerva told him she'd written and begged Diana Iverley to join the party. She said she needed her sister's support when tossed into the position of hostess to scores of strangers. He had no argument with that. But where Diana went, so did Sebastian.

He was doomed.

Chapter 23

Blake's reaction to the political gathering was so different from hers she might have laughed, had it not filled her with new doubts about the future of their harmonious relations. Where she was thrilled at the prospect of entertaining a houseful of party luminaries, he looked as though he'd rather spend the summer in a dungeon, complete with torturer and rack. At least he didn't go so far as refusing to hold the party, which he had every right to do.

But it put him in a foul mood. It came as little surprise when he announced he would leave for Shropshire immediately. With guests arriving in less than a month, he claimed he needed the extra time to see to a hundred and one matters pertaining to the Mandeville estate.

"In that case," she said rather sniffily, "I'll remain in London a few extra days. I need to consult your mother and work on the invitations. Will you take Hetherington with you, or may he stay and assist me?"

"Hetherington is all yours. I'll take Blenkinsop. I will be working with the land steward at Mandeville and have no intention of giving a second thought to politics until I absolutely have to. Are you sure you won't come with me?"

She was tempted. "I have to see the modiste about half-mourning gowns. I have nothing suitable to wear."

"You'll enjoy that," he teased, drawing a smile. He was now aware of her dislike of dress fittings. "Or I shall, seeing you in them." He kissed her ear. "And out of them."

So they parted on good terms and she missed him, especially at night, but she got on splendidly with Hetherington. The secretary knew everything and everyone and between them they honed the guest list to the few dozen most vital allies and worked out the endless details of entertaining such an enormous group, even in a house as vast and well staffed as Mandeville.

She was resting in the duchess's sitting room one day, hers alone since her mother-in-law had left for Scotland. An hour of leisure would have been an excellent moment for a chapter or two of Scott. Lascivious thoughts were interrupted by Filson.

"Your Grace," he said. "A caller has asked to see you. A Mr. Thomas Parkes."

How odd. She still wasn't receiving casual callers and could think of no reason why the Member of Parliament for Gristlewick should wish to see her now. "Did he say what he wants?"

"At first he asked for His Grace. When he heard His Grace had left town, he said only that the matter was urgent and could not be entrusted to Mr. Hetherington."

"Show him up. No, wait. I'll see him in the morning room. I'll be down directly."

Minerva wondered why she didn't feel awkward meeting the man she'd once planned to marry. It seemed like a year had passed rather than a few months. She felt no trace of regret for the loss of her future as Mrs. Parkes.

"Your Grace," he said with a deferential bow. "May I offer my felicitations on your marriage and my condolences on your loss."

"Thank you, Mr. Parkes. What can I do for you?"

"I intended to speak with the duke, but it occurred to me, since my acquaintance with him is slight, that it might be better to see you. The matter is delicate."

"I see."

"It's about the vacant seat at Warfield Castle."

"Are you looking to make a change, Mr. Parkes? I thought your situation as Member for Gristlewick was secure. I believe it's already been decided who will have Warfield Castle."

Parkes nodded. "Geoffrey Huntley. That's what I wish to speak to you about. Huntley must not have it."

"Why not?"

"Because he is not reliable. He is no friend to the cause of reform and will not vote as we would wish. In days past I had the honor of learning your views and trust me, Duchess, they are very far from Huntley's."

"I don't understand. Naturally I am sorry to hear you don't think Mr. Huntley sound in his opinions, but as member for the duke's borough he must vote as he is told or risk losing his seat."

"Apparently not, and that is the reason I was relieved to speak to you and not to the duke. According to a reliable source, Huntley has been boasting that the new Duke of Hampton will support him, whatever he does. That he could even take a place in the government without forfeiting the duke's favor because they were intimate school friends. I don't need to tell you how close things will be after the election. We cannot afford to lose a vote. I beg you, Duchess, speak to the duke and persuade him to give Warfield Castle to someone else."

"Is Sir Gideon Louther aware of this? I understand he favors Mr. Huntley."

"I would have spoken to Sir Gideon, had it not been for the report of Huntley's friendship with the duke. I thought it better to be direct."

Minerva found the business very odd. Did Huntley really put so much store in the strength of his friendship with Blake? She had the impression—based on a certain irritation in his manner when the topic arose—that Blake wasn't in fact fond of his former schoolmate. She needed to get to the bottom of the matter before she left London.

"I must speak to Mr. Huntley. Much as I respect you, Mr. Parkes, it would be wrong to destroy a man's future on hearsay."

At her request, Huntley called the next day.

"My dear Duchess. What an honor to receive your invitation! What a pleasure to meet you again! May I felicitate you on your happy new position?"

Minerva drew back. Huntley, whom on the occasion of their meeting at the theater she'd found quite amiable, was standing a little too close. She withdrew her hand from his, before he should take it into his mind to kiss it, and wished she was wearing gloves.

"I assure you, Mr. Huntley, there is nothing about the late duke's death that is cause for celebration."

"Of course not, Duchess. I meant your marriage. It pleases me greatly that my old friend Blake should have found such a beautiful bride." His brown curly hair and round face gave him an appearance of youth and openness, but his manner struck her as devious. She strove to keep an open mind, in case her feelings had been prejudiced by Parkes.

"Your acquaintance with my husband goes back to Eton, I understand."

"More than acquaintance. Our friendship. Blake used to say he could never have survived school without me."

"Naturally life at Eton must have been dreadfully hard for the heir to a dukedom."

"Exactly," Huntley said, as though her sarcasm had sailed over his angelic head. Apparently he didn't think her very bright.

"And out of his very great affection and gratitude you are to have a seat in Parliament."

"Exactly! Thus ensuring my *eternal* affection and gratitude. He couldn't have a more reliable ally in Parliament than a friend from his youth."

"I suppose," Minerva said carefully, setting him a test, "Warfield Castle isn't as valuable as it once was."

"What can you mean, Duchess?"

"Correct me if I've misunderstood, but I believe the rotten boroughs will be abolished when reform comes to Parliament. Your safe seat will disappear."

"My dear Duchess," Huntley began, making her itch to slap him—she wasn't his dear anything. "If you don't mind my saying so, you are naïve. Yes, there is a great deal of talk of reform. But in the end, why would the Duke of Hampton, or any great nobleman, willingly relinquish his power?"

Sometimes looking like a doll could be used to advantage. She gave him the benefit of her most candid gaze. "Do you suggest the reform party is disingenuous?"

"I'm sure there are many good souls in the party who truly believe reform is in the interests of the country. We know better. England is better off if the great families continue to hold the reins of government. Look what happened when they let the common man run matters in France."

"You are very good, Mr. Huntley, to explain this to me. I am, indeed, naïve. Just an ignorant woman, alas." She feared she was overacting but he seemed to drink it in. "Am I to infer, since the two of you are such very good friends, that your views are also my husband's? He doesn't tell me much about his political business." She fluttered her eyelashes and tried to look stupid.

"He has not said so in so many words. But I know Blake very well. He will give lip service to reform but, in the end, I know how he will wish me to vote."

Minerva hardly trusted herself to speak. She waited a couple of minutes, as though in deep cogitation. Did Huntley think her a fool? Or was he so sure of Blake's complete loyalty that he felt he could safely betray the party? Deep down she also feared Huntley was telling the truth. Not that Blake was selfishly opposed to reform, but that he cared too little for the issue. That in the end he would hesitate to punish any of his followers who voted against it.

She needed to get the unctuous fellow out of her house before she gave into the urge to hit him with a poker. "I'm glad we've had this conversation, Mr. Huntley. I have been naïve, as you put it. But no longer, I promise you."

Huntley bowed low over her unwilling hand and she was certain she detected mockery in the gesture. "If you have any doubts at all about what about what I have said, you can ask Blake."

Since her husband was over a hundred miles away, she would have to wait. She relieved her annoyance by hunting down Mr. Hetherington and having Huntley struck off the guest list for Mandeville.

Chapter 24

It was good to be home. And he was home, Blake realized. Fond as he had become of Devon, the varied greens of Shropshire and Mandeville's rolling acres spoke to him the way the coastal landscape could not. He spent several days riding around his lands, inspecting fields and woods, farms and cottages, and talking to his tenants and dependents. To be in charge, to make decisions, initiate improvements without permission, was a heady power.

The only drag on his satisfaction was how he missed Minerva. He found himself composing accounts of his activities in his head. Reluctant for his own reasons to discuss the political affairs she loved, he'd enjoyed the perspective she'd brought to their discussion in the carriage crossing northern France. And though he was finally getting the kind of extended physical activity his body craved, it didn't stop him wanting her.

He'd moved into his father's rooms. The late duke hadn't been at Mandeville since the previous autumn and somehow his presence in the private ducal apartments seemed weak. In London Blake had found it hard even to enter the room where he'd witnessed his father's death. Sleeping under the elaborate red velvet hangings of the Mandeville bed felt like easing into his father's position without disrespect.

He wished he didn't have to occupy the bed alone. The mattress was firm and comfortable and completely suitable for energetic activity.

The afternoon Minerva was expected he meant to stay near the house, to greet her on the portico steps upon her arrival at her new home, but she arrived earlier than anticipated. He'd just returned from the stables when she swept into the estate office like a blond tempest, trailing bonnet strings and a long gauze scarf in her wake.

He scooped her into his arms for a lingering kiss, which she returned warmly, until noticing the presence of the land steward.

"We're not alone," she murmured.

He gave her another quick kiss before she pulled away. "I'm glad to see you, Minnie. I've missed you. How was your journey?"

"Don't call me that in public," she said, though without much heat. He did believe she was coming to like the name.

"Let's go somewhere private then." Firmly he led her in the direction of the hall and the grand staircase.

"You hardly let me say a word to poor Mr. Hudkins," she complained. "I've known him for years. He was embarrassed."

"Let me show you to your rooms. They're next

to mine." He was about to raise the interesting topic of his bed, and its remarkable size, when he noticed that his bride no longer looked happy. In fact he was fairly sure something had upset her very much.

"I need to speak to you about something," she said. "Something important and extremely disturbing."

"We'll go to my sitting room, then. Your rooms will be full of maids unpacking." And his sitting room was right next to his bedroom, he didn't add.

It took a long time to get anywhere in the huge house. Minerva answered his trivial questions about the journey with diminishing patience and by the time they entered his room she was like a steaming kettle. Blake searched his mind for what might have set her off. He prepared for a harangue on the pernicious actions of someone, most likely a member of government. A smile tugged at his lips and was hastily quashed. His duchess looked very appealing when enraged, but not in the mood to appreciate levity or compliments.

"What has you so overwrought?" he inquired.

Her forehead creased in a ferocious scowl, so at odds with her porcelain beauty. "Warfield Castle," she said and his heart sank. Surely she had no objection to Huntley? No one did, except him, and he wasn't saying. Nonetheless, it made him anxious even to approach the topic of his nemesis.

"What about it? It's all settled."

"You cannot give that seat to that man. He is a villain."

She was, of course, absolutely right. He spoke

carefully. "Huntley? What makes you think that?"

"He will vote against a reform bill and claim it is your wish."

"Will he?"

"He virtually told me as such. And I have it on good authority he will accept a place in the government, doubtless in exchange for his vote."

So that was Huntley's game. Blake had wondered why he was so anxious for the seat in Parliament, which came with no income unless he won a government position. Even if their party won the election, there was a long list of candidates for lucrative places, most of them with better credentials than Huntley. After so many years in opposition, the scramble for patronage was going to be vicious.

"If he does so," he said with all the calm he could muster, "he won't hold onto his seat beyond the next election. I shall dislodge him."

"Will you? He claims that no matter how he votes you will never desert him." She moved close and took his hand, looking up into his face with troubled eyes. "Why would he believe that? Is the friendship of this man so important to you?"

Blake stared back into her blue gaze and his heart sank. He couldn't have written the names in Greek, or spelled them in English, but he knew what it meant to be caught between Scylla and Charybdis. If he stuck by his promise to Huntley and dismissed her concerns about his motives, Minerva was going to be furious with him. In the end she would be proven right too. He didn't know how his father and Gideon had come to be fooled, but Blake knew Huntley to be rotten through and through. As rotten as the borough of Warfield Castle. Not that he hadn't been deceived himself. For fifteen years he'd believed the fellow his good and loyal friend.

In a minute Minerva was going to ask him to dismiss Huntley, to change his mind about Warfield Castle. That dismissal would be followed shortly by a full and public account of the educational shortcomings of the Duke of Hampton.

The ignorance of Lord Blakeney would have been cause for gossip, that of the Duke of Hampton would be news. He could see the caricatures in the print sellers' windows, mocking his inability to read a book. Imagine the items in the newspapers: "We hear the new D___ of H____ is an unlettered fool."

Blake had always believed with his father gone that he would no longer care what anyone thought of him. Alas, that wasn't true.

"I owe Huntley a favor," he said, hoping she'd leave it at that.

Not a chance. "What kind of favor? What hold does he have over you?"

Could he bring himself to confess the truth, as he'd lost the chance with his father?

He remembered Huntley's cruel imitation of Blake's pathetic attempts at reading.

He remembered the constant complaints of his tutors, his schoolmasters, and his father. *You're lazy. You don't study. Why won't you apply yourself?*

And Minerva's words on a Parisian street. *You don't even try.*

What was the use?

"I don't know whether your opinion of Huntley's intentions is correct," he said. "I don't know how we can know. But he can have the seat. I gave my word."

After refusing to see reason, Blake avoided her for the rest of the day, claiming business in some far-flung corner of the estate. Dinner was an even more formal affair than it was in London. If she'd expected to dine with her husband tête-à-tête she learned her mistake. At Mandeville it was the custom for gently born retainers to dine at the duke's table.

The Duke and Duchess of Hampton were prevented from airing their differences by the presence of the land steward, the chaplain, the librarian, the keeper of muniments, Mr. Blenkinsop, and Mr. Hetherington, lined up on either side of the table in the misnamed small dining room, a chamber large enough to hold most of the ground floor of Wallop Hall, the ancient manor where Minerva had grown up.

The comparison was inevitable in Minerva's mind. With the exception of the two London secretaries, all the men at the table were frequent visitors to her parents' house and to other houses in the vicinity of Mandeville. She knew them as social equals, older gentlemen who merited her deference. Now they were her husband's servants and, she supposed, hers.

They seemed as thrown by the situation as she and it was up to her to break the ice.

"Have you made any new acquisitions, Mr. Lindsey?" she asked the librarian, a friend of her father's.

"Thank you for asking, Your Grace," replied the elderly man, who had called her Minerva since she was old enough to lisp a greeting. "You must see the additions to the map collection I have made on His Grace's behalf this year. His late Grace, that is. I hope the new duke will be interested too." He sounded about as dubious as Minerva felt.

"My sister and Iverley will be joining us next month. I know *he* will want to see them." She spoke with special clarity and glanced up the length of the table to see if Blake heard her. Sufficiently miffed at him to be solidly in Sebastian's camp this evening, she was glad to detect a twitch of discomfort.

"Excellent. I'd like Lord Iverley's expert opinion on the provenance of several pieces. How do you find Mr. and Mrs. Montrose?"

"I haven't seen my mother and father for some months. I had hoped to call on them this afternoon, but His Grace was otherwise occupied and they will expect to see us both when we call the first time since our marriage." She smiled sweetly at her husband and raised her voice a notch. "But no matter. Doubtless the duke will have leisure to attend to me tomorrow. Or next week."

Mr. Lindsey shifted in his chair and Minerva felt ashamed for involving the old man in her quarrel. "I spent the afternoon touring the house with Mrs. Courage and settling into my rooms," she continued more quietly. She managed to get through the rest of the meal with propriety, though not much wit.

"Minnie?"

She thought about pretending to be asleep. She wanted to see him and she wished he'd go away. It would be easier if the decision wasn't hers.

"Minnie?" He came closer. "You're still awake. I just want to say I'm sorry."

She'd behaved badly this evening too—not as badly as him over Huntley—and owed him an apology back. "Hmph" was all she could manage.

The mattress dipped. "I have a good reason for giving Huntley the seat," he said as he joined her under the blankets, his chest against her back. "But I can't tell you. In the future I may be able to, but not yet."

"What—"

He cut her off. "Please don't ask me now. Let's be friends again."

His arms came about her and his lips started nibbling at her ear. As usual, it felt good. Very good. But she was furious at him. A so-called "good reason" was no reason at all. He was prepared to share her bed, but not his decisions.

She loved it when he kissed her neck. And when his hand found the neck of her nightgown and dipped inside. "Oh, Minnie. You have the loveliest little breasts," he breathed. They loved him back, swelling under his questing fingers.

She ought to tell him to go away, rather than let her anger be overcome by his wicked touch. She stopped herself from arching into his hand.

She didn't want to encourage him. She wasn't in the mood tonight. How could he be such a dolt as to think she'd forgive him for handing a parliamentary seat on a plate to one of his drinking companions?

Good Lord! How could he possibly think she would, under the circumstances, allow him to suck on her nipples? In just a minute she was going to push him away. The way her heart pounded and little streaks of bliss shot down into her sex was really quite irritating. A mere animal reaction. Quite despicable.

But wait, her brain chimed in through a mist of desire. She herself had been less than perfect this evening. Quarrelling with Blake always made her behave quite horridly. Instead of apologizing she could let him do what he liked to her. That was only fair. And as long as she didn't actively participate it wasn't like giving in.

She repelled the part of her mind that told her the argument was specious nonsense, and concentrated on resisting the urge to turn into his embrace and rub her aching groin against him. It wasn't easy and required her to stiffen every muscle in her body.

At once she was free. Blake rolled away and sat upright. "If you want me to leave you alone, I will."

"I didn't say that."

"You didn't have to, Minerva. Obviously you're very angry."

She flopped onto her back. "I know my duty. You are my husband and I won't turn you away."

"Thank you, but no thank you. I'm not interested in bedding a woman who merely endures me."

"I'm perfectly willing to welcome you in my bed."

"Welcome! Some welcome. A carriage shaft would be more responsive!"

Frustrated desire, combined with an obscure sense that she might be in the wrong, frayed her temper. "I suggest you go to the stables then. It's where you'd rather spend your time anyway, since the well-being of your horses is so much more important than the well-being of the country."

"The trouble with you, Minnie, is you think you know everything. Everything must be done the way you want it. Just once I'd like you to trust that I know what I'm doing."

That was so unfair! She'd spent weeks keeping her thoughts to herself and refraining from interfering in matters she was far more qualified than he to decide. She buried her head in the pillow to stop herself screaming at him in unseemly rage.

"So, Minnie? What do you say to that?"

"Go away, and don't call me Minnie."

"Fine, Duchess. And welcome to Mandeville." He stamped out of the room, making an impressive series of thumps considering that the floor was extremely well carpeted.

Chapter 25

Minerva walked through the massive front door of Mandeville House and saw two horses awaiting her. One, led by a groom, bore a sidesaddle; the other carried the duke.

"I heard you were riding to Wallop Hall," he said once the groom had helped her mount. "You should have let me know. I'm sorry about yesterday afternoon. I should have thought you'd want to visit your family."

"I'm glad you've made time to accompany me," she said coldly. "My parents would be concerned if we didn't come together on this occasion. Not to mention the whole neighborhood."

She questioned whether Blake understood what a seven-day wonder their marriage must have been in Shropshire. That Miss Minerva Montrose, the younger daughter of an ancient but decayed family, had caught the Duke of Hampton, the blazing sun around whom much of the county revolved, would have been a cause for marvel.

"I imagine there has been some talk about us," he said with a faint smile. "Naturally they must be concerned about you. But they received me very graciously when I called on them last week."

"You never mentioned that."

"We've hardly had the chance to exchange news. Of course I called," he added with a touch of impatience. "I hadn't seen them since I married their daughter."

"Thank you," she said. "It was good of you to do that. Everyone will hear about it." There was no need to add that the new Duke of Hampton's condescension would silence any questions about the propriety of his duchess. "How was the visit?"

"At first they were polite but wary. It got better."

Minerva could imagine. Her parents weren't overly impressed by dukes, certainly not by ducal heirs who compromised their daughters. Never in favor of Diana wedding Blake, they'd been delighted when she married Sebastian instead.

The three-mile ride passed in silence, but not a hostile one. While they waited for the park gate to be opened, Minerva had occasion to observe her husband in full daylight. His color was better than it had been in London but his face still seemed drawn, cheekbones etched higher than ever, the faint crow's feet more pronounced. On horseback he appeared completely at home, without the caged-lion look he sometimes wore indoors. Sensing her examination, his dark blue eyes met hers with a grave intensity that made her blush, without having any idea what he was thinking. The clank of the iron gate intervened and they cantered along the lane and down the oak-lined drive to her childhood home. Wallop Hall, an ancient ivy-covered manor, though small and shabby compared to the glories of her new habitations, looked very familiar and dear.

Mr. and Mrs. Montrose came out to meet them, accompanied by the usual complement of overenthusiastic dogs. With a bounding heart she flung herself down from her horse into her father's arms.

"My dear, dear child," he said with a hairy buss on each cheek, then held her by the shoulders at arm's length and examined her face intently. "How are you?" This was most unlike her dear Papa, who tended to live in his own world. He was worried about her.

She summoned a happy smile. "I am very well and so glad to be home." She looked sideways at her husband, who was patting one of the ebullient foxhounds. "Blake and I had a wonderful time in France."

Over lemonade in the untidy drawing room, Minerva caught up on family news and talked about Paris. Blake offered an occasional observation. As soon as he mentioned the visit to Chantilly Mrs. Montrose lit up and dragged him off to her own stables to inspect a horse with a bruised knee, leaving Minerva alone with her father, who regarded her with a look of crafty sheepishness only he could manage.

"Will you come out to the hall to be weighed?"

"That's not fair, Papa! You promised me and Diana that married women didn't have to."

Several years before Mr. Montrose had acquired a scale and a hobby of recording the weights of his family and visitors, all under the guise of slightly dubious scientific research.

"Please, my dear. I have a particular reason."

She never could resist him; he had a childlike capacity for happiness when his eccentricities were indulged. So she climbed into the swinging seat and let him adjust the weights on the bar.

"Are you well, my dear child?" he asked. "I haven't heard you speak about any aspect of public affairs since you arrived. Don't tell me my little Min is turning into a domestic creature."

"With half the opposition party arriving at Mandeville soon, it's rather a relief to talk about dogs and the weather and your latest invention."

He wrote the weight in his record book. "Two pounds less than last time." He sounded disappointed. "Are you eating enough?"

"I think so. I've been busy."

"Down you get, take off your shoes, and stand on that board over there."

"Papa! Why?" What new madness was this? "I'm a duchess now. I don't have to take part in your experiments."

Naturally her father was unimpressed by her new rank. "I'm going to measure your feet."

That didn't sound too bad. "Why?"

"I want to see if the feet get larger as people get heavier."

"But I just got lighter."

"That may change very soon. Is Blakeney—Hampton, I mean—looking after you?"

Realizing what he meant made her blush, which he observed with satisfaction. "Are you perhaps, you know, in a delicate condition?"

"Papa! It's much too soon." Her courses had occurred since the last time she and Blake shared a bed. Unless they made up their present quarrel she wasn't going to be a useful subject for her father's researches. She bent to unbutton her half boots while he fussed with his measuring tools.

"You know, my dear. I'm pleased with your husband, far more so than I expected. Your mother and I were concerned about your marriage but now I have hopes. Blakeney seems to have grown up in the last two years."

Blake had displayed a generosity of spirit in accompanying her today after yesterday's bitter exchanges. She didn't believe the careless, selfish man who'd wooed Diana would have behaved so well.

"I think you're right, Papa. But I fear our concerns in life will never match."

He regarded her quizzically. "Because he loves hunting? Like your mother?"

"You don't care much for horses or dogs, do you?"

"Not much, but since they make your mother happy, they make me happy too. She feels the same way about my inventions."

Could it be as easy as that? Minerva didn't think so. Whether he wished it or not, Blake had been born to a great position. He couldn't in all conscience shrug it off. He owed duty to a greater good than his own desires.

Mr. and Mrs. Montrose had always seemed a bit of a joke. He was dedicated to the invention of mechanical devices, most of them unsuccessful, useless, or both. Mrs. Montrose was a noted breeder of foxhounds and Master of the Mandeville Hunt. Even men who were neither outraged nor derisive at the aberration of a female master could rarely refrain from a jest or two at her expense.

Neither seemed bothered by the world's opinion of them, and they showed no hint of awe at his elevated status. He wondered if they would have greeted his father the same way. With more formality, he guessed, but little more reverence. These people didn't give a damn that he was a duke and the richest man in Shropshire. All they cared for was the happiness of their daughter. It would be nice to have a family who offered such unwavering support.

On his earlier call they'd received him with reserve, but apparently he'd managed to allay some of their doubts about him as a husband. It hadn't been hard to convince them that he, at least, was entirely reconciled to his marriage. That was before bloody Huntley raised his head again, leading to yesterday's unrapturous reunion with his wife. Minerva had put up a good front but he wondered, as he examined the gelding's injury, what she was saying to her father.

Mrs. Montrose gave him a quick tour of the neat stables, which he noted with amusement were better cared for than the manor. On the way back to the house he enjoyed an excellent discussion with her about horse feeds. Entering the hall they found his father-in-law on his knees and his wife shoeless and holding up her skirts to calf height. She really had the prettiest ankles.

"All done," said Mr. Montrose, rising to his feet.

"There you are, my dear. Is the horse all right? Fetlock was it? I've been measuring Min."

He beamed at his wife and she smiled back. They seemed a mismatched couple: he stout and bewhiskered, she tall, slim, and fair, an older version of Minerva with a weather-beaten complexion. At that moment he observed the depth of their affection, despite disparate interests that they pursued with great enthusiasm. Neither could he doubt the deep pride and love they shared for each of their six children.

With instinctive accord they looked at their younger daughter, just so damned happy to have her in the house with them. He stood aside from the contented little group and felt envious.

Blake had always refused to feel sorry for himself. Aside from the frustration and shame of his struggle with the written word, he had nothing to complain of. He was handsome, rich, and heir to a dukedom. Women pursued him and men envied his prowess as a sportsman. What right did he have to be unhappy? He'd always shied away from the fact that, with the exception of Amanda, he had no true intimates. Friends by the dozen, yes, and acquaintances by the hundred, ever ready to share a lark. But no one who knew him, no one with whom he shared his secrets. For his secrets had prevented him from forming close friendships.

And this fact was, perhaps, as much of an obstacle to good relations with his wife as their divergent tastes and interests.

Chapter 26

That afternoon Hetherington kept bothering him about the forthcoming descent of ravening hordes of politicians. "Ask Her Grace," he said as often as possible. His secretary was usually happy to do so. He had developed quite a tendre for Minerva as well as respect for her perspicuity.

"We're getting perilously close to full up," Hetherington told him. "Some of the single gentlemen will have to share rooms. We'd better make sure we know which groups they belong to."

"Ask Her Grace. She'll know," Blake said. Then added, with a touch of malice, "Put them in rooms with people they disagree with. Either they'll come to an agreement or they'll kill each other. Either way we're better off."

Sharing of rooms was a sore point since he was not sharing one with his wife.

"Tell me, Hetherington," he said. "What did my father think of this reform business? He can't have wanted to give up the control of so many parliamentary seats."

"His Grace took some time to come around, sir.

But in the end he saw the future of the country was more important than his own interests. Even the interests of the Vanderlin family."

"Fancy that."

"And if I may observe without disrespect . . ."

"Be my guest."

"His Grace, being no fool, saw which way things were going. Knowing that change was unavoidable in the long run, he preferred to influence its course."

"An astute observation on my father's character, Hetherington, and not one he'd object to."

Blake could imagine his father's response to the game Huntley was playing. He'd tell the scoundrel to go to the devil and then use his influence to crush him into the ground.

What a weak fool he'd been, to let Huntley play him. By giving in without a fight he'd shown himself unworthy of his father's respect, and of Minerva's too. It was time to take control of his own destiny.

"Hetherington," he said before he could talk himself out of it. "I'd like to dictate a letter. To Mr. Geoffrey Huntley."

Half an hour later he entered the duchess's sitting room and found her seated at her desk, writing. She looked an ideal of feminine serenity, her golden hair swept back from her face, her posture straight as she covered a sheet of paper with her neat, effortless script. The contrast between her fair beauty and her clever, unpredictable, sometimes cantankerous character never failed to intrigue him.

"You win, Minerva. I've written to Huntley to tell him he can't have the seat."

"Why?" she asked, without looking up. She didn't even put down her pen. Cantankerous.

"First you want to know why he should have it, and now you want to know why not. Can't you just accept that you are getting your way?"

"Are you doing it only to please me?"

"What would be wrong with that?"

Minerva stopped writing and stood up. "This is a serious decision that should be made from conviction, not to get into your wife's bed. You said you don't want me to lie with you out of duty. Well, I don't want you to agree with me out of lust."

He strode over, took her shoulders, gave her a quick hard kiss, then let her go. "You know what, Minnie?" he said. "Sometimes you give me a pain in my belly. You just got your way. For once could you say 'thank you, dear husband' instead of arguing with me some more?"

He took a step back for her eyes were stormy, then turned to sky blue summer. She nodded.

"You were right about Huntley. He shouldn't be in Parliament."

"Thank you, dear husband," she said. "And I'm sorry for my own behavior. I had no right to be such a Tartar."

Like a man making an apology she held out her hand, but he caught both of hers and they stood for a minute regarding each other in rare harmony. Blake felt a surge of optimism for the future of the challenge he'd set himself that morning: to prove to his duchess that he was capable of fulfilling his inherited duties with honor, and to win her admiration. When Huntley began to talk and the truth came out, perhaps she wouldn't despise him too much.

"Come and sit with me," he said, drawing her over to a sofa. "I want you to help me understand the politics of reform."

"Really?" Her eyes gleamed as though he'd given her a wonderful present.

"I'm going to have to listen to dozens of people talking about nothing else over the next week, so I may as well know what they're saying. I gather no one can quite agree on what a reform bill should contain. Let's start with you. What would you like to see?"

"Oh, I'll never get my way. My sympathies lie with the Radicals. Nothing less than universal franchise for all adults."

"No property qualification at all? You'd allow even the poorest men to vote?"

"Not just the poorest men. Women too."

Blake let out a shout laughter. "And why not? Look at us! You're far better able to make an informed decision than I."

She was smiling at him now and he felt like a genius. "Perhaps it's as well, Your Grace, that you don't have a vote."

"Merely a seat in the House of Lords. Dear me, how will England survive?"

"Because you are a good man and good men are always needed." He felt like a god. "And," she added with a naughty little grin, "because you have me to advise you."

He lifted her hand, turned it over, and pressed a lingering kiss into her palm. "Nonsense, my dear. You'll destroy the very fabric of society if you get your way, and plunge us into a French Revolution. I'll end up hanging from a lamppost and you will go to the guillotine."

"I have no worries. I'll be knitting while heads roll."

"Do you know how to knit?"

"No, actually."

"I knew there had to be an end to your accomplishments. No knitting, no mercy. And all because, through no fault of your own, you ended up a duchess."

She didn't appear too sorry about it. She looked at him with a naughty little smile. "Shall we share a tumbril, do you suppose?"

"What exactly is a tumbril? I've never been quite sure."

"I believe it's some kind of cart."

"Pity. I was hoping it was some kind of bed."

"I could be wrong." Her voice emerged in a bare whisper, which he took to be a very good sign.

"You know, Minnie. There's a tumbril in my quarters. A very large one. Would you like to see it?"

"That would be very educational. Never let it be said I cannot admit when there's something I don't know."

Under the circumstances he was more than happy to let her have the last word.

Chapter 27

Eighty-three guests, including wives and political secretaries, but not personal servants and the occasional child, were expected. Although the staff at Mandeville was well accustomed to such epic gatherings, Minerva was kept busy planning the care, feeding, and entertainment of such a crowd. Her days were occupied settling a thousand little details. Bed and table linens, china and glass, soap and candles—all these were needed in quantities she'd never even conceived of. Then there was the food and drink. The home farm's population of pigs, sheep, cattle, and chickens would be severely depleted. The head gardener—an old friend from Minerva's youth—had his minions ready to harvest fruit and vegetables by the hundredweight and deliver baskets of fresh flowers to the house every day. Cartloads of supplies arrived from the grocers and other merchants of Shrewsbury. The bills, which Minerva dutifully examined in carefully summarized lists, were staggering. She was thankful the preparations of the stables for dozens of visiting horses and carriages and the selection of hundreds of bottles from the wine cellars did not fall to her lot. The stable master and wine steward reported directly to the duke.

Something was bothering the duke. On the surface he seemed cheerful enough, but Minerva had become sensitive to Blake's moods. She knew he wasn't looking forward to the house party, but that wasn't the trouble. It was something to do with Huntley. With great difficulty she'd bitten back her questions about the hold his former schoolmate had over him. Ever since their engagement she'd suspected Blake had a secret. He might be persuaded to tell her if she insisted; she'd always been good at arguing her friends and family into submission. But Blake could be incredibly stubborn. She also learned every day that marriage wasn't the same as dealing with a recalcitrant brother. She wanted to win her husband's trust.

Gideon and Maria Louther and their children arrived in advance of the main party. Escaping the company of Maria, whose temper tended to be querulous, she rode over to Wallop Hall to see Diana and Sebastian, who were spending a few days with the Montroses before coming to Mandeville.

"Frankly, darling," Diana said, as they sat alone in the drawing room, "I thought Sebastian and Blake would do better with four or five score other guests to separate them. I had a hard time getting him to agree to come. He's only doing it for your sake. Now tell me, how are you and Blake getting on? Your letters have been most uninformative."

"Quite well," she said.

"Do I detect a blush? That's a good sign. You must tell me all about being a duchess."

"Could we please forget I'm such an exalted being? You knew Blake well. Certainly better than I did before I married him. Did you ever hear rumors of anything odd in his past?"

"What kind of thing?"

"I don't know, but it has something to do with a man called Geoffrey Huntley who was at Eton with him."

Diana shook her elegant head. "I never heard of him. What makes you suspect anything strange?"

After a brief account of the Warfield Castle story, Minerva frowned ferociously. "I have this feeling Huntley has a hold over Blake for some reason. I know I have the key to it. I've noticed things ever since our engagement, times when Blake seems to be dodging the issue, trying to deflect my attention, but I can't put my finger on it."

"You could ask him."

"I want him to tell me because he trusts me."

A broad smile crossed Diana's face. "Well, well. Who would have thought it?"

"What?"

"Never mind. But I think I'd better tell you about something that happened between Blake and me."

Minerva felt a moment's panic. The short-lived betrothal between Diana and her husband had never bothered her before, but she felt a stab of irrational loathing for her sister, not unlike what she'd experienced when she saw him speaking to Desirée de Bonamour in the Tuileries Garden.

"After Sebastian and I married, Blake borrowed a large sum from me."

"That is odd. If there's one thing I know it's that the Vanderlins have plenty of money."

"That is why I suspect he wanted the money for something he didn't want brought to his father's attention. I thought perhaps he had a gaming debt, yet Blake never had a reputation as a heavy gambler."

"No, he doesn't much like cards. I suppose he might have bet on a horse race."

Diana nodded. "He used to enjoy a bet. Even though he sold his hunters and gave up his London house, it still took two years for him to pay me. That's why he went to live in Devon, to save money."

"I never asked him why he did that." Minerva shook her head in amazement that she'd missed the connection. She'd scornfully assumed he'd been banished by his father and never given it another thought.

"I know the duke was less than generous in his allowance to Blake." Diana smiled wryly. "My fortune was a big part of his attraction to me."

"And he wouldn't let himself remain in debt to you . . ."

"No."

"The question is why he needed such a large sum. Let's say it was Huntley. If Huntley is blackmailing Blake, he may have decided this time he'd rather have a parliamentary seat than money."

"But what could Blake have done that he had to pay so much for Huntley's silence?"

"Of one thing I am absolutely certain," Minerva said fiercely. "Nothing dishonorable. Blake is a good man. And if Huntley thinks to harm him, I shall have something to say about it."

Diana's revelation explained why she'd felt a pall of anxiety hanging over Blake in recent days, a sense of impending doom. One night she'd tackled him directly about it and he said crossly that the prospect of a hundred near-strangers invading the house was enough to give anyone a sense of doom. She couldn't get another word out of him. There was one thing she could do to make the party, in a small way, less of an annoyance for her husband.

"Where's Sebastian, Diana?"

"Reading in the summer house."

The summer house was rather a grand term for a rickety rustic shelter the other side of the shaggy lawn. She found Lord Iverley escaping the afternoon sun with his nose buried in a book.

He looked up at her approach, peered owlishly, and retrieved his spectacles from his pocket. He couldn't see more than a few feet ahead without them. "Min!" He was always pleased to see her.

"Good book?"

"Miss Appleton's *Early Education*. She has some interesting ideas about reasoning with infants."

Dear Sebastian. Always looking for the answers to life's mysteries on the printed page. "What does Diana think of it?"

"She tells me not to worry so much."

"I want to talk to you about Blake."

Sebastian made a noise that meant he didn't

want to discuss something and looked longingly at Miss Appleton.

"When you come to Mandeville this week, I want you to be polite and make an effort to get on good terms with him."

"That's what Diana keeps telling me. Do I have to?"

Minerva put her hands on her hips. "He's not only your cousin, he's your brother-in-law."

"Yes, damn him. And we know how that happened."

"However unfortunate the beginning of our marriage, we're bound for life and we're both trying to make the best of it."

"Is *he* trying to make the best of it, Min, or is it just you? Does he treat you well?"

"Yes, he does. Whatever happened between you and Blake in the past, I want you to forget it." She wasn't privy to all the details of Blake and Sebastian's feud, only that it went back to childhood. She'd always taken Sebastian's side. Now she felt sure the fault wasn't one-sided and Blake must have good cause to dislike his cousin.

"I no longer dwell on our boyhood quarrels," he said stiffly. "We simply don't have anything in common. I've often wondered if the man can even read. But there's no reason I can't be polite."

"Good. Now you should try and do better than tolerance. You know, we always made jokes about how stupid Blake is, but we were wrong. Just because he's not a great reader doesn't mean he lacks intelligence. I find him to be knowledgeable in many areas and capable of acute observation." She put her hands on her hips and glared down at Sebastian. She realized she'd articulated an opinion that had been forming over many weeks.

"Don't look so fierce, Min. I take your word for it. I'll try to make Blake my friend. Only for your sake, of course."

"For my sake and for yours. He's your closest relation, Sebastian."

Sebastian started laughing. "To think I'd ever see the day. Minerva Montrose, defending Lord Blakeney."

"It's not funny, Sebastian. Everything is different now."

Since Sebastian was a man of his word, she was satisfied with their conversation. But something he said preyed on her mind as she rode home through the park.

I've often wondered if the man can even read.

He'd been joking. It was the kind of sniping remark he and Blake made about each other, the sort of thing a bookish man would say about a sportsman he disliked.

And yet . . .

It was incredible. And it explained so much.

Minerva had never seen her husband in the act of reading, not once. Not a pamphlet, not a novel, not even a menu.

But he could write, proven by a single brief and misspelled note. It was the only time she'd ever seen more than his signature. When he'd had occasion to contact her in the short weeks between their betrothal and wedding, a servant had delivered the message verbally.

Of course he could write. How could a man of

his station manage without that most fundamental method of communication?

Her head buzzing with speculation, she handed over her horse to the waiting servant. With a hasty "later" to a request for consultation from the housekeeper, she tore upstairs with unseemly haste and dismissed her waiting maid. Instead of tossing it out when she packed to leave Paris, she'd tucked Blake's note into a drawer of her jewel chest.

The sight of it drew an involuntary smile and a shiver of pleasure. The morning she'd received it was the day they'd first lain together. How foolish she'd been to be so upset by a little pain. Whatever educational shortcomings Blake might have, he knew how to make her happy in bed.

She unfolded the half sheet, recalling how hard it had been to decipher. At the time she'd assumed he'd written in haste. Perusing it now she doubted it. There were none of the ink splatters common when pen was dragged across paper carelessly. Now that her suspicions were aroused, there seemed something premeditated about the chaotic sprawl, as though it were deliberately ill-written.

Deflection.

She recalled at least two occasions when he'd used a physical advance to get away from the subject of reading, once when she'd outright asked him to take a turn at reading aloud. In each case she'd had the impression he was avoiding something.

Yet he could write, a little. So he must be able to read too. A little. The secretaries' brief summaries, Amanda's little capitalized notes.

She passed through the small antechamber dividing the duke and duchess's suites into Blake's bedchamber. Nothing here. He slept in her bed. His sitting room was almost as neat, with none of the clutter of paper that her maids constantly, and to her annoyance, tidied up in hers. While she never had fewer than a dozen books in her room at any moment, she found just two here.

Two books. Her heart lightened. Her suspicions were crazy and unfounded. She'd always known he wasn't bookish, but that didn't mean he couldn't read.

One was a recently published work on agriculture, almost new. Bound in the printer's boards, the pages were uncut. Only the first few had been slit open with a paper knife so he hadn't got very far into the tome. The other was her wedding gift. The binder had trimmed the pages and gilded the edges, but the bookmark proved he'd progressed less than a chapter since she last checked. Yet he'd told her once he was enjoying it.

Minerva could barely take in the implications of her discovery. How could Blake be virtually illiterate? Anyone could read if taught. Her studies told her that even those born in the lowest circumstances could be educated. That the heir to a dukedom should fail must be attributed to only two causes: gross stupidity or extreme idleness. Neither explanation fit the Blake she'd come to know and value. She wanted to ask him, demand the truth, but how could she insult him so? Suppose she was wrong? He would rightly be mortally offended by such a shocking accusation.

And where did Huntley come into the picture?

Her reeling brain refused, for the present, to make any sense of his involvement and she had no leisure to consider it. The housekeeper needed her and tomorrow almost a hundred guests would fill the house, requiring her attention as a hostess and her political acumen in solving the quarrels that were the reason for the house party.

Besides, what she'd said to Diana was true. She wanted Blake to trust her.

Chapter 28

"I think it would be quite wrong to extend the franchise to tenants. Freeholders are the only ones who can be trusted to have the interests of the country at heart."

Blake had forgotten the name of the fellow in the yellow waistcoat who harangued him. Another man lingered nearby, anxious to favor the Duke of Hampton with his impressive opinion. A politically-minded earl, one of his father's oldest friends, was headed in his direction.

Everyone wanted the duke. They wanted to know his thoughts on the important subjects of the day. Not because his views were of any inherent value, but because he had things they wanted and they were trying to find out what they had to do to get them. Blake realized to them he wasn't a man; he was a title and a position in life. To add to his disquiet was the knowledge that many of these men were acquainted with Geoffrey Huntley. Every time the post came, one of them could receive a letter with the sorry tale of the new Duke of Hampton and his long unsuccessful struggle with the written word.

Despite his complete idiocy when it came to the Greek language, by listening in class (though usually pretending not to) he'd managed to imbibe a fair knowledge of classical culture. One story had always resonated with him, never more so than now. He completely sympathized with the man who lived with the constant threat of death from a sword hanging over his head by a single thread. There were moments when Blake was tempted to slice through the thread that held his personal Sword of Damocles and let it fall, publicly destroying any notion that he could adequately fill his father's shoes.

Since the only strategy he'd found to deal with Huntley's threat was to prove to the world that he was a worthy occupant of the title, he suppressed his boredom and listened carefully while saying little.

In the library, where several dozen were gathered this wet Wednesday morning, he looked around for the only person whose company he desired. Over the shoulder of his tormenter, his height much shorter than his speeches, he found Minerva at the other end of room, engaged in a group of chattering politicos and bargaining radicals. She was beautiful and bright-eyed, a lavender-gowned beauty in a sea of coats and breeches, and having the time of her life. His mood softened a degree at her obvious happiness, which he had no wish to interrupt.

He drank in her slender fairness, apparently so frail when compared to the dark masculine hues that surrounded her, but deceptively so. Minerva,

Duchess of Hampton, was strong, keen-witted, and cunning as any man. She was speaking to a group of men and, though she was far from earshot, his inner ear could hear the low-pitched clipped accents with which she delivered her cogent, intelligent, and mercifully concise arguments. His heart swelled with pride that this remarkable woman was his. How could these fellows not fall on their knees before her and agree to whatever she asked?

Another fellow joined them, added something to the conversation. The men all started talking at once and distress was written over her features. How dare they? His fists itched to knock down the lot of them.

"Excuse me . . ." he cut off Mr. Yellow Waistcoat. "I've remembered an appointment." He cut through the assembly to her side.

"Blake," she said softly. Her use of informal address in public, as much as her convulsive grip on his arm, confirmed her unhappiness.

He kissed her hand, a real kiss so that his lips brushed the soft skin of her practical hands. "Minerva," he said. "Present these gentlemen to me."

Doubtless he'd already met them but he didn't care. Men who upset his wife didn't deserve his consideration.

She listed their names and they all bowed eagerly and started to talk, but fell silent when he raised his hand. "I'm sure you've expressed your opinions to the duchess and she's more than capable of conveying your arguments to me." When one of them had the temerity to demur he looked down his nose at the man and composed his features into what he hoped was the expression his father had used to depress pretensions. "Her Grace has my ear," he announced. That was all. No doubt anyone who didn't hear him say it would have the report before the longcase clock struck the quarter hour.

"Please accompany me to the study, Minerva. I wish to consult you on a matter of importance." He bowed formally, offered his arm, and the two of them walked the length of the library, the assembled men hurrying aside to create a path for their progress. He would have laughed, but tension rippled through her hand to his. The rosebud lips were thin and pale, the china blue eyes brimmed with frustration.

The visible effort it required to maintain her dignity might have amused him had she not been genuinely distressed. Then any impulse to laugh shriveled.

Huntley. Had the weasel's letter arrived? Had one of those fellows told Minerva the truth?

To his utter amazement, when they reached the study she burst into tears. His fearless, confident Minnie wept as though the world had ended.

He took her into his arms and held her close, dropping helpless kisses into her glossy braids. He'd happily kill the man who'd upset her, but he feared that would mean suicide. As her sobs subsided she drew back and groped for her handkerchief. He took it from her convulsive grip, tilted her face, and carefully dabbed away the tears.

"I'm sorry," she said with an endearing sniffle. "I just heard something terrible."

He waited, helpless, for her next words. What

could be more terrible than learning that her husband was a fool?

She opened her mouth, as though afraid to speak. A first for Minerva.

"I . . ." she began. "I . . . told Edward Jones he could have Warfield Castle."

"Is that all?" Searing relief mingled with an undercurrent of something akin to regret that his secret had not been exposed. "I'm sure he's a good fellow."

"He is. But I just learned Gideon had promised Lord Waterbury he'd give it to Mr. Sanborn. Now the people on both sides are furious. I've made a terrible mistake. I thought I'd made a clever move, but I've made things worse."

"I'm sure it's not so bad, my love." The endearment dropped from his lips unplanned and pleased him.

She shook her head with a despondent pout. "I never knew hosting a political gathering could be so maddening."

"Come here," he said, pulling her back into a loose embrace. "Tell me all about it." He stroked her back and she gradually relaxed in his arms, settling her cheek against his chest with a gusty sigh.

"I spent an hour this morning talking to three men whom I admire. They are intelligent and thoughtful and have the best interests of the country at heart. But each one of them thinks that he, and he alone, is right."

"We all think we're right, Minnie. Even you."

Her little chuckle reverberated into his chest. "True. But at least I admit the possibility of a different point of view."

"Must be because you're not a man."

"If that's what men are like, I'm grateful I'm female."

"I'm certainly grateful for that." He dropped a kiss onto her hair.

"There are reasonable men. There must be."

"Of course there are. Me, for example."

"Oh, you don't count." That didn't sound like a compliment. On the other hand she put her arms around his waist and snuggled into chest. "Sir Gideon is working hard to forge a compromise and I'm trying to help him. If the reformers cannot agree on the contents of a bill, there's no chance of even introducing it in Parliament, let along mustering the votes to pass it. The object of this gathering is to bring everyone together. If it fails they'll all go away."

Though nothing could make Blake happier than to see his house shot of every last gabbling guest, not even for a moment was he tempted to say "Good." Minerva's wishes were more important than his.

"I'm failing," she said. "I always thought I could help important things to happen and it's all falling apart. It's much more difficult than I imagined."

He found he couldn't bear to see her humbled. He wanted his bossy, overconfident Minnie back. "My dearest girl! You mustn't blame yourself. You're new to this game. Besides, it's not your sole responsibility."

"Someone must try," she said fiercely.

His father would have succeeded. Blake felt his own inadequacy keenly. The heritage and future of his family was now on his shoulders. Political influence was only a part of it, and not a part he was suited to by inclination or talent. Nonetheless, while the power existed it was his duty to wield it, well and responsibly. Like it or not, he alone was Duke of Hampton.

"What can I do?" he asked.

Minerva tilted her head and looked at him with an arrested expression. "You are Hampton," she said, echoing his own conclusion. "They will listen to you."

"What do I have to contribute to the discussion? If they were all as clever as you claim, they'd be following your advice."

"Thank you." She smiled for the first time. "They find it hard to look beyond the fact that I am a woman, and a young one too."

Swinging her by the waist, he moved over to an upholstered window seat. Once he had her ensconced on his lap, fragrant and shapely, he was tempted to initiate some serious kissing. But he had work to do and his industrious resolution wasn't entirely motivated by his need to impress her.

"So, Duchess, what should I say to these recalcitrant fellows?"

He could almost hear her brain churning. "They're all madly curious to know your opinion, because you never express it. There's a good deal of speculation about which side you support."

"Hah! I hardly even know which side is which."

"Being mysterious is effective. It makes people suspect you are a deep thinker."

"In that case I shall continue to keep quiet, lest they learn otherwise."

Minerva cupped his cheek with her hand. "I'm

beginning to think your native common sense has much to offer."

The glow in her blue eyes pierced him to the soul. A casual caress and a few words of praise from Minerva meant more to him than the extravagant attention of a dozen beautiful women. He wondered how he could be worthy of her. He could never be his father, sweep into an assembly and sway men's opinions by the power of his personality and brilliance of mind. But he did stand in his father's place and perhaps he could fool people into believing him a worthy successor to the late duke. But if he were to retain even the minimal respect he now enjoyed, he couldn't afford to let them know how incapable he was. Men who now regarded him as a leader would laugh at his ignorance.

And the damnable thing was they could know any day. Even now, Huntley could be spreading the rumor.

She was frowning again. What now?

"Warfield Castle. Whatever shall we do?"

"Gideon had no right to make that promise without consulting me."

"Nor did I. I'm so sorry."

He could see her pride and self-confidence were badly shaken. Where once he'd have taken pleasure in seeing Minerva brought down a peg or two, now he wanted only to restore her happiness.

"You had every right. I told them back in the library that you have my ear and I mean it. Anything you do, I'll back you to the hilt. And before you point out that I should make decisions based on merit, let me assure you that I have far more faith in your ability than Gideon's."

Chapter 29

He'd given her everything she'd always wanted. Thanks to Blake, she now had influence she'd scarcely dreamed of. And the dreams of her girlhood had never been modest.

But she was greedy. She wanted more. A true political partnership with her husband had always been her goal in life and simply ruling through Blake was not enough. How much greater the satisfaction would she gain from exercising power with his full participation. If her theory about him was correct—and she was more and more sure of it—it explained his long disengagement from ducal and national affairs. Whatever the cause of his inability to read, it didn't matter. With her help he could overcome it. She wanted the role she guessed had been Amanda's.

She demanded it. It was her right. Not as his duchess but as his wife.

Blake didn't trust her enough to confide in her, and she understood why. Throughout their acquaintance she'd underestimated and scorned him. When she thought of their quarrel in the streets of Paris, the way she'd railed at him, she was ashamed.

A demonstration of her changed sentiments was in order. If she hadn't lured him to speak by the time their guests left, then she'd raise the subject herself. In the meantime she'd use some of the feminine wiles she'd learned from Celia and Diana. That naughty book of Celia's had given her lots of ideas she hadn't been able to imagine putting into practice. Now she looked forward to it.

Gideon wasn't happy about Warfield Castle but Blake told him firmly that his decision was made and he should live with it. To his surprise his brother-in-law gave in gracefully. The late duke's assessment had been correct: he was a follower. To assuage any resulted discord between Gideon and Minerva, he suggested they work together to soothe bruised feelings among the competing parties.

That worked well. The pair of them huddled in conversation in a corner of the drawing room for at least an hour after dinner. That he'd been able to find a solution to her dilemma pleased him, but if he hoped for a physical demonstration of his wife's gratitude he was disappointed. She informed him with a modest smile that he shouldn't come to her room that night. From which he deduced that the next Duke of Hampton did not yet exist, even in embryonic form. It wasn't the lack of a potential heir he regretted.

He felt restless and not at all like going to sleep. He couldn't even get a game of billiards without having the satisfying clunk of ivory balls disturbed by speculation and horse trading, not alas of the equine variety. He prepared for bed, let his valet help him into a light banyan suitable for a summer evening, and dismissed the man. The sight awaiting him when he opened the door to the duke's bedchamber drew a happy smile. He felt better than he had in days.

The duchess was draped across the giant bed. By the light of a few carefully placed candles he absorbed the curves of arms, waist, and hips, admired the long golden hair draped over her shoulders and barely covering the peaks of her breasts. She wore not a stitch of clothing but an emerald necklace and a pair of almost matching bracelets.

"Good evening, Duchess," he said. "May I compliment you on your dress?"

"Someone with excellent taste selected this ensemble."

"When I saw the necklace in the shop I thought it would suit you. The effect is *just* what I had in mind."

She raised her brows. "You thought *I* would wear it like this?"

"A man can always hope."

"I don't believe you ever thought of me unclothed. Not back then, when you bought *me* the necklace." Thus she averred her certainty that he'd chosen the emeralds for her, not for another woman. And though she underestimated a man's capacity to imagine a woman naked, almost any woman, his wife was the only one who now interested him. His smile broadened.

"Lately, Minnie, I find I think of little else. Especially when I'm surrounded by our tedious guests."

"I noticed you weren't enjoying yourself so I thought I'd try to cheer you up."

She looked pointedly at the area below his waist, showing through the opening of his blue cotton robe. The evidence that he had, indeed, cheered up drew a smile he could only describe as lascivious. He cheered up even more.

"What did you have in mind?" he asked, striking a pose that revealed the length of his body. He'd noticed before that she enjoyed looking at him and her blatant ogling aroused him to an anticipatory ache.

"Join me in bed and you'll find out."

He dropped his robe to the floor, swung up onto the high mattress, and stalked on hands and knees across the linen expanse of the great ducal bed to where she lay.

She was a banquet for his delectation and he contemplated which part to taste first. She lay on her side like a goddess, Venus rather than Minerva, one arm supporting her head, the other resting along the line of her hip, the hand a partial fig leaf to her sex. She raised it, revealing to his eyes the nest of blond curls. It was tempting to tuck in but he was in no hurry.

He dipped down for a kiss, sampling her with slow thoroughness, tracing the bow with his tongue and sucking tenderly on the plump lower lip. "You're so sweet, Minnie," he murmured.

That was the wrong thing to say, or perhaps the right one. She set her palm to his forehead and pushed. "I am not sweet."

"I beg to differ." Sweet wasn't the right word for

her character, but she possessed far more softness than she admitted to. And there was no other way to describe her taste.

"I want you on your back." Within seconds she had him spread-eagled on the soft cloth, and she'd taken his position on hands and knees, her eyes raking his body.

His chest shook with laughter. "I see the forceful, demanding side of your character has invaded the bedchamber."

"Do you mind?"

"Far from it."

In the bedroom, if nowhere else, she'd always let him lead, but he had no objection to her taking a turn. Their roles were reversed so he was now the feast. And he knew that he was a lucky, lucky man.

She started at the neck, nibbling and nuzzling, then worked her way down his torso. She seemed fascinated by the contours of his chest, honed by years of strenuous exercise.

"Why do you have such beautiful muscles?" she murmured between licks.

"So that you can kiss them," he said.

"Thank you. You've spent your time well."

And it continued, thrilling him with touch and foolish, arousing words. As her fingers, palms, and lips explored his rib cage his straining cock knocked against her firm little breasts. A little pant of surprise, and she raised her head to regard it, her lips pursing into a perfect O. Sitting back, her knees on either side of his legs, she wrapped both hands around it and experimented, pushing up and down to expose the tip.

"Hmm." She gave the matter some consideration and for once he didn't want to tell her she thought too much.

Would she or wouldn't she? He didn't expect it, neither would he ask. He realized he'd never, in all his many and varied relations with women, had greater joy in bed than with his inexperienced wife. Still, he yearned for her mouth on him and his cock jerked in her grasp.

His breath caught, her lips parted, her head dipped. A red tongue emerged and brushed the tip, arousing a shudder of delight. Then she took the entire head into the wet heat of her mouth and he was in heaven.

She had no skill. How could she? As far as he knew this wasn't something you could learn from a book. But trust his Minnie to give it her best shot.

After some delightful and maddening experimentation, she caught on and imitated the rhythm of coitus. In very little time she had him groaning in pleasure and thrusting back, though he tried not to go too far. A fierce grip on his thighs kept her from losing balance and being thrown off by the convulsive heaves of his hips. Before he completely lost control he brushed aside the wild golden hair spread over his stomach.

"No more," he rasped and raised her head.

"But . . ." Before she could argue he sat up in one forceful move, lifted her by the waist, and brought her down to straddle his lap. Though they'd never made love in this position either, she understood at once, without words, what he wanted. Holding his cock, she guided herself into place and took him in, welcoming him with slick warmth that left no doubt of her own readiness and desire. She put her arms about his neck and whispered how much she wanted him, how good he made her feel. His racing heart lurched and the fleeting notion crossed his fevered mind that if he died now he'd depart this world entirely happy.

"Minnie," he whispered. "My Minnie." He held her tight and would never let her go.

The possessive words went straight to Minerva's heart. Too moved for more words, she expressed her feelings with deep, fervent kisses as she rode him in time to his own thrusts. Breast to breast in a fierce embrace, she was lost in the intensity of their congress and an intimacy greater than anything she'd ever felt with another soul. Tears pricked her eyes as she approached the apex.

"Blake," she whispered. Then shouted his name again as her head jerked back in bliss. As delight continued to ripple through her body he turned her on her back and drove to his own finish.

They lay together afterwards, exchanging lazy caresses and soft kisses. "Thank you, Minnie," he murmured. "I cannot describe how much better I feel."

Minerva couldn't recall ever feeling better herself. "I know this party isn't your idea of fun. Thank you for putting up with it. And for supporting me today when I made that stupid mistake."

"Just as long as *you* are enjoying yourself. You appeared to be this evening."

"I was," she said. "I am enjoying it, for the most part. But I didn't expect so many fruitless arguments. Some of these men behave like quarrelling children. Don't they understand than none of them is going to get everything he wants and that they need to compromise?"

He pecked at her nose. "Are you telling me that a nineteen-year-old female has more sense than the combined male wisdom of the party?"

"Yes, actually."

"I'm not surprised. You're worth a dozen of them, Minnie."

"Why, thank you."

"*You* should be Prime Minister."

"That's what I've always thought."

"But I'm extremely grateful you can't be. If anyone should seriously recommend extending the franchise to women I shall have to oppose it." He kissed her in a spot in the middle of her rib cage.

"I thought you agreed with me in all my goals."

"Not when they run counter to my self-interest. As Prime Minister you'd never have time for interludes like this one."

It was hard to muster any outrage while he paid delectable attention to her breasts. "Don't you think that's rather selfish?" she said between gurgles of pleasure.

"I've always been a selfish man."

"I used to think so, but I've changed my mind." She made to stroke his head but he raised it, knocking her hand out of the way.

"Why?" He regarded her intently.

"Well, first of all you could have refused to marry me."

"I said I was selfish. I hope that doesn't mean I'm not a gentlemen."

"You didn't have to buy me emeralds."

"I like giving people presents."

Blake, she knew, didn't really possess the endless self-assurance and arrogance he showed in public. He appeared embarrassed by her praise.

"And you wanted to give Warfield Castle to an old school friend." She awaited his response, suddenly hating her stratagem of trying to coax a confession from him. The connection between them felt deep and honest and beyond the need for manipulation. But still she didn't demand the truth. More than ever she longed for his trust.

For a moment she thought she had it, that he was on the brink of saying something momentous. Then a grave expression turned quizzical. "You're extolling me for that? For Huntley?"

"You were wrong about him, but the impulse was a generous one."

"By all means give me credit for my errors."

"And you took my side over Sir Gideon's about his replacement."

"I'll admit to that act of benevolence. It was a great sacrifice for me. And I've been amply rewarded. Now I believe it's time for me to repay the favor."

He started kissing her again, this time on her stomach which set her laughing and wriggling with pleasure. "You like that, don't you?"

"You read me like a book."

He raised his head, looked at her oddly, opened his mouth as though he had something to say, but nothing came out. Instead he returned to his previous activity. Intelligible conversation came to an end.

He almost told Minerva the truth. He wanted to and he would, soon. His desire not to keep secrets from her overcame his fears of rejection. He trusted her to treat him kindly. In fact he woke up the next morning feeling so well he wouldn't care if everyone knew. He went out to the stables and the world seemed a new place. Pale sunlight washed the cobblestones of the yard; brilliant cerulean blue framed cheerful, fluffy clouds; and birdsong competed with the whistles of the grooms and stableboys at work.

The only thing that could improve the morning would be the company of his wife. But she'd kissed him tenderly and returned to her room to gird herself for a morning persuading a trio of recalcitrant M.P.s to behave.

Galloping up Mandeville's famous avenue of beeches, he felt deep content. He was doing what he loved, and so was Minerva. And later they'd come together and share their joy and their love.

He drew his horse to a halt at the apogee of the avenue, crowned by a Roman style arch. He was stunned.

He loved her. He'd fallen in love with Minerva. His breath was as challenged as that of his panting steed and he had a moment of sheer panic that settled into satisfaction. It was a joy to love. He felt as triumphal as the arch behind him. He wished he had a rapier to wave, a trumpet to sound, an enemy to slay on behalf of his lady.

Of course he wouldn't mind charging down the hill and putting a few politicians to the sword, but he didn't believe his love would appreciate that gesture. More likely causing grievous harm to a member of the reform party would lead to his summary eviction from her bed. Although he believed Minerva had grown fond of him, and she certainly found him physically appealing—she'd never made a secret of it—he didn't flatter himself that she returned his feelings. He had some work to do there, and revealing his cretinous inability to read a simple handwritten letter wasn't going to achieve his ends. He needed to bewitch and enrapture her until nothing she learned of him could make a difference.

He knew it could happen because it was the way he felt about her. She was clever and funny and beautiful and stubborn and outspoken and a complete thorn in his flesh and he adored her. No matter what she did, he would always adore her. How he would bring her to that same happy state he had no idea. But he wanted to start his efforts at once.

He needed exercise and after several days of rain he was behind on the schedule of land inspections he'd set himself. So though his heart jumped with impatience to behold his beloved again, he made himself complete his work. Neglecting his duty would not, he fancied, impress Minerva. Besides, he took pride in his stewardship of his family acres.

By midmorning his need to set eyes on her was a physical ache. He trotted along the stable road, letting his horse cool down, despite his haste. Quite a decent beast, one of his father's saddle horses. Nevertheless the horseflesh at Mandeville wasn't up to his standards. He looked forward to the arrival of his French purchases, which had crossed the channel and were making their slow way to Shropshire.

At a curve in the road a man emerged from a stand of laurels and walked out into his path. His heart sank. Whenever life seemed particularly good, his nemesis turned up to spoil it.

The first thing he thought when he dismounted was how short Huntley was. Perhaps he'd never noticed before because Huntley had never boxed or fenced with him. He looked positively disreputable, his coat unbrushed, neck cloth askew, and boots scuffed. Very unlike the dapper aspirant to Parliament who'd talked his way into Vanderlin House and a rotten borough a few weeks ago.

Blake stood by his horse, waiting in silence for Huntley's new demand.

"You've ruined me," he said, brimming with resentment. "The bailiffs have taken almost everything and there's one more creditor who'll do far worse if I don't come up with nearly two thousand."

"Been gambling in low places again? I'd say you've ruined yourself."

"I'll take five thousand pounds for my silence. Then you'll never hear from me again. I promise." Even now, Huntley tried to feign sincerity, but his façade was slipping. Blake saw nothing but low cunning, tinged with desperation.

"Why should I believe you?"

"This time you can. I intend to leave the country. There's nothing left for me here."

And there was nothing left for Blake but to tell the blackguard to go to blazes, as he should have years ago. Yet curiosity held him back. A lingering memory of old affection meant he wanted to know what had gone wrong. Though there was nothing Huntley could say to change his mind, he wanted to understand why the most important friendship of his youth had turned so sour. "Why did you do it?" he asked. "If you needed funds you should have asked."

Huntley's civility grew as bedraggled as his linen. "I knew you'd never dare ask your father for the kind of money I needed to pay off my debts of honor. With *your* honor at stake you'd go to the duke. Turns out I was right."

"You got a lot more than you needed."

"My father sent me to Eton as an investment. That beating I took for you was my first expenditure of capital, you might say." He sniggered unpleasantly. "What a lode of gold I hit. Not just a duke's heir, but an idiot with a secret I could help him keep. I thought I was made for life."

"You were a fool. You could have been."

"I should have been," Huntley almost shouted. "But you betrayed me. I was no longer any use to you and you discarded me for other companions. Men of birth, not a mere merchant's son. You couldn't even let me have Warfield Castle. Such a small thing and it cost you nothing. As an M.P. I couldn't be imprisoned for debt, and I had it parlayed into a nice little government sinecure."

Blake had heard enough of Huntley's self-serving blather. "I shall never give you another penny. Do your worst." He loomed over the creature, who snarled and spit with rage, his beatific features no longer disguising the rottenness of his heart. "You'll find the Duke of Hampton's worst is a lot more potent than Geoffrey Huntley's."

Huntley launched one last insult. "It's your wife who's given you the courage, I suppose. I was indiscreet with her. I never thought to see you, of all men, living under petticoat rule."

Even through his exasperation, a smile intruded. "You have no idea," Blake said, more to himself than to his taunter.

"Under the thumb of a lowborn creature you had to wed because you were caught debauching her."

That was quite enough and it ended quickly. A quick right to the jaw wiped the sneer off Huntley's face. He slumped to the ground, out cold. Blake dusted off his hands and grinned.

He returned to the stable and summoned the head groom.

"There's an unconscious man near the laurels. Take two of the lads and dump him out beyond the gates. I want him off my land."

Hitting Huntley had been remarkably satisfying. He should have done it years ago. While it might not be the method his father would have used, he felt the old man would have approved. He'd told Blake he must be his own kind of duke, and apparently that meant using his skilled fists when the case demanded it.

As he walked back to the house the high noon sun emerged from behind a harmless white cloud and bathed him in its light. Symbolically he felt his father's blessing touch his brow. More than ever he wished he'd had the opportunity to confess to the duke. Instead he would confess to his wife, throw himself on the mercy of the woman he loved. This very night, after they retired, we would tell her everything.

In the meantime he needed to solve the problem for which this gathering at Mandeville had been assembled. And because real life hadn't magically transformed, he'd better do it soon, before his guests heard from Huntley. He trusted Minerva's response, but not that of the world. His moment of wielding his inherited influence might be only too brief.

Chapter 30

The table in the state dining room at Mandeville was very long. Occasional oases of feminine colored silks punctuated the sober attire of the political males who made up the majority of the seated diners. Diana, perfection in red, sat halfway up on the left, vainly trying to make polite conversation with one of her neighbors. Minerva saw her exchange amused shrugs across the table with Sebastian, who wasn't even trying to make himself heard among the babble.

Most of the guests were talking. At once. Loudly. Minerva's debut as a political hostess was about to degenerate into a brawl.

Her gaze traversed yards of gleaming mahogany, past silver and crystal and porcelain, and found her husband seated at the head of the table on another ducal throne. The stark black coat and black mourning neck cloth only enhanced his golden beauty. He sat still, silent and utterly dignified, an island of calm among bellowed opinions and fraying tempers. Minerva's stomach fluttered and she felt most peculiar, as though she'd fallen from a great height and was tumbling head over heels into a bank of clouds. Her chest tightened and she could hardly breathe. It was too far for real eye contact, but she knew when he noticed her looking at him. They exchanged something, a wordless thought that cut through the cacophony. He nodded at her and rose to his feet.

At first only those sitting nearest him noticed, then quiet traveled through the ranks. Minerva's squabbling neighbors were the last to know and stop in mid-dueling sentence. Only the discreet clatter of dishes broke the silence as the footmen continued about their business.

"Gentlemen," Blake said, "I have welcomed you to Mandeville as my father would have, even though my family is still in deep mourning, because the cause of parliamentary reform was dear to his heart."

A murmur of approval was quelled with a frown. "I can't speak with certainty for the late duke, but knowing my father I'm reasonably sure he'd be appalled at what I've been hearing today. He knew, I know, you all know, that there is no single view of reform. Whatever happens will be too much for some, too little for others, and not exactly what anyone wants."

Minerva's heart swelled with pride. It was exactly what she would have said, and already had, to her husband. But the tone of voice was all his and so was the look. She'd seen Blake bored, she'd seen him sulky, and she'd seen him arrogantly scornful. Lately she'd got to know his better side: charming, attentive, funny, and capable of causing a good deal of pleasure. But now he stood at the head of the table and exuded the raw power of generations of dukes.

His voice managed to be calm, well bred, and utterly reasonable, but underlain with threats of unspoken retribution. The familiar deep tones held a new edge that seemed to stroke the base of Minerva's spine.

"Let's be reasonable, gentlemen. Every one of you knows how hard it will be to introduce a reform bill in Parliament. That bill won't go as far as most of us would like but it will be better than the present system. Imagine you are called upon to vote on a reform bill with these provisions." He raised a forefinger to the fascinated assembly. "One. Extend the franchise to small landowners, tenants, and householders in the boroughs. Two. Abolish the rotten boroughs and pocket seats and give their members to large towns that are now unrepresented. Three. Make it less difficult for those enfranchised to actually vote." He glanced around the table, daring anyone to argue. No one did. How could they contradict that steely gaze? Breathing became a labor for Minerva.

"Who will vote against it?" No answer. "Good. Now stop arguing and reach an agreement. If you're still fighting at breakfast, you may all summon your carriages and go home."

She shouldn't approve, of course, even if the result was desirable. The Duke of Hampton had treated them to a show of aristocratic potency that reminded them the age of the nobility had not yet passed. Even as her principles abhorred it, her brain applauded and her body reacted in the most extraordinary way.

Every arrogant word had ripped through her body like a hot caress. She looked at her husband and heat flooded her abdomen. She wanted to stand up and cheer. Then throw herself on him and take him. Now.

After a minute or so, conversations resumed. The tone was low and civil and serious, but she barely noticed. She muttered some politeness to her neighbors, rose to her feet, and walked the length of the room to where Blake waited and watched her, his head tilted in question. She curtseyed.

"Your Grace," she said. "I believe our guests have much to discuss among themselves. Shall we retire?"

He offered his arm, his only answer a glow in his impossibly dark blue eyes. Surely he could hear her panting. Surely everyone could.

She couldn't fall on him. The passages and halls were full of footmen. "Where?" he asked.

The house was too big and their beds too far away. "Your study," she said.

She closed the door and reached for the fall of his evening breeches. She wasn't feeling subtle. He stiffened beneath her touch and by the time her fingers, lent efficiency by desperation, had seen to the buttons, he was hard and ready.

Wildly, she looked around.

"Desk." He answered her unspoken question, guiding her backward and pulling at the satin skirts of her gown so that by the time her behind hit furniture he'd found her drawers and ripped them off.

She feared they were damp, for she was insane with lust. With easy strength he lifted her onto the desk.

"Quick," she commanded, rustling her skirts out of the way and spreading her legs. For a few seconds cool air soothed her burning entrance but this wasn't the relief she wanted.

"Whatever you say, Duchess."

Holding her firm with his steady sportsman's hand at her back, he guided himself into place, entering her with one powerful thrust that elicited an unbidden scream of satisfaction.

It was fast and noisy and without finesse. She clawed his neck with her nails, made her legs a girdle around his waist, and clenched her inner muscles to hold him tight each time he entered and withdrew. She approached her peak with unprecedented rapidity, driven by his steady strokes and inarticulate groans. She screamed again, and the explosion of sound enhanced her excitement, bringing her ever closer to the brink.

"Oh my lord, Minnie," he rasped and bent her back over the desk, pushing her knees to her shoulders and bearing down with harder thrusts. She went over the top just as his movements became convulsive and, with a shout to challenge her own final shriek, he released his hot seed and pulled her into his arms.

Half lying on the ancient oak desk of the Dukes of Hampton, a surface even wider than the one at Vanderlin House, they clutched each other until their panting subsided.

Minerva was the first to speak. "You are magnificent."

He grinned and looked modestly pleased with himself. "Anything to please Your Grace." He kissed the tip of her nose. "That was the most fun I've had all day."

"I didn't mean *this*. Much as I enjoyed it." She stroked his cheek and pouted her lips to reach his, in case he didn't think she appreciated *this*. "I meant earlier, in the dining room. I do believe you may have saved the day."

"The ideas and words were yours. All I contributed was a voice."

"At exactly the right moment. You served notice that the new Duke of Hampton has taken up the mantle of the old."

Blake stood, leaving her cold. She stumbled to her feet and smoothed her petticoats and skirts. He turned his back on her, but she didn't think it was modesty while he fastened his trousers. "I'm not my father," he said.

She put her arms around his waist and rested against his back, willing her warmth to relieve the stress she heard in his voice. "You are more than worthy to be his son."

"I can't be like him. I don't even want to be. I'm not going to lead the party and I'll never be a member of the government, let alone Prime Minister. I wish I could be the man you want, Minnie, but I don't have it in me."

"You are the man I want. You don't have to be anyone different."

His hands found hers and squeezed them. "Truly?"

"Truly."

"I want to do what's right but there are things my position requires that I'm simply not suited for. All this political business."

"That's why you're lucky to have me."

"I can feel you smiling against my back."

"You've just made me very happy."

He twisted in her arms and gathered her into his. "You just made *me* very happy. Very happy."

"That's not what I meant . . ." Her protest was interrupted by a warm open-mouthed kiss. "What I meant—" she began when she was able. But he cut her off and sealed her lips with a finger.

"Hush. I know what you meant. We make a good team. When it comes to politics you supply the brains and I provide the muscle."

"You read my very thoughts."

It wasn't the first time she'd talked of him reading her. *You read me like a book,* she'd said last time.

This was a perfect moment for Blake to make his confession. While he sought the right words, her attention was distracted. "Oh look. We've knocked your papers all over the floor."

"Leave them . . ."

Too late. She gathered up the scattering of reports his secretaries and land agents had left on his desk, each with its brief summary.

"Why—" she began.

He could see it in her face, knowledge and doubt at war. With her intelligence the right conclusion was inevitable. The thread holding up the sword unraveled and he waited for the inevitable crash.

"It doesn't seem possible and yet . . ." she began.

"You've guessed."

"You *don't* read. *Can* you read?"

"I can read."

"I've never seen you do it. Not even a menu."

Stripped bare and vulnerable, he somehow found the courage to speak plainly and admit, without prevarication, what he'd hidden so long.

"I can read," he said, "but not well. I was never able to learn. The Duke of Hampton is an idiot and you married him."

Her beautiful face blazed with an unfathomable emotion. Seconds passed like hours and he had the thought that his heart might fail and he would die before she spoke.

Of all her possible reactions he would never have dared imagine what happened. The papers she clutched drifted to the floor. Two steps and his hand was pressed between both hers and she engaged him eye to eye, hers bluer and fiercer than he'd ever seen.

"Don't you dare call the man I love an idiot."

A rushing filled his ears. He must have misheard. When he opened his mouth nothing came out. "Love?" Finally one croaked word.

"I love you, Blake."

His eyes stung. "You can't."

"As you know very well, I do not take kindly to being told what I can and cannot do. It's taken me a long time to realize it, but I love you." A dazzling smile lit her face and the room seemed full of sunshine. "I love you."

His arms slipped around her and he buried his face in her hair. "Oh God, Minnie. I love you too.

So very much." He feared he would weep. He'd cried in her arms before, the night of his father's funeral. This time his tears remained unshed. He merely held her tight and relished her slender strength, her sweet clean scent, the silken hair tickling his nose.

"Oh, my goodness!" she said, her voice rich with the same incredulity he'd felt when he'd discovered his feelings. "Who would have ever imagined it? We love each other. After loathing each other for years."

"You were the most impossible girl I ever met."

"And you were the most despicable man in the world."

They laughed shakily and kissed and exchanged disjointed murmurs of disbelief and happiness.

Chapter 31

Minerva was transformed, not into a different person but a new, better version of herself, all her rough edges rubbed away. Seated on a sofa, wrapped in his arms, she felt as soft and tender as a kitten.

"Why didn't I know how wonderful it is to be in love?" she mused, languorously unwinding his neck cloth because gentlemen's clothing swathed him too thoroughly and she wanted to soak in the warmth of his skin. "If I'd known I would have tried it before."

"I'm glad you waited."

She cast aside the muslin strip and drew back a little to admire the effect. With his shirt open he looked younger and ridiculously handsome.

"You're too far away," he said and held her close as though he couldn't bear to have an inch of space between them.

She stroked the corded column of his neck and traced the line of his jaw, relishing the masculine abrasiveness. He gave a smile of unalloyed joy, having lost the guardedness she hadn't known existed until it disappeared. Blake was all hers now: hers to love and hers to know. And she wanted to know him, every inch, inside and out.

"How did it happen?" she asked. "Why didn't you learn to read? I want to understand."

"It's a long story." He caught her hand, kissed the fingertips and she glowed with pleasure that he finally trusted her.

He described his early struggles, his utter bafflement at the sight of the alphabet, and his eventual limited success with Amanda's help.

"What did your tutors do?" she asked in wonder. "They must have been incompetent fools."

"They beat me. Unable to believe I was almost incapable of learning the most fundamental skills, they complained to my father that I was lazy. More beatings. I lived up to my reputation for idleness and refused to pay any attention to my lessons."

"Better to be called lazy than stupid?"

"Exactly. I did the minimum amount of studying to get by."

Her heart aching for the misunderstood boy, she tightened fierce arms about his waist. "The neglect of those in charge of your education is appalling. I'd like to meet some of those tutors and give them a piece of my mind."

"I can't blame them. Everyone else learns to read without any difficulty."

"You went to Eton and Oxford without Lady Amanda, how did you manage?"

"Oxford was ridiculously easy. I was heir to a dukedom. I don't believe a single one of those dons ever uttered a peep when I spent three years without reading a book or writing a word. Eton was harder." His voice darkened. "That's where I had the great good fortune to meet Geoffrey Huntley."

"So that's the reason for your friendship. He helped you at school."

"It's not as simple as that. We met when we were both placed in the Lower Greek. For me Latin was bad enough, but Greek was impossible. How could I learn a second alphabet when I had so much trouble with one? We were set a test and I left my page blank. To this day I remember the schoolmaster's words, his cane already in hand. 'Your ignorance is exceeded only by your impertinence. Come here.' I was ready to take my punishment and, I hoped, be ejected from Greek class forever, when Huntley spoke. 'That is my paper, sir. It is I who deserves the beating, not Blakeney.' "

Minerva knew how her brothers would react to another taking blame for their offenses. "What a filthy thing to do."

"Naturally I couldn't let him do it and both of us were beaten, he for lying. But I was grateful to him for trying to help. We became friends and I confided in him. With his assistance I did just enough to convince my masters that I was merely the laziest and worst behaved boy in the school. I trusted him."

"And he betrayed you."

"I thought he was my only true friend. I'd have done anything for him."

Minerva heard the pain in his voice. "And so you hesitated to trust anyone else with the secret. How horrible for you."

His mouth twisted into a humorless grin. "I'm the last person to deserve pity. I was born to every advantage. There's no reason in the world I shouldn't be completely happy. And I was, once I left Oxford and no longer had to pretend to read and write. I had a few good years. The sporting Lord Blakeney, hard riding and hard playing, always up for a lark. You hated him."

She kissed his cheek. "That's because I didn't know him. What happened with Huntley?"

"After Eton we remained on good terms, though our intimacy was less. We met in London from time to time but he got in with a gaming set. I heard his losses were heavy, and he'd been cut off by his grandfather. I didn't pay much attention. You know how one hears these things. A couple of years ago we ran into each other and he invited me to dinner in his rooms. I was reluctant—had a more attractive invitation that night—but he pressed me."

"And you couldn't say no."

"We dined, we drank—a lot—and we played piquet. I lost."

"A lot?"

"Not more than I could afford. He wrote up my vowels for me. Joked that he knew what a piece of work it was for me to write even the simplest letter. I signed it."

"Without reading it?"

"I looked it over. The sum looked right. The next afternoon he came to collect his debt. I had the bank draft ready. 'Blake, old fellow,' he said. 'You're missing a nought.'"

"He cheated."

"Yes. He'd written the I.O.U. for ten times the amount and I hadn't noticed."

"Surely you didn't have to pay him! He *cheated*."

"It was a debt of honor."

Her blood boiled. "Dishonor, you mean."

"Indeed. But he had my signed note."

"You could tell people he miswrote it, expose him as a villain."

"And if I did that I would have to expose my inability to read."

"You could say you were drunk."

"I considered that, but Huntley said if I accused him of cheating he'd spread the tale of my illiteracy to the world."

"Perhaps you should have let him."

"I didn't want my father to know."

"I see." Picturing herself in a similar situation, she knew she could have gone to her parents and received nothing but support and love. "You couldn't trust him not to despise you."

"I wish I had. But at the time I couldn't go to my father for the money. I couldn't bring myself to tell him that his son, in addition to disappointing him in every possible way, had managed to lose a fortune at cards. So I borrowed it."

"From Diana. She told me last week."

"It took me two years to repay her but I came back this spring, free of debt. My time away from London wasn't all bad. After years of self-indulgence, looking after the estate gave me something worthwhile to do. My plan was to come up for the season, take a holiday from responsibility, and enjoy having money again. I intended to spend a lot of it at Tattersall's, then retire to Devon and breed horses."

"Poor darling," Minerva said. "You found yourself a beautiful mistress and ended up with a scold of a wife instead."

"Perhaps I should thank Huntley. He was at your ball, that night at Vanderlin House. If he hadn't upset me I wouldn't have got so drunk and I might not have mistaken you for the Duchess of Lethbridge."

"Thank goodness I had a migraine. Otherwise I might be betrothed to Mr. Parkes now." She almost made a provocative remark about the loss of the M.P. from Gristlewick, but caught herself in time. Their love was too new and Blake's self-regard too battered. It would take time before she could make that kind of joke without danger of hurting him. Shifting around, she threaded her arms round his neck and gave him a long, lingering kiss. "I love you, Blake," she whispered. "I am so happy we found each other."

"I love you too, Minnie."

"I'm proud to be your wife."

He pulled her on to his lap and reveled in the way she fit against him. He was light-headed, floating on air, dizzy as the bubbles in champagne. A corner of his mind knew his troubles weren't over. The terrible truth that had dogged his life hadn't gone away, but for an hour he could pretend nothing would ever go amiss again. Minerva's head rested on his shoulder, her hair tickled his chin, and her scent flooded his senses, telling him he was at home.

"Huntley will tell the world. Ever since I took the Warfield Castle seat from him I've been expecting it."

"You did that for my sake."

"For yours, but also because you convinced me it was the right thing to do. I have responsibilities beyond my own pride. This evening I saw exactly what I can achieve through the respect my position inspires. I'm afraid that will disappear once the party discovers the new Duke of Hampton is a dolt. You've allied yourself to a declining power."

"We'll come up with a way to stop him, together. You're not alone anymore."

"I've probably made things worse." He described the morning's encounter with Huntley and to his pleasure Minerva crowed with delight.

"I wish you'd done worse than knock him out. I wish you'd torn him limb from limb."

"Is this my sensible Minnie speaking? I thought you believed in a rational and humane approach to criminals."

"That's all very well in theory, but if anyone attacks the man I love I have no mercy."

To which there was only one response, and it didn't involve speech.

Chapter 32

Blake liked to ride before breakfast. His wife did not. Even in her short tenure as duchess she'd developed the habit of drinking copious amounts of chocolate while reading in bed. He had no doubt he was about to become accustomed, for the first time in his life, to a bedroom strewn with reading matter of all descriptions. The morning after his great confession he returned from his dressing room and found her supported by a bank of pillows, cup in hand and her nose in a newspaper. Her perfect nose. Bending down to salute it, he somehow got involved in a much more thorough kiss.

"Lucky my cup was almost empty," she said when she was able. "Have a good ride. I shall go down shortly and find Gideon. See if your good work last night has paid off and everyone's ready for compromise."

"Come with me."

"Oh, why not? Our guests will still be here in a hour or two."

"Worse luck."

What a great day it was, hardly a cloud in the sky. He loved and was loved and in a day or two his unwanted guests would all leave and he could settle down and enjoy the resumption of his honeymoon. Meanwhile he had Minerva all to himself. She looked splendid in a dark blue riding habit and a pert feathered hat.

"You ride well," he said as they pulled up at the apex of the avenue and looked down at the sprawling mansion.

"My mother's approach to girls' education may have been unorthodox, but she didn't tolerate a bad seat on a horse."

"I'll have to find you a worthier mount. The stock I bought in Paris should be here any day, and I intend to buy more. My father's judgment of horseflesh was no more than adequate."

"I'd like that."

Her smile made him want to sing. "It was on this very spot, yesterday morning, that I realized I loved you."

"For me it took a little longer. It had been coming on for a while, but I knew at dinner last night, just before your big speech." He found it deeply moving that she'd loved him even before he made his big political gesture. "You beat me by a few hours," she said with a provocative little grin.

"It's not a competition."

"No, it isn't." The glance they exchanged singed him to his toes.

"I'll race you to the grotto."

* * *

Though long familiar with the Mandeville Park, Minerva hadn't considered its possibilities for erotic encounters. Not so her husband. A grassy glade behind the lakeside folly provided privacy and a comfortable surface for a heated joining that left her boneless.

With clothing in disarray, they lay hand in hand, staring up at the inconsequential clouds while they recovered their breath.

"How have you managed all these years without reading?" she asked, breaking the contented silence. "I can't even imagine how hard it must have been."

Blake rolled onto his side to look at her. "Once I accepted that I would never be able to learn things from the written word, I found other ways of gaining information. When I concentrate I can remember almost anything I hear."

"Is that how you learned French?"

"My father hired a native French tutor for conversation. But I can't read a word of it."

"I know. You made me order dinner from that impossibly long menu."

"While you flirted with the waiter, you minx."

Minerva discovered she enjoyed flirting, with Blake. "He was very handsome. Especially the moustache with the twirly ends."

His eyes told her she would pay for that remark later and she looked forward to it. For now he continued in a serious vein. "At least we were taught to *speak* French. The classics were hopeless. I became very good at appearing not to pay attention in class, but in reality I listened closely so I know enough Greek and Roman history not to appear completely ignorant."

"That was clever. Throwing in the occasional classical allusion would reassure anyone who suspected."

"I've expended much ingenuity devising means of disguise. I'm so glad you know, Minnie. I should have trusted you. I thought you'd despise me when you found out."

"Never," she said, reaching up to stroke his jaw. "What you've told me fills me with awe."

He shook his head. "But, Minnie. Reading is the first thing every child is taught. How come I'm the only one that couldn't do it?"

Realizing he voiced his deepest fear, that he was inherently damaged, she sought to reassure him. "There are lots of things that lots of people can't do. I can't carry a tune. What about you?"

"I can sing well enough."

"Can you shoot straight?"

"Yes."

"I can't."

"You're a girl."

"Diana can. Will and Rufus taught us both to use a pistol. I was hopeless."

"But anyone can read."

"How do you know? Perhaps the world is full of people who can't and cover it up, just as you have."

Never had it occurred to Blake that others might be in the same position. He'd always believed only the poor were unlettered and that he, with all his advantages, must be deeply flawed. That it might not be his fault was hard for him to grasp. Yet Minerva, with her brains and knowledge, said it could be so. Better still she accepted him as he was.

"Let's hope our children will be like you," he said.

"If any of them are like you I shall be even prouder of them. Any child of ours will have the help of his parents that you never had. You aren't alone anymore."

She stroked his hair absentmindedly as her features set into the frown that betokened deep thought. He couldn't believe his luck that he'd won the love of this amazing woman. "I've been thinking," she said finally. "If Huntley exposes you he'll get the satisfaction of revenge, but nothing more. Far more likely he'll come back with another demand."

"I made myself fairly clear when I told him I wouldn't pay him a penny."

"He won't dare approach you in person, that's certain. The demand will come by some other means, which means we have time to come up with a plan. After our guests leave, we'll hunt him down and crush him like the worm he is."

"I can't wait. Speaking for myself, I wouldn't mind the opportunity to pound him into the ground like a fence post."

"Much as I share the sentiment, if we're going to keep your secret, we'll have to be more subtle. Let's look into *his* private affairs. He'd had large gaming debts in the past. If he's short of money again we could push him over the edge into debtor's prison, or drive him out of the country."

"He could still talk."

"He must be persuaded not to. Let's discover his guilty secrets. Threaten to expose them if he talks."

"I'm not sure there's anything to be found. I know him well, remember."

"Then we'll meet fire with fire. Spread some really appalling rumors about him."

"Do they have to be true?"

Minerva smiled happily. "This, my darling, is not a moment to be honorable."

Minerva returned to the house alone to resume her hostess duties, while Blake saw to some estate business. He returned at midday and went to look for her. He expected to find her chatting with happy politicians, intently discussing the coming election and their plans for its victorious aftermath. He threaded his way through the library, shaking off some overblown praise for his speech at dinner, but couldn't find his duchess. He emerged at the other end of the room and found Sebastian Iverley alone in the librarian's office.

"Have you seen Minerva?" he asked. He'd seen little of his cousin in the course of the house party. Sebastian, it occurred to him, had been guardedly cordial during a few brief exchanges.

"I should think she's in there with the mob. That was quite a speech you made last night."

Blake nodded. Was that approval in Iverley's voice? Before he could reply they were joined by one of the footmen, who appeared agitated.

"Your Grace. I've been following you through the library. It's Her Grace."

"What about Her Grace?"

"I delivered her a note earlier and she went out."

"Did she say where?"

"She said she was walking to the Italian Garden and ordered me to report to her in half an hour for further instructions. When I arrived she wasn't there, but I found this paper caught between the fingers of a statue of a Roman gentleman. It's addressed to Your Grace."

Blake prayed this wasn't what he suspected, that Huntley had contacted her and she'd gone to face him alone. It was just like Minnie to go marching off in a state of righteous indignation without considering the consequences. Hell and damnation!

"Thank you, James," Blake said. He stared at the letter. Why had she *written* to him? It wasn't sealed, merely folded. The single sheet was filled with words in capital letters. It didn't help having Sebastian Iverley looking on as he tried to read. He took a deep breath and tried to relax.

"HAMPTON," it began.

Minerva wouldn't address him as Hampton, but he knew who would. Someone who knew he had trouble reading ordinary handwriting. His gut clenched. He dragged his eyes down the sheet and almost at the bottom, because he expected it, he saw the word "HUNTLEY."

The letters danced a fandango on the page and he knew it was hopeless.

"Sebastian." He handed the letter to his cousin. "Read this."

"What?"

Blake took another deep breath. "Read it, damn you. Tell me what it says."

"The writing seems clear enough to me."

Blake grabbed his cousin's neck cloth in his fist. "Look here, Owl. Minerva may be in trouble and I cannot read this note. I can hardly read a damn word. I never could. So read the bloody thing aloud before I throttle you."

Sebastian made a choking noise. "Can't read it if you strangle me." Blake had to hand it to him. As soon as he was free, without stopping for any tiresome questions, Iverley read the letter.

" 'Hampton. I have your bride. If you wish to see her returned to you undamaged, bring five thousand pounds in notes, gold, or jewelry to the Mausoleum. Come alone and unarmed. If anyone else approaches the duchess will suffer. You have until six o'clock. Geoffrey Huntley.' Then there's a postscript. I recognize Minerva's hand, even though it's also written all in capitals. 'Everything he says is true. He has a pistol. Minnie.' "

The two most famous educational establishments in the Thames Valley had at least taught him many colorful oaths. Blake made use of them all.

Sebastian didn't waste time with any irrelevant questions. "What shall we do to get her back?"

"I'll get the money together. I'd rather we didn't have to, but I'll pay it if I must."

"Good. Do you have enough on hand?"

"I think so."

"You'll have to go alone. That's why he chose the Mausoleum."

Of all the temples and follies in the five-hundred

acre Mandeville Park, the Mausoleum was the only one that stood atop a bare hill. Huntley would be able to keep watch in every direction and see anyone approach long before they reached him. A covert attack was impossible. Or so he believed.

"I will. But the blackguard made a mistake. He doesn't know there's an underground passage from the grotto that leads right into the crypt of the Mausoleum."

Sebastian nodded. "What do you want me to do?"

"We'll gather some men and you shall lead them through the passage. Then wait. The access from the vault is through a trapdoor leading to a niche on the right-hand side of the building, cut off by a wrought iron gate. It's never locked but the hinges rattle. If you hear them, come out and attack Huntley. But I won't signal unless I can be sure Minerva is safe. I'd rather pay twice as much than put her at risk."

"Huntley will probably wait for you outside. Could we creep up from below? If he's holding Minerva inside we might be able to grab her there and then."

Blake considered it, then shook his head. "We can't risk it. Remember, Minnie says he's armed. If I can distract or disarm Huntley I'll try and rattle that gate. And for God's sake, come up if you hear shooting."

"Before you go may I ask one question?"

"Make it quick," Blake snapped.

"Does she really let you call her Minnie?" Every syllable expressed Sebastian's incredulity. Blake had just been forced to reveal his lifelong shame to his lifelong enemy and that's all he had to say?

"Yes."

"She must love you a lot."

Despite his fear for Minerva's safety and his fury at himself for underestimating the level of Huntley's desperation, he allowed himself a strained smile. "I believe she does."

And suddenly Blake was glad it had been Sebastian who'd been there when the note was delivered, his cousin to whom he'd had to reveal his inability. Not only was Iverley his first cousin, as his brother-in-law he was doubly kin. There was no one else who had Minerva's interests more fully at heart and her protection was the only thing that mattered.

"You do realize, don't you," Sebastian said, "that Minerva will probably try to *help*."

He was right. He knew her only too well. "I just hope, Sebastian, that you are wrong this time."

Chapter 33

Minerva was furious. At Geoffrey Huntley, and at herself for not guessing his intentions. She would have attacked him with her bare hands had they not been tied behind her back. And it was perhaps as well she was gagged, because she had a great deal she wished to say, none of it polite. Huntley might shoot her out of sheer exasperation if she were allowed to speak.

Her captor was jumpy. While he made her write her postscript to his ransom note, he'd threatened to shoot her when she had tried to delay, knowing the footman would be coming out to find her. She wouldn't have put it past Huntley to shoot the man. So she'd meekly allowed herself to be covered with a cloak to hide her identity and led, with the barrel of the gun jammed into her ribs, along a deserted route to the Mausoleum. Then he'd bound and gagged her and sat her down with her back to the huge sarcophagus that stood in middle of the square building.

There was nothing for her to do but wait for Blake. He'd come, she knew, and he'd bring the money. But she hoped he wasn't going to give in to Huntley's blackmail without a fight. Unfortunately she'd given him some incorrect intelligence. She thought her kidnapper only carried one gun. Now she knew he had a pair of pistols. She prayed Blake hadn't made any plans based on the supposition Huntley had but a single shot at his disposal.

It was a long wait in the somber edifice, whose thick stone walls repelled the heat of the sun. Dressed in summer muslins she was disagreeably chilled. After an hour or two her bottom felt as cold and hard as the marble floor. Huntley appeared to be feeling the strain of the wait. Most of the time he was outside, presumably on the lookout for Blake. Then he'd return and brandish his pistols at her in a manner that, she had to admit, unnerved her. He might be irrational enough that the sight of an innocent gardener would be mistaken for proof that Blake disobeyed his demands.

She had no idea of the time and the dim light through the small clerestory windows told her only that the afternoon was progressing, not how far.

Huntley came in again, his eyes as wild as his hair. "Almost six o'clock," he said, on the edge of hysteria. "Not much time left."

She cursed her gag, wanting to point out that five thousand pounds was a lot of money to find in a few hours. Midway between quarters, there would be few rents coming into the estate. The majority of the sum would have to be in silver and jewels. She had no idea if there was a jewelry collection at Mandeville to equal that in London. Most likely not. The only valuable gems she knew of were her emeralds. She'd be very sorry to lose them.

"He'd better not be playing with me, Duchess, because if I'm ruined I'm taking you with me."

Alone again, she heard a scratching noise beneath the floor. When she was a small girl, exploring the Mandeville Park as the local residents were permitted to do at certain times, her brothers had told her the Mausoleum was haunted by the ghosts of those whose bones lay in the vault. She knew it wasn't true, of course. Merely a tale to tease their little sister. The Vanderlins were buried in the churchyard at Duke's Mandeville. Nevertheless, she felt a little uneasy. Especially when she considered the alternative. She'd sooner be confronted with ghosts than rats.

Expecting Blake to arrive at any moment, she wanted to be prepared, in case she could play a part in her own rescue. Her feet weren't bound and if she could manage to stand, tied hands or not, she might be able to inflict some damage by kicking. Alas for that plan, she'd developed pins and needles in her right foot. She was still wriggling her toes when she heard voices outside.

"Go to hell, Huntley." Blake's deep tones were unmistakable through the partly open door. "I'm not giving you a penny until I'm sure that the duchess is unharmed. If you've harmed a hair on her head I'll tear you to pieces, and if you shoot me I'll do it from beyond the grave. And I can do it too. Believe me."

She managed to roll over onto her knees, then struggled upright, resting her head against the marble sarcophagus for leverage.

The tall door creaked further open. "Are you all right, Minnie?"

But the minute she put weight on her right side, she discovered her foot was still half asleep. She gave a gagged shriek of pain as her ankle collapsed under her and she staggered a few steps, unable to use her bound arms to keep balance, before crashing against an iron railing or gate in a dark corner. She was rudely pushed aside when the gate opened and men poured into the building, led by Sebastian. The invasion within was greeted by a gunshot without.

Blake walked up the steps leading to the Mausoleum's portico, trying to talk calmly to Huntley, who was blathering like a madman and waving his pistols around in a way that made Blake extremely nervous. As he reached the top, Huntley demanded he throw the bag, containing thousands in gold and jewels, onto the ground. But he wasn't about to hand over the booty without making sure Minerva was safe. Besides, the heavy sack was his only weapon.

Huntley laughed like a maniac. "I've ruined you anyway," he screamed. "I've written and posted letters to *The Times* and *The Morning Post* and *The Gazette,* telling them all about you."

That's when he told the other man to go to hell and dared him to kill him.

"Are you all right, Minnie?" he called into the building.

The scene erupted into chaos. As Sebastian and his men appeared, a bullet tore into the wooden door, just above Blake's head. He felt a sting in his upper arm, a fraction of a second before the sound of another shot. Huntley was out of firepower. With enormous pleasure, Blake spun round and started beating the blazes out of him until a pair of arms grabbed his shoulders.

"Stop it, Blake, you're hurt," Sebastian said.

"I am now," he replied, flinching at the pressure on his wound. "Let go. That's devilish painful."

"You're bleeding. One of the bullets must have hit you."

"Flesh wound. Let me finish this."

His intention of reducing Huntley to butcher meat was interrupted by a furious guttural noise. He turned to find Minerva, her hands tied behind her back and her mouth in a gag. Nevertheless she managed to express herself quite eloquently.

Letting Huntley slump half conscious to the ground, he was about to embrace her, then stopped. If he didn't love her so much he'd kill her.

"I have two things to say to you, Duchess." He folded his arms and looked down at her. "First, I am never letting you out of the house by yourself again. You simply cannot be trusted not to do something foolish and get yourself into danger."

She growled ominously.

"Secondly, if you do find yourself in a dangerous position, you will not, repeat, not, attempt to save yourself. You may be the brains in our partnership, Duchess, but I am the brawn. Any fighting that's needed falls into my purview. Understood?"

He turned to his cousin. "Sebastian," he said, ignoring the rumble of resentment emitted by his wife. "Thank you."

"That's all right. I owed you one for introducing me to Diana."

With that Blake knew he'd been forgiven for the cruelties he'd inflicted on his cousin in the past. His own resentment had disappeared too. There was no need to say any more. They were men.

"Would you and the servants deal with this piece of vermin? I'm going to take Minnie back to the house."

"I'm not sure she's in the mood to go with you, old fellow." Sebastian grinned broadly.

"Too bad."

He snatched his bride by the waist, slung her over his shoulder, on the unwounded side, and marched down the hill. As soon as they were out of sight, in the shelter of a stand of beeches, he stopped. Her kicks had almost subsided and the timbre of her throaty communications had changed.

"Are you going to behave now?" he asked with mock sternness as he slid her to her feet. He was fairly sure she was laughing. She nodded. "Turn round."

The knot tying the cloth gag was tight and took a minute or to work loose. "Yech," she said in disgust, when he finally freed her.

"Keep still. I should have borrowed a knife from one of the men. The knot on your wrists is worse than the gag."

"Don't you dare do that to me again."

"I think you rather enjoyed it."

"Humph."

"I thought so. I'll be happy to accommodate you anytime. There you are." The ropes fell away.

She spun round, doubtless ready to say something acerbic, and her mouth fell open, horror replacing indignation on her face. "Oh my word! You're wounded. My poor darling, there's blood all over your coat. We must get you to a doctor at once. No wait, I must bandage it. I'll use my petticoat."

She raised her skirt and would have slipped off her undergarment, which he would have quite enjoyed, but he really couldn't have his wife wandering around the park in nothing but a transparent gown, especially when there wasn't the slightest need.

"Stop, Minnie. It was only a graze."

"Are you sure?"

"It isn't even bleeding anymore."

Her forehead creased, she eyed it with misgiving, gently touching the torn cloth with her finger and confirming that the blood no longer flowed and was already drying. "Does it hurt?"

"A little."

"Is there anything I can do?"

He held her close and basked in the relief that she was alive and unhurt. His hands traveled down her back, below her stays to her waist, to feel the warmth of her skin through the light cloth of her garments. Her vitality of body and spirit flooded his senses. "You can kiss me," he said, his voice hoarse with emotion.

Cradling his head as though it were a precious and fragile treasure, she pulled it down to meet her parted lips. Soft heat filled his mouth and what started as the merest touch grew deeper. He'd never experienced a kiss of pure love but he had no trouble recognizing it. Pure love and, he knew with a profound conviction, a mutual joy that they had found each other and were alive for a shared future.

He drew back to feast his eyes on her beloved features: pale flawless skin with pink-tinged cheeks, perfect straight nose, bow-shaped mouth of dark rose, and eyes like a clear sky, flashing with passion for life and for him. How had he ever thought her insipid? Minerva would doubtless continue to drive him wild, and not always with desire, but she would never disappoint him. His heart lurched with dread that he might have lost her.

"How did it happen, Minnie? How could you be so stupid as to let Huntley seize you?"

"When I received his note I thought he must be trying to get the money from me, since he failed with you. I never thought he'd *kidnap* me. I was very sensible, you know. I told the footman to come and find me."

"You have to stop thinking you are invincible."

She looked quite unabashed and her mouth took on a mulish, very Minerva-ish set. "I just intended to slow him down, persuade him to wait while we made our own plans. I couldn't allow him to ruin your life."

It was his turn to be unimpressed. "I can save myself. Next time, tell me before you go off on a mad adventure."

"So that you can stop me?"

"So that I can go with you."

Her smile lit his heart. "Agreed. Perhaps we'll

find ourselves a convenient screen to hide behind."

There was no answer to that but another kiss, until she remembered his wound and insisted on going back to the house to have it cleaned and dressed. They wandered along the shaded paths hand in hand, fingers enlaced.

"What shall we do about Huntley?" she asked.

"Sebastian and the men will bring him back and we'll have to decide. He said he'd already written to the newspapers. Who knows, for once he may have spoken the truth. Will you still love me if all the world knows I can't read?"

"Of course I will."

"In that case I don't care."

Chapter 34

The yearling was a beauty: a glossy bay, polished mahogany with points of ebony. Minerva stood quietly at the railing and watched him canter around the paddock, detecting the power and grace of a future champion.

The man holding the lunge in the center of the ring was a thoroughbred too, as golden as the horse was dark. She could never have enough of looking at the Duke of Hampton, who managed to look ducal even with buckskins and top boots splashed with mud and engaged in a most unducal task. With as much concentration as Minerva would devote to a new edition of the *Edinburgh Review,* he put the unbroken colt through his paces with gentle command, beating time on the earthen circuit with a long whip. The appearance of heedless arrogance that used to mask his inner uncertainty had given way to confident authority that reflected ease and, she fancied, deep happiness. That she had contributed to and shared that happiness made her chest swell with reflective joy.

Sensing her presence he looked up and returned

her smile. Her heart turned several somersaults. He brought the colt to a halt, patted his neck, rubbed his nose, and murmured lavish praise. "Enough for today," he said and nodded at the waiting groom to take the youngster, then loped to the fence and vaulted over to join her.

"He's doing well," she observed.

"Brilliantly," he said, with a boyish grin. "That one's going to win the Derby, I swear. I can't wait till the fellows in the Jockey Club see what I found in France."

"Have you settled on a name yet?"

"I'd like to name him after you. Minerva's something. What's the goddess's symbol?"

"An owl."

"Minerva's Owl! I wonder what Sebastian Iverley would think. He may have forgiven me for the past but I'm not sure he'd appreciate the compliment."

"What about Minerva's Shield? Though that's really naming him after yourself, since you take care of me so well."

"Minerva's Shield. I like that. In honor of you and because I will always be there to protect you." Their eyes met in a moment of deep and wordless communion. Longing for his touch, clasped hands were all she could allow herself in the presence of the groom. "I sincerely hope," he added sternly, "that rescuing you from peril won't be necessary again."

"Not unless Huntley returns. I doubt he'll dare, though I still wish we could have delivered him to the magistrate."

"Into the hands of English justice? I thought you disapproved."

"I cannot conceive of a fate bad enough for him. I wouldn't even mind seeing him rotting in the hulks."

"I appreciate your thirst for revenge. Putting him on a boat to New York with a little money seemed a tame solution, even to avoid scandal." Not caring about the servants, he kissed the tip of her nose.

"That's another thing," she said. "I was thinking today how unfair it is to inflict Huntley on the Americans. What did they do to deserve him?"

"By all accounts they're a very capable lot. I'm sure they can survive him."

They'd reached another paddock, containing a mare and foal. Minerva laughed at the ungainly little filly with its spindly legs and soft fuzz. "Is this one a Derby winner too?"

Blake shook his head. "Not bred for the turf. If she turns out well I shall give her to you, since you've agreed to join me in the hunt."

"Mama is going to die of shock."

"You can tell her later. I met her when I was riding out this morning and asked her over to see the French horses. She's prepared to set foot in Mandeville now that there's no chance of having to meet any of our political guests. She and your father and Stephen will dine with us tomorrow."

"You and Mama get on far too well together."

"Indeed, Mrs. Montrose and I find ourselves in agreement on almost every subject. Lord, Minnie, I thought those politicos would never leave. It was such a marvelous feeling to wake up this morning and know we had the place to ourselves."

A relative state of isolation, given the presence of over a hundred servants under the roof of the great house, but Minerva appreciated the sentiment. Even she'd been sick of company when the last straggler departed, a full week after the designated date for the conclusion of the gathering. Most, however, had left when expected, including the Louthers, who were back in London.

Minerva tried to coax the foal to come to her hand, but it skittered away. "I had a letter from Gideon today. Apparently the letters Diana wrote in strictest confidence to several of her dearest friends have born fruit. Gideon says it's all over London that Huntley was madly in love with me and tried to abduct me." She paused to lend drama to the tale they'd all concocted and which Diana had brilliantly embellished. "Seems he came to the ball at Vanderlin House, hoping to win my affection, but the poor man never even had the chance to dance with me because I slipped off to the library to meet you."

"Is that what happened, you saucy minx?"

"He was driven mad with envy and disappointment when I married you."

"I don't blame him."

"Out of the kindness of your heart you were ready to give him Warfield Castle. But, knowing him as you do, you detected the signs of increasing derangement and you couldn't send him to Parliament."

"No indeed," Blake said. "There's never been a madman in Parliament."

She grinned back at him. "Driven over the brink, he tried to ruin you and seize me for his own."

"And I nobly declined to prosecute him because of our long friendship."

" 'The quality of mercy is not strained.' "

"And of course to save the delicate nerves of my duchess from the distress of appearing in court."

Minerva snorted.

"You mean people actually believe this utter nonsense?" Blake asked.

"They may have their doubts, but it's a good story. Once the newspapers hear it they'll forget that dull stuff about you being a bit slow in school. Everyone in London will be talking about our version of events. Besides, Huntley has disappeared and they all want to be invited to our dinners and assemblies. It's in no one's interest to believe him."

"Are we going to give a lot of dinners and assemblies?" He sounded so mournful Minerva had to laugh.

"Dozens of them," she said, tucking her arm into his. "All season long. I shall be the greatest political hostess London has ever known."

"I'm glad to see recent experiences haven't diminished your confidence in yourself." Then, more gravely. "You must do what you want and I shall do my humble best to support you. It's in my best interests to work hard for the reform of Parliament and then I'll never have to think about rotten boroughs again. I'm afraid you will feel the loss more than I."

"That's not likely to happen soon, alas. Gideon also writes that the Prime Minister has reorganized the cabinet and buttressed his support. There won't be an election this year after all."

"I'm sorry, Minnie. You must be disappointed after all your efforts to unite the opposition."

"That's all right. Next year things may be different. There are no permanent victories in politics, neither are there permanent defeats. Things change all the time. It's what makes it so fascinating."

"My father said the same thing. I suppose he was a very wise man. I wish I'd known him better."

Blake had told her about his last conversation with the late duke, on his deathbed. That he'd never had the chance to explain himself would always grieve him, but Minerva believed the duke would have understood. He could remember his father with love.

Arm in arm and in comfortable silence they strolled toward the house, the raised portico of the garden front looming ahead of them. Instead of climbing the stairs to the upper terrace, Blake guided her into the walled rose garden. A quick glance confirmed the absence of gardeners. A smile formed within her.

"Let me see," he said, tilting her chin with one hand. "No election means there's no reason for us to go to London until Parliament meets."

"I'm afraid not. What a pity."

"We could stay here all summer and autumn." His arm snaked around her waist and pulled her close.

"We could."

"Or I could go on a horse buying trip. Would you come with me?"

"I might enjoy it. Especially if it were to Paris." As long as they were together and his touch made her body hum with excitement, she wouldn't much mind where he took her.

"I've heard Paris is a lovely place to spend a honeymoon."

And though she couldn't have agreed more, he stopped her reply with a thorough kiss. But Minerva had learned that it wasn't always a bad thing to be deprived of speech.

Epilogue

London, a few months later

The carriage stopped at the entrance to Westminster Hall. The Duchess of Hampton straightened the Duke's neck cloth, needlessly since his valet had turned him out perfectly as usual. Minerva wished there was something more she could do. She knew how nervous Blake was on the occasion of his maiden speech in the House of Lords.

"You will be brilliant," she said for the ninetieth time. "Don't forget to look at your notes from time to time."

"I won't," Blake promised. "But if anything could dispel the rumors that I can't read it will be this. There isn't a member of either house who'd believe I could make an hour-long speech on criminal justice reform without reading it. I just hope I won't forget my words."

"You won't. We've practiced it so often, you know it as well as Edmund Kean knows *Hamlet*. They'll see that the new Duke of Hampton is as impressive as the last."

"I wonder what they'd all say if they knew you'd written it."

"Most of it. You contributed some important ideas."

"You give me too much credit. If I have anything of value to say it's due to my duchess."

Minerva laughed. "*That* they would never believe." She gave him a quick kiss, careful not to muss him. "Thank you, my darling."

"What for?"

"I've always wanted to give a speech in Parliament. Through you I realize my ambition."

"I only hope I can represent you well. Persuade a few of those fellows to change their minds."

"If you don't, we'll keep trying, even if it takes years."

"I'll put up with them for years, as long as I have you for even longer." He pulled her to him for a more thorough kiss, apparently not caring if he was mussed. "I'd better go in."

She watched him enter the building, his tall figure relaxed and confident. He exchanged a few words with the doorkeeper, then disappeared inside. The coachman drove her home to Vanderlin House to await the reaction to the speech. She wished she could be in the House to hear him, but no matter.

How could she complain about a little thing like that when she was the luckiest woman in the world?

Author's Note

When I decided to write a book with a political setting, I looked at events in England in 1822, the year of this book. I quickly realized that politics, while engrossing for those involved, is incredibly complicated and mostly lacking in the kind of dramatic incidents that would enhance a romance without overwhelming it. The most thrilling event of 1822 seems to have been The Great Cabinet Reshuffle. Excited? Neither was I.

I'd already invented the Vanderlin family, a ducal dynasty (inspired by the Dukes of Portland) at the very center of English political life. So I decided to unhitch my tale from history. I took a single important issue, that of Parliamentary reform, and wove my tale around a simplified version of the subject. In the U.S., every ten years, congressional and state legislative seats are reapportioned according to population changes recorded by the census. Early nineteenth century England had basically gone without reapportionment for five hundred years. Thus "rotten boroughs," with a handful of inhabitants, sent members to Parliament while big cities had none. The Great Reform Act finally passed in 1832, though the result was hardly what we'd recognize as democracy. In fact the main provisions were similar to those Blake outlined in his dinner speech.

The word dyslexia didn't exist in the Regency era, neither did any concept of the condition. I'd like to thank my friend Sandy Dickson, teacher and dedicated reading specialist, for her insights into the struggles of a boy born with dyslexia at a time he could expect neither help nor sympathy.

Miranda

*G*ive in to your Impulses!

These unforgettable stories only take a second to buy and give you hours of reading pleasure!

Go to *www.AvonImpulse.com* and see what we have to offer.

Available wherever e-books are sold.

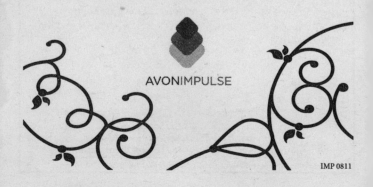

AVONIMPULSE